NATURE OF THE LION

SHADOWS OVER AFRICA

T.M. CLARK

WILDE PRESS

NATURE OF THE LION

Published by Wilde Press

Edited by Creating Ink

Cover designed by Mecha

Cataloguing-in-Publication details are available from the National Library of Australia
www.librariesaustralia.nla.gov.au

ebook © Published 2024 ISBN 978-1-923129-01-6

Paperback © Published 2024 ISBN 978-1-923129-02-3

Hardback © Published 2024 ISBN 978-1-923129-22-1

Previously published by Mira, an imprint of Harlequin Enterprises (Australia) Pty Ltd.

GENERAL FICTION

This book is written in English as used in Britain and Australia. It has not been Americanised.

ABOUT THE AUTHOR

Zimbabwean-born T.M. Clark combines her passion for storytelling, diverse cultures, and wildlife with her love for the wild in her captivating multicultural books.

Writing for both adults and children, T.M. Clark is the author of Shooting Butterflies, Tears of A Cheetah, Child of Africa, Nature of the Lion, Cry of the Firebird, and the critically acclaimed My Brother-But-One, nominated for a Queensland Literary People's Choice Award in 2014. Her children's picture books, Slowly! Slowly! (a 2018 CBCA Notable Book) and Quickly! Quickly!, are beloved by young readers and are companion pieces to Child of Africa.

When she's not writing thrilling adventure stories, T.M. Clark is dedicated to helping other writers. As the coordinator of the CYA Conference (www.cyaconference.com), she provides professional development for both new and established writers and illustrators. She also co-presents at Writers as Sea (www.WritersAtSea.com.au), guiding writers on their creative journeys.

Tina Marie loves mentoring emerging writers, indulging in chocolate biscuits, and collecting books for creating libraries in Papua New Guinea. Her new novel, Daughter of Africa, is set to release later this year, continuing her commitment to captivating stories with an African heart.

Visit T.M. Clark at tmclark.com.au and follow her on social media.

facebook.com / tmclarkauthor
instagram.com / tmclark_author
amazon.com / stores / author / B018N3D2QY
bookbub.com / authors / t-m-clark
goodreads.com / tmclark
linkedin.com / in / t-m-clark
mastodon.au / @tmclark
pinterest.com / TMClark_Author
tiktok.com / @tmclark_author
threads.net / @tmclark_author
bsky.app / profile / tmclarkauthor.bsky.social

ALSO BY T.M. CLARK

ADULT NOVELS

- Child of Africa
- Cry of the Firebird
- My Brother-But-One
- Nature of the Lion
- Shooting Butterflies
- Song of the Starlings
- Tears of the Cheetah
- The Avoidable Orphan

PICTURE BOOKS

- Slowly! Slowly!
- Quickly! Quickly!

WILDE PRESS

DEDICATION

To Shaun, with love as always.

'Return to old watering holes for more than water; friends and dreams are there to meet you.'

Old African Proverb

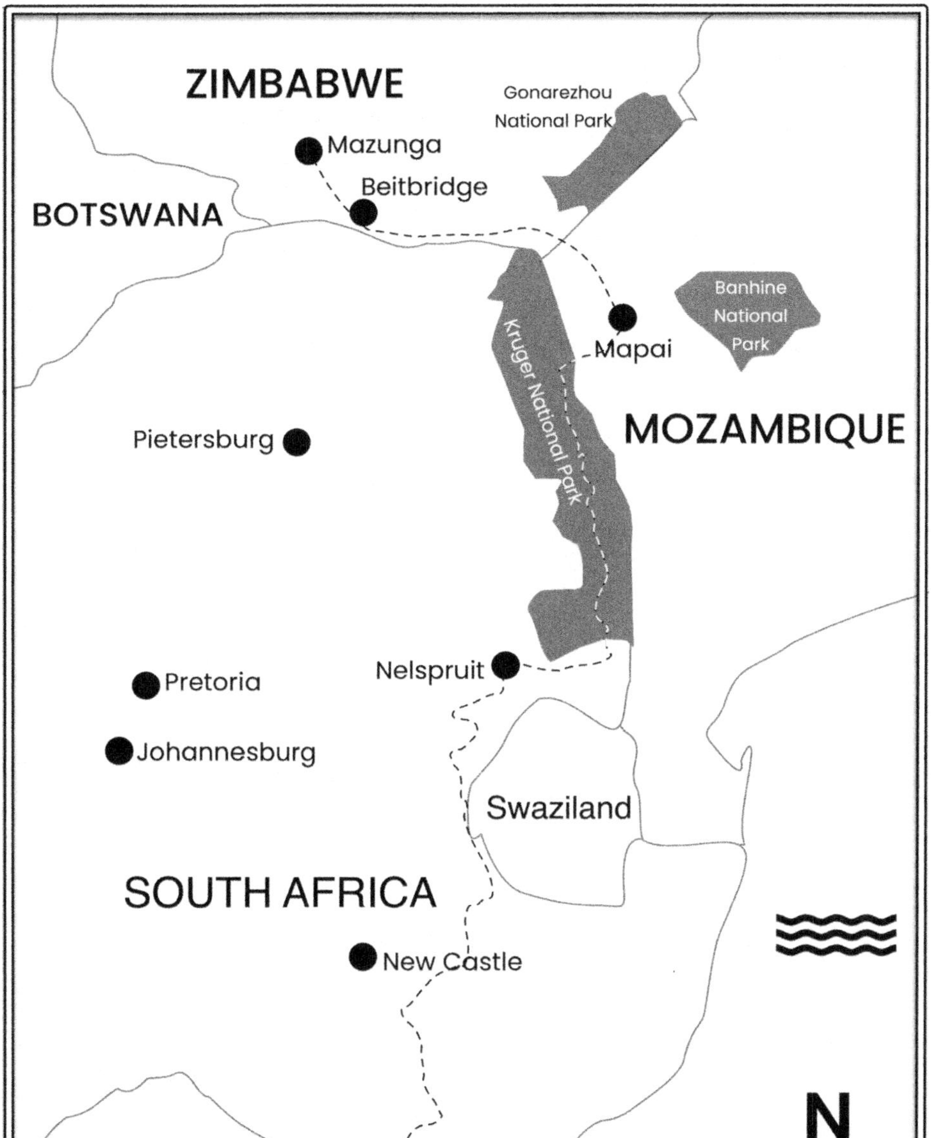
ZIMBABWE
Gonarezhou National Park
Mazunga
Beitbridge
BOTSWANA
Banhine National Park
Mapai
Kruger National Park
MOZAMBIQUE
Pietersburg
Pretoria
Nelspruit
Johannesburg
Swaziland
SOUTH AFRICA
New Castle
N
LESOTHO
Pietermaritzburg
Durban

PROLOGUE

MATOPOS HILLS, ZIMBABWE, 1973

The balanced granite rocks on top of the hills of the Matopos defied logic, but they formed the perfect game funnel. The emerald-green trees, hiding the sandy soil beneath, kept the temperatures at least a little cooler.

Mike rode his horse, Rebel, further into the thick bushes. 'Stick really close, Chloe,' he instructed in a whisper.

'Yes, Dad,' Chloe said, edging her horse, Mongoose, nearer to his until they almost touched.

Slowly, they walked forward and broke through into a clearing where the herd boy had seen the horses at sunset the previous night. The chances of them being in the same place were slim but a good starting point.

Mike and Chloe saw eight horses, not yet aware of the humans' presence, grazing on the sweet grasses. Mike smiled when he heard the quick intake of his young daughter's breath.

The stallion stood slightly away from the herd, a proud bay, curving his neck as he looked around, watching for danger, smelling the morning breeze —as he should, for the area was crawling with leopards. The rocks and caves here were a perfect hiding place for them.

'Old Man Tyrrell has been telling me about the wild horses of the Matopos for years, but I wasn't sure if they were a legend or a figment of his imagination,' Mike admitted quietly.

'They're beautiful,' Chloe said.

Everything horse looked beautiful through the eyes of an eight-year-old. Mike smiled, but realised his daughter was right. There was a dappled grey mare flecked with dirt—she looked tri-coloured, but Mike suspected he would find her only grey and black once they cleaned her. The foal close at her side was almost black. Its short, stumpy tail, small mane, and knobbly long legs were evidence of its young age. It stamped its hoof, getting rid of whatever was bothering its leg. The foal looked ready to take on any predator in a race already. Mike was sure, given time, the foal would lighten to the same beautiful grey as its mother. Standing with the mare was a palomino that shone almost golden in the early-morning light, two chestnuts with black manes and tails, and a skewbald. Mike had always had a soft spot for paints. Having grown up on cowboy and western stories of the great American-Indian horses, and what they could endure, he was happy to see that even in his Rhodesia, the breed was strong enough to survive wild in the bush.

'Please, can I have the palomino? It's so pretty,' Chloe said. 'I can call her Honey?'

'Let's see how healthy she is when we get her home. It's important to remember that these horses come at a price. I had to shoot Mr Tyrrell's menace leopard that was eating his stud Brahman calves. These few wild brumbies are payment for our help.'

'Bush bartering,' Chloe said, her eyes focused on the horses.

'I don't want you to think that we're just taking these horses from the wild. Everything has a price. Old Man Tyrrell and his boys had killed several leopards that were not the one causing him trouble; that's why he asked for help.'

'I know, Dad, you and Enoch are always helping the farmers.'

'It's the right thing to do, sweetheart. Sometimes when men get old, they forget how to ask for help. They get stubborn,' Mike said.

'You're never going to get old and stubborn, are you, Dad?' Chloe asked.

Mike almost laughed aloud but held it in, careful not to disturb the horses. He wished he could tell her no, but he tried really hard not to lie to his daughter.

Despite the predators that roamed the Matopos, these wild horses had survived for more than three generations—Old Man Tyrrell swore they were already on his grandparents' farm when he lived there as a boy.

'You ready? We're going to drive these horses north, into the funnel we've built to narrow the valley,' he said, quietly thanking his friends for the cloth borrowed from Brady Barracks in Bulawayo.

'What happens when the horses get there, and they don't know what to do?' Chloe asked.

'Old Man Tyrrell is waiting there with a lead horse. When this little band arrives, he'll release that schooled horse to make sure the wild horses end up inside the boma. That way, they won't hurt themselves. Then after we have them there, we'll funnel them down the cattle chute to load onto the truck.'

As if sensing his life was about to change, and he was about to be taken from the wilderness, the stallion whinnied.

'Come on, we need to get them moving,' Mike said as he took out his .303 rifle and shot it into the air. The sound echoed around the *kopjes*. Rebel and Mongoose stood still—they were used to the sound as they had been trained as hunting mounts.

The wild horses ran from the noise, the stallion leading the way, although one of the bay mares quickly caught him up and began to lead the charge. Mike could see the strength in her muscles as she pounded the ground with her hooves. 'She's like the wind,' he said.

Mike clicked his tongue, and Rebel broke into a trot. 'They've run towards Enoch,' he told Chloe. 'We have to help him press them towards those twin hills.'

He glanced at his daughter. She was seated well in her saddle, Mongoose still close to him. He looked north-east—Enoch was riding to his flank, keeping the horses heading in the right direction. He slipped silently through the bush, almost ghosting Mike and Chloe. Xoline, Enoch's son, was to the west, his horse helping to maintain the herd on track into the funnel.

Mike watched as the wild stallion left the big bay mare to lead the escape. He doubled back behind his herd, getting ready to challenge the danger, then stopped. His nose flared, and with his neck arched he pawed the ground, then reared up. He exuded raw power.

Mike shouted, waved his arms, and the stallion snorted, turned and ran behind his mares again, his flight sense winning over his fight sense.

Despite the bush, the horses weaved their way forward, following the big bay around thornbushes and under low-hanging branches. They were magnificent, never once misplacing their footing, even when they ran over the exposed granite.

A little steenbok female, with her beautiful tawny-orange fur, was surprised from her hiding place. She ran next to the horses in a zig-zag pattern, trying to escape the mayhem. Mike slowed Rebel down in an attempt to give the steenbok a place to escape from the herd. She stopped and looked back at her pursuers. The distinctive marks in her ears, like black fingers, helped to camouflage her in the bushveld. The steenbok could sense that while she wasn't the target of the trap, it was time to flee. She bounced off again, then disappeared.

They slowed their horses and looked around.

'Where did she go, Daddy?' Chloe asked.

'Not sure,' Mike said, then smiled when he spotted her. 'Look, the clever little thing has hidden in an antbear hole.'

'But she's a buck,' Chloe said.

'Animals have more intelligence than people give them credit for. She found a way to escape her pursuers; that's all that matters to her. There is a time to run, but then there is also a time to hide. We would've ridden past and not known she was there.'

Chloe grinned.

'Come on, we have to keep the horses moving,' Mike said as he kicked Rebel in the sides with his heels.

By the time they got to the funnel, the horses were tired, having run for a good forty minutes at a steady pace through the bush.

'Look how Mongoose is sweating,' Chloe said.

Rebel's skin was also lathered. 'Good boy,' Mike said as he patted the horse's neck.

Enoch closed the boma behind the seven horses, Xo right next to him. Their horses hadn't fared any better and were also slick with perspiration.

'Xo and Chloe are in for a long, slow walk after rubbing down these horses to make sure they don't pull up lame,' Enoch said.

'The wild ones are really fit; they've hardly broken a sweat,' Mike said.

'They didn't have to carry the weight of a person on their backs, now did they?' Chloe said.

Old Man Tyrrell climbed up the side of the boma. 'Told you they were here. Aren't they beautiful?'

'They are,' Mike said.

The horses milled around in the boma; the lead horse had stopped and was eating from the lucerne bale that was attached to the side, next to the fresh water in the bathtub that they'd brought in, his presence helping to calm the wild horses. The fact that he was gelded and didn't challenge the stallion also helped.

The white of the stallion's eyes still showed, and he baulked at the food, but the smell of fresh water had him sniffing the air, and soon he dipped his head down to it and drank deeply. The big bay followed his lead.

Mike looked at the bay mare. She was beautiful, and she could run fast. 'Maria,' he said aloud. 'After the wind in *Paint Your Wagon*, that's what you're going to be named.'

'Which one, Daddy?' Chloe asked.

'The big bay next to the stallion. She's a keeper.'

'Maria and Honey. They're friends, right?' Chloe said.

'Of course,' Mick said, ruffling his daughter's hair.

'Right. Breakfast,' Old Man Tyrrell said. 'They can stay in the boma for the day, and when it's cooler tonight we can herd them down the chute and you can drive them home. From then on, they're your problem. Nice foal you captured there. You see it run? Those legs were born to make it eat up the miles.'

'No track for him,' Mike said. 'I'm almost sorry to bring his free running years to an end.'

The foal, as if knowing that he was the centre of the conversation, lifted his head and tail, pranced around a little and stamped his foot, before running back to the protection of his mother.

Mike said quietly, 'Diablo. There's a devil in that horse, just waiting to be unleashed as he grows into his power. One day, he'll raise hell.'

6TH SOCIETY

RULES OF THE 6TH SOCIETY, BERN, SWITZERLAND, 1984

General Member: All persons granted membership into the 6th Society must comply with all by-laws as defined below. Failure to comply will result in a member's immediate termination.

1. No talking about the 6th Society to any person who is not a member.
2. Never acknowledge a 6th Society member outside the safety of the organisation.
3. Only one of the six elite hunters of the organisation can verify a 6th trophy.
4. Never leave your bullet behind.
5. Only one chance to harvest the 6th trophy; if you refuse, your hunter will silence you.
6. Only one 6th trophy per year per member.

Elite Hunter: Only six professional hunters will be appointed membership into the 6th Society at any one time. They must comply with all by-laws as defined below. Failure to comply will result in an elite hunter's immediate termination.

1. No talking about the 6th Society to any person who is not a member.
2. The hunter must ensure the personal safety of the member at all costs. If the hunter is unable to do this without jeopardising the safety of the organisation, the hunter is to take whatever steps necessary to ensure the anonymity of the 6th Society.
3. The hunter is to verify all 6th trophies and to retrieve the bullet. The hunter must also ensure the carcass is disposed of and not traceable back to the member or the 6th Society.
4. The hunter must guarantee that the member hunts mature male specimens only.
5. The member is only allowed one chance to harvest the 6th trophy; if a member refuses, the hunter must terminate the member immediately.
6. The hunter has the discretion of harvesting additional trophies personally; however, they must be reported to the organisation on completion of the hunt.

CHAPTER 1

6TH SOCIETY HEADQUARTERS, BERN, SWITZERLAND, 1984

The building owned by the 6th Society looked the same as many others in the old medieval city centre of Bern. They had been rebuilt after the major fire in 1405 and had stood undefeated on the hill ever since—surrounded on three sides by the river Aare—sharing the space as they shielded the cobbled road.

Except for the old stone carving of a huge eagle-owl that stood sentinel on its lintel above the door, the entrance was as nondescript as all the others in the side street of the financial district. All were made of the same large sandstone blocks, with nothing to reveal what was taking place within the solid walls. The security cameras—discreetly concealed in the owl's eyes—watched the goings-on of the tourists and locals who walked past it each day.

Douglas Smith, known in the organisation as Hunter #4, walked along the corridor behind a woman who wore a long, flowing purple robe. The fabric looked soft, like velvet, and it moved with her every step, as if it was liquid wrapped around her slim body. He found it totally inappropriate for the organisation, but he had never seen her wear anything else in the four years he'd been coming to the headquarters. Her hair was covered by the hood, and he'd never got a good enough glimpse of her face to say he would be able to recognise her in the street, or to see how old she was. She had neat hands, with a deeper skin tone than the Europeans. Her nails, which were immaculately clipped, were devoid of paint or polish.

She motioned him into the Hall of the Hunters for the yearly gathering of the hunters. She'd been part of the Society as long as he had, perhaps longer. He didn't know for sure.

The only time she talked to the visitors at the lodge was to greet them in French when she opened the door, usually before they could even ring the doorbell, and to ask them for their coats and instruct them to empty their pockets before walking through the metal detector just inside the front door. But he was sure that though her French was polished, it was not her native tongue.

The elders were already seated, their black clothes blending with the dark décor of the room. Four of the other 6th hunters were also present. Thankfully, he was not the last one to arrive.

She motioned to the chair assigned to him. Douglas nodded first to the elders then to the others seated at the table, before he lowered himself onto the velvet-cushioned chair that he knew was no Napoleon III rip-off, but a genuine antique from his reign, gifted to one of the 6th Society members.

The purple-robed woman walked out the door, closing it silently behind her, her bare feet making no sound on the plush carpet.

'Good morning,' said the female council elder at the head of the table. She wore her long hair in a neat bun on top of her head, and he could see that it was streaked with grey. She also wore distinctive round John Lennon glasses. Douglas hadn't realised that there had been a leadership restructure since their last meeting. He wondered what else had changed.

'As you may be aware, our previous leader passed away earlier this year. I have been voted the new chairperson by the elders of the 6th. The first item on the agenda is a serious matter. It is not common for the elders to have to address the hunters as a group at the annual gathering, but it is not often we have news like this.' She looked gravely at each of the hunters. 'Hunter #5 showed leniency in offering a member a second chance on a hunt. Furthermore, she was unable to eliminate the member because she had begun a close relationship with them. This jeopardised the 6th by allowing the member time to leave evidence that could damage our organisation. In the end, the member turned #5 into the police in Germany, and the council has had to eliminate both #5 and the member.'

She paused for a moment, giving what she had said time to sink in.

'This type of collaboration between hunter and member should never happen. We feel it necessary to remind you that the rules are in place for a reason. They are there to protect the Society. If the client cannot make a kill or chooses not to complete their hunt, then the penalty must be carried out immediately. Hunter #5 has been replaced, and you will meet the new hunter soon.'

There was silence around the table.

'On a more positive note, your lists of members for the next year are in the folders in front of you. We also remind you that all copies of faxes used in communications both to and from us must be destroyed after you have the information you require. Any questions?'

Again, there was silence around the table.

'Let us proceed.'

The hunters nodded and opened their files.

The meeting had adjourned, and the elders had left the Hall of the Hunters. The silence in the room was shattered when Hunter #3 slammed his hand on the table. 'Hunter #5 would never have talked. It's a pity they eliminated the member because I want to kill him with my bare hands.' He was a tall Icelander, his blue eyes piercing. His accent was strong, and his skin so white it was almost translucent.

'Agreed,' Douglas said, 'but right now, we need to focus on what the council is reminding us of. There are no second chances on a hunt. Either the member kills or we eliminate the member there and then.'

'Yes,' Hunter #2 said.

Douglas looked at her. She was a German woman who wouldn't look out of place on a magazine cover. She'd been one of the 6th hunters since before he'd joined.

'Aye,' Hunter #6 said. The man was tall and broad, and his almost bald head had wisps of red sticking out where he had shaved it close to his skull.

He had a large wiry beard to match, looking as if the hair had slid off his head and onto his chin. One could almost expect the man to wear a kilt, no matter where he was, Scotland or abroad.

'Not that I needed it,' Douglas said, 'but consider me reminded. It would be inconvenient if I have to shoot my own clients on a hunt. Becomes bad for regular hunting business when a client gets shot, but the rules are the rules.'

'They did not say they had to be shot. Any accident could happen,' Hunter #1 said, his Brazilian accent as thick as the black hair on his head, but his English perfectly pronounced.

'Every time we lose a hunter, they remind us of the rules. Each and every one of us knew what was at stake when we became 6th hunters. Losing a member isn't good for anyone's business reputation, so we need to protect our client, no matter what. If that means we need to help them over this decision on the hunt, then so be it,' #2 said.

Hunter #6 nodded his head. 'Most of us hunt in the jungles and the wilds of the world. But #5 was a specialist in the urban environment, and she got caught there. Cornered like a rat. I think that #5's experience was an exception, and we haven't been given all the details.'

'In reality, how many failed members have we had to deal with? They know the consequences when they pay their fees. I've never had a client I couldn't ease into obtaining their trophy, even if the hunt took a day or two longer. A much better outcome for all—as opposed to losing a client,' Douglas said. 'There is a good reason that the council recruited each of us for this job: we are professionals.'

'I have not lost any,' #2 said.

'None,' #6 said.

'None,' #3 said.

'None,' #1 said.

'We must not allow this to happen again,' Hunter #6 said. 'I have seen the occupants of each of your chairs change. All have been good hunters, but this is the first time that I have heard of a client being responsible for an empty chair.'

'Then we need to be more careful, help each other to ensure it doesn't happen again,' Douglas said.

'Agreed,' #6 said. 'Anyone ever needs help, or finds themselves in a similar situation, let's call on each other to sort it through as the hunters, before the executives step in.'

The door opened, and in walked the woman in purple. All the hunters turned to look at her.

'Your discussion has been interesting,' she said.

Douglas clenched his fists. He had always suspected that their hunters' talk time was being monitored. He guessed nothing was secret or personal within the walls of the headquarters, so why wouldn't the executives listen in on the hunters' gathering, too?

She sat down at the head of the table, her movement fluid, graceful, and removed her hood.

'I'm sorry that Hunter #5 did not feel she could confide in the Society of her change of heart. And that she did not ask for help. However, it is good to know that none of you let her down either. It is sad that she did not feel she had friends in her colleagues to call on to assist her with her problem.' She looked around the room, taking the time to look at each hunter's face.

The hunters all remained silent as they stared back at her.

She continued, 'The Society realised that in our own small way, we need to extend our relationship with the 6th Elite Hunters in this changing hunting environment. From now on, if a hunter needs help in any way, personal or professional, they only need to fax and ask. I will always be on your side, and I will do whatever it takes to help you.'

'Who do we address the fax to?' #2 asked. 'Until today, we have never seen your face, much less been introduced to you by name.'

'You may call me Kupua,' she said.

'Kupua?' Hunter #6 said. 'Like the demigod monster that appears in different kinds of bodies?'

'I'm impressed,' she said, yet her eyes were steely. 'But make no mistake; I live up to my name.'

CHAPTER 2

CROCODILE BRIDGE, KRUGER PARK, SOUTH AFRICA, OCTOBER 1986

There would be no debating it'd been a harrowing night out. As the morning sun touched the tops of the mopani trees, Nick stopped the Land Rover when Khululani tapped twice on the dashboard and pointed.

Nick squinted through his windscreen, then grinned as he reached for his camera and climbed out. Resting it on the open door, he looked through the viewer and took a series of photographs. 'The lack of sleep last night was worth it when we get to see Mbulala moving her cubs outside the fence line for the day again.'

'*Yebo*,' Khululani said as he took the binoculars out of the cubby hole and stood on the other side of the Land Rover with them pressed to his eyes. He clicked his tongue. 'She has blood on her face; she must have joined her pride for the hunt last night.'

'Look at those fat spotty bellies; they've obviously just finished nursing,' Nick said, taking another photograph.

Khululani nodded. 'Soon these cubs will be big enough not to hide anymore, and she will stop using our workshop area and fuel drums, and we can mend the fence.'

'I'll miss photographing them here,' Nick said. 'We've built up quite a collection.'

'It's an expensive habit, your photography, having those films developed,' Khululani said, just as one of the cubs started to pounce on their mum's tail that flicked up and down, the only acknowledgement she showed that she knew they were being watched. Finally, she relaxed and began to groom herself, and then each of her cubs, washing them in the early-morning light.

'It's worth it, just look at them,' Nick said. 'One day there won't be any lions left in Africa, and at least then I will have proof that I saw them in real life.'

The lioness got up, her nose clean of blood, and slowly walked away. For a moment, the cubs continued to play, then as they realised their mother was moving, they ran to catch up and fell into line behind her. They slowly headed away from the workshop, and the complications that being in close proximity to the humans could bring, back through the fence and into the bush.

Nick stretched and put his camera on the seat. 'Just as well, my eyes are battling to stay open. Let's put these tools back in the workshop, then I'll drop you at the compound. I vote we both take today off to sleep. I think we've earned it.'

Nick was dragged out of a deep sleep by his phone ringing. 'Hello.'

'Hey, *boet*. Sorry, man, it's Dave. I need your help. There're tourists who've broken down just north of the Crocodile Bridge near the Lindanda Memorial. When one of the safari vehicles drove past, they found the idiots sitting outside their vehicle. The driver told them to get inside his 4x4—or get back inside their car—till they could contact us. Anyway, they insisted they were okay, and their vehicle would be fine once it cooled down.

'The driver reported it when they got into Skukuza campsite, and I sent some rangers to check them out. They found the vehicle abandoned. Those tourists have been missing for about four hours, and we need you to come and find them. I lost their tracks close to the Mozambique border.'

Now fully awake, Nick squinted at the clock. Two pm. He'd only got to bed just before five that morning, after helping fix a ranger's vehicle that had broken down while chasing a hippo that had raided farm lands back into the reserve, and then having to help him get the lumbering mass of blubber back where it belonged before the farmer shot it.

He ran his hand over his stubble. 'I'm on my way.'

'I owe you. I need you and your boy to find them. What idiots go walking in a national park with lions when they're visiting a lion attack memorial? I've been driving around since they were reported. I really expected to get out there, throw a tow rope and bring them into the camp.'

'I'll get Khululani, then we'll join you.'

'Do you want to know where I am?'

'Meeting me at Lindanda Memorial, obviously. I'm sleepy, not stupid.'

Dave chuckled. '*Ja, boet.* See ya soon.'

Nick climbed out of bed and hit the shower. After dressing in his khakis, he nabbed a packet of chocolate Romany Cream biscuits and a couple of Cokes—he needed something in his stomach to get him going—and headed out the door, grabbing his hat on the way. He made sure both backpacks were sitting in the back of his Land Rover, and that he had fresh water in the canisters hanging on the outside. Climbing in, he opened the windows to let out the hot air trapped inside. He drove around to the workshop, looking for Khululani, who, if he was awake and at work as Nick suspected he would be, was hopefully servicing the lorry that had broken down when the men were out collecting wood from a big mopani tree that had been struck by lightning. Given that the tractor had blown something the week before, and was still being repaired, taking the lorry had seemed like a practical solution, until that had also broken down.

He found Khululani lying under the lorry. His black legs were recognisable. Lighter than the rest of him, they held a shiny glow to the damaged skin, and were laced with a patchwork of scarring. He refused to wear the long pants of the overalls issued by the Kruger Park management. Instead, he would cut them into shorts so that they didn't irritate him by rubbing on his scars.

Nick didn't have an issue with this. Still, some of the other senior rangers did as it made Khululani look different to the others. Because of that, he hadn't progressed up the ranks. He'd remained a junior ranger, on a junior's pay, despite his ability to do everything well, aside from sitting the ranger's exams. Khululani was illiterate, and that above everything else was probably what was holding him back. Nick was working on that one, and soon they would surprise those idiots who sat in their office and thought that literacy was the most important skill in the park.

There was so much more to being a good ranger. An overall approach was needed, or an alternate way for Khululani to take those exams.

'*Woza*, Khululani, time to finish up here. We need to head into the park,' Nick called out.

The trolley under the lorry zipped out, and Nick saw the familiar wide grin on Khululani's face, which he always wore when he was going into the bush.

Of all the rangers, Nick knew that Khululani loved the animals and the bush with the deepest passion—as if every animal or tree belonged to him. If you took the time to listen to the older man, he'd tell you stories of the rangers in the past, and how they'd had prison gangs working to clear areas to erect the fences to keep the game inside and safe. He'd tell you of the many *deurlopers* that came from Mozambique to work in the gold mines of Johannesburg, and how they'd saved many of them after they'd been treed by lions—and buried what was left of the not-so-fortunate ones. Khululani's face was creased with the years spent labouring in the hot African sunshine, and yet when he smiled, it was a face that was grateful for his full life.

'You came to save me from this white man's work and take me into the bush? Twice in twenty-four hours?' Khululani said as he approached the Land Rover, cleaning his hands on an old rag.

'Sure did. We've got a couple of lost tourists to find.'

Khululani continued to grin as he walked towards the Land Rover, then gathered himself to climb into the tray at the back.

'Get in the front,' Nick said. 'We need to talk about these idiots walking around in lion country unarmed.'

Khululani nodded and got into the passenger seat, closing the door with a loud bang.

Nick drove off, thinking about the friendship he experienced with Khululani. Not so long ago, he'd done everything possible to keep others at a distance. Not so surprising for someone from his background, really. Not with his useless father, and his mother's inability to stand up to his drunken, thieving ways. Nick had been happy when the bastard had eventually abandoned them and disappeared into Africa somewhere. Nick didn't know if he was still alive, and he didn't care. By the time he was five, he'd been smacked across the head enough times and told that cowboys didn't cry, to know that he dared never show any emotions when his father was around, sober or drunk. His mother's friendship with Sarah Mitchell had been his saviour in a time when a boy needed a decent role model and mentor. Mike Mitchell had been everything that Nick had wanted his father to be and more. But even Mike had let Nick down.

Enoch had always been at Mike's side, and Nick had had a deep respect for both of them, to the point that he had even rushed to enlist into the Grey's Scouts as soon as he was of legal age to serve with them. He had put them both on a pedestal so high that when they tumbled off, they had almost crushed him with their fall.

Though guilt still ate at him for not doing more on the day Mike had been hurt, the resentment he had felt at the time had simmered close to the surface. He had chosen to leave Zimbabwe before he did something he would regret, to cut all ties and start a new life in South Africa.

Away from the heavy burden of being let down. Away from those he'd once believed in.

To others it had appeared that he had run from the demons of war, and the loss of his country to a man he had never even heard of before the elections. Nick had never bothered to correct them. His reasons were more personal than that. He'd walked away from a friendship that had been born in blood and trust but shattered by gold. Gold that was supposed to be the noblest of metals, but which to him represented the stain of betrayal.

He had shied away from relationships and forming connections with others, remaining aloof and reserved. Alone. Until Khululani had saved his life. Nick had accepted the position in Kruger National Park as a chance to start again, but he hadn't been prepared for what being back in the bush would really be like.

Hours of alone time to think on the past, to mull over and over what had happened. But within the first week of Nick's arrival in Kruger as a ranger, Khululani had appeared at his door after work and told him they needed to go walking in the bush together. Instead of telling Khululani to get lost, Nick had accompanied him, and then again, the next day. Soon they had got into a routine. After the work was done, he wouldn't even enter his house. Instead, he and Khululani would walk for a few hours.

To anyone watching, Khululani was teaching him the South African names of the trees and plants, and the history of the park. What Khululani had done was to give him a new purpose in life, to protect those animals, plants and people within the fence. A different country, a different fence, but the task was just as vital. But to Nick, even more importantly, he'd learned to love Kruger Park with the same fierce passion that Khululani did.

'How's the lorry going?'

'That axle is *ifela*. Dead. I can't fix this one. We need to get a new one, or newer at least. Jeremiah has a brother who works at a scrap yard in Pietersburg; he says he is sure he saw a truck just like this last time he was there. He wanted to call him tonight on the telephone if you let him.'

'Sure. We need it up and running again, and we don't have lots of money in the budget, so we must *maak 'n plan*.'

Khululani nodded. 'What about these tourists?'

'We don't have much information—two of them, disappeared early this morning,' Nick said.

Khululani clicked his tongue. 'Inthunzi Zingela could have them by now. We could be looking for two dead people.'

The Shadow Hunter, as the black people called him, was the whispered foreboding to whoever went missing around the national park area lately. No one ever saw him, but the body count of those found with bullets dug out of their heads was adding up. As far as Nick knew, the police in the area were not getting any closer to solving the mystery.

'Do you know how many people have already walked over their spoor?' Khululani asked.

'Too many. Dave Muller and whoever was with him lost the tracks; they called us in.'

'Always, when the other trackers give up, they call you and me. The grease monkeys do their jobs and save their bacon again.'

'True. But I'd rather talk to an engine and hear it purr when it's fixed, than have to listen to the constant chatter of the tourists like parrots screeching in my ear.'

Khululani laughed. 'One day you will meet the one woman whose voice does not annoy you, and then you'll think differently.'

'Not likely.' But an image of a beautiful sixteen-year-old girl surfaced in his mind. He blinked and shook away the memory.

'Did you pack the water?' Khululani asked, still smiling.

'Don't ask stupid questions.'

The Land Rover always had jerry cans of spare diesel and water. Along with his shotgun and hunting rifle, and enough ammo to bring down a small herd of buffalo if needed, his emergency backpack was always ready for days just like this, when he'd be out looking for tourists and could end up spending the night out. He'd rather be prepared than end up in the bush at night with no provisions.

Khululani had once told him a story about a man who'd been driven mad with thirst and chewed on a tree for moisture, as he'd seen the bushmen do. Only he didn't know the plants of the area—the sap had been poisonous and caused hallucinations. He'd thought that the buffalo around him weren't real and had tried to pat them on the hindquarters, to tell them they were no trouble to him. He didn't remember them attacking him, or the men who'd found him a day later lying battered and trampled in the veld. Nick was always doubly cautious about the water after hearing that story.

On arriving at the memorial, they chatted briefly to the other ranger, then got to work. Nick handed Khululani a .303 rifle, and he took the other one from the cab of his Land Rover. He'd trusted his life to the accuracy that Khululani had with a rifle more than once while walking in lion country.

Nick's tracking skills were good—having practically grown up on Mike's farm in Zimbabwe and hunted for the pot from an early age—but Khululani's were better. It might've been the twenty-nine years more experience he had on Nick, but the man could find the proverbial needle in the haystack. Together, they'd become well known for finding lost people inside the Kruger.

They circled around.

'Here,' Khululani said, pointing out the heel imprint in the sand. 'And here. A smaller print. A woman.'

Nick nodded.

'That way, towards Mozambique.'

They headed into the bush. He could see where the other rangers had lost the spoor and turned back.

'Here. This is where they went wrong. Now we look together,' Khululani said, and they changed from single file to walking abreast a few metres apart.

Only a little way further, Khululani said, 'Two walked this way, one on each side of the dirt road, in the track indentations made by the vehicles. Here, they walked into the pack of lions. The tourists ran that way.' He pointed. 'Into the bush.'

'The lions didn't give chase,' Nick said, reading the tracks in the sand.

Khululani laughed. 'Perhaps they were too surprised by two people walking into their dining room while they were eating,' he said as he pointed to the fresh zebra carcass.

The carcass was barely bones; a brown hyena crunched on the cartilage in a rib cage, and a few vultures hopped around, their necks still bloody from the feast they'd enjoyed, bellies too full to allow them to take to the skies.

'I wonder what's moved the lions on?' Nick asked. 'They should be here defending their kill so they can eat again.'

Khululani took his floppy jungle hat from his head and wiped his brow with it. '*Eish*, keep an extra eye out.'

This was where the footprints became faint and harder to follow once they'd plunged into the veld. Knob-thorn trees dominated the area which had obviously received good rains, as it was lush, green and well grown.

'They have several hours on us,' Nick said as he took a small swig from his water bottle, the heat of the day still burning down on them.

'They are scared. They tread softly, not sure where to put their feet. We will catch them quickly. Maybe before the next pride of lions,' Khululani said.

'They've turned again and headed south here,' Nick said.

Khululani nodded. 'Perhaps they have found the river and will follow it, hoping that it joins the Orpen Dam.'

'We can hope they headed for water; perhaps they will wait in the shade or find a decent tree to climb and wait for us,' Nick said.

'I will not put my money on them waiting,' Khululani said. 'My hope is only that when we find them, they are still alive, and we are not the ones having to see inside their heads. Look—there are other tracks; someone might be following them. I cannot be sure as they crossed the tracks. Two people, one carries something heavy, and is tired, the other walks easier. They are both still fresh. We will need to watch if they cross again, or if they fall in behind the tourists.'

'You think it could be the Inthunzi Zingela?'

Khululani shrugged his shoulders. 'I do not know, but there are others walking in the park, and that is never good.'

They tracked southwards, and too soon dusk was upon them.

Nick spoke into his radio. 'Dave, come in.'

'Nick.'

'We followed their prints a lot further than your team, but we still have no visual. We're going to stop for a while and see if they light a fire,' Nick said.

'Okay, we'll camp at Tshokwane,' Dave said.

'There's another set of footprints crossing theirs, coming from the Mozambique side. Might check those out once we have the tourists.'

'Damn it. I'll let headquarters know. Chances are it's poachers, but it could be the Shadow Hunter.'

'Don't even jinx us with thinking that. We haven't found a body inside the park; they've all been on the perimeter. It's going to be really dark out here, and he's the last thing we need to be thinking about.'

'*Ja, boet.* Take care out there. Goes without saying that if they walk into camp, let me know.'

Nick smiled. 'Khululani and I like nights out in the open in the middle of summer with all the mosquitoes as much as you love losing tourists.'

'Aren't you the funny one,' Dave said, then ended the transmission.

The sky was alight with a million stars, but storm clouds threatened in the distance. Lightning flashed, and the world shuddered at its ferocity. Nick watched Khululani climb up a big knob tree, as high up as the branches would hold his weight.

'I can see a fire—don't know if it is *deurlopers* or tourists—about two kilometres south of us.'

'Hopefully it's the tourists. You up for the night walk?' Nick asked.

'As long as we are armed and they are not, we do not have a choice, do we?' Khululani said.

'Guess not. Come on, get down from there and if we're lucky we'll get to them before the rain hits.'

Amazed at how agile Khululani remained, Nick watched him descend the tree faster than he'd climbed it. They walked in silence, listening to the night sounds of the bush, where crickets chirped, cicadas screamed their never-ending serenade, and the frogs joined in the night chorus. The deep *hoot-hoot* of an eagle-owl sounded as he voiced his disapproval at the men; their eyes strained to see him in the branches of a nearby tree.

'*Maywe, Nkhunsi,*' Khululani warned.

Nick had heard this often: an owl being a messenger of death from an evil person. 'Don't go all superstitious on me,' he told Khululani. 'We could see their fire, they're alive. We've watched many eagle-owls without dying.'

'You know the Shangaan belief. There is death coming …'

Nick knew when Khululani got his mind set on something, he wouldn't let it go. 'Let's pick up the pace and make sure it's not our tourists and it's not tonight, then.'

They only had to stop once for a large herd of buffalo to pass by, but the herd seemed to have a destination to reach before the rains came too, so they weren't delayed for long.

They came up a small incline and could see the fire clearly. Anyone covert wouldn't have had a fire. Poachers wouldn't build a fire at all. *Deurlopers* might have tried for a smaller one. Tourists build theirs big, having no idea that a rhino would try to put it out for them during the night.

'Smell that?' Khululani asked, sniffing loudly.

'Just the smoke.'

'In the smoke. Tamboti. Cover your mouth and nose,' he warned as he pulled his hankie from his pocket and tied the knot behind his head.

They heard the vomiting of the tourists before they saw them, standing side by side with the toxic fumes from the wood washing over them as they continued to stay as near to the fire as they could.

'Good to see you two are alive,' Nick said, 'we've been looking for you all afternoon. I'm Nick, and this is Khululani. First thing we need to do is sort out your toxic fire.'

They began pulling the logs off the fire and throwing sand onto them to stop them from burning any further, smothering the flames and ending the poisonous smoke. Nick then threw on pieces that were safe to burn.

The woman sat down where she was and sobbed while continuing to sporadically throw up.

'I'm Herbie, and this is Floss. Thank God, you found us.'

Nick took a bottle of water from his pack and handed it to the tourists. 'Sip it slowly.'

'Thank you,' Herbie said, and gave it to Floss first.

Nick smiled. They'd be alright.

When the fire was banked and casting a warm light, the tourists sat huddled together, sipping at the water. There was nothing Nick could do for them to help with the nausea; their own bodies needed to fight the poison. Herbie had commented that he was dizzy.

'It's one of the effects of burning Tamboti,' Nick told him. 'Just sit there and rest. It'll start to clear out of your system now that the smoke's gone.'

They heard a distinctive *whoop-whoop* of a brown hyena close by, and the serenade of the night animals continued. A far-off cry of a jackal had Floss snuggling tighter into Herbie as the fire popped and crackled, sending sparks high into the sky and lighting up the small group around it.

Nick got on the CB radio. 'Dave, we have them.' He explained where they were and about the Tamboti intoxication. 'They should be okay by morning, and we'll walk them out. Think it best if we just camp here for the night.'

'*Lekker, boet.* See you at sunrise,' Dave said.

After putting away the radio, Nick looked around the spot where they would be camping. There was no natural shelter from the rain coming, but at least the ground was almost flat. Khululani and Nick set up their small two-man tents and threw Nick's sleeping bag into the one that Herbie and Floss would use. It would depend on the rain if Nick and Khululani even bothered getting into theirs. Although they were both tired from the previous night's excursion, they would take turns to stay awake, on guard, against any predators approaching the camp.

Nick stepped away from the fire and shared the food out onto the two plates. He passed one to Herbie. 'You need to try to eat. That is for both of you.'

'What is it?' Floss asked.

'Smash—a rehydrated powdered potato with a bully-beef topping. Think of it as bangers and mash with a bush twist.'

Floss pulled a face.

'You have nothing in your stomach. Your body needs some food to enable you to walk out of here tomorrow. It's a long way back to our *bakkie*. You'll need the energy.'

Floss took the fork and tasted it. 'It's not too bad.'

Herbie took the fork. 'Not bad at all.' He started to load it into his mouth.

'Slowly,' Khululani warned. 'You need to eat slowly, or it will come back up again.'

Herbie nodded. 'Tell you what, when we're back in camp, I'll buy you two a proper meal of bangers and mash to say thank you.'

'Deal,' Nick said.

Khululani was making the tea while they ate. 'Drink this,' he said, putting a mug next to each of them. He'd left the teabags in to make it extra strong and added lots of sugar along with the powdered milk. Khululani's one vice was that they always carried powdered milk when they went out. Nick had become accustomed to seeing him eat his from the packet.

After dinner, the tourists disappeared into a tent, and soon they could hear Herbie snoring. Khululani and Nick continued to sit on their packs, in front of the low fire, late into the night. When the thunder, lightning and cool rain drenched the camp and put out the fire, the rangers took turns being on watch until sunrise.

After all, in lion country, you slept with one eye open, or you died.

CHAPTER 3

PIETERMARITZBURG, SOUTH AFRICA, NOVEMBER 1986

'Get your *kaffir* driver to park in the road next time,' Meneer Botha shouted, adding to his already foul monologue of where and what he thought black people should and shouldn't be allowed to do. 'Next, he'll be thinking he can sit at your table and eat like a civilised human, too, just because he knows how to drive.'

'Ignore that racist bastard,' Chloe said quietly. 'Don't react.'

Enoch opened the passenger door, and she got in. He walked around and climbed in the other side, shook the umbrella and put it against the door.

Huge raindrops shattered on the windscreen as the thunder crashed overhead. Chloe shook the tiny bit of rain from her hair as a dog would from its coat.

'You sure you have everything? Nothing left behind?' Enoch asked.

'I've got everything, although I'm happy to be leaving that racist pig behind.' Chloe looked at the building which had been her share house at Pietermaritzburg University for the past three years—it hadn't changed since she'd enrolled for her Bachelor of Commerce degree, and she was pretty sure it would look exactly the same when she came back next year to start her honours. The yellow briar roses bloomed across the front of the building, a pretty touch to the Dutch Gable residence she had been assigned to by the university.

'Come on, let us go home.' Enoch started the *bakkie*, and a loud backfire and belch of black smoke came from the exhaust, but he didn't put it into gear.

Chloe groaned. 'Still not fixed?'

'Not yet. I try—but we need a new vehicle, not a fix.'

'Wish it wasn't so low down on the list. At least we won't have to pay accommodation fees for three months.'

'Truly. It will be good to have you home for a while.'

'Home ...' Chloe sighed. 'How is he today?'

'He was alright when I left this morning.'

'Only because you guys are there with him all the time.'

'True. On Wednesday, he had a bad turn while we were out. Ethel tried her best, but she could not stop him hitting his head on the floor when he fell. It took us hours to calm him down when we got home. Unfortunately, he had to get stitches again.'

Chloe shook her head. 'What would I do without you guys there to watch over him?'

'I will always be there for you and your dad; you know that. Besides, in one more year you will have an honours degree, and then you can get a good-paying job.'

'I know, but I still feel bad having to leave Dad with you so much. I can't thank you enough for always being there for us.' She reached over and squeezed his arm. 'I worry that I'll forget what Mum and Dad were like.' She didn't elaborate that what terrified her was not remembering how kind her dad used to be, and how—after her parents had read her a bedtime story—her dad would tuck her into her bed so tightly she could hardly breathe, and he'd smother her with kisses, knowing that she couldn't stop him.

Enoch smiled. 'I remember when he would ride with you doubled up on his saddle, on Diablo or Maria. Not because you could not ride, but just so that you were together.'

'And on the tractor,' Chloe said, 'ploughing rows and rows of straight lines, and then when the beans had started growing, we'd spend hours watching the herds of impala and kudu that fed on them. Ah, man, I'm remembering aeons of time on the old Massey Ferguson.'

'You see. You are not forgetting. It is all there in your head, and in your heart.'

She smiled. 'Sometimes I still see Dad as he was before the accident.'

'He is in there. Yesterday I told him I was fetching you, and this morning he went into the garden where he picked a rose from the bush for you. Ethel found him in the kitchen, shredded by the thorns—it took her some time to get him cleaned up.'

'He's getting good at giving her the slip.' Her eyes filled with tears.

After her father had been injured, he had changed. At first, they'd thought that he only had a head injury, but it had turned out that he'd also suffered spinal damage. A combination that had left him with a confused mind and trapped inside a body that would often not obey him, especially on his left side where he had limited movement.

He had difficulty concentrating for any length of time, and while his long-term memory was fine, he had shown minimal capacity to process anything that had happened after the incident. Most days he struggled to remember if he'd eaten lunch. He'd lost nearly all ability to speak and needed assistance with almost all his day-to-day activities. In older times, people would have said he'd become 'simple'.

The doctors had said he was suffering from cognitive impairments due to the severe brain injury, and a spinal cord injury at the C5 vertebra. They'd warned Chloe of the possible change in his behaviour once the swelling in his brain went down, that he might become increasingly aggressive. That if his voice returned, he might become very vocal, yell and swear, and possibly possess an explosive temper. Or that he might retreat totally into himself, completely withdrawn from the world. There had also been multiple warnings about his spinal injury, that his breathing would always be weak. The paralysis on his left side might improve, and he may regain some of the movement in his arm, and perhaps bend his elbow, but more mobility on that side was unlikely.

When she'd travelled down to South Africa, she'd employed a nurse, who had taken care of her father's everyday needs twenty-four hours a day. Chloe had shared that responsibility with her while they checked with doctors in Johannesburg, and then Cape Town to see if there was any hope for rehabilitation. At just sixteen years old, she'd had to switch places with her father; she had become his guardian and carer.

Eventually, they'd ended up at a brain injury hospital in Howick, and the doctors there had advised her to put her father in permanent care. Even threatened to take him away from her. Still, she'd insisted that in less than a month, more adult help would arrive. She'd have the support of others who'd ensure that he would be more comfortable at home than in an institution. The doctor had given her time to consider both her and her father's futures, and time was what she'd needed while Enoch and Xo made their way through the bush with the horses to join them in South Africa.

Things were pretty much the same five years down the track.

'Come on. Let us get home so Mike can remember with us, too,' Enoch said as he put the *bakkie* into gear, just as another round of thunder shook the vehicle. 'Your suitcase is going to be saturated by the time we get to the farm.'

'It all needs to be laundered anyway,' Chloe replied as she dug out the belt from behind the seat.

Enoch put on his flicker to move out from his parking spot close to the door. Dependable Enoch who had never let her down. Enoch, her father's best friend. And his son, Xoline, her best friend.

She remembered so clearly her drive across the Beitbridge border five years ago, into the land of apartheid. Where everything she had known as normal had changed so dramatically.

In South Africa, Enoch and Xo were viewed as nothing more than servants—or workers at best. They were considered to be her driver and the horse boy, not part of her family. But skin colour did not define a family for Chloe. Together with her father, Enoch and Xo were all the family she had left, other than Aunty Grace, who had stayed behind on their farm in Zimbabwe.

'Last chance to wave goodbye to all your friends,' Enoch said.

'If I hug one more person, I might just stick to them I'm sweating so much.'

'The horse trough is nice and clean; you can have a splash when you get home,' Enoch said.

'Thanks. Bet it was Xo who removed the slime and frogs for me.'

'Of course.' Enoch smiled and slowly edged the yellow Datsun *bakkie* out of the parking. 'Ethel is too busy with your father to help clean outside the house.'

A horn blasted behind them.

'Come on, *kaffir*, I don't have all day!' Meneer Botha shouted out of his window.

'One day, I am going to shove my fist down the throat of that fat son of a —'

'Stay here,' Chloe said as she opened her door, and was out as Enoch grabbed at the air where her arm had just been.

She stormed to where Meneer Botha hung out of the side of his Mercedes-Benz. She watched as his hand beat his annoyance on the thin metal.

'Meneer Botha, I don't like the way you speak to Enoch, and I'd appreciate it if you'd stop treating him like a second-class citizen. For three long years we've put up with your racist slurs whenever he fetches me, and in all that time has he done anything to you?'

'No, but —'

'No buts! Can you remember any time when he hasn't gone out of his way to help your family, despite your horrible behaviour? Do you remember when you had a flat tyre going up Fields Hill, and we brought Melissa to you so you didn't need to travel back to Umdloti in the dark? Enoch drove her there, despite making himself late for a cattle pick-up. Even though you never bothered to thank him, he has been nothing but a gentleman towards you.'

'You told him to drive Melissa there —'

'No. It was his idea. I had an assignment due and just wanted to go home as fast as I could. That was Enoch's good heart helping your family. Believe me, Enoch is a better man than you. He's not someone who should have to put up with the way you speak to him. He fought in the war in Zimbabwe alongside my dad, and he's part of our family. I ask you to show him the same respect and courtesy that you would show my dad, because I'd like to believe that my friend has a decent father, even though this side of your character says otherwise.'

'I … I …'

'I'm not asking you to apologise for behaviours gone, Lord knows that would never happen, but I am asking you to be a better person and to not disrespect Enoch again.'

Meneer Botha's face was now red, and Chloe could see he was near his breaking point of humiliation.

'I'll leave you to think about the way you treat people. I hope that from now on, you'll show the community that perhaps deep down inside you're a kinder and better-mannered person than the one we've seen over the last few years.' Chloe looked past Meneer Botha to where her friend sat. 'Bye, Melissa,' she said, before she turned and walked back to where Enoch stood under the umbrella at the back of the *bakkie*. Immediately he sheltered her with it, allowing himself to get wet as he walked her towards the passenger door. She turned around and shouted, 'Good luck for the holidays!'

'Why are you wishing her luck?' Enoch asked.

'You've met her father; don't you think she needs it?'

'Good point,' Enoch said as he opened her door. Once back in the driver's seat, he released the handbrake, placed his foot on the accelerator and drove out of the gates, another backfire covering the Botha's car with black exhaust fumes.

'Do you want to tell me what you said to Meneer Botha? He looked ready to burst, his face was so red.'

'We were discussing the correct way for him to address his betters, that's all.'

'Did not look like it from where I was standing.'

She grinned.

Enoch smiled and switched on the windscreen wipers as the rain turned into a torrential downpour.

She turned her head to look out of the side window as the rain splattered against it.

The rain stopped as they turned right off the main road and onto the dirt one that led towards their smallholding. Chloe began to fidget.

'What is wrong?' Enoch asked.

'I don't understand, men like Meneer Botha or Sebastian. We've never done anything to them, so why won't they just leave us alone to live our own lives?'

'They do not think like you and me. They see the colour of skin as a measure of character and a means to judge who a person is. They are too stupid to see the truth.'

'True, but it makes me feel bad for you. Them not being able to see you for who you really are makes me so mad.'

Enoch looked over at her. 'Chloe, I have never treated you as anything other than the daughter I never had. It is not important what small-minded men think, just that I have done my best by you, that you are a daughter both Mike and I can be proud of.'

'Oh, Enoch,' Chloe said.

For as long as she could remember, Enoch had been a second father to her. He had taught her to drive when she was only fifteen so that she could get her licence as soon as she turned sixteen. He'd also drilled her in unarmed combat skills, making sure she and Xo kept their tracking up, so that they knew how to disappear in the bush if they needed, for survival.

'I'm not sure what I would do without you and Xo.'

'You would be fine. You are mature beyond your years. You had to grow up fast with your father but know that Xo and I will always be there with you.'

Enoch stopped at the gate. The sign on the small farm was old, but you could still read 'Amalfi' quite clearly. The 'No Trespassers' sign next to it was newer. Despite their best efforts, her father had a habit of disappearing on them, but he never seemed to go outside the gated area. Trying to keep people out went some way to ensuring that no one accidentally left the gate open, which helped protect her father.

Chloe climbed out, pushed the gate open and waved Enoch through. As he went past her, she put her hand out and begged for money, as many of the black kids used to do on other farms. He playfully slapped her hand. He stopped on the other side to let Chloe climb on the back. Standing up, she took the elastic out of her hair and let the wind comb it as he drove the last stretch. She could smell the freshness after the storm and the familiar aroma of home. Her house came into view, and she smiled.

The thatch-roofed cottage was painted white, the beams under the windows stained black, in the Tudor style popular with many South African farmers. The garden that surrounded it was meticulously groomed; it reminded her of Delaware, the home they had left behind in Zimbabwe. That was why she had chosen to settle here. When she saw the picture of the house five years ago, she had negotiated to lease the farm and they had lived here since.

Accessing superior medical care in South Africa had been the main objective of leaving Zimbabwe, but always in her mind was what she'd seen on the night her dad had been hurt. She had a deep-seated dread that the police would come looking for him, because of what he and Enoch might have done.

She was almost certain that she'd seen Enoch bury someone that night. But when she'd asked him about it, Enoch had told her to drop the subject and never bring it up again.

The huge oak trees that surrounded the lawns had bright green leaves of summer on them already, and at the bases of the trees there was a mass of bright fuchsias covered in their little lantern flowers which danced in the wind. The wire fence that separated the garden from the farm was strung tightly, keeping the sheep and horses out of Xo's masterpiece. Washing flapped in the wind on the line and wood smoke curled from the donkey boiler at the back.

Chloe jumped off the *bakkie* as soon as Enoch stopped the vehicle in its parking space in the workshop area at the side of the house.

Xo was waiting as always when they drove in, waiting to catch her when she jumped off the *bakkie,* wanting to hear about her week at varsity and to help carry her bag into the house. He would wait while she changed and kicked her clothes in a pile in the corner of her room, and then race her to the paddock and call their horses, if he hadn't already got them ready and waiting in the stable.

Friday was steeplechase afternoon, when she got to ride freely and feel Pampero's strength under her as they raced around the small farm over the ever-changing course that she and Xo had constructed.

'I'm home,' she said, giving him a hug.

CHAPTER 4

Douglas stared down at the fax and then at his diary that he was trying to concentrate on, but the image of the two game rangers who had interrupted his opportunistic hunt last month niggled in the back of his mind. Demanding he correct what was denied him.

He'd been with a Polish client, Aleksy Bargiel, and they'd followed the targets from the Paul Kruger gates when the odd tourists had pushed in front of them to pay for entry. Douglas had planned on using the park to cut down the time to get to Komatipoort before they went into Mozambique, where the 6th hunt was going to take place.

Rude, obnoxious people who cut in and had no manners deserved what they got in life, and if he had any say in the issuing of karma, it would be a lead present.

He'd casually started up a conversation with the couple, telling them about the Lindanda Wolhuter Memorial, and how they had to visit it. How it was best viewed late in the day when the golden sunlight lit the area where the ranger had once fought off the two lions that'd attacked him just at sunset, before dragging him off into the bushes, and how despite that, the ranger had managed to stab the lions with a knife and kill one. How he'd climbed into a tree in order to survive in the bush, until his colleagues came and took him to safety.

Douglas had set them up perfectly. He'd even ensured they'd have engine trouble by slamming a screwdriver into their radiator. But those rangers had robbed him of his kill, just as a cheetah is often robbed of theirs by another predator.

Except the game rangers were not apex predators. They were just guards. But there was something about the way those two worked together, how they'd found the couple, the way they seemed as one with the bush, that had had him backing away from his first instinct—to hunt them, too.

He could have instructed Aleksy to take the black ranger as his 6th and he would have had the white one as a bonus kill for himself. It wasn't often that he got the opportunity for multiple hunts in one day. But he hadn't.

And their images continued to burn in his gut. He'd made the right choice to abandon the hunt. But one day soon, he would finish what he'd started. Because Douglas Jones always finished what he started. It was who he'd become. A man that had been created in the back alleys of Manchester's slums, and the corridors of the community home he'd been sent to at the age of fourteen.

He shook his head to try to dislodge the memories, but it was too late. At times, as now, they came flooding back …

The train tracks that led through the dockside warehouse of Stalford Docks hadn't been used in over ten years. Not since they began to use the huge containers on the bigger ships that couldn't make it up the canal, which was too shallow to accommodate them. The merchants who'd stored their cargo here had left long ago, leaving behind a derelict dockside building, with damp rising into the red brick mortar from the ground level, and the rain slowly collapsing the slate roof from the top. In a place where unemployment continued to rise, and the slum areas around Salford continued to degenerate, the condemned building was used by the youngsters in the area who needed a place to hang out. To hide away from the ugly places where they lived.

Graffiti covered the walls inside and out and the doors no longer shut; some of the hinges had long rusted through and fallen off. No one cared. They just added to the industrial mess with their own discarded cigarette butts and newspapers that once had wrapped greasy fish and chips.

Eric sat by the door, swinging his chair backwards on one leg, perched precariously, as if by magic. He held the position as he spoke with Tommy, Douglas's best friend, who was also there to negotiate what they needed to do to join the Dead Snakes gang in Manchester. In front of them sat Joe, who claimed to be the local leader. He was about twenty years old, had terrible acne, and all Douglas could look at were the pus-filled sores on his face, and wonder if he squeezed those whether the pus would hit the mirror with the pressure release. He realised that Joe was talking again, and tried to concentrate on what he was saying.

'You'll have to prove yourself before you can join. You have to be guerrillas. We expect you to be able to do things. Things that need you to be fit and strong. At your age, you might not be … let's say, *physically mature* enough. I'm not sure you can do it …'

'We want to join now. Tell us what to do? We're ready for the initiation,' Douglas said, adding his cigarette butt to the pile on the floor.

'Yeah,' said Tommy, 'we're ready. We've done everything you asked us so far. Everything. What else do we need to do to prove ourselves?'

Joe said, 'I've seen other boys unable to complete their tasks. They get caught and rat to the police. They never get to do the fun stuff like blow something up.'

'We won't rat,' Tommy said.

Joe looked at them. 'Under the Barton Road Swing Bridge, there's a man who's a nobody. He's old and dirty. Says he was a pilot in WWII. Nobody will miss him when you beat him to death.'

Douglas leaned forwards so that all four legs of his chair touched the floor. 'That all?'

Joe said, 'Kill the Royal British Navy pilot, and you're one of us.'

'Thought it'd be something hard,' Tommy said. 'What-ya-say, Douglas? You and me, we can take him!'

'Might be,' Douglas said. 'How long do we have to complete the initiation?'

'Tonight.' Joe sniffed hard and sucked snot down the back of his throat in a guttural snort.

Douglas nodded. 'And if he's not there?'

'He'll be there,' Joe said. 'He's there every night. He ain't got no place to go.'

It seemed like a simple enough initiation, but Douglas and Tommy hadn't counted on being set up. No sooner had they begun their attack on the old man than the police were there shouting at them and hitting them with their billy clubs.

'Keep your hands in the air,' the copper yelled. 'On your knees!'

Douglas could feel the roughness of the man's hands as he jerked first his left arm and then the right, to snap on the cold handcuffs.

'On your feet,' the copper shouted as he dragged him up by his arms, pulling them further up his back, causing Douglas to cry out in pain. The copper marched him to the waiting paddy wagon and practically threw him inside.

Douglas rolled on the floor and used the bench on the side to help him stand. He turned around when he heard a groan from outside. Tommy didn't look so good. The copper had smacked him hard with his billy club when he had found the boys attempting to beat up the old guy. While Douglas had immediately disengaged, Tommy had refused to stop kicking the beggar, who had given them as good as they managed together to give him, and kept kicking Tommy back. The copper had gone in hard to break them up. It was amazing that Tommy was standing at all. He had a cut somewhere in his hair, which was obviously still open as blood poured down his face. He was also handcuffed.

'Stop fighting and just get in, Tommy,' Douglas said. 'Once you're in, that jackass won't hurt you anymore. We'll sue them for police brutality.'

The tall copper laughed loudly. 'You think you can report us for brutality? Dream on, you little shits. Have you seen that poor old guy you beat up?'

'I hope he dies!' Tommy shouted.

'Don't talk,' Douglas said. 'Don't say another word to these pigs.'

The copper smacked Tommy on the head with his wooden club again, causing him to fall to the floor. 'Yeah, you little shit, listen to your buddy here. Don't talk, because believe me, when we get to the station there'll be plenty of talking going on. Most of it will be the magistrate putting you in an adult prison cell for this.' He slammed the door closed.

Tommy groaned.

'You okay?' Douglas asked.

'My head hurts. Why didn't you fight back, Douglas? Why did you just give up?'

'Because I needed my mind to fight another day,' Douglas said as he looked at the ugly purple egg forming on Tommy's forehead.

'What happened? He was supposed to be a nobody, not someone who knew how to fight. He kicked our arses. I think Joe set us up. He wanted us to be caught; it's like me mum says, you can't trust nobody but family.'

'Bullshit,' said Douglas, 'being part of a gang might be the only thing that'll save us now.'

'Hell yeah, and only if we don't talk.'

Douglas nodded.

Tommy swayed, then sat down. 'I don't feel so great.'

Douglas heard the copper return to the van, then he slammed the front doors as he got in.

They braced themselves for the bumpy ride they knew was coming. This was not the first time Douglas had travelled in the back of the paddy wagon. He was sure it wasn't going to be the last, but as the van went around the corner. His head hit the side. He hoped to hell that he would actually make it to the police station without them killing Tommy and him on the way.

As it turned out, Tommy was dead by the time they reached the police station. The beating he'd received from the coppers had caused a brain aneurysm, and he died in the back of the paddy wagon that fateful night. The only silver lining was that this helped Douglas receive a softer sentence, because the magistrate felt that he'd had it bad enough with losing his best friend. She was wrong about that, but Douglas didn't bother correcting her.

Finally, at the age of sixteen, Douglas walked out of his community home for the last time, and his mother wasn't there to meet him. In fact, she'd only visited once during the time he'd been there, and only to tell him how disappointed she was in him.

He went to his family's terrace house to find it'd been demolished as part of the slum clean-up taking place. Bare ground and rubble were all that remained. He found himself walking to the old dock area, hoping that Joe would be there.

He had a score to settle with him.

The building on the pier that the Dead Snakes had used was still there, with a few new slogans scratched into the bricks and painted over the walls. Cigarette smoke came from inside, and music blasted from a radio.

'Password?' a young boy playing pointsman at the door challenged.

'Fuck off,' Douglas said, easily pushing him aside as he walked in.

Joe was in the same place Douglas had last seen him two years before. Only this time, Douglas realised what he hadn't noticed before. There were no older members in Joe's gang of Dead Snakes supporting him, only young boys and girls between twelve and fifteen hanging on his every word.

'Still working the same old tricks, I see,' Douglas said as he approached Joe.

Joe's chair tumbled backwards as he stood up and took a step away from Douglas, putting out his arm.

'Who're you sending to the community home this time?' Douglas asked, looking around. 'What did he promise you? The same that I was promised before they threw me in that children's jail? To run with his gang? To have money to take you away from the slums?'

He looked around; the kids were all silent. 'He promised me that, too. And he made me promise not to snitch, never to tell anyone. Do you want to know why?'

No one answered.

'Because he takes a kickback from the coppers for every street kid that's convicted and put in there. Don't you, Joe?'

Joe had backed up and was now against one of the walls. 'That's not true. Alfred Weasel went last week, was initiated and he got to leave Manchester, his pockets filled with money after he passed his initiation.'

'Alfred,' Douglas said. 'About this tall,' he indicated with his hand, 'hair a bit long and blond, thin, worn sideways. He likes to make it flick a little, curve on his forehead, to cover up a red birthmark across the left side of his face?'

'Yeah, that's him. How do you know him?' asked one of the kids.

'He entered the community home right before I left. He didn't snitch by the way; he kept quiet about the Dead Snakes, so you guys can trust him when he gets out. But the guard, the fat one, he talks all the time. He's the one who said that as long as Joe keeps supplying them with new fodder for the principal, then the old man wouldn't care if the guards had a little fun on the side. Alfred was too pretty to not be someone's bitch in there.'

Joe paled and looked at the window to see if he had a clear run.

Douglas stepped into his escape route. 'Do you know what a little fun on the side is, Joe? Do you understand where these men stick their cocks?'

'Don't … Don't believe him,' Joe stuttered. 'He … He's lying …'

'Let's test me, then,' Douglas challenged. 'See who tells the truth, good Joe with his promise of the gang and the free ciggies, or the kid who served his time and was set up to go to jail by Joe? Give me a name of any of the boys before him who were initiated and got away that you can remember.'

'David Wellington,' one of the boys said.

'Dark hair, fifteen years old. His mum lived with her family on Common Street. He was sent to the community home for assault and battery.'

'No way,' said the kid who had supplied the name, shaking his head.

'Another one?' taunted Douglas.

'Simon Adams and Colin Martins,' one of the girls said.

'Simon was tall for a fifteen-year-old. Red hair and lots of freckles. Talked with a lisp from a cleft palate. That Simon? I didn't meet Colin. Simon said he was let off because of his important lawyer, and the whole family moved away from Manchester. Apparently, his family had a bit of money, and they spent it all on keeping him out of jail.'

'That's him.'

Joe went to move away, and Douglas shook his head. 'I wouldn't try to leave if I was you, Joe. You see, funny story. Simon and Colin's initiation was just like mine and Tommy's. They were sent to kill the old war pilot under the bridge, to finish him off. Only no one is finishing him off, are they? That's your old man, and he's in on the scheme. He used to box. Anyone attacking him thinking they'll kill him, and pass "initiation" will fail. We got lucky because we were pumped on drugs the night. We did it and were invincible, but the others—none have been as lucky. They've got you to make sure he isn't hurt too badly, to call the coppers so that they come at the right time. Then the coppers send the violent offender to the community home, and you and your father get paid by the guards for filling their quota. They need new kids to replace ones who leave, and what better way than to get those who think they're joining a gang? Ones who'll be silent and follow instructions after you've groomed them.'

'They get a better future there than here in the slums.'

'Bullshit. No one deserves that. They're not better off. Do you think Tommy is better off? The cops killed him! Is he better off?'

'Tommy wasn't meant to die.'

'But he did. And that's because of you, Joe, isn't it?'

Joe was waiting for Douglas to jump him, to hurt him.

'You're a worm; nothing. These kids will go out there and spread the word that you're nothing, that there's no such thing as the Dead Snakes gang, and they'll tell everyone what you did. You'll never send another kid there, and so help me, if I hear that you have so much as passed a shit near those guards, you'll die. Understood!'

Joe stood against the wall, visibly shaken.

'You're disgusting,' Douglas said, and turned away, but as he began to walk towards the door one of the kids shouted a warning, making him spin back around.

Joe had the leg of an old chair and was running at him.

Time slowed down as if he'd had a shot of drugs. While he could see Joe coming, he took time to think. He'd watched many fights in the community home. He'd even been in a few. He had to deflect Joe and make him fall hard, hit the floor first to give himself the advantage, because Joe was still older than he was, and probably stronger.

Douglas ducked down, easily avoiding the chair leg as Joe swung it like a club. He stepped closer and crouched to put his shoulder low into Joe's belly to flip him over. A move he'd learned early on in the community home, taught by some of the older kids, to help the younger ones fend off the guards and wardens.

Douglas lifted Joe without too much trouble, but Joe got up and came back at him.

One of the kids threw Douglas a metal bar, which he caught mid-air. Now they were both armed.

Joe rushed at Douglas, and Douglas sidestepped him; he followed through by hitting Joe's departing exposed back with the pole. A sickening crunch was heard by everyone in the room.

Joe screamed in pain, but anger overruled. 'I'm going to kill you,' Joe howled as he ran at him again, the chair leg raised like a club. Only he tripped as he got close to Douglas, and he flailed his arms around madly, the chair leg flying out of his hands. Douglas instinctively lifted the metal pole and dug his knee into the concrete, making a pike.

And Joe ran right straight into it.

Douglas let the rod go, and Joe slipped to the floor, his body at a strange angle as it rested on the rod.

Blood welled out of Joe's mouth as it worked like a fish on a riverbank. Opening and closing as he struggled to breathe, his blood pooling around him. No sound came out of his mouth, no scream of agony. Only silence.

Joe's body twitched as Douglas stepped back. Watching, adrenaline pumping through his veins, his mind tried to process what had just happened. Waiting for Joe to try to turn onto all fours, waiting for the chance for him to expose his head, his kidneys, and his stomach for a good kick while he was down. Yet Joe didn't move.

Douglas stood there, waiting, but Joe was never going to get back up.

Slowly, the awareness of the situation hit. The night sounds of the city, a far-off hooter of a ship in fog, the water lapping against the loading dock, the hushed sound of every other child standing there, breathing, and the overriding sound of his own blood pumping through his ears, the beat steady but racing.

'Go get an ambulance,' Douglas heard one of the other kids call the door watcher, who ran off instantly.

He noticed the movement of the girl that came towards them. But the sound was still muffled in his ears as she asked, 'Joe, can you hear me? Joe?'

A deafening silence answered her as she tentatively put her hand over his mouth to try to feel his breath. 'He's dead.'

Douglas's legs collapsed beneath him, and he vomited. He hadn't meant to kill Joe. That'd been an accident.

He began to shake, realising that unlike the intentional attempt on the old pilot, this time there were witnesses to what had happened. He knew that there was a chance they would try to pin this on him.

He knew from experience that, even if his legs had wanted to work, he shouldn't leave the scene. He also knew from listening to the other kids in the community home that the best thing to do would be to just sit there, to make sure he didn't fight when the coppers came. That way he might not get a beating.

'It wasn't your fault,' the girl was saying. 'Everyone saw Joe come at you. We all saw it was his fault.' She lifted her voice. 'Didn't we?'

A murmur rose from the kids still gathered there, from those that hadn't already silently slipped away into the night.

Douglas threw up again. He'd killed a person. This time, he'd passed Joe's initiation with flying colours. Only there was no gang to join, and he didn't want to anyway. Not with Tommy dead. That one was on Joe. Joe's death was also on Joe. It wasn't his fault that Joe had come at him, and that the accident with the steel bar had happened.

As he looked at Joe on the timber boards, for the first time, the blood of another human on his hands felt right.

He tried to tell himself it was justice for Tommy, but in his heart, he knew better.

Douglas threw another log on the fire, and stared at the fax he'd received from the 6th headquarters again. They'd changed his client list, requesting an assessment hunt by an American client.

Man, he hated the Americans. Somehow, they always managed to mess with his carefully planned schedule. He would have to fit in the three-day hunt back-to-back between the German client, Heinz Koch, and Nicole Schaffer, the woman who was after leopards and due on the last Friday in November. The hunt required the setting of bait to coax a leopard into the area, and he would have liked more time preparing for that. Now he would have to leave it to his tracker to get that first bait done. He sighed, acknowledging that sharing responsibility had never been his strong point, but admitting that the addition to his schedule was tight but doable.

The client to be assessed couldn't have come at a worse time. He frowned, thinking about the increase in demand from the general members of the 6th in the past year. His hunting grounds were shrinking, and he wondered how he would fit in even more harvesting with his normal animal-hunting clients. He had no idea.

Already he was on the lookout for new 6th hunting grounds—even if it wasn't a permanent one, he needed to visit a different area for his next 6th hunt. Two bodies, including the one he'd chosen to take for himself during the last hunt in Phalaborwa, and now two more, in the same place would attract unwanted attention.

That was why he always rotated his hunting grounds, leaving some fallow for a few years before returning. He had different hunting grounds in Angola, South Africa, South West Africa, Botswana and Zimbabwe. Where there was still place for people to go missing without the authorities coming after you. Other hunting grounds had been shut down permanently because they had become too populated.

He'd even chosen to stop hunting on the Transkei coast, one of his favourites, and his more military-style one, adjacent to District Six, near Cape Town. The urban sprawl and settlements had become a problem in both areas, because with them had come more South African Defence Forces—SADF—and the bright-eyed conscription boys strutting around in their brown uniforms, poking their noses into everyone's business. Phalaborwa had become like that now, with too many police around.

His most frequented stomping ground was still right here, just outside of Coutada 16, in Mozambique. It was convenient and close to the lowveld in Zimbabwe where he conducted most of his professional animal hunts. He often came here alone to think, and to satisfy his own craving for a kill, after his paying clients were on their planes and flying back to their meaningless lives somewhere in the world. The need to show his dominance often came after he accompanied a 6th hunter on their harvest. He just liked to know there was nothing anyone could do to punish him for it.

Originally, he had been looking for elephants when he'd come into the granite *kopjes*—which his tracker had called the 'work migration route'. At first, he hadn't believed his old tracker that there were migrants walking through the bush, but now he knew better. The bush was never quiet, and you were never alone out there.

The perfect hunting ground for the 6th hunts.

Five years later, the area was as productive as ever. The stem of migrations through the bush had never slowed, regardless of the dissident wars, civil war or the racial violence in South Africa. There was a vein of people there, just waiting for him.

If he brought the woman client here, he could fit in the assessment of the American client, too. But that would mean he couldn't take a 6th of his own in the morning as it would leave two bodies for the scavengers to clean away and dispose of too close to each other. Once he killed here, the bush talked, and the area would be devoid of movement for a while. He needed the area to have traffic within a month to bring the woman here and harvest her 6th.

The thought of how to further streamline his process, to fit in more 6th hunts, filled his mind.

He had always set up his hunts with time at the end for him to provide a guided tour through different parts of Africa. Sticking as close to the truth as he could, with only a slight smokescreen, had helped him be a successful 6th hunter. His clients hunted the animal trophies in legitimate concessions, and then afterwards, got a few days of a one-on-one guided tour with him in a game reserve and finally their 6th harvest.

He took his weapons-cleaning kit from his backpack and, stripping down his hunting rifle, he began giving it a thorough clean, the smell of the oil soothing his mood.

He noticed movement in the bushes below his elevated camp, and taking his telescopic sight, he looked through it. He could see a herd of elephants passing on the trail, migrating just as they had before humans came into the bushveld and built roads. Their great grey bodies so quiet as they trod softly on the sun-baked ground. The huge matriarch at the front had impressive tusks, and if he had a hunting client with him, they might have gone after her for the trophy, but today he just admired her from afar, and watched as she led her small herd northwards.

He followed behind the herd with his scope, looking to see if anyone was using the well-trodden trails, but couldn't see anyone. Tonight, he would look for small fires along the trail, and that would give him an indication of anyone in the area.

A fleeting thought crossed his mind that he would love to be free to spend more time exploring Africa—go to Kenya to see the great migrations of the wildebeest and zebra herds as they crossed the Maasai Mara, or go scuba diving off the Berbera coast of Somalia and explore the coral reefs in the Gulf of Aden. And just for once, do it without the 6th breathing down his neck.

But the only out for a 6th hunter was to die. It was a job for life.

CHAPTER 5

Chloe climbed out of the Datsun after grocery shopping at Checkers. 'Come on, slowpoke, if we hurry up and unload, we can catch some of that re-run of last night's third test match. Bet you Imran Khan wins it for the Pakistani team in the end.'

'No way. Malcolm Marshall is going to bring it home for the Windies.'

'Seriously?'

'Yes, seriously, just like seriously we did not really need that Milo—you wanted it, and I didn't,' Enoch was saying.

'Need. Want. It's basically the same. Besides, it gets drunk before it goes hard, so what's the problem?' she argued.

'Ten rand,' Enoch lamented, 'that could have bought us sweets to eat while watching the TV. Instead, all our money is gone on Milo.'

'You're just a sore loser because I got to choose the luxury this week,' Chloe said, grabbing a few of the bags off the back, before realising that Enoch was no longer listening, but walking to the rear entrance of the garage.

She frowned. 'Where's Xo?'

'He should be here.'

'Xo,' she called.

Silence answered.

Enoch frowned. 'Something is not right.'

They walked towards the house and caught a glimpse of a green *bakkie* tucked in next to the workshop.

'Shit,' Enoch said. 'That drunk prick Sebastian is here again.'

'Can I throw him out this time?' Chloe said.

'Fine, just do it fast. We do not want Mike upset,' Enoch said through clenched teeth.

Sebastian Smith was their extremely racist neighbour, and a member of the white supremacist—bordering on neo-Nazi—separatist political party Afrikaner Partisans. He was a stereotypical *boer* in every way, right down to wearing only khaki shorts and a shirt. Aged about fifty, Sebastian was under the misconception that he could visit the farm anytime he wanted to, and say whatever he wanted to his '*when-we*' neighbours. He revelled in trying to cause mischief for Chloe with the doctors, regarding Enoch and Xo living inside the house with her, because as far as he was concerned, under the laws of apartheid, black and white people couldn't live in the same place.

Mike seemed to hate Sebastian with a passion. Once Mike had hobbled in from his room to see Sebastian in the kitchen, giving Ethel a mouthful. Mike walked up to him, took a pan that was hanging on the rack near the stove, and managed to clonk the unsuspecting Sebastian on the head with it.

It was the most violent thing they'd seen Mike do since the incident, and if they needed any further proof that they didn't need Sebastian in their space, that was it. Although, if Enoch was honest, he was happy to see that Mike had controlled his muscles and been coordinated enough to actually pull it off with his one working arm.

'I hope he has not got too many drinks inside him,' Enoch said as they ran towards the stables.

Tanked up, Sebastian often came spoiling for a fight. They'd called the police multiple times for help. But they always seemed to take their time, as if Sebastian wasn't a real threat to them.

Sure enough, Xo was standing inside Sirocco's stable, and Sebastian was leaning on the stable wall just outside the door, as if needing to be propped up.

'You need to know your place, boy, and it's beneath a white man's. You *when-wes* mustn't get too comfortable in South Africa. Soon all you foreigners will be running back to your own countries when we bring in some proper laws to *beheer* your kind. When one of *my* people retakes control of South

Africa. We have a promised nation here. A white man's land. None of this leniency nonsense that the current government was starting to show towards you black terrorists —'

'Sebastian! What are you doing here?' Chloe said.

He spun around, staggered a little, and clutched at his chest. 'Hello, Chloe. You're home from shopping already?'

'Don't hello Chloe me, get back in your *bakkie* and leave. You're not welcome here.'

Enoch stood like a granite wall behind her.

'I was just *terugkeer* one of your sheep that got through the fence and was mingled in with mine. Can't a neighbour be neighbourly?' Sebastian said. Now that he was propped up against the wall again, he was standing okay, but he still held his chest.

Enoch looked at Xo, who rolled his eyes. 'The sheep isn't one of ours. I told him. He brought over a merino, we only have dorpers. It's in the back of his *bakkie* still.'

'You accusing me of not knowing what your sheep look like? I'm going to *bliksem* you now, you dumb *kaffir*,' Sebastian said, trying to get into the stable, but every time he went near the door, Xo would tickle Sirocco's tummy, and the beautiful horse would pin his ears back and attempt to take a bite out of Sebastian. Even in his liquored-up state, Sebastian seemed to realise that the horse was not something to trifle with and he retreated.

Enoch frowned, remembering how many hours Xo and Chloe had spent teaching the horses tricks when they were still in school, and exactly how long Sebastian had been coming around to their farm, still spouting the same bull-shit all these years later. The kids had grown up, but Sebastian hadn't changed.

'Sebastian, just leave,' Chloe said, 'before Dad sees you. I don't need him upset.'

'I'll go, but you need to keep your *kaffirs* in check. This one,' he pointed to Xo, 'thinks he's white. Watch them. They're going to steal everything from you,' Sebastian said with venom in his voice.

'I'm going to call the police again,' Chloe said.

He staggered and started to walk past her, but stopped.

Mike had just hobbled through the door.

'Shit,' Enoch said.

Mike looked at Sebastian, and he rocked on his feet. A strange sound came out of his mouth. It was simultaneously mournful and sadistic. Almost otherworldly.

'Your spastic father is in my way,' Sebastian said to Chloe. 'I can't leave if the old fool is blocking my path.'

Chloe bunched her fists. 'Enoch, can you escort Sebastian out? I'll walk Dad back inside.'

However, Mike was not budging. Even though he was not as muscular as he had once been, he was still strong. Enoch and Ethel made sure that he did his exercises every day as the physiotherapist had instructed.

'Come on, Dad, let's go inside. I know that Ethel was making some nice *vetkoek* today; let's go see if they are almost ready.'

But Mike wouldn't move even when she took his hand in hers and tugged on it. He remained rocking, watching Sebastian.

'Stupid old fool,' Sebastian said as he attempted to pass, but instead, he pushed into Mike, who made the sound again, only this time it was a little louder.

'Do not touch Mike,' Enoch warned.

Sebastian stepped backwards, then in all his drunken wisdom, decided to take a step closer to Mike, only to find Chloe standing between them. 'Get out of my face, now,' she told him. 'Touch my father or me again, and I'll make you pay for it.'

Sebastian seemed to understand that Chloe's cautioning was real. But he wasn't about to lose face to a woman.

He lifted his finger and poked it into her chest. Just once.

Chloe reached forward, and Sebastian screamed.

'I warned you. Loud and clear,' Chloe said as she let his hand go, his finger hanging limply where she had dislocated it at the knuckle. It'd be useless until a doctor put it back in place.

Sebastian bull-charged Chloe, who was still standing in front of Mike, taking down her lighter weight easily.

As they tumbled backwards, Enoch watched in horror as Sebastian's head slammed into Chloe's face, causing her head to snap back into her father's; Mike's head smashed into the hard cement floor as they landed on top of him.

'No!' Enoch roared as he grabbed hold of Sebastian by the belt and lifted him off Chloe and Mike. He tossed Sebastian away from them as if he was a rag, and not a one-hundred-kilo farmer.

Sebastian recovered faster than Chloe and Mike, and while Enoch was asking Chloe if she was okay, he went for Enoch. But his movements were slow, and his arms flailed wide of their intended target. The dance of a drunk man.

Enoch smashed his hand into Sebastian's face, and the man dropped.

'Xo, get out here. Help Mike and Chloe,' Enoch instructed as he walked towards Sebastian, not wanting to take his attention off the man again. Enoch grabbed some of the rope from the rack opposite the stable.

But as Xo came out of the stable, Sebastian caught his foot with his hand that wasn't damaged and tugged.

'Dad!' Xo called.

Enoch grabbed the shovel next to him and hit Sebastian on the side of the head. This time he didn't get back up.

Despite wanting to check on Mike and Chloe, he checked Sebastian's vitals first. *Never leave yourself vulnerable to another attack*, the voice of his Grey's Scouts instructor echoed in his head. *Don't turn your back on the enemy until you know they are dead.*

Enoch put his two fingers onto Sebastian's neck. He had a pulse. He was unconscious, and a large hematoma was already forming on his temple. 'That is going to hurt. At least you will be out for a while.'

Turning his attention to Chloe, he checked her pulse, too.

It was fast but steady. She had a bloody nose from taking the impact of Sebastian falling on top of her and had bitten through her lip.

He picked her up and cradled her in his arms against his chest. 'You gave me a fright,' he said softly, wiping his fingers over her nose to remove some of the blood. 'He is asleep now. He cannot hurt you again, angel.'

But she didn't come around. 'Xo!' he shouted at the top of his voice. 'Xo, *woza*!' Then he turned back to the girl in his arms. 'Come on, Chloe, do not make us have to take you to hospital unconscious. Come on, wake up!' He could hear the difference in her breathing as she began to surface.

'I have got you; you are safe,' he said, and she wrapped her arms around him without opening her eyes.

'Enoch,' she sobbed. 'I hurt!'

'I know. I am sorry I was not quick enough, but he is down now.'

He felt her pull away from his chest. Her eyes were partially closed already, too swollen to open properly. Looking around through slitted eyes she asked, 'Where's Dad?'

'He is here next to us; I will have to take him to the hospital. He will be alright, but he hit his head when you fell.'

Tears leaked from underneath swollen eyelids, and she attempted to sniff.

'Yuck,' she said as she tasted blood.

'Spit it out, do not swallow the blood or you will vomit later.'

'Dad,' Xo said quietly next to him, putting his hand on his father's shoulder.

'You alright, Xo?' Enoch asked.

'I'm okay. I was grooming Marin when Sebastian came at me. That stallion kicked him double barrel in the chest. I got into Sirocco's stall, and he'd only just got up and continued his sermon about how useless I was when you guys came home. That kick was direct and hard. I can't believe he got up again, and then still tried to fight.' He took a breath. 'Chloe's a mess.'

'We need to get them to the hospital—get Chloe in the front of the *bakkie* and keep her awake. I will put Mike and Sebastian in the back,' Enoch said.

'Are you okay, Dad?' Xo asked.

'Just my pride is dented for not having protected you guys from this shitbag.'

'Thank goodness,' Xo said as he hugged his dad and Chloe. 'Come on, let's get you some help.' He lifted Chloe into his arms and carried her to the *bakkie*, then quickly climbed into the driver's seat, and the *bakkie* started with its customary backfire. He reversed it out of the workshop and up to the stables, then tossed in some blankets to cover the back and used one to create a pillow.

'Take his feet,' Enoch said as he bent low and lifted up Mike. Mike was almost as tall as Enoch's six foot one, but not as broad, even when he had been at his physical best. He was a heavy man to lift.

They dragged him onto the back of the *bakkie* and curled his legs up inside the bin area. Then they rolled the still-unconscious Sebastian—now securely tied up—into the horse blanket and loaded him into the back, too, before closing it.

'Drive fast,' Enoch said. 'Mike is in bad trouble.'

CHAPTER 6

Africa Top 6 Trophies List

1. Leopard
2. Lion
3. Buffalo
4. Rhino
5. Elephant
6. Man

CHAPTER 7

Douglas stood quietly in the back of his *bakkie,* his viewing platform in the absence of one being provided at the pan. The sun had risen, evaporating the dew drops, and giving a promise of a hot day filled with bright sunshine, and later thunderstorms with life-giving rain. And in anticipation of the coming deluge, fat-bellied impala strutted around, waiting to give birth in a synchronised breeding strategy as old as Mother Africa herself. In front of him, the elephant drank deeply from the waterhole. The beast was old; his age showed in his sunken face, in the discolouration of his long tusks, and the tattiness of his ears where the edges had been torn away over time as he'd walked through the bushveld. The elephant seemed aware of Douglas and his team—as was befitting such an old soldier—but he clearly didn't believe there were any threats to him here in the reserve where he ruled by size alone.

'He's magnificent,' the German hunter, Heinz Koch, said. 'I can see why you brought me here; it was worth the long trek.'

Douglas smiled and patted him on his shoulder. 'I'm glad you like him. But we can't hunt him in here. We're still within the boundaries of the Kruger Park. Good news is, he's migrating north. This is the last stop in the national park that the elephants make before they push down the fences and cross over into the hunting concessions.'

Heinz nodded. 'And this is why you come highly recommended. This elephant will make a fine trophy. One I'll be proud to hang on my wall.'

'Come,' Douglas said, 'we can follow him for a while in the vehicle. It'll be another day before you can think about getting your rifle out, but he's yours.'

Heinz got ready to jump off the back of the *bakkie*. He was only about five foot six, with short blond hair, and a little on the tubby side, but he made up for the lack of height in personality. They'd been together for three days while the German was getting over his jet lag, and Douglas already knew that he was an excellent marksman. He'd passed the shooting tests he'd been given when they had zeroed the weapons at eighty metres. Using the bonnet of the *bakkie*, with a rubber mat thrown over it to keep the heat off the hunter and any scratch marks off the paint, the man had hit the mark that Douglas had chopped into the tree.

Heinz Koch's guns were well cleaned, and it wasn't from lack of use—rather from someone who knew how to maintain and care for them and respected them as if they were an extension of himself. The normal test of five to six shots per weapon had been done, but Heinz had done more, not caring about the cost of the ammunition because he genuinely enjoyed his rifles.

Heinz turned back towards the elephant and lifted his hand, pretending his arm was a gun. He made a bang sound, then blew on the tops of his fingers as if clearing gunpowder, before putting away his imaginary weapon, much like a five-year-old playing at cowboys would. He grinned at Douglas.

There were only two items left on Heinz's list. The elephant was the last animal. Douglas was looking forward to the hunt already. The almost sixty-year-old man's juvenile excitement had him laughing. Most of his 6th clients were too serious to fool around like this.

'After the elephant, then we get to hunt the apex predator?' Heinz asked.

'Show me your skill with this elephant, clean shot. Drop him with one bullet, and then the hunt can begin.' He stood next to his vehicle, getting ready to leave, then noticed that a Parks Board vehicle had just driven into the area, and parked near the windmill that was not rotating, despite the gentle wind. The lifeblood of the pan's water supply, the windmill pumped the water from deep inside the earth to the surface and into the catchment area, creating a year-round water supply for the animals.

Another reason the animals in the Kruger Park were always in such good condition. Not that it mattered now. With the recent rains, the grass was green, and the thick bush was becoming denser by the day. It was a season of growth and expectation in the bushveld.

He watched to see who got out.

It wasn't long before he was rewarded with seeing the tracker from his previous encounter in the park, and the white ranger who walked alongside him. They were far from the last place they had happened upon each other, and he very much doubted that the rangers had even known Douglas and Aleksy had been there, just a distant whisper in the sands, if, and that was a big if, they had seen their tracks at all.

He got into his *bakkie* and drove around the pan, right past them. He raised his hat in a polite greeting, and then left.

He had followed many an elephant on this route, and the trophy was always worth the few days' wait. This elephant would travel out of the park before he would meet his maker.

CHAPTER 8

Chloe woke from a place where there was no pain, where there was no sound, only silence and clouds. She could hear someone breathing close by, but she couldn't open her eyes to see who it was. She could feel pain in her arm, but couldn't move it, and her leg throbbed. She kicked out.

'Chloe?' Enoch's gentle voice broke into her confused world.

'Where am I?'

'You are okay; you are in the hospital. They had to give you an anaesthetic and set your nose because it was broken and sew up your leg. Good news is that other than some grazes and scrapes, you are going to be okay, but they want to keep you here for a little bit to make sure.'

'Dad? Is Dad here with me?'

'No, my *umntwana*.' Enoch's voice broke as he used his strongest endearment for her, and a sob escaped him. 'He is at home. Xo and Ethel are looking after him.'

'Is he okay?'

'The doctors said that his head is bleeding inside again, and there is nothing they can do for him. He is comfortable for now. We always knew that a hard knock on his head was never going to be a good thing.'

'But he's alive, he can heal again.'

'The doctor said he should, given time,' Enoch said. 'Sebastian—he did not make it.'

'Sebastian died?'

'The doctor said that the bleeding inside his chest, from Marin kicking him so hard, is what killed him. He did not have much time before his body would have given up even before he picked a fight with us.'

She couldn't breathe. 'I think I'm going to be sick.'

Enoch attempted to put a kidney dish in front of her, but he wasn't quick enough; it splashed over the sides and onto the bed. He pressed the button to call the nurse to her room. 'I have to go now, Chloe; I will be back when there is no nurse here,' he said and was about to sneak out when a black nurse arrived in her pristine white uniform.

'Out, you cannot be here,' she hissed. 'What you thinking? A black man being in a white girl's room? Out before Matron sees you!' She turned her back on him, expecting that he would leave.

'Hello, Miss Mitchell,' she said, looking at the chart. 'I'm Baleka, your nurse this morning.' She turned back to Enoch, who was standing just outside the door. 'Out. I see to her and tell you all what is happening outside the gate. If Matron finds you in here, *pas op* lots of trouble!'

'Please let Enoch stay, please,' Chloe begged.

'No, Miss Mitchell, he cannot,' Nurse Baleka said. 'Come on, we gets you cleaned up before Matron says I'm doing a useless job.'

'Can Enoch come visit me later?'

'I don't know what happens on your farm, Miss Mitchell, but he not come inside here. Black people go to their own section in the hospital and not by the white people's ward. He knows that.'

'But Enoch's family …'

'Shush, girl. *Thula*. Never says that to anyone, you hear me? You gets him hurt bad. The police, they make him disappear if you says something like that. Thinks before you speak. Matron can come in and talk to you soon.' She dropped her voice to a whisper. 'You haves to protect him; there is Afrikaner Partisans people in this hospital. They hear, and they do bad things to him.'

'Oh, okay, understood,' Chloe said, and Baleka helped her move to the chair before she remade her bed with fresh sheets.

She hated South Africa and its stupid apartheid laws.

Chloe sat in her wheelchair, her head still bandaged, while Xo went to fetch the *bakkie* and bring it closer. Despite her being discharged, the hospital had insisted that she remain in the chair until she got to the car.

The receptionist stopped the porter from taking her further.

'I made this for you.' She handed her a *melktert* in cling wrap. '*Ons is jammer.* You need to know that the *vrous* of the town are *jammer* for what happened to you. Smith had no right trespassing on your *plaas* like that. You should never have been put in that *situasie*, and it was a good thing that your *kaffir* protected you and your pa from him,' Mevrou Van Vuuren said.

Chloe frowned as she accepted the tart, wondering what else was being said around town about the attack. She knew the townsfolk meant well, but she wished they would just back off and leave them alone. She was so tired of defending her family.

Nurse Baleka had been right to warn her. While she was in hospital, the state mortuary had issued the death notice after the autopsy on Sebastian, which said that he had died of pulmonary contusion caused by a blunt force to the chest; a farming accident. Baleka had warned her that some people didn't like the outcome.

The Afrikaner Partisans membership was strong in Pietermaritzburg, and in their small community of Howick. Chloe had come to realise that many of the people she was around were supporters of this extreme far-right group. They had an insane idea that a friendship between a white and black person was wrong. They believed that people were not equal, and that the government should not be granting any power to any Indian, or coloureds. That they could even think that the world, which had sanctioned South Africa so harshly already, would ever allow an independent *Boerestaat* for Boer-Afrikaner people only, was ludicrous. There were also rumours that they had begun killing non-whites—yet, nothing was being done to stop them. They could make her life, and her family's life, difficult if they wanted to because the police turned a blind eye to whatever they were doing.

'*Ek is jammer*, about what happened to your pa, must be so hard for you. Please know that you have *vriende* here. Not everyone is out to find a *sondebok*.'

Scapegoat? Chloe's survival instincts bristled. She was being told something here, but her brain wasn't functioning on all cylinders.

'If there is anything we can do to help, please let us know,' Mevrou Van Vuuren said. 'Your pa, he's not an active part of our community, but he's good with horses; everyone knows that he can settle a green horse down in no time and is no threat to anyone. Which makes what happened so sad. It's almost like the horse was protecting him from Sebastian.'

Chloe smiled. It hurt. 'Not quite, but thank you.'

Mevrou Van Vuuren nodded.

Xo was outside, waiting for her. He stood by the *bakkie*, jungle hat in hand. As the orderly pushed Chloe's wheelchair to the car, he opened her door as a chauffeur would. He made sure that she was safely buckled into the passenger's side, before he climbed into the driver's seat and started the *bakkie*.

They'd been friends for as long as she could remember. One of her best memories was of when she was about ten and he was eleven, when he'd come to rescue her after she had run away from home. Only this time, he hadn't taken her right back to her mother. Instead, he'd walked with her further from the house, showing her how beautiful the bush was, and started to teach her what plants to live on if she was out there alone. He had known how to make a bird trap with grass, and he had shown her how to peel the hairy skin from a prickly pear without a knife. She remembered the sweet juices running down their faces when she'd done it right. Chloe had always known that no matter what, she could trust Xo.

He sat back. 'I'm twenty-two years old, and I don't know what to do. I don't know how to help him.' Xo wiped his face with both hands. 'The police are questioning Dad every day about what happened, and I fear soon he won't come home, even though he didn't kill Sebastian.'

Chloe looked at Xo. At six-foot tall, he was built like men were supposed to be, broad shoulders and slim hips, with a face that smiled often and a wicked sense of humour. She'd seen him laugh and cry, but she'd never seen him like this. Not even when they had got into serious trouble for taking their horses into the Communal Land and been late coming home, causing their dads to send out a search party for them. His face always showed hope. Trust. Love. Now it just showed despair. He was hunched over the steering wheel and wore the face of a man admitting defeat.

'What? Come on, that's ridiculous! The report said it wasn't his fault!'

'He's black. Sebastian was white. How many times have you witnessed the racism yourself against us?'

'Too many times. This is madness, dammit!'

'The apartheid system is going to swallow Dad up as if he was an activist.'

'But they can't do that!' Chloe protested.

'You and I both know that the police can do anything in this country. There is a state of emergency on; normal rules don't apply anymore. Dad is going to be made an example of for killing a white man, and they'll put Marin down too, now that the report is done. They'll say he's a menace, a dangerous horse.'

'We can't let this happen, Xo,' Chloe said.

'There's no way to stop them,' Xo admitted. 'Dad and I have no rights here, and we don't have money to fight them with a lawyer. I'm out of ideas.'

Chloe watched his face break, and it made her heart ache. But there was something they could do. It would be tricky, and it might have other consequences, but she would do it to save Enoch. She pushed the old vision of the silhouette of Enoch burying someone deep in the ground from her mind. She couldn't let the uncertainty of that shadow haunt her now.

'We've no place here anymore. We must go home to Delaware,' Chloe said. 'I know we came here for the good of my dad, but we need to go back for the good of yours. Before they lock him away forever.'

Xo looked at her. 'Are you serious?'

'Of course I'm serious. I can't sit here and watch them take Enoch away. He's like a father to me.'

'How do we just leave?' Xo said.

'We get in the truck with our horses, and we go.'

'Bringing three horses 1500 kilometres through the bush wasn't easy, Chloe. Have you forgotten that Dad and I had to get a South African dompas to travel? When we crossed the Limpopo and got to Dad's friends' farm in Masisi, he had to sign the papers to say we had his permission to travel, and that we were taking his horses to Howick. Every place we stopped, the farmer had to sign to give us permission to continue travelling. As if we were their possessions. Every police officer or defence force person who stopped us along the way treated us like we were nothing.'

'But you're everything to me. You gave up your own freedom to come here and help me look after Dad. Now it's my turn to help. I'm serious, Xo. We need to leave South Africa and go home.'

'I would say that only Dad and I go, but your dad and mine—I would never try to part them. That friendship is set in stone. My dad won't leave yours. You're right; the only way to save him is for all of us to leave.'

'The receptionist at the hospital, she was trying to warn me. Something about a scapegoat. Now you tell me about the police, and alarm bells are ringing in my head. We need to leave and leave now. And even if we're wrong and they don't come after your dad, they're going to destroy Marin. I can't let them do that.'

Xo nodded, then took a deep breath. 'You think you are up to it? Now? Despite your injuries?'

'They wouldn't have let me out of the hospital if they didn't think I was going to be okay. Besides, this is your dad's life we're talking about. I have to be. It's going to be a long trek. I'm just glad that this time we'll travel together. It'll be easier for us to get to Messina in the horse truck, so most of the journey is done, and the only part you and Enoch need to do is cross the Limpopo with the horses again. It'd be so much simpler if the border hadn't been closed five years ago and the horses had come in with papers.'

'The horses were never going to get clearance to come through the border into South Africa in 1981, and getting the horses back through the border now is not going to happen. They have to go through the bush.'

'Have you forgotten there are crocs in the Limpopo?' Chloe said.

'And there're lions, leopards and hyenas in the bush around that area, all along the Limpopo, down to where we cross the river. There's the South African Defence Force doing their patrols, and terrorists from both sides in Mozambique. There're going to be more people in the bush than last time—and that's before we cross back into Zimbabwe with the Red Brigade and the dissident war going on. When we came into South Africa, they weren't expecting black people to cross the border to get away from Zimbabwe. There was already a stream of white people trying legitimately to cross over to deal with.'

Chloe nodded. 'I hope that now they're still going to be too busy with all the people leaving Zim to realise we're jumping the border back the other way.'

'We can only hope.'

She smiled, then winced at the pain. 'Leaving our horses behind isn't an option this time either, so we don't have much choice to get back over the border, except through the bush.'

'Your ability to just take a situation, make a decision and run with it amazes me. You used to be the wild child, and yet you see straight to the heart of any problem and find solutions so easily.'

'And it's got me into trouble many times, too. You know there's one thing when we get home to Zim that'll make life a lot easier for us. My dad's bank accounts that he couldn't empty when we left. We can at least go home to decent money again, and we won't be living this existence that we do now.'

'I've heard living expenses have gone up a bit in Zim, and you'll also have to buy your dad's medication there,' Xo warned.

'There's enough in those accounts, Xo. And there's Delaware, with Aunty Grace keeping that going. I've done three years of an accounting degree–I know that we should be better off at home in Zim than we've been here,' Chloe said.

Xo nodded and put the *bakkie* in gear.

'I think the quicker we have your dad away from here, the better. Let's go home. We'll tell your dad what we decided—when he objects, we can tell him it's two to one, and he's outvoted if he says no.'

CHAPTER 9

Enoch's head ached. The police had roughed him up a bit this time, trying to intimidate him. But eventually, they'd let him go. Another day to be grateful for—because their warning not to leave town was clear.

He was living on borrowed time.

He looked at the man sitting at the dining-room table, refusing to eat, pushing away Ethel's arm. In the week that Chloe had been in hospital, Mike had deteriorated before their eyes. His clothes hung from him, and he had become a ghost of the man who used to fill them. Enoch couldn't quite believe that this was all that was left of his friend.

Forty-nine years had passed too quickly; the end for Mike was coming fast. Who knew if his friend was trapped inside his damaged brain. Enoch knew that despite any change in Mike, the doctors would not operate on him again. Mike was more fragile than ever before.

But it was having Chloe in hospital that had caused Mike to lose heart. Taking him to visit her had been a mistake. It would've been better to tell him she was away at university because it was after that visit that he'd stopped eating; he thought she wasn't coming home. Thankfully she would be here soon, and she'd get Mike to start eating again.

Mike's expression was just vacant; it was like he'd simply checked out. The last knock on his head had caused swelling again, making him even more mixed up. It was ironic. He'd survived the Rhodesian Bush War relatively unscarred, despite seeing horrendous things that no man ever should. Bodies pulled apart by men like wild dogs, people on poles as if they were pieces of meat, even men hung from trees like cocoons, when Buffel had lost his mind and snapped during one of the Grey's Scouts' contact with the guerrillas at Shilo Mission. Before that, none of those men in the unit had any inkling that their fellow scout was so screwed up in the head that he would actually commit such atrocities against another human. Yet Mike had been the one to show compassion and try to guide Buffel to someone who would help his mixed-up mind. They had faced mortar attacks and been shot at numerous times. They had lost fellow Scouts and heard horses screaming until they'd been silenced by a gunshot, and still Mike had been the strong one.

The Mike he knew had died the night they had taken Andy Pryor's gold. It had paid for Sarah's life but cost Mike his.

Enoch needed to honour Mike's living spirit and take him back to his farm in Zimbabwe, take him home to Sarah. He wasn't going to live long. It didn't matter that they hadn't been near home in all these years. Enoch had always thought that Delaware would be the place where they'd grow old.

'Sarah, you will not know the man I bring to rest with you,' he said aloud. 'But I will keep my promise and bring him home.' He and Mike were blood brothers, an oath they had sworn long ago as young boys.

He could still remember the slide of the hunting knife against his palm that had cemented their pledge all those decades ago. As the blade had stopped moving, a single drop of red had splashed onto the cow-dung floor of the tack room of Delaware's stables.

'*Eish*, it burns,' he said.

'You sure that knife is sharp enough, Enoch?'

'On my life, I swear it. Look, mine is done.' He proudly displayed his hand.

'Okay. Now mine.' Mike held out his hand.

Enoch shook his head and offered the knife to Mike as blood ran down the handle and dripped onto Enoch's foot.

'You do it. If you tell the *baas* I cut you, he will beat me.'

Mike shrugged. 'Guess that's true. Give me the knife; you're bleeding all over the place.' He took the handle and gripped it tightly. He took a deep breath, then he relaxed his hand over the blade, just as Enoch had done, and pulled.

For a moment there was no pain, and then the burning began.

'*Einahhh!* Quick, put our hands together,' Mike said as he held out his hand to Enoch, and as they joined hands, blood dripped again onto the floor.

Enoch stared at their hands. One the colour of dark coffee, and the other white, despite Mike's suntan.

'Now we are blood brothers forever,' Mike said.

'Always blood brothers, you and I,' Enoch nodded. 'No boarding school and no government can ever tear us apart.'

The burning in Enoch's hand had stopped. Now all he could feel was the pulsing of his blood and Mike's. He stared at their joint hands as if something might change due to having some of Mike's white blood run into his body.

'You think the blood has passed from me into you?' Mike asked, as if he'd been thinking the same thing.

'How would I know? You're the one who knows things like that from your fancy school,' Enoch said.

The boys pulled their hands apart, and when the air got into the cuts, they both applied pressure to their wounds.

'*Sheeesh,* that hurts worse than a Matabele ant bite,' Mike said, and Enoch looked at his hand. The cut was deep, the white edges had split apart, and swelling had started. Blood still oozed out, but it no longer ran freely.

He passed Mike a piece of a hankie he'd cut in half with the knife. 'Press this into it and we can tie it off. That way, by suppertime, your mother will not notice the cut. If she does, just tell her you cut yourself by mistake when we were sharpening the hunting knives. Do not tell her what we did; the adults will not understand.'

'And yours?' Mike asked.

'Mine is black; no one is going to notice if I have a cut on it or not,' Enoch said as he wrapped the other half of the light-blue faded material around his own hand. 'It will be okay.'

'Good. Would hate to have my blood brother die from bleeding,' Mike said, then slung his arm over Enoch's shoulder. 'Come, if we're quick, we can still catch the tractor to the dam where my father is fishing.'

They ran out from the old *ikhaya,* down towards the compound.

'Enoch,' Mike said suddenly, pulling on his arm to stop him. 'Promise me that no matter what happens, first you'll be my brother, then you'll be my friend.'

'I promise,' said Enoch.

'Me too,' said Mike.

A sound outside the dining room brought Enoch back to the present; he wiped his eyes, clearing away the old images.

Xo walked in with Chloe. He had to tell them they needed to leave. To flee. He just had to find the right words in his pounding head.

Chloe rushed in and gave her dad a hug, then she turned to Enoch. 'It's good to be home.'

'Dad,' Xo said, 'good to see you home.' He touched his shoulder.

Enoch flinched.

'What happened? What did they do this time?' Xo asked, frowning.

'They were having a pissing contest,' Enoch said. 'Excuse me, Chloe, Ethel, that was not for your ears. I am sore and tired.'

'With reason too, by the look of it,' Chloe said, and she touched her forehead to his instead of hugging him, unsure where he was hurting, a gesture he was grateful for.

She sat down next to Mike. 'Hi, Ethel,' she said as she took the plate from her and began feeding her dad.

Mike opened his mouth, and he ate like a young child, chewing and swallowing slowly. 'Thanks, Ethel, for looking after Dad while I wasn't here,' Chloe said as she passed her the empty plate.

'I'm happy to see him eat; he's not been eating well,' Ethel said.

'I see that,' Chloe said as she picked some invisible fluff off Mike's shoulder. 'He has no choice now; his bossy daughter is home again.' She patted him on the arm. He took a while as he fought for control over his muscles to put his hand on hers.

Enoch laid his head on the table and released a sigh. Perhaps he had been overreacting. Perhaps Mike was going to be okay. He looked up at Xo and Chloe to see they were both looking at Ethel, and it didn't look like they wanted her to bring them food. They were waiting for her to leave the room.

They wanted to talk too. Even he couldn't be reading those signs wrong.

'Ethel, we will do the dishes tonight. Take the rest of the night off—you need a break,' Enoch said.

'Are you sure?' she asked.

'I am sure. You have your church meeting tonight, so go and get ready and Xo will run you there in the *bakkie* so that you are not late. My head is pounding, so it is best he drives you if you do not mind.'

'Thank you, Enoch,' she said, already undoing her apron ribbon.

'Of course, Dad.' Xo grabbed a bread roll from the middle of the table. 'Chloe, don't you and Dad eat all the dinner before I get back, I'm starving. Come on, Ethel, shake a leg. That preacher will be singing a song for your sins if we are late,' he called as he shoved the bread in his mouth.

Mike was already in bed and fast asleep when Enoch, Xo and Chloe sat in the dining room.

'We need to leave, go home to Zim,' Chloe said.

'I agree with Chloe,' Xo said.

Enoch nodded. 'You know what? It must be what is right because as I sat at the table tonight, I was thinking that we need to take Mike home. We have to leave this place, go back to Delaware.'

'That was too easy,' Chloe said.

'No. Not easy. It is a necessity, and we are all in agreement,' Enoch said.

'Yes,' Xo and Chloe said in unison.

'We need to go soon. Like tonight. Tomorrow, I dread the thought of the police taking you away and hurting you again. I hate the thought of them coming to shoot Marin. We need to leave immediately.' Chloe's voice was getting louder and louder.

Enoch nodded, and he put his hand on Chloe's arm. 'Keep calm. Nothing is ever accomplished when we are uptight and rush things. Besides, my head is still sore, and shouting is not helping it.'

'Sorry,' Chloe said. 'I didn't mean to shout.'

'I know. The question is, when do we leave? And how do we get back?' Enoch asked.

Chloe kept her voice low. 'Xo and I spoke about this on the drive here,' launching into an explanation of what they had discussed.

'That could work. You are licensed to drive the cattle truck so you and Mike can drop us, and then take the excess baggage with you and go through the Beitbridge border post. Just past the airport on the Fort Victoria Road—no wait, it is now called Masvingo. You will need to take the turn-off to drive through to Chipise and down to Sengwe. From there you will find a small road heading south. You will need to trust your instincts to fetch us as close to the Limpopo as you can, without bringing attention to the fact that you are down there in the first place, and obviously looking for something.'

'That's a good idea—I like it,' Chloe said.

'What about Ethel? Do we ask her if she wants to come with us, or leave her here?' Xo asked.

'We give her the choice. I don't think she has much family, so she may want to come with us,' Chloe said.

'I am not so sure. If she wants to say goodbye to anyone, she could jeopardise our leaving. I think that if the SAP got wind that I am leaving town, they will issue an arrest warrant. They are too determined to pin Sebastian's death on me.'

'I know,' Chloe said, having witnessed the South African Police in action, 'but Ethel has worked for us nearly the whole time we've been here. She came to us because she wanted a family to look after, so we need to return the kindness. We need to ask her. I depend on her to help Dad.'

Enoch nodded. 'I have to be guided by you on this one. I would leave her behind if you were not championing her. I worry that if she is with us and we get caught, she will be in the same amount of trouble as we are, and she does not deserve that.'

'There's other logic to my reasoning—if she's with us, I can help watch for lions and other dangers. I can carry a gun and help protect us. I won't be the one always looking after Dad. Three of us doing the protecting is better than two. Besides, we all know Ethel cooks so much better than I do.'

Xo grinned. 'What? You don't want to be the little woman?'

Chloe threw a cushion at him.

Xo said, 'When do we leave?'

'Tomorrow night,' Chloe said. 'That way we can go into Pietermaritzburg in the morning and buy some supplies, and if anyone sees me, I'll just tell them I'm stocking up the house after being away for a week. No one will suspect anything.'

'How about this?' Enoch said. 'We pack tonight; it will not take us more than three or four hours. We only take what we really need, and then we stop on the way for any supplies, and to clear out our bank accounts in Vryheid in the morning. Chloe, do you have any unpaid bills in town?'

'No. And the rent here is paid, so we won't leave a debt.'

'Fine. Then all we need is what we really feel is essential, the rest is just possessions and can be replaced. The horses, any tack and feed that needs to go. Chloe, make sure you have our Zimbabwean bank books and passports, and all of Mike's medications,' Enoch said.

'Let's do this,' Xo said.

CHAPTER 10

Chloe went to her room and stuffed her clothes into the only suitcase she owned—they all fitted in with ease. Not that she thought they wouldn't; she wasn't one for excessive clothing. Everything was functional and long-lasting.

First packing the pictures of her mother and a few of her knick-knacks, she put her mother's wedding band on her right hand, and frowned at how it looked on her finger, before removing the gold ring and hanging it on a chain around her neck, with her father's, not sure why she hadn't put them together until today. Moving into her father's room, she opened his chest of drawers and looked through his clothes, deciding what she wanted to take.

'Let me pack this up,' Enoch said from the door. 'It cannot be easy for you, bending over with your nose still healing.'

She shook her head. 'It's not, but I've taken the drugs the doctors gave me—they've dulled most of the pain. You okay?'

'I will be. Once we get over that border and are home in Zim. I know it is not perfect what we are heading into—the war is raging in Matabeleland—but it has got to be better than being hunted for a crime I did not commit,' said Enoch.

'Even in death, Sebastian's being a *doos*,' she said.

'Do not swear. It is not nice,' Enoch said automatically, causing them both to smile.

When she'd packed them all, she took the bags to the cattle truck outside. Xo and Enoch had already started to load the front section with feed and hay. She left her bags there and began transporting the saddlery and all the tack she could take from the stables and piling it up next to the truck.

'Good thing we only have five horses,' Enoch said. 'We need to take all this, but it is going to make the journey slow. Xo, it is time to go fetch Ethel. Take Chloe with you so that you can talk about the offer in the car, but make sure she knows that if she does not come, she cannot tell anyone where we have gone, and if she decides to come, she cannot call anyone to say goodbye.'

Two hours later, Ethel stood next to the cattle truck, her eyes large, carrying two Checkers packets containing all her belongings.

'I don't suppose you have a passport?' Enoch asked her.

Ethel shook her head. 'I have my dompas.'

Enoch nodded. 'Then you will need to cross over some of the bushveld with Xo and me. Have you ever ridden a horse?'

Ethel shook her head again.

Chloe swore that her eyes grew even larger. 'We'll put you on Pampero; she's very gentle. You'll be fine, Ethel, trust me. She's like riding a big barrel because she's pregnant.'

'You sure about this, Ethel?' Enoch asked. 'This is your last chance to change your mind.'

'You are my family. I go with you,' she said. 'I must look after Master Mike.'

Chloe smiled. 'Did you get the CB radio home base packed into the truck?'

'Yes,' Xo said. 'We're almost done.'

Xo and Enoch loaded her father's ex-Grey's Scouts horse, Diablo. The horse was so battle-hardened that he went up the truck first and was tied up in his own cornered section without any problems. His beautiful grey-dappled coat shone. Next into the truck were her pregnant Arabian chestnut, Pampero, and the bay stallion Marin. Followed by Xo's horse, Sirocco, a white-and-brown skewbald with a long mane and tail, and finally, they loaded Kimberlite, the horse that had kept Enoch safe all those years ago, a black horse, with one white sock.

'Go on, my boy, we are moving again,' Enoch said gently, and Kimberlite neighed softly as if answering back.

Chloe watched Enoch check the horses one more time to make sure they were secured into their stalls, and then he closed the big door with Xo's help.

She looked around.

The truck stood silhouetted against the dark night sky, and the stars shone brightly. She felt alive for the first time in many years.

They were going home.

'It's twelve-fifteen,' she said. 'A brand-new Friday and a good day to move.'

'If we push through, we might be able to get just this side of Messina by sundown. The horses are fit, and they are conditioned well for travel. I know that we will be pushing them, but I am sure they will be okay because it is a cool evening,' Enoch said. 'We can figure out our border crossing once we know if the SAP put out a bulletin on us. Let us see how far we get. We have the horses' vaccination papers, and we can probably pay for stock permits if we get stopped. If we go through Nelspruit and up that way, we will be able to rest once and still make the border tomorrow.'

'And if the SAP does put out a police bulletin? Then what?' Chloe asked.

'We will hear about it on the CB. We will be listening. If it happens, we can use the back roads and stay close enough to Swaziland, then we can cross the border and get into Mozambique through the bush. It will be easier to avoid the landmines and freedom fighters in Mozambique than get away from the SAP; they are a lot less organised there.'

Chloe checked that her dad was buckled in properly in the middle seat as Xo was helping Ethel into the front to be next to her dad. She touched his arm before climbing out of the driver's side to take her place with the horses in the back of the truck.

'Well, this is it. Onwards and upwards to our next adventure in our lives.'

'Shhh. Listen,' Chloe said. 'Turn that up so we can hear in the back.'

Enoch turned up the volume on the police radio.

'... Believed to be travelling north in a ten-tonne truck, registration NP 464,' the voice said.

'That's us!' Chloe said.

'Considered armed and dangerous.'

'Now what?' Xo asked.

'They cannot identify us. Not after that visit to the scrap yard outside Vryheid. Our truck is from the Transvaal, right down to the disk for the dashboard. And they have no idea how many people are travelling together. They will also assume that Chloe and Mike would be in the front, and us blacks in the back, so to have me driving and Ethel in the front, we can drive past any police station, and they will not realise it is us,' Enoch said.

'How far are we from Nelspruit?' Xo asked.

Enoch heard Chloe rustle the map she had resting on the hay bale.

'An hour away,' she said.

This is where they'd planned to drop in on an old Grey's Scouts friend, Nigel Smoothy, on his citrus farm just outside of town. His farm was situated between Karino and KaNyamazane, a little towards the Kruger Park, but off the main freeways. They'd planned to rest there for an hour or so before pushing on past the R40 and into the Northern Transvaal in the cooler part of the day. They'd already spent just over thirteen hours travelling, including their four-hour rest stop in Vryheid to sort out all their supplies.

'We stick to the plan, meet Nigel at his place, and figure out our next move from there,' Enoch said.

'You sure that Nigel will still provide us sanctuary?' Chloe asked.

'We will have a rest, but we cannot stay there long. After we leave Nigel's, I think that we head east. If we cut across, perhaps we can get close enough to the Komatipoort border post. We can ditch the truck and go through the bush if necessary. It will be heavy going, but we can make it,' Enoch said.

Chloe looked at the map. 'Or we can telephone Nick Davis. He's at Crocodile Bridge. Here.' She showed Xo on the map. 'He said I could call on him if I ever needed help.'

'Chloe, how well do you think you know Nick?' Enoch asked.

'Come on, Enoch, he was always around in the holidays with his mum when we were growing up. Until she died at least and then it was just him. Xo and I spent lots of time with him. He was always nice to me,' Chloe said. 'I remember he was at our farm the night Dad got hurt, but he left for South Africa soon after that—and he's the only person other than Aunty Grace who sends me a birthday and Christmas card every year.'

'Hold on to that memory of him,' Enoch said. 'Because I'm not so sure he will help us. He believes that your dad and I dragged the Grey's Scouts' name into the mud the day your dad got hurt.'

'Did you?' she asked.

'In a way. But it was not because of what he thought.'

'What happened?' she asked.

'It is a story for another day,' Enoch said.

'I just think that if we can get him to help, perhaps we could get further north before ditching the truck. Having a game ranger with us might work to our advantage if we have to go into the bush,' Chloe said.

'We are getting desperate enough that I am going to say something I never thought I would say. Ask him for help, but I doubt that he will,' Enoch said. 'Especially now that we are on a bulletin.'

CHAPTER 11

MOZAMBIQUE HUNTING CONCESSION

Douglas ground his teeth but grinned politely. He'd known from the moment the man had opened his mouth that fitting a three-day hunt into Coutada 16 concession in Mozambique, right before the leopard hunt in Zimbabwe coming at the end of the week, was a mistake. His latest hunting client, Payden Martinez, was from the South in the United States, and his nasal accent was getting on Douglas's nerves. Even if the money was good.

'When?' Payden asked as the elephant thrashed his way through the hunting concession. Though his larger tusks were heavy, he held up his head regally, as if he was the king of the bushveld. The trees in his path were merely an inconvenience as he made his way northwards on his migration. He was in musth, and the dark stain ran down his light-grey skin.

'Soon. There's a waterhole not far from here. After he drinks, he'll cross into the hunting concession, and you can claim your trophy,' Douglas said. 'This isn't the first bull we have waited for to come north, and they are worth waiting for. Trust me.'

'He's taken his sweet time getting here,' Payden said.

'Good things are worth waiting for,' he repeated. 'You couldn't ask for a better specimen for your collection.'

Payden nodded. 'I know. He's worthy of the wall in my den.'

'That he is. Another old man of the bush. This area is known for these big tuskers.'

'You sound like you're sorry he'll die,' Payden said.

'I'm not sorry that he won't suffer what old age has in store for him, that he'll slowly starve when his teeth are so worn out, he'll no longer be able to chew his food. Not sorry that when he lies down the wild dogs might tear him apart. No, he'll be spared that. But I do have total admiration that he's been on earth for many years and has won the respect of all who have met him. See how his ears are torn and the scar lines on his rump? Probably from a lion attack when he was younger.

'He's seen so many changes in his life. So many places where he used to migrate that are no longer accessible because of fencing and years of war; he has heard the thundering landmines and pop of gunfire. If he could talk, he'd probably tell us stories that might make the beer sour around the campfire.'

'Put like that, I can almost feel sorry for him. Almost.'

'But?'

'I'll still be able to appreciate him when I sit in my den and look at his head hanging there with all the other trophies I've collected—from the first squirrel I killed. My rhino will be dwarfed by his head,' Payden said. 'My black rhino is impressive. Truly. I got him up in South West Africa. The hunting outfit there said that it would be in the top ten all-time record books. Most of my trophies have reached our club's Gold Medal standards or higher. I won the biggest rhino trophy from our club that year.'

Payden was someone who sat at the far left of the trophy hunters. The group that was excessively obsessive about their trophies, and only the trophies. In his years as a professional hunter, Douglas had only ever met two or three people like this. Most trophy hunters had a huge respect for the environment and the animals they took from it.

Payden was simply a killer. Always after something bigger and better than what he had. Never going to be happy that he'd hunted every species in the world. He would probably be one of those to move on from his wish list of shooting every species, to trying to eat them all ...

A chill ran down Douglas's neck at the thought.

Having been asked to assess if Payden was ready to be approached about joining the 6th, Douglas would be sending his recommendation that they stay far away from this man. He didn't trust him, and he doubted that he would stop at just one kill of a 6th trophy per year. Worse. He wouldn't keep the existence of the 6th Society a secret because he liked to brag. He was too full of self-importance and pride not to crow to the world that he could kill humans and feel as little remorse as if they were animals themselves.

'Don't worry, this elephant will be one of your best trophies,' Douglas reassured him.

'Too true,' Payden said as he broke a large thorn from the acacia tree to use as a toothpick.

They walked downwind from the elephant. While they could see him and certainly smell him when he defecated in a large pile, he didn't know they were there.

Douglas's tracker, Virgil, motioned them forward. 'Come, this way,' Douglas said, 'we'll bypass the waterhole and set up on the other side. Once you've shot him, I'll radio my boys to bring the *bakkie*, and we can save that trophy for you.'

They trudged along the sandy path that led past the waterhole, Douglas ever alert to other game that might catch them unawares as they moved through the bush. Finally, they crossed a large trail intersecting theirs. 'He'll come along this route.'

Virgil turned and walked north on the path until it went through a thicket of *wag-'n-bietjies*. 'Here, *Baas*.'

Douglas nodded, and they set up just on the other side. Close—within eighty metres, but not so close that if Payden didn't drop him in one shot, Douglas wouldn't have a chance to react and set off a second bullet.

He had known hunters who had been trampled at this stage of the hunt. Hunters who had thrown themselves in front of a charging elephant to save their client from being crushed. He never wanted to be in that situation because he didn't believe he would make the right choice. An ordinary hunter could leave an area and reinvent himself, get a new identity if he wanted to.

But not a 6th hunter. You died protecting your client or you died at the hands of the 6th for not protecting them well enough. He didn't need to test the theory, he had seen it in play already.

He closed his eyes and thought of the only other time he'd been forced to make a choice, and while he had known then it was the right choice—it had brought him to Africa after all—he still hated that a woman had been the driving force behind the decision.

Judge Barbara Joyce.

She'd sat in her courtroom and supposedly given him a choice. Did he want to spend more time in the community home? Or did he want to enlist and serve in Her Majesty's Service?

There was no choice. In the army he would get to be deployed overseas, see the world. It was a no-brainer, really.

He found he was grinning as he remembered those first few years in the military. His training, shooting a gun for the first time, and then finally being sent with the UN peacekeepers to the Zimbabwe-Rhodesia election. To ensure it was fair and free.

At the time, he hadn't understood the implications of the election. To him, it had just been his deployment. Coming on the cusp of when he needed to decide if he was going to stay in the army as part of the infantry, or as he liked to call it, 'cannon fodder'. It was his ticket to freedom.

Or so he'd thought as he quit the army and began his new life in a beautiful new country, filled with possibilities, exotic animals and opportunities for a man to make something of himself.

Payden's nasal accent brought him back to the present. 'Here he comes.'

Douglas could see the elephant as he walked along the path and hear Payden as he drew in a ragged breath.

Virgil was nodding. The elephant was almost in range.

'Easy, take your time. He'll walk right in front of us, then you can take him. A side brain shot,' Douglas said.

The seconds ticked slowly by as Payden lifted his rifle—so did Douglas. His heart rate elevated. He controlled his breathing. *In. Out.*

Douglas whispered, 'Remember to look for the crease of the ear. Visualise the target inside that. The trophy is yours. Take the shot.'

Payden settled his rifle into his shoulder and squeezed his trigger. The weapon discharged and recoiled, slamming into Payden. The American stood his ground, absorbing the impact.

The old bull took half a step and his legs crumpled beneath him. A direct shot through the brain. The rugger shot was clean. Perfect. Skilled.

Payden began to walk forward.

'Wait,' cautioned Douglas as he watched for any movement, any sign that the elephant bull was only injured and would get up and charge them.

It stayed still.

Virgil, his rifle still held to his shoulder, walked slowly forward.

Douglas could see that the elephant bull was dead. Still, they needed to check. Many hunters had assumed no movement meant dead. Virgil's job was to make sure.

Virgil reached the elephant and put his rifle in between its eyes, where he knew that it would penetrate through the pachyderm's thick skull and into its brain. Then he kicked the elephant.

Nothing.

He gave a thumbs-up sign to Douglas. There had been no need of a 'make sure' shot, as Payden had been the perfect hunter. One bullet, one animal. Just the outcome that a professional hunt should have. An elephant deserved a quick death; that was the least that Douglas could give him.

'He's down,' Douglas confirmed.

Payden approached slowly.

'Jelly legs got you?' Douglas asked.

'No, caution and common sense. Had an onyx in South West Africa a few years back that gored the tracker who checked on him. Figured if a local can make that mistake, an ex-Brit and his tracker can too.'

Douglas shook his head, as if he hadn't already had to caution against the man rushing in, and now he was making out like waiting was *his* idea. Instead of belittling Payden, he carefully chose his more professional answer. 'Not likely, but it's good to be cautious. Your elephant is dead. Make no mistake, your shot was true. Congratulations! This is quite a trophy you have bagged.'

Douglas took his radio out of his pack and relayed his location to his skinners. They'd bring in the *bakkie* and collect the elephant. There was much to do to ensure the trophy wasn't damaged.

'Do you want pictures?' Douglas asked.

'Hell yeah,' Payden said as he dug in his pack for his camera. 'I get photos with all my kills.'

Douglas looked through the lens and pressed the shutter to record another moment for Payden to frame and put on his wall. Another reason why Payden would never be invited to join the most elite club in the world.

CHAPTER 12

North American Top 6 Trophies

1. Moose
2. Bison
3. Grey wolf
4. Grizzly bear
5. Polar bear
6. Man

South American Top 6 Trophies

1. Wild boar
2. Water buffalo
3. The red stag
4. Père David's deer
5. Jaguar
6. Man

CHAPTER 13

Nick heard his phone ring as he came into the house after fetching the second-hand axle for the truck. Having spent most of Friday in the city, he was now ready for a long hot shower and a drink, despite it being only three-thirty.

'Nick here.'

'Hi, it's Chloe—Chloe Mitchell. Mike Mitchell's daughter.'

Nick froze. Then his brain seemed to kick into gear, a million thoughts racing through it: she'd used his number! Was she alright? Did she need help? Did she still consider him a friend? Where had the years gone? She sounded so mature?

'Nick? Are you there?'

He realised he had been quiet for too long. He cleared his throat. 'Ah, Chloe, nice to hear your voice.' He took off his hat and tossed it towards the lounge chair. It caught the wind underneath it, sailed a little, and missed entirely, landing on the floor. He had done that shot a million times and never missed. He looked at his shaking fingers.

'Dammit,' he muttered, rubbing the back of his neck.

'Pardon?' Chloe said. 'This is a terrible line.'

'Ah—that wasn't for you, just something that happened here.'

There was silence on the other end of the line.

He opened his mouth to say something, then shut it again, not quite sure exactly what to say to someone he hadn't seen for five years.

'Is this a bad time?' she asked.

'No,' he said, and even he could hear he'd said it a bit forcefully. 'It's fine. I'm fine. How are you?' Then he realised she hadn't asked him, and he smacked his own forehead with his hand. He was making a total botch of talking to her, as if he was a nervous teenager, and it made no sense to him at all. This was Chloe, whom he had seen grow up. Chloe whom he'd almost had as his ward …

'I'm good. I know it's been a while since we spoke, but I was wondering if you meant what you said, you know … that if I ever needed anything, I just had to ask …' Her voice faded.

Nick held his breath. He'd almost stopped himself from writing that offer in the card earlier in the year, but he'd meant it because he couldn't bring himself to hold it against her that her dad and Enoch had caused so many problems.

He took a deep breath and then exhaled. 'I did. What's the problem?'

Her voice sounded sweet—innocent, as if somehow, she'd managed to remain unaffected by the cruelty that had happened to her so early in her life.

'I need—we—need your help. Enoch told me I have to tell you that he's travelling with Dad and me, and he understands if you don't want to help us.'

Nick ran his hand over his face. Chloe wasn't her father or Enoch, and she had nothing to do with what they had done. When he had seen her last, she had been sixteen and innocent, protected and beautiful. He hoped that even now she was unchanged by life, but he doubted that she had remained unaffected with everything he knew had happened with her moving Mike to South Africa. 'Tell Enoch to remember that time heals. What's happened?'

There was a pause as she relayed his message, then she came back on the phone.

'We need help getting home to Delaware.'

The sucker punch to his stomach was unexpected. Delaware was where he'd thought all the pressures of war could miraculously be lifted, but from where everything he held dear had been ripped apart instead. Where lies, deception and destruction had ruined his most prized friendship.

She was returning to Mike's farm. The farm where Nick had been a witness to a great secret he still didn't know how to deal with.

No, the secret he could process. It was the reasoning behind it that he still didn't understand.

He cleared his throat as he sat down on the floor, knowing now that this call would take time. 'Are you crazy?' he managed. 'Why?' Then he had a thought. If she was with Enoch and they were in trouble, and travelling with her dad despite his condition, perhaps she shouldn't be telling him anything where someone could listen in. 'Where are you?'

'Near —'

There was a muffled noise and then she came back on the line. 'Enoch said to tell you we're with the father of Destiny's Folly.'

That was a horse's name he hadn't heard in many years. Nigel Smoothy had a place outside KaNyamazane. She was closer than he thought. 'Stay there. I'm coming.'

What had he just got himself into? The last time he'd crossed paths with Enoch something illegal had been going on. And it seemed that way again now. But if Chloe was heading home, and he could get her to trust him enough to let him accompany her—them—then the chances of him getting to the bottom of what had happened back in 1981 might give him closure. God knew he needed closure.

It was his duty—no it had almost been his duty—to protect her once, and he was damned if he didn't still feel responsible for that promise now, even though Mike and Enoch were both still alive.

It was dark by the time he got to Nigel's farm. There was no gate on the citrus farm, and as his Land Rover rattled over the cattle grid, he couldn't help but wonder if the shake-up of his body was the universe telling him to wake up, to walk away while he still could.

The dogs that greeted him at Nigel's house were Great Danes. Over-friendly and not vicious at all, they shoved their heads through the window and licked his arm. The brindle dog was taller than its tan companion with a pink collar, and while the female kept her head through the window, mournful eyes watching his every move, the brindle one put his head in and out and looked expectantly at the house. He needed to push them aside to get out, and while they didn't jump up on him, they were very much in his space, sniffing him.

When Nigel opened the front door and whistled, both dogs quickly loped back to him, their agile bodies covering the short distance to sit on either side of their master.

'You look like a statue from Ancient Egypt with those next to you, just not enough gold dripping from your clothes,' Nick said.

Nigel grinned and put his hand out to shake Nick's. 'It's been too long. Come in.' He clapped Nick on the back and led the way into the house.

In the lounge, he saw Colette, Nigel's wife, and he kissed her on both cheeks in greeting. Colette was of French descent, and while she put up with Nigel's colonial ways, including living on the farm, she still kept an elegant aura around her that shrieked sophistication and mystique. Her voice still carried that breathless accent as she spoke. 'Good to see you, Nick. You don't visit enough.'

He smiled. 'You know how it goes in the bush, always some tourist losing themselves, some hippo needing to be chased back into the park …'

She laughed, the sound light.

He looked past her to where Enoch, Xo, Mike and Chloe—with her long black hair looking unruly and unkempt—stood. But it was the bruising on her face that his eyes focused on. Her nose had obviously been broken and reset recently, the deep purple around her eyes testament to the pain. Her left cheek was also blackened, as if she'd been in a fight with a truck, and the tell-tale scab on her lip showed where her teeth had obviously been forced through the flesh and a surgeon had sewn her back together.

What the hell was going on?

Her dark eyes, skittish as a newborn impala's, stared back at him. And then she smiled, broad and spontaneous. It dominated her face and brightened up everything in the room, and he knew that he'd made the right decision to help her tonight, no matter what Enoch had got her into.

Enoch stepped forward, hand outstretched.

Looking away from Chloe, Nick gripped it in a tight shake, then shook Xo's hand. Chloe surprised him by throwing her arms around him as she said, 'Thank you for coming to help. I told Enoch you would.'

He held on to her for a brief moment, trying to comfort her, to be worthy of her gratitude—when all he had done was drive a few kilometres down the road. He could feel the blush start in his chest and flush up his neck and into his face. He couldn't remember any other girl throwing herself at him in quite the way she just had—without any reservation.

She'd always been like that with him. Natural. No falseness. Perhaps that was because he'd last seen her as a child, but now the body that pressed against his was that of a grown woman.

He nodded and stepped away quickly, feeling the echo of where her hands had drawn across his body as they parted.

'Your face—what happened?' he asked, unable to contain his concern any longer.

'Long story, another time,' she said quickly.

He nodded and put his hand on Mike's shoulder. 'Good to see you, Mike.'

Mike slowly lifted his right hand and moved his fingers in a small almost wave, but he didn't respond verbally, yet Nick could have sworn that he saw a flicker of recognition cross his face.

His heart broke when he thought of the corporal he'd known and the shell of the man who now stood in front of him.

Guilt bit deep in his stomach that he hadn't done enough to stop Enoch and Mike that fateful day, or that he hadn't gone with them. Perhaps if he'd been there, the outcome might have been different. Perhaps if he hadn't been so proud —

'Come through to the dining room. We're about to eat. I've set a place for you,' Colette said as she seated everyone around the table. 'Nick, what can I get you to drink?'

'Just a Coke, thanks,' he said, wanting to keep a clear head.

'This is Ethel,' Chloe introduced the woman as she sat next to Mike. Ethel was obviously used to Mike, as she fed him, then cleaned his face, before she got her own plate.

The roast dinner was scrumptious, and Nick ate with relish as he realised just how hungry he was for a home-cooked meal.

No one said a word during dinner until Colette got up. 'I guess you're dying to know what's going on, Nick,' Colette said, 'I'll leave you all to chatter amongst yourselves. Nigel was always the one who was into the cloak-and-dagger stuff. The less I know, the less I can tell anyone who asks. You know me, I'm a total gossip. I'll be in my sewing room, darling.' She kissed Nigel on the cheek and left.

Nick watched her go. He knew that Colette and Nigel were from different backgrounds, and he also knew that Colette had gone against her father's wishes to marry him. She was a French diplomat's daughter, and Nigel a humble farmer, but they had a love that not even years of excommunication from her parents could break.

Nick shook his head. He'd watched people since he was a boy, always wanting to know their story. It was what had got him into trouble in Zimbabwe in the first place. Wanting to know what made Mike and Enoch so close, why they were inseparable and why it made them such a formidable force together. Even though he had been around them since he was a boy, and growing into a man, he had noticed that their friendship was different to many others around. They shared a brotherhood, and he knew that for a short while, he had also been part of their coalition. A member of their pride.

'Nick? You here or somewhere else?' he heard Nigel ask.

He nodded, bringing his attention back to the present.

'You need to know what is going on before you agree to get involved,' Enoch said. He went on to explain what had happened with Sebastian.

Nick clenched his fists and his nails bit hard into his palms. If Sebastian hadn't already been dead, there was a danger that he'd have driven to Howick to teach him an important lesson about respect of women, and of humans in general.

He understood that while Enoch had done everything he could to protect Chloe and Mike, they were living in South Africa, and apartheid and racism were the way of life. Enoch was black. Sebastian was white. Add to that, he sounded like a radical Afrikaner, too. It was typical that a minority group could damage the reputation of the majority. He'd worked with, and knew, plenty of amazing Afrikaners. They were not all like Sebastian.

'What are your plans?' Nick asked.

'We want to cross through the bush near Komatipoort, into Mozambique and travel up to Zim, then through Gonarezhou National Park, and home,' Enoch explained.

Nick shook his head. 'That area near Komatipoort is crawling with SADF at the moment. There was an upsurge of *deurlopers* with the increase of RENAMO—the Mozambican National Resistance—movement in the area. FRELIMO—the Mozambique Liberation Front—is pushing down, and they're pushing back, but it's taking its toll on the citizens who are coming to South Africa. Despite apartheid, they still think they'll have a better life here.'

'They probably will. Safer anyway. Poor bastards, they are caught in the middle of a war zone, and all they want to do is live a normal life,' Nigel agreed.

'There's another option. Travel through Kruger. I'll join you. We can switch your truck with a Parks Board vehicle. And then we can go as far as we can in the park, and through to the other side into Coutada 16.'

'But that's FRELIMO country,' Nigel said.

'And hunting country. Yes, but if we can get one of their uniforms from the RENAMO guys I already know, and pay for a guide through the area, then we can get past. If we can get the RENAMO guys to send word that something big is passing through, then everyone, including the South African hunters in that concession, will turn a blind eye. There's a pontoon service in Mapai to cross the Limpopo, but it's not big enough for the truck. Lucky the rains haven't been good, so we might get away with an ox or two helping us through that river. I have seen them take army trucks through like that. Once across, we're back in RENAMO territory and can go into Zim south of Gonarezhou without being spotted.'

'And you know this route because?' Enoch asked.

'You really don't want to know,' Nick admitted with a shake of his head.

'Actually, I do,' Chloe said. 'Are you going to get us all killed?'

Nick chuckled at the irony of this. But then he looked at Chloe's face and knew that while she might appear outwardly soft, inside she was a survivor. A fighter. Someone he'd be proud to know as an adult.

'Nothing like that,' he reassured her. 'I often travel with the SADF soldiers. We've been that way a few times. Khululani showed me the route when I was first getting to know the park. The Malawian and Zimbabwean workers use it to come through to the gold mines in South Africa. It's an old migration workers' track. Used for many years, but many have fallen there, too. There are sometimes mines, depending on whether FRELIMO or RENAMO feel like being nice and letting them through to work or not. It won't be easy, but it'll keep you away from the SAP.'

'And you think we can go all that way undetected?' Chloe asked.

'It can be done, but horses in the park will be the tricky part. We'll have to stop to rest them, stretch their legs, let them recover before pushing on. It'll add time. Lions will be drawn to the smell—there haven't been horses in Kruger for years. There are enough service roads for us to travel on to get all the way through, and I have a few co-workers who'll help us if we need it, but we are going to have to keep our presence in the park as inconspicuous as possible.'

Chloe looked at Xo and Enoch.

Enoch shrugged his shoulders. 'You hold all the cards this time, Nick. We are in your hands.'

CHAPTER 14

Douglas waited for his next client at Klein Knapview airstrip, knowing that she had had to go through Bulawayo airport first. Fridays were always a busy day for the staff at the airport processing people through their counters, but for some reason, being the last Friday in November, the process was taking longer than normal.

While most of his schedule from the 6th was worked out a year in advance, there was no contact with the 6th's clients until a few weeks before each hunt. They were just a name with a list of the animals they wanted to shoot. Headquarters organised all the import and export permits for the guns and the trophies. The 6th clients had to use their real names because of the legalities of the arms importations and exports at the end.

Everything was organised by fax through the secretaries of the 6th Society. The system had been set up long before he'd been invited to join the 6th—that the clients would provide their names, and as much factual information as possible. He'd found that the easiest way to hide his 6th trophy hunting was to have a proper trophy-hunting front, like the Lindani Conservancy in the lowveld of Zimbabwe that hired him on a regular basis, and to run his 6th clients and the normal clients from the hunting companies he contracted to. Alongside each other, but never together.

It was also a convenient way for him to assess other hunting clients and report the information to the 6th if he thought that any of them might be worth approaching to join their elite clientele.

When the pilot landed her little plane on the airstrip, he was ready for his next client. Pushing away from the Land Cruiser, he walked to the plane once the pilot had stopped the propellers.

A woman climbed out of the passenger door and stepped in front of him. She pushed her dark glasses up on top of her head. She was about five foot seven with mouse-brown hair, green eyes with bags under them, and a pleasant enough face. 'Hi. I'm Nicole Schaffer.' Her South African accent was thick.

She didn't put her hand out to shake his, and when he glanced down, he could see she was missing the last two fingers on her right hand.

'Douglas Jones,' he said, nodding instead.

Nicole smiled.

'Thanks,' he said to the pilot when she came around and deposited the client's case by his feet.

'Weapons on the other seat, one second,' she said, opening the door and giving him the client's guns.

'Thanks,' he said again, and the pilot returned to the plane.

Douglas walked to his Land Cruiser, and carefully put the hunting weapons in the front seat between where he and his client would sit. Only after they were secure, did he go and fetch her luggage. Nicole Schaffer was still standing where he'd left her.

'We need to move, come over to the *bakkie*,' he said.

They walked together to the vehicle before he turned around and signalled to the pilot that they were safely out of her way and not about to cause any obstruction.

She saluted him through the windscreen and started her engines, then she turned her plane around. He watched her taxi, then run her little plane down the dirt field, and up over the trees at the end.

The warthog that lived on the other side of the airstrip ran to its hole, its tail up like an aerial, as it always did whenever a plane came or went.

Douglas put the cases in the back, then climbed in. Nicole was already seated, waiting for him. He gave her a folder with the itinerary.

'Everything is in here. The leopard hunt, and then our free time when I'll be your professional guide in a game reserve. Are there any questions before we join the men in the camp?' he asked.

She let out a quick breath. 'You need to know I'm only here for the hunting, nothing more. My husband knows that my passion is hunting, but he doesn't share in the sport. I've told him I wanted another leopard—the one I have in my trophy room is small and was the first of the big five I shot a few years ago.'

He nodded his head, understanding what she was saying. She was not after anything other than the thrill of the hunt. He liked her already.

'I've organised for the baiting of your leopard. We've permits on this property for those, but our 6th will not be inside the fence of this concession,' he said. 'When we hunt your leopard, it'll be a normal professional trophy hunt, with trackers and skinners and a nice hunting lodge. When we go after the 6th, it is only you and me. No tracker, no porter for your bag. We carry in what we carry out.'

She nodded. 'I expected as much.'

'Does your schedule still allow ten days for the hunt?'

'Yes, and I've added two extra in case. I'm happy to sightsee for the last two or more if we don't need them, but I would like to get home for the public holiday on the sixteenth if I can. Showing people pictures of a safari is always better than showing them pictures of a trophy hunt. It's becoming more and more socially unacceptable in the circles I move in. There's no regard for those of us who know that it is we hunters who invest the most in conservation, and make sure that there are animals left to shoot. I suppose I'm preaching to the choir here.'

Douglas had heard it before, but never quite so eloquently. Many people always banged on about how hunters killed everything, but it was true that they also spent a lot of money on that privilege. Trophies were expensive, and much of the money spent was filtered down through the hunting communities, and into the grassroots of those communities where the hunting took place.

At the same time, the people who were complaining about the hunting were the ones still buying the kudu and eland biltong. Hypocrites.

He prided himself on being spared that social taboo. He was a hunter, and that was all there was to it. If those with a gentle constitution couldn't handle it, they would never cope with knowing that he loved being one of only six 6th-appointed hunters in the world. And he couldn't live without those kills.

Hunting an animal was easy. They ate, you fed them, you shot them. Game over. A man who knew he was being hunted, that was a different story. The realisation that he was about to die. The chase. That look in his eyes knowing that you were about to end his life, and you held the power to decide if he lived or died and there was nothing he could do about the outcome. That moment when it was over, and you had taken that life, not because he deserved it, but because you deserved it.

That was what he was in hunting for.

He seriously didn't care about all the other arguments around money, conservation or even the newest term, sustainable tourism.

'You are,' he said, realising that he had been quiet for a bit long. 'And an invitation to play tourist and sightsee is always welcome. Anything particular in mind?'

'I heard Zimbabwe Ruins were stunning, and Victoria Falls.'

'I'll organise charter flights. First, we zero your rifles. Any blood show and my tracker will report it to management, and you'll pay for a trophy even if we can't find it afterwards.'

She nodded. 'Fair enough.'

'I assume you realise how dangerous a wounded leopard can be? As your professional hunter, I can tell you that I'll try to protect you, but I'd rather you didn't put me or my tracker in that position in the first place. If you want that trophy, and the cover story, you need to shoot true on your leopard.'

She nodded.

He started the *bakkie*, and they began their drive to the camp.

Nicole was a great shot. She didn't even adjust her scope on her .404 Jeffery. He could see that the gun was not new, and it was well cared for; the wood shone with the gloss of a weapon polished often. She loaded it with Douglas's own hand-loaded bullets. He cursed that ammunition wasn't allowed on the planes and knowing that a lot of the hunters brought in .404s, he'd hoarded many original Kynoch bullets to reuse. There had been a decline in commercial bullet manufacturing for her weapon of choice, and he was still expected to have the hunter's chosen ammunition on hand when they needed it. Making bullets was a skill he'd learned, an art that he was proud of.

She hit the mark that he made with his axe on the tree three out of three times, at about eighty metres. Given that the hide was probably on the thirty-to-forty-metre range, he was more than happy that she could shoot well enough to take on the leopard.

'We use that weapon, then,' he said.

'Yes, but I need to check this as well,' she said, removing a 30-inch-long shotgun out of her bag. She loaded it with number two shells, and then took a shot at the tree.

She blasted a hole in it. 'It's also good.'

'Not too many hunters carry a shotgun in case they don't make the kill shot. They're always so certain that they'll make it. You shoot well, and you carry this backup in case the leopard charges you. There must be a story behind that ...'

'I lost my fingers to stupidity. I'm not losing my life to it as well,' she said.

Douglas looked at her. 'Yet you still balance your weapon perfectly.'

'It took a little practice. Before I started hunting, I used to do enduro motor biking. I had a bad fall, and my fingers were crushed. The doctors couldn't save what was left,' Nicole said. 'Now I hunt. The adrenaline rush is better, and I get a lovely trophy for my room instead of leaving bits of myself in the bush.'

Douglas didn't ask her any further questions. 'Right—let's go bag an impala and re-bait. That leopard has been sniffing around an empty tree after it finished its last bait. Let's give it something to keep it there, shall we.' He shouted out into the camp, 'Virgil! *Woza*.'

Virgil ran from an *ikhaya* at the end of the campsite and greeted his new client with a grin.

'Nicole, this is my tracker, Virgil.'

Virgil looked at her when she didn't put her hand out. He reached out and took her right hand in both of his.

'*Salibonani*. Welcome to Zimbabwe; I am happy to be your tracker.'

Nicole stood there a bit dazed as he let her hand go and ran to sit in his seat on the front of the *bakkie*.

'Hop in,' Douglas said, and she shook her head slightly before climbing into the front passenger seat.

'Don't mind Virgil, we recently did a bit of hospitality training; he's just really keen to show that he learned something there.'

Nicole half smiled.

Douglas smiled in satisfaction. They would be alright on this hunt; there was more substance to Ms Nicole Schaffer than her wafer-thin body and missing fingers.

They drove down to the waterhole.

'This is an artificial water source. There's a borehole that pumps the water from deep in the ground up into the dam daily. This waterhole is the lifeline to this section of the conservation, as without the water source, the game would drift off in the bush, looking for another water point, and they would have no animals in this area year around, just dry thornbushes.'

'It's cleverly done. If you hadn't told me I would have thought it was natural,' she said.

'This section of the conservation used to be a cattle farm. It's better now that it's back to the natural bushveld.'

Nicole nodded.

'Look. Impala,' Douglas said, pointing.

There were always plenty of impala coming in for a drink. The herd was larger than he was expecting, and while they were calm, they were still constantly looking around, checking for predators, their tails flicking at the summer flies. The familiar brown antelope with the big ears milled around, some drinking while others nibbled the short grass on the side of the dam, upwind from the *bakkie* and not aware of their presence.

Virgil sat on the front. 'There's a big ram in there, but he's good for breeding, so the one on the outside, who isn't quite as large, is a good one for the baiting if we're not doing a trophy today.'

Douglas watched as Nicole removed her weapon from its bag, and then he stood next to her as she chose.

'Virgil has a good eye,' she said.

Douglas was watching, but before he could even check that she knew which part of the vital organs she was aiming for, she'd let off her shot.

The large male dropped down onto its knees and fell over. The rest of the herd scattered, barking and running in all directions.

They drove up to the carcass. Douglas looked at the dead impala: it had a clean shot through the head. For only his second female client ever, Nicole was proving to be quite an interesting hunter.

Virgil loaded the impala into the back of the *bakkie* before seating himself on the front bonnet seat. He pointed left, and Douglas followed his instruction away from the waterhole and back towards camp.

Once there, Virgil helped Simon, the skinner, take the impala to the skinning tree.

'We can have a drink while we wait if you don't want to watch,' Douglas suggested.

'I'm interested to see how they do it. The last hunt I did for a leopard, I wasn't involved in the baiting at all, so it's fascinating to be here from the start.'

'Okay,' Douglas said. 'I'll just go get us some drinks; we can stay here. Coke or alcohol?'

'Coke,' she said.

He returned with two bottles of Coke and a bottle opener. 'To the start of a successful hunt,' he said, clinking his bottle with hers.

She took a sip. 'Why did they catch the guts in the buckets?'

'To use for draglines,' Douglas explained. 'To attract that leopard.'

'Draglines?'

'To get the leopard's attention and show him where the meat is hanging in the tree.'

She nodded.

Virgil and Simon dumped the headless carcass into the *bakkie* and loaded the buckets onto the back. Virgil sat in his seat and pointed forwards to Douglas as they left the camp. They made their way to where his team had previously baited the leopard. Once they were sure that the leopard eating was a big tomcat, they had constructed a rough hide, just for this client.

They parked near a big tree, and Virgil came to the *bakkie* tray and took the back part of the carcass on his shoulders.

Simon was ready with two large buckets.

'Bring your weapons and be vigilant. The leopard is active in this area, and we don't want to walk into a snarling animal before we're ready to shoot it,' Douglas said, taking the lead. Nicole followed, with Simon and Virgil coming up the rear.

'Here,' Douglas said. 'Look, this is his spoor.'

Nicole took a bullet and put it into the imprint in the sand, an easy way to measure a decent-sized print and know that if the print was bigger than the bullet, then the animal was at least a shootable size. It was 3.5 inches, so big enough. Now they just needed to make sure it was not a female.

The light was starting to fade a little as Virgil climbed the tree and hung the whole ribs to tail and hind legs of the impala in the tree. He positioned it close enough that the leopard would be able to stretch out its claws and grab it, pulling it onto the branch.

They began to set the drag lines.

'Can I do one of those? There are five or so to do, aren't there?' she asked.

'You know you've paid for us to do that,' Douglas said.

'I know. I want to be part of the hunt from beginning to end, not just shoot the leopard and have nothing to do with the preparation.'

'Your choice. Get one of the buckets that Simon has carried from the *bakkie* and copy what Virgil's doing. You're not like some of the other hunters who come through to shoot their big five trophies at all,' he said.

'Why be stereotypical?' she said as she followed Virgil's example. Walking about one hundred to one hundred and fifty metres away from the trees, they began spilling the blood and internal organs of the impala as they walked towards the tree again, so that the leopard would follow the scent to the main meal waiting for it.

'It's all set,' Douglas said. 'Your tree is baited, and your leopard should come again. Now it's just a matter of wait in the hide and see.'

On day three, the tracker told him that the bait had been hit, and they moved into the hide for the day and night, with Douglas explaining to Nicole that she had to be as quiet as she could.

Virgil woke him from his dozing at five-fifteen am the next morning. Douglas reached over and shook Nicole awake. 'He's here.'

She startled when she heard the baboons barking a warning to all in the bush that there was a predator around, then pulled the blanket she was wrapped in around herself to keep warm. She had slept fully clothed, with her boots on.

She sat up straight in her deck chair. For a moment she looked disorientated, then she was once again a cold killer as she reached for her .404 Jeffery and stood up.

'Leave that,' Douglas whispered. 'At this time of the morning you've time to watch him. He'll be here for a while. Enjoy the show. Wait for the sun to get a little brighter, and there'll be no shadows dancing over your scope. The bush is dense, so he thinks he's safe to eat in daylight hours. He's used to eating here and not being disturbed.'

She nodded and looked out of the hide. The leopard playing with the impala carcass was huge.

For over an hour they watched him as he manoeuvred his meat to the tree, and then began to dine.

'What keeps falling from that carcass?' she asked.

'Maggots,' Douglas said. 'If we were downwind, you'd be smelling a very ripe bait now.'

'Thanks for making sure we were upwind, then,' she said.

He smiled. Despite bait checking twice a day from four till ten in the morning, and again from three to seven each evening, she was still in good spirits.

Sometimes, this part of the hunt was when the true nature of the hunter would begin to show itself, the part that the client usually tried to keep hidden. The impatient, oh-God-I-hate-that-rank-smell-and-just-hurry-up-this-is-boring part.

The light improved and slowly the sunshine filtered in through the treetops. The leopard's coat sparkled in the morning light, a deep yellowish-orange tinge along his back.

'Now is a good time, when you're ready,' Douglas said. 'We've checked. He's a tom, and all yours.'

She lifted her rifle and positioned herself for the kill. At her feet she had her trusty shotgun loaded with SSG, a high-energy-hitting power buckshot, just in case. She placed her Jeffery's barrel on the makeshift rest they'd fashioned from sticks. Douglas stood next to her, his own rifle ready, too. Virgil stood with his shotgun in position.

Her breathing was ragged.

'Relax, there's no hurry. He'll be here for a while. Get your breathing under control. Remember, this cat is at an angle up a tree, not directly on, so you need to adjust how you shoot it.'

She answered him with a flat stare.

'Head shot or heart?' he asked.

'Heart. I don't want to damage a rosette on his head, even if a good taxidermist can repair the damage. He's too beautiful.'

'Good choice. Remember, the cat's internal organs are further back than an antelope's. You can't use the front leg as a judgement. Count backwards three to four ribs, about one-third of the way into the body as it's slightly quartering.'

He heard the shot, followed by the deadened sound of a large cat falling from the tree, and then running.

'*Jislaaik*, I missed? I heard him run. Really?'

'You got him. About twenty feet out there is a dead cat. Wait here. Whatever happens, don't move. If I'm wrong and he's only hurt, he'll certainly charge Virgil and me.'

He took the safety off and walked out behind Virgil with his shotgun.

There was silence, and all he could hear was the blood pumping through his own veins as he held his weapon ready, in case the leopard was alive. It could rip him apart. He didn't know a single hunting story where the wounded leopard had not come out fighting for its life. They were notorious for it.

At almost twenty feet, he released his breath. The leopard lay still.

Virgil poked it with his shotgun. It didn't move.

'She can shoot well,' Douglas said. 'He's a massive tom.'

Virgil grinned.

'All clear,' Douglas called. 'Come out the front, under the tree and keep walking, you can't miss us.'

She joined them a few minutes later.

'Looks like you shot him straight through the lungs and the heart. He was dead before his muscles knew he was dead. He didn't suffer,' Douglas said. 'Congratulations.'

She grinned as she looked at her first trophy for this hunting trip.

CHAPTER 15

Just before six o'clock on Sunday, as the sun was setting and the gates were about to close, Nick slowed the truck down a little and waved at the ranger on duty at Crocodile Gate, Kruger Park. The ranger, seeing who was driving, lifted the boom. '*Hamba kahle*, Ranger Nick,' he said as they drove through.

Nick heard Chloe release the breath she'd been holding and smiled.

Enoch, Xo, Ethel and Mike were in the back, trying hard to keep the horses quiet as they passed. He kept the truck going at an even pace so that the weight of the horses wouldn't shift and there would be as little noise as possible.

The trucks had been a problem at first. Nick had wanted to use an actual Parks Board truck, but with a new axle, Khululani said he wouldn't get that truck going for at least a week, and having to wait at Nigel's was not going to work—Chloe stood out like a red tomato on the citrus farm.

Usually, there were only two white faces on the farm, Nigel and Colette. Now there were four, and that would cause lots of excitement and whispering by the staff. Even with the bruising on her face, Chloe's features were distinctive enough that if anyone saw the bulletin, they'd recognise her. Colette had suggested that Chloe needed to change identities for a while.

They didn't have a wig, so they cut her hair short. It was no longer the black veil of beauty it had been. Then they bleached it, causing it to turn carrot orange. Wearing men's clothes, and with her hair cropped against her head like a pixie, she could easily pass for a young male. Except to him. He would recognise her anywhere.

It was the ideal disguise to get her through the bush. It made Nick a little happier about the trip. Protecting a white female in a war zone was never going to be easy. If things went south, the chance of her being raped was high, but if she looked just like another ranger, it would make it all a lot less stressful if they came across an enemy out there. Having a damaged old man and his maid along for the ride was not going to be a picnic in the park either. There was no way that he could disguise Ethel, but he hoped that perhaps she would be protected by her age, and the attitude of respecting one's elders within a tribe would still be in play in Mozambique.

He wondered if he'd taken on more than he was capable of delivering. All their lives were now in his hands. His responsibility.

'I knew that my acting in plays would be of help to me someday,' Colette had said, laughing when Nick had commented how good the disguise was.

Problem number one had been solved, leaving them with problem two. But the solution turned out to be a simple one—disguise Chloe's truck.

Nick drove her truck into the workshop at Crocodile Bridge, and Khululani and his boys repainted it to look like it belonged to the Parks Board, giving it a distinctive logo on the doors, sides and tailgate. Once it was ready, Nick and Khululani switched the plates with one of the broken Parks Board vehicles. He also added a much-needed slatted rooftop storage area. They filled four 44-gallon drums with diesel and hoisted them up top and made sure that a decent syphon hose was also put into the truck, so that they didn't need to bring the drums down. They would be able to top them up as they passed through any sites that had diesel. He'd also added a hitching rail along both sides, so they could easily tie the horses up if needed. Finally, Nick's last addition had been the upgrade on the two-way radio installed into the back to talk easily between cab and those travelling with the horses. The one that Chloe had been using was not as good as the ones they had in the workshop.

When they were ready, Nick had fetched his precious cargo and driven back into the park, all within two days. There were some perks to being in charge of the maintenance garage of the Parks Board fleet. The two days had given him the time needed to organise leave for himself and Khululani. They had a month, though he hoped to be back well before then.

Khululani sat next to Chloe, who wore old overalls he'd scavenged from somewhere that just about fitted her, a cap pulled low over her forehead and sunglasses.

Nick had tried unsuccessfully to tell Khululani that what he was doing might get them fired, but the older man had grinned and said, 'I am your tracker. When you go into the bush, I come with you.'

Nick smiled, thinking how lucky he was that Khululani had decided to stick with him, and not kick his sorry butt to the kerb from the day he had arrived at Kruger.

'Last chance to change your mind, Khululani. I can drop you here at the camp, and you can pretend you had nothing to do with me and this trip. You can tell Gladys in the office that she can tear up your leave request,' Nick said.

'I have not been on a journey in a long time. If you tell me to get out, I will. But I would rather stay and see these old friends of yours and their smelly horses safe. And know that if you throw me out, I will follow you—you are going to need me on this adventure.'

'Don't say I never gave you a way out,' Nick said. Now they were off, about to start one of his most dangerous journeys.

He'd had to drive over the Crocodile River bridge in full view of anyone watching, and that was just the start. He would continue to break the park's night-driving curfew throughout their journey. All he could hope was that when people saw it was a Parks Board truck, most wouldn't give it another thought.

'Turn the radio up; we need to try to monitor where everyone is,' he said.

Chloe turned up the sound and got the map and her pencil ready.

The temperature dropped only a few degrees as the sun disappeared, and they crawled along. A ranger called in to his station that his walk on the Wolhuter Trail was late getting to its rest camp; he suspected it would take another half an hour. Apparently, one of the tourists had fallen and hurt his leg, causing a delay.

Chloe put a cross on the trail that Nick had marked on the map.

Another ranger reported into Skukuza Rest Camp about a water pump they were experiencing trouble with, and that they would be getting back later than expected.

'As long as we drive steadily through the camp here and take the service road to bypass Lower Sabie Rest Camp, we should be okay. We're meeting an old friend on the Mozambique border, opposite Tshokwane. Once we have the uniforms of the ROMANO and FRELIMO with us, then we press on to the N'wanetsi Viewpoint. There we can stop at the picnic site to get the horses out and rest them before pushing on again to get to the Sabie River. The bush there is thick enough for us to wait out daylight hours without being seen by the public. Driving in the heat of the day, unloading and loading horses, even in a Parks Board vehicle, will attract attention. It'll be slow, but we will get where we want to go.'

'As long as this truck holds out on the road—that place is near where John broke the axle of his truck,' Khululani said.

'No reason it shouldn't. It's a solid old thing. Besides, I'm a better driver than he is,' Nick said.

Khululani laughed, and Nick filled Chloe in on how many vehicles John had crashed, and how Khululani was always fixing them up so that he didn't get into too much trouble with management.

They lumbered up a small incline, the gears grinding as Nick changed down. 'Shit, the rangers all across the park must have heard that.'

Chloe looked out the front windscreen. 'I've never been to the Kruger National Park,' she said. 'But I've heard other students talk about their holidays driving around and looking at the game, and the elephants of Kruger. Do you think we'll see any of the Magnificent Seven?'

'The story of those elephants comes from a really smart marketing department. They elevated elephants to celebrity status to try to save their lives. We've a big problem with poachers in the park. Many come in from Mozambique, but some from South Africa, too. It's one of the reasons I chose to travel with you. Extra protection. They come armed with AK-47s, and they mow down our elephants and chop out the ivory. The campaign hopes that when a poacher sees one of these big tuskers, whether he's in or out of the park, they'll know that the wrath of the people will come down on them, so that they don't kill the bull.'

'Does it work?' Chloe asked.

'We'd like to think so. Not too many have been killed by poachers recently. Most have died from natural causes.'

'What's the difference if the poachers do it or you guys kill them? You cull the elephants anyway—they're all dead in the end,' Chloe said.

'When we do it, the money is put back into the park—to make it better, improve the park and the camps, make new much-needed camps, pay the wages of the rangers, build new fences. When the poachers do it, it's for personal gain.'

Nick slowed as about forty zebras and wildebeest crossed the road in front of them, then he waited for a lone giraffe as it ambled down the road. He followed at a safe distance, at the same speed as the magnificent animal, until it eventually swished its tail and veered right off the road.

'We'll see elephants—don't know if they'll be the giant tuskers though,' he said.

'Have you seen the hall where all the Magnificent Seven pictures are? Is it true that they have the tusks of the elephants who were in the pictures? Are they all dead?' Chloe asked.

'I have, and no, not yet, but they are old. That's why they're so magnificent. There are younger bulls coming up, taking their own places in their greats list, but nothing will stop people marvelling at the Magnificent Seven.'

'Have you seen them all?'

Nick nodded. 'I was lucky enough to see them all alive. Khululani and I went looking for each and every one, and we have photographs of them. They are not the best pictures, but they will do to prove we saw them during our lifetime. I made copies for Khululani; I think that was the first time that he ever possessed a photograph of his own. Now he has multiple albums, and we both take the photos. He likes to share his albums with the staff who work in the lodge and don't get to go out into the bush much.

'We've started a Sunday drive club, where we take anyone who's not on duty out into the bush for a few hours, so that they can experience what everyone else does. He and I think the same: unless your local population loves the game and wants to protect it, you'll never stop the bush-meat trade. It's seen as a commodity, but if they can see value in it and develop a relationship with it, then half your battle is won. Same goes for the poaching for rhino horn.'

'What were the Magnificent Seven really like?' Chloe asked.

'Big. Old. Extremely large and heavy tusks. I imagine that long ago when the slave traders raided these areas of people, and they collected ivory, that much of what they took was from elephants like those guys. These days there are far fewer big tuskers. I don't know if it's a certain DNA within them that's been hunted out, or if it's an age thing, where they are not getting as old as they once did. But most elephants we see don't get anywhere near the length or weight of the tusks of those old guys.'

'It's really sad that they have to die just for their teeth,' Chloe said.

The radio crackled to life just as they crossed the river near the Tshokwane Picnic Site. Dave was out on patrol with a unit, and had spotted their lights and was reporting their movement heading north.

'Shit, keep quiet,' Nick said, taking the radio in hand. 'Dave, it's Nick, I'm the lights you see.'

'*Izzit.* Seriously, *boet*? Aren't you supposed to be on leave?'

'*Ja*, man, Khululani got the truck working, and we were testing it by going to Satara to collect a Land Rover they were having trouble with. Stupid thing broke down again, but he got it running so I figured I'd push through. Also got held up with a night patrol of a huge herd of buffalo.'

'You're lucky it wasn't a black rhino. Was in that area today and there was one pissed-off old *oke* strutting his stuff,' Dave said. 'Don't know what pushed his buttons, but he was *gatvol* of the world around him.'

'Haven't come across him yet.'

'As long as you're good, you take care with that truck, *boet*,' Dave said. 'Have a *jol* on leave.'

Party? Yeah sure, if only Dave knew …

'We will, good night,' Nick said, and ended the communication. 'That was a close one. I just hope as we press north that the other rangers along the way are just as trusting.'

They lapsed into silence, and while the lights of the truck picked up the odd spotted hyena, or a nightjar sitting in the road, the animals stayed mostly in the bush. Slowly Nick turned east, towards the service roads and the Mozambique fence line.

He stopped where he knew the park ended. He was certain he was in the right place because he could see a few men with flashlights and a Land Rover blocking the road, their AK-47s pointed at his truck.

He cut the engine.

'General Vareya is the commander of a RENAMO stronghold adjacent to this part of the park. I'll go speak to him; he knows Khululani and me. It's a good thing Enoch and Xo thought to pick up some whisky. Don't come out unless I tell you, and keep your dad quiet; I'm not sure they understand brain damage, so if he won't talk to them, they might see it as being rude,' he warned Chloe.

He jumped down, slammed the door closed, walked to the back of the truck and got the bottles from Enoch; then he and Khululani walked confidently towards the armed blockade.

Nick's heart beat loudly and all he could hear was the blood rushing through his ears, but he stayed on the road and forced one leg in front of the other, hoping that this was the right person meeting him and that Khululani's message had got through to the general in the short amount of time they'd had, and not someone else about to ambush them.

'This is good that it is you, Khululani,' General Vareya said as he stepped out from the armed group. Vareya was about sixty. He was well built, and his origins were from further up Africa, probably Kenya, unlike the Makuleke people who were employed at the park. He was taller than most of the men around him, too.

'*Yebo*, Vareya, it is good to see you,' Khululani said. 'I was not sure that my message had been received, or if you would help me.'

'*Eish!* I owe you. Perhaps now we can call it even. You saved my life once before, and the lives of many of my men; this is the least I can do when you call for help,' General Vareya said.

'Believe me, I appreciate it,' Khululani said as he shook hands with the general. Vareya was looking stressed in the lamplight, his hair greyer than when Nick and Khululani had seen him last, and perhaps a bit leaner, too. He was an active general, one who led his troops by example, and ran with them when he needed to, rather than sitting in some office commanding from afar. Nick admired him for that selfless determination, and that he still believed in a cause.

'Nick, good to see you. But I cannot believe that Khululani dragged you into woman troubles. Here I thought that his womanising days were done, and he would die saving the Kruger Park with you.'

Khululani smiled. 'There are not many secrets left between this boy and this old man. But I need to tell you that these woman troubles are Nick's, and I share them because he is my brother.'

'That is good to know. I was wondering why you had woman troubles at your age.' General Vareya laughed. 'Your troubles. Nick's troubles. They are the same-same. I have something that you need. This is Filipe. He is like a son to me. Take him with you as your guide for when you cross back into Mozambique. He has both our uniform and the FRELIMO one. He can fit in with both our factions; we call him the chameleon. He will get you safely through Coutada 16 and those FRELIMO bastards.'

'You're giving us a guide?' Nick asked.

'Khululani has helped me in the past. Without him, I would have been captured and tortured by FRELIMO. That debt needs to be taken seriously. All my men can see that I pay my debts.'

'Thank you,' Nick and Khululani said together.

'It is a deal, then. Pass over that whisky. It has been too long since I had some good stuff, and I see you brought me cigarettes, too. Ah—South African Dunhills, one of my favourites.'

'I remembered. I do not forget much either, just like you.' Khululani laughed and handed over the bottles.

'We cannot guarantee when we'll get Filipe back to you,' Nick said. 'Does he understand what might happen if he's captured here on South African or on Zimbabwean soil? When you cannot help him?'

'He knows. He is willing to risk his life for you and Khululani because I have saved his life, too. Now I want to meet this lady who you men are willing to get into so much trouble for.'

Nick shook his head. 'Can you guarantee she'll still be safe if you have seen her face, and you get captured?'

'No. You are correct. Perhaps better to send her my regards and tell her one day we will dance at her and Nick's wedding, in a more peaceful time.'

Nick smiled. An image of Chloe with her natural black hair against a white wedding dress filled his head, but he shook it away, instead hoping like hell that she couldn't hear the conversation, because he didn't want her sprinting like a cheetah to get away from him.

They shook hands, and Filipe—who was dressed as a game ranger in khaki overalls—walked with them towards the truck, his small pack all that he carried.

'You can travel in the back for now. You're not afraid of horses, are you?' Nick asked.

'I have donkeys in my hometown near Vilankulos,' Filipe said, and as they neared, Nick heard the distinctive sound of hunting rifles being unloaded.

Evidently, Enoch and Xo were watching out for Chloe even from the back of the vehicle. A white man going across the countryside in and out of Mozambique and border jumping was madness. Escorting a young white lady and her five horses across that same land was an absurdity. Trusting General Vareya's 'son' to see them all the way through Mozambique safely was total lunacy.

They continued to trek north; the going was slow, and eventually, Chloe nodded off to sleep. Nick watched as she fought it but ultimately was lulled by the hum of the diesel engine. He tried hard not to pull away when her head rested against his shoulder, not used to the heat that she generated against him but getting used to the idea of always having her there with him really fast.

'Wake up, sleepy head; we're almost at the Nwanetsi River. You guys are going to need to offload the horses to rest them,' Nick said reluctantly a few hours later. The moon was close to setting in the west.

'Sure,' Chloe said, taking Nick's offered hand to avoid tumbling out of the truck.

He noticed how warm her hand was, and that she didn't rush to remove it from his, before she began stretching and rubbing at her leg where the stitches obviously still irritated her.

Nick had already begun opening the back and securing the flap so that the horses could be unloaded. The darkness of the night showed that it was just before dawn.

Ethel got out first, guiding Mike, her arm tucked into his. She carried out a camp chair with her, and while she attempted to get Mike to walk for a little while, she soon gave up. He was tired, so she seated him instead, right next to the ramp going into the truck, and started to rub his legs.

'How's he been?' Chloe asked.

'He slept most of the way, which is easier for him. I think it is better for him in the back here where he has more room, and he seems happy to be with his horse,' Ethel said.

Chloe smiled. 'He has always loved Diablo; from the first time he saw him.'

The horses pranced and neighed softly, wanting reassurance from the humans that this was a safe place to offload. They were stiff from the long trip and just needed to be walked a little to loosen up.

'Chloe, this is Filipe,' Nick said, introducing the guide as he climbed out of the back.

'Nice to meet you,' she said, shaking his hand. 'I take it Enoch or Xo told you that he doesn't talk?'

'Yes. I'll be very careful with your father,' Filipe said.

Xo and Enoch walked out Kimberlite and Diablo and gave her the reins for Pampero as they passed. Nick took the lead rein for Marin and was soon walking him. Khululani backed away when Xo offered him Sirocco, but Filipe keenly took him instead.

'Khululani wasn't part of the unit in Zimbabwe; I met him here in the Kruger,' Nick explained. 'We don't keep horses in the park—the lions think they are just plain-looking zebras and easy pickings.'

'As long as some lion doesn't decide to come while we're walking the horses, then that's a good thing, right?' Chloe said.

'I know it's a dangerous park. The lions bite. The crocs bite. The leopards eat everything, and the elephants and rhinos like to run all over you. But hey, if you don't bother them, they won't bother you,' Nick said.

Chloe shook her head. 'Even I know that's rubbish. I bet you anything, if a lion came now, you'd say it's my fault for parading the horses around.'

'Probably,' Nick said with a small smile. 'This really is lion country, so keep an eye out for movement. The horses will spook if they smell one.'

'It seems like a lifetime ago that we spent hours training them, making sure they understood that the scent of a lion was dangerous, and they needed to alert us. I am sure it is not a smell that a horse would forget,' Enoch said.

'Right,' Chloe said. 'Lions for real.'

'Princess, we never imagined it would be easy, so not sure why you are suddenly baulking at lions now that we are in the park,' Enoch said.

Filipe chuckled, as did Xo, although he did try to hide it behind his hand.

'Perhaps because I've never had to get up close with a lion like you lot. I don't know the smell of them, or how big they are. We've kind of been busy the last few years, so I haven't had the chance to get back into the bushveld and learn the tricks of how best not to be eaten by a lion.'

'Chances are they will give us a wide berth if we do encounter them. You really do not have to worry much about them. Just be alert, that is all,' Enoch said. 'How is Pampero doing?'

'She's managing. I can't believe that she's travelling so well pregnant.'

'As long as she does not get too hot when we are travelling during the day, she should be fine,' Enoch said. 'Xo, I need to put down a water trough. Take Kimberlite and Diablo and walk them while I organise it.'

Chloe had zoned out a little while she was walking but was soon pulled back to the present with a strange whinnying coming from Kimberlite. The sound was low, as was the tone of the vibration. She'd never heard him make a sound like that. 'Enoch,' she called, 'listen to Kimberlite.'

His ears were pinned back, and while he was tossing his head constantly, the low murmuring that came from him was disturbing her. His eyes were rolling around as if trying to see everywhere at the same time, almost like a chameleon, but white with fright.

'Something is out there he doesn't like,' Enoch said. 'Come on, let's take his warning and get the horses back into the truck. Ethel, get Mike inside the cab.'

They loaded the horses and were still standing in the back of the truck when Nick's powerful torchlight fluttered over eyes in the bush not too far from where they'd been. They looked at the creature and it looked back defiantly, despite not being accustomed to having night lights shone in its face.

'There's the source of his skittishness. A honey badger,' Nick said.

The small mammal stood about twenty-five centimetres tall, its silvery-white bank of fur covered it from the top of its head to the top of its short tail, and the creature had almost no hair on its fat legs. Its shiny black nose clearly visible in the spotlight, the honey badger stood its ground, watching them. Challenging them to interfere with its journey.

'I've never seen one of those in the wild. I did see one dead after it had got into our chicken run at home, and it killed every single one. Dad shot it, and Mum was so mad at having to get all new chickens as hers had been good layers,' Chloe said.

'They are vicious,' Khululani said. 'You will hear the nice stories of the relationship between the badger and the honeyguide bird—I have never seen it myself in all my years in the bush, so I do not think it is true. But I can tell you if you see one, get away from it as fast as you can.'

'Really?' Chloe said.

'Absolutely. You see these legs.' Khululani pointed to his scarring. 'That is what happens when you stumble into its burrow. Run because it will attack you and keep attacking you. I was lucky. I survived.'

'And the honey badger?' Enoch asked.

'Nothing penetrates that skin, except maybe a bullet or six. I eventually managed to club it on the head and ran away. But it got my *takkie* as I was running, and was hanging on, not letting go. Luckily my shoe came off, to be left behind.'

'What'd it do with your *takkie*?' Xo asked.

'When I was healed, I went back to that place. There was not much left. There was no body of the honey badger either; I think it survived.'

Nick shook his head. 'All these years and I never asked what happened. Are you telling us the truth or just a ranger's tale?'

'This is no ranger's story,' Khululani said. 'But it was a very long time ago, when you saw many more honey badgers than you do now.'

'How old were you when it happened?' Chloe asked.

'I think I was maybe fourteen,' Khululani said.

'You've had those scars since you were so young,' Chloe said.

'Scars are survival victory medals worn on your body, and I am proud of mine. Why do you think I never cover them up? I learned a lesson that day. You never give up—you give one hundred and ten per cent of your strength to a fight. Do not quit, not until you are dead, and you have taken your last breath. You never stop fighting,' Khululani said. 'Despite the years gone by, I still have a healthy respect for the honey badger. See, I am still up here in the truck, and not getting down on the ground.'

'Respect?' Enoch asked.

Khululani chuckled. 'Perhaps they are the one animal I am scared of.'

While they had been talking, the badger had come closer, got a stronger whiff of their scent and turned its back. It walked away, disappearing into the bush on its stubby legs, its swagger as it did so bragging to the humans that they had survived an encounter with probably the most fearless creature in the whole of Africa, and they'd been the ones to give way.

'Is it gone?' Chloe asked.

'You can't be certain,' Nick said. 'Just because we can't see it doesn't mean it isn't there.'

CHAPTER 16

She'd thought that cutting through an elephant fence that served as the border between South Africa and Mozambique would've been more difficult, but Chloe watched as the men quickly dismantled a section of it to allow them to pass on to the south of the Shingwedzi River with ease before they headed eastward.

The track wasn't much, and certainly not well maintained, but then it wouldn't be. It was a smuggling route for vehicles stolen in South Africa and taken into Mozambique.

She'd been on edge since they drove in the Kruger two days ago, and she really needed a bath. Stuck in her same overalls day in, day out, no amount of deodorant was helping her body odour.

The men were ripe on the nose, too, but Filipe was adamant that she mustn't shower and smell like a female when they hit FRELIMO territory. Just in case. He had even told her to start using the men's deodorant.

Nick had kindly offered his spray when she had turned her nose up at a roll-on that Xo was using. Even in the bush there were some limits with sharing your almost-brother's deodorant. She discreetly sniffed her arm and smiled. The faint smell of the deodorant reminded her of Nick.

Filipe was small for a black guy, really short compared to Enoch and Xo. He almost looked like a schoolboy, except for the tell-tale signs of ageing around his eyes and the white in his hair. He was wiry and as nimble as anything. And bossy.

She'd seen him with the fence; this was work that he was used to. Despite his AK-47 hanging from his shoulder, he wielded wire cutters like a professional. Ordering everyone around to go faster, work harder. Even telling Nick and her what to do. That was something she wasn't used to.

It amused her to watch Nick bristle.

'Don't react,' Chloe reminded him. 'He's not doing it to be nasty, but because he wants us to succeed, to get through into Zim no matter what. He'll have to answer to General Vareya personally if he fails.'

She knew that they needed him to guide them through a quicker journey. But Filipe was just so … military.

'We are clear; drive her through,' Enoch called, breaking into her thoughts.

She breathed a small sigh of relief and released the brake, put her truck in gear and slowly edged forward, through the narrow gap between the two poles. She knew that she would fit, but making sure the whole truck kept true and didn't scratch if she went at an angle was taxing her skills.

Finally, she let out her breath; she was through. She stopped a little distance away and made sure that the handbrake was on. She was so tired.

Looking in the big side mirror, she could see that her bruising was at last going yellow and fading. A good thing as her pain meds had run out. Her lip itched from the internal stitching the doctors had sutured, but the line on the outside was neat and given time the scar would fade. As for her orange hair, that would grow out thank goodness, because she didn't like that one bit. She pulled her jungle hat back on her head, covering it.

Taking a deep breath, she pushed the door open and jumped out to rejoin the others.

Nick swore. 'I never thought I'd see the day I was cutting a hole in the same fence I've helped mend so many times before.'

Chloe smiled. She hadn't heard him swear often, so it added weight to him doing it now. She knew that he was as angry and tired as she was. Frustrated with their situation.

'Relax, Nick, we are going to restring,' Khululani said.

Filipe looked at them, shaking his head. 'That's a waste of time.'

'Not a waste. It will keep the elephants inside the park,' Khululani said. 'Better on the South African side. They might die to poachers, and sometimes they get culled, but still, they die fast. Not like getting massacred in Mozambique for meat for the troops, with no care if they suffer or not.'

Filipe turned away to avoid an argument, but he clearly was irritated that he wasn't being obeyed.

Chloe chewed on her lip as she watched him. While he'd shown he was a peacemaker at heart, Filipe obviously was not happy about the talk of his people massacring animals for food.

'Fixing it would be great, even making it almost fixed, but it is not happening,' Enoch said. 'We do not have wire pullers with us.'

'But we can at least try to pull in a few of the strands,' Nick said.

Filipe turned back to them. This time his voice was more forceful. Cold. Military once again. 'This needs to look like a vehicle theft, that you have come through and driven deep into Mozambique. Only a ranger would fix an elephant fence. A hijacker would not stop to fix it—they cut it and drive through. If you try to fix it in any way, it'll make your crossing different to the hundreds before you. The SAP will know it was you who came this way, and not someone stealing a vehicle. General Vareya told me that Miss Chloe is wanted by the SAP for saving a black man's life. If you make this crossing about the elephants, then we'll have the SAP joined by the SADF and the FRELIMO soldiers will follow too. They will all know that someone who is travelling this way belongs to the Parks Board. They might want to question you all. Only if this looks like a stolen vehicle, will you be safe from the SAP. This is Mozambique, and the South African law no longer holds here. But if they want you badly enough, then they will send the soldiers from the SADF after you: the Recces. You are not safe till you're in Zimbabwe, where even they do not dare tread because of the Red Brigade. You must do everything not to let them know we crossed here.'

They all stopped what they were doing and looked at him.

'Fair point,' Chloe said. 'I vote we leave it. I can think of nothing worse than anyone from the South African military catching up with us now that we've crossed into Mozambique.'

'Fuck it. Let's get out of here,' Nick said.

Filipe nodded. 'Enoch needs to drive now. Nick, you must go in the back with Miss Chloe, Mike and Ethel. You and Xo need to keep the women and Mike safe. I have Khululani and Enoch in Parks Board overalls, and me looking like a FRELIMO, but you and Miss Chloe and Mike, you are white, and no one will expect you to be here. This is not your war on this side of the border.'

Nick nodded, as did Chloe.

Nick put his hand gently on the small of her back to guide her towards the truck, and she didn't immediately step away. It felt like a motion done without thought, but it brought him close enough to her and she found that she liked that. A lot.

As the tail of the truck closed her in with the horses, she sat on the feed bags and wondered how she was going to get through another two days cooped up inside the box. Xo and Enoch had managed so far and refused to switch with her when she'd suggested it. Now she watched the unchanging inside of the truck, instead of the scenery and the wildlife as they passed it by. The time was measured by how many sweat droplets rolled from her arms and dripped into the hay spread across the floor.

The truck groaned and creaked under them as they pushed further into Mozambique. She thought about how little they knew of Filipe, and yet they'd all had to put their trust in him.

He was RENAMO, sworn enemy of FRELIMO, but he seemed to be able to move between the two as if he belonged to both factions. At least she hoped he did; they had yet to test his disguise. Filipe's bag was tucked away under the truck, where—hopefully—no one would find it. His RENAMO and Parks Board uniforms were directly below her feet.

She supposed she needed to believe that he was on their side and trust him.

Nick and Chloe looked up and over the metal through the breathing holes in the truck, as they came to a stop at a roadblock in the middle of nowhere.

'This is the safari company road to their camp. I need to speak with these men, tell them that I'm transporting something important. Then we'll have no more stops,' Filipe said into the radio.

'Leave your weapon,' Enoch suggested. 'It makes you look hostile.'

'That would be like stripping me naked,' Filipe said, then the radio cut out.

Chloe could hear him climb out and slam the door, and she adjusted her height to try to see better. Nick helped her gain her balance a little higher up on a bale. Despite him taking his hand away once she was steady, she could still feel the lingering warmth.

Her heart pounded as Filipe appeared in front while he walked closer to the roadblock. She looked at Xo. He was still. Composed. Watching the happenings, but she noticed that he'd got one of the hunting rifles ready while she'd been dozing, and it was pointed at the guards, just in case. Sweat ran down his face in rivulets. He was clearly more anxious than he looked.

Nick was also ready. The intense expression on his face as he watched the goings-on outside made her wonder again what it was that he and Enoch still had to settle. She adored Enoch, and as she became reacquainted with Nick a little more every day, she was coming to realise that they were very much the same. Both were determined men. They had obviously put aside whatever it was for the journey, so she wouldn't ask either of them, but she was curious. She remembered that there had been a closeness between Enoch, her father and Nick when she was a teenager, and yet now he seemed to tolerate their presence rather than be happy with their company.

She also chose not to ask why they hadn't got a rifle out for her. After all, she needed to be silent and ensure that she didn't give any reasons for the guards to come and look inside the truck.

Turning away, she slid carefully down the bale to check on her dad, but Ethel already had her one hand on Mike's arm and her other showing him to be quiet with her finger over her lips. Chloe hoped that her dad still understood that sign. But given that he was not known for making much noise, she wasn't that worried about the sounds, more that he would want to move.

Thankfully, she'd noticed that since he'd sat on the hay bale near Diablo, they had travelled better. It was as if the man and the horse—which he'd bottle-fed as a foal after its mother had died in transit after being captured in the Matopos, and had grown old together—were taking comfort from each other. Diablo had carried Mike through his war years. Now the horse rested his velvety-soft nose in his hand and blew gently, as if comforting her father.

She climbed back onto her bale and watched as Filipe spoke with the men, shaking their hands one by one.

The sweat had started to roll down Chloe's face, and she wiped her head on her shoulder. With the truck not moving, the back was quickly heating up even more than it had been while in transit. It seemed to be taking forever for Filipe to come back, although she knew that it was only a few moments.

As if knowing of their obvious discomfort in the hot parked truck, Filipe came to the back and opened up the small side door. She could only see the top of his head, but when he walked back to the men, she could see that the price for the talk was only a single bottle of whisky and a carton of cigarettes, both of which he handed over to the guards.

There was lots of back slapping going on, and finally he returned, and the men moved the barrier to the side of the road.

'Drive, Dad, get us the hell out of here,' Xo said quietly as the door closed, signalling that Filipe was back in the truck. 'Don't stop till we get to Mapai to cross the river.' Slowly, he lowered his rifle and held it between his legs, not ready to let it go.

The breeze began circulating inside the truck again as they bounced slowly along the bush track.

'That was tense,' Chloe said.

'Guess Filipe was convincing enough,' Nick said as he put aside his rifle. 'Now we have to see how fast the news travels in this part and if we are going to get anyone else sniffing around us.'

They continued to drive for another few hours, but they could see that the horses were tired, restless. They were kicking at flies and baring teeth at each other, not something they did often.

'Dad, we need to find a place for the horses to walk around. They have had enough,' Xo said into the radio.

'We just passed a small, abandoned village. It is probably a good place here,' Enoch said as he slowed to a stop under a large tree.

Even though Chloe knew that no one was in the burnt-out shells of the *kraals*, it still upset her to see them as they drove past. Where once families had worked and played, the dirt was blackened from the flames that had ravaged the mud huts, easily destroying the thatch. The mud bricks still stood, despite the fire that had consumed the buildings. Only a few had crumbled and fallen inwards, bowing to the savagery that had befallen them. A row of pottery containers that had been used to store food or water for a family had exploded in the heat outside of one hut. Chloe turned away when she saw a pile of charred corrugated iron, too distressed to look anymore.

Enoch opened the back, dragging her thoughts away from the village.

Khululani was standing with him, with Filipe to his left, a large grin on his face and his AK-47 slung on his shoulder.

'I have no idea what you're finding to smile at,' Chloe said.

'I'm looking at the real precious cargo, and I'm thinking that the men of FRELIMO will not believe it when word gets to them that this was only a lot of horses.'

She shook her head.

'You just keep believing that's the precious cargo and we'll be fine,' Nick mumbled as he helped Mike and Ethel out of the back.

'It's not the horses, it's the people, isn't it? Something else is special—your lady love, as Vareya called her. Other than the police chasing her, and her orange hair.'

Nick grinned back.

'Hey, the hair will grow out eventually, once I'm safe in Zim. But why do you insist that I'm anyone's lady love?' she asked. 'Have you seen any of us do anything remotely romantic?'

He shook his head. 'Just because a love is not in the open, does not mean it is not real, and not there.'

Enoch laughed as he led the first horse down the road. They each took their horses, and while Khululani kept watch for lions and leopards, they watered them and walked them for a good two hours under the trees.

Mike wandered around a little with Ethel watching him like a hawk, before she settled him into his sleeping bag under the vehicle, and he slept for almost the whole time they were walking the horses. Ethel sat in the deck chair, constantly checking that he was still alright, and no ants or scorpions had crawled onto him.

'We need to drive for another few hours, then make camp before dark. We cannot drive through this area at night; we will hit a landmine for sure,' Filipe said. 'I remember that there is another burnt-out, abandoned village about three, three and a half hours away up this track. If we can get there, at least we can have a solid wall behind the truck for better protection tonight.'

Nick nodded. 'Let's load up again and get moving.'

'Can you smell smoke?' Enoch asked.

Khululani sniffed. 'Cooking fires.'

'Perhaps the people have returned to the village?' Enoch said.

'Or soldiers,' Filipe said. 'We need to check it out before we drive in there. There could be danger for the truck.'

They stopped on the rough track and let the others out of the back.

'That village isn't abandoned anymore,' Enoch explained. 'Filipe wants to go and have a look, make sure it's safe to approach.'

'I will go with him,' Khululani said. 'It is better to have two sets of eyes and ears in the bush when you think you might be walking into danger.'

Nick nodded. 'I agree, so while Khululani and Filipe go on reconnaissance on foot, we need to keep watch over the truck. There is no place to hide in the open bush, and while people could sneak up on us, if we sit on top, we should have a height advantage and will see anyone approaching.'

'How am I getting my dad up on top and off again?' Chloe asked.

'You're not. Ethel and Mike can make a small camp and get comfortable in the shade of the truck. I don't expect them up here. We'll watch in case something like a hyena comes sniffing around.'

Enoch nodded. 'Right, let us get ourselves ready. I will see to Mike and help Ethel. Xo and Chloe, start your watch up there.' He pointed to the roof. 'Make sure you have extra ammo with you.'

Just as the sun set, Nick saw Khululani reappear from the bushes.

'The villagers, they have returned recently, but they are still shell-shocked from the last attack that happened.' Khululani said. 'They have a few *nguni* in their boma, and they have horns. Putting the horses in with the cattle as a place to stay for the night is not a good idea. The cows do not know the horses; they might hurt them. And they have dogs; I doubt they are vaccinated; if one bites a horse, they could get rabies. Better to stay out here than go into the village and share their fire.'

'We make camp here,' Nick said.

'Agreed,' Chloe said.

Khululani nodded. 'Filipe has gone to check that the message he sent to the FRELIMO camp, just past the village, has got through. He said if he is not back by nine o'clock that we must take it that his message was not received and make ready for an ambush. He said this FRELIMO, they come in the night, so nobody sleeps.'

'Shit,' Enoch said.

'At least we can sort of prepare,' Nick said. 'If I was in their shoes, I would mortar the truck first, so we need to build a boma and get the horses out. Did you notice any ditches or gullies when you were walking?' Nick asked.

'About three hundred metres to the right, there is a small riverbed which is dry,' Khululani said.

'Let's get the horses out and walk them there. Hopefully, we can find a place not too far away that we can corral them in. There are enough thorn-bushes to make the boma. It won't be bulletproof, but it can keep out the predators,' Nick said.

'They will stay when instructed. They are all trained, except maybe the mare Pampero; she has not finished her training yet with Chloe and me,' Enoch said.

Nick nodded. 'Lucky, they had you to train them, then, because if they bolt in this countryside, we'll never catch them.'

'It is mostly Chloe's hard work. I help, but she is the horse whisperer now,' Enoch said.

'Really?' Nick asked in surprise. 'She's better at training horses than you? I find that hard to believe. You were pretty spectacular in your day.'

Enoch said, 'She inherited Mike's soft touch, although he still stands there and somehow even without words commands them to calm down. It is amazing what he can still do.'

'Once we're finished making the boma, then what?' Chloe asked.

'You and Xo stay with the horses and out of sight,' Nick said. 'Take your dad and Ethel with you down to the river, and keep the horses quiet. Us three will protect the truck. That way you two women are together, which makes it easier to protect you both.'

'I can do my share of protecting, thank you, Nick,' Chloe said. 'Ethel and I aren't exactly useless.'

Nick shook his head. 'You know that's not what I meant. I know you're capable of protecting yourself.'

'Fine, but Chloe and I are taking the fuses and relays with us in case they come and try to steal the truck,' Xo said. 'I'm not walking if I can possibly help it. Not here in Mozambique. Too many landmines from what you guys say, I like my feet. I want to be much closer to home before I have to get on a horse and ride through the bush again. They are not taking our truck for a joy ride.'

'Not a bad idea,' Enoch said. 'Right, let us get those pangas and gloves out of the back now, and walk the horses down to make that boma. Nick, can you stay with the truck for now, so "our friends" do not try to steal everything instead of destroying it.'

'Okay,' Nick said.

'We have the two-way radio with us, but if you are unable to get to that can you make a loud animal sound to alert us that you have company, friendly or not?' Enoch asked.

Nick put his hands to his mouth and whistled like a guinea fowl. *Ripppeee-peeep-peep.*

'That will do for friendly. Have not heard any of those the whole day,' Enoch said. 'And for unfriendly?'

He made the sound of Egyptian geese. *Hoot-hoot-hoot.*

Chloe heard it clearly: the call of the Egyptian geese. She knew it was Nick; they were far away from any open water.

'Stay here, you two. Keep the horses quiet and do not come out of this boma unless you see me, understood?' Enoch instructed.

'Yes,' Chloe and Xo answered together.

Khululani and Enoch closed the boma from the outside. 'Remember, this is real, not a drill. Shoot to kill, my children.'

Chloe strained her ears to hear what was happening. Other than the call to say they had unfriendliness approaching, they'd heard nothing. No call on the radio, no further bird calls.

As always, Ethel had her father organised on his chair and was standing near him. Chloe wondered how she would've managed the trip if Ethel had said no and made a mental note to remember to thank her again as soon as she could.

They heard Enoch call, and they peeked through the thorns and saw Enoch and Filipe as they came out of the bush towards them—talking loudly.

Behind them walked six soldiers. All armed with AK-47s, they were relaxed and carried guns on their shoulders, not at their hips.

Their uniforms matched Filipe's FRELIMO outfit.

Filipe called out, 'They are here to watch the camp, so we can all sleep. They came to protect your horses. You can stay in the boma and keep the horses company. They will stay on the outside and patrol to keep the wild animals away.'

Chloe dug Xo in the ribs. If she spoke, they'd know she was female. She motioned for him to answer.

'*Yebo*,' Xo said. 'Thanks for the heads up.'

Filipe was smiling, looking his part as the one who was in charge of transporting precious cargo through the FRELIMO countryside. Chloe was relieved that he hadn't told them about her at all. He seemed to be keeping his side of the bargain.

She realised that she was starting to trust the little Mozambican.

CHAPTER 17

Enoch stared into the fire. His hunting rifle was next to him, and somewhere out there, soldiers patrolled around them.

Not so long ago, it had been Mike and him doing those patrols, around Mike's men, protecting their unit, being the soldiers. Fighting for what they both believed in.

Nick had been one of the men he and Mike had protected, and Enoch continued to try to protect him, even after everything that had happened since. So many secrets hung between them. Silently being eroded by time.

They had survived that war, and it was only afterwards that life had gone wrong for them. But if he was honest, he was grateful not to be separated from Mike. It was never easy to walk away from your best friend, and he hadn't had to.

When he had chosen to go to South Africa and live with Mike nearer the brain hospital, he had known that there were hard times ahead of them, and he was certain that he and Xo would be subjected to racist behaviour. Mostly it had been tolerable. Well, except for having to flee for a crime he didn't commit.

He threw another stick on the fire. It had been worth it. Now if they could just get home again to Delaware, and Chloe could learn about her ancestry, along with all the family secrets, he knew that they would be just fine. Making sure she and Xo were safe, that was payment enough for all the hardships he had endured and would continue to endure.

If he could rewind the clock, would he have done it any differently?

The day that Shilo Mission was attacked. The memory crept into his head …

Enoch watched as the silhouetted vultures glided on thermals in large circles around the mission. The brilliant blue sky behind them was marred with smoke coming from the still-smouldering buildings they were there to check on. The vultures appeared immune to the acidic smell as they danced with the wind, their large wings spread widely. Their patience was amazing. Waiting for the opportunity to land for their feeding frenzy below. They were one of his favourite species in the veld. The vultures and the mighty eagles. The watchers of the sky.

His people had a belief that if you ate vultures' brains—dried, smoked and mixed with mud—you could dream of the future. That the bird gave the gift of foresight. His people thought that they could dream where their next food source was, and those people could travel great distances to find it. They also thought it would give you stamina in the bedroom.

Enoch didn't believe any of it; they were just amazing birds as far as he was concerned. He and Mike had spent hours watching the ugly creatures on Delaware when they were younger, how they had been so patient waiting for an animal to die before going in. They would clean up the messes in the veld, making sure that the rabbits and diseases like anthrax didn't get a chance to spread.

Much like he and the Scouts were doing today.

'There it is,' Mike said.

They were checking in on the mission that had been attacked, making sure that if there were any terrorists still there, they could be captured and interrogated. To find out more about why they were attacking the missionaries, the soft targets, and why suddenly the rules of war had been changed: the church was no longer a sacred place, and its people no longer respected.

Mike was now his corporal in the Grey's Scouts, and he rode just behind him, with Buffel to the front and Nick to the side. Any other time, Enoch would be asking if Mike saw the birds, but a silence had descended over the small group of men, even before the mission station came into view.

This was precisely the type of attack that Mike had said would happen when communists—whose fanatical belief in their regime of not practising freedom of religion or speech, and having a state own and control everyone and everything, like in Russia—came to try to take their beautiful country from them.

Corporal Mike Mitchell signalled for everyone to follow him as they approached the eight-foot-high security fence around Shilo Mission. Zach and Henny, the youngest in the team of six men, had been instructed to stay near the gates. Despite having completed their initial military training, Mike was always sensitive about having the green recruits in an unpredictable situation; he was still getting them 'battle easy', as he would say. Enoch and Mike hadn't been as fortunate when they started in the Grey's Scouts just a few years before.

As they rode into the mission, Mike took point and rode up the stairs of the church, and Buffel was on the left flank to circle around the back and then enter from that side. Nick swung right towards the missionaries' houses, and Enoch rode even further right to circle around the back of the school rooms. Each had been assigned their duties before they had got to the mission. They had done this formation before; this wasn't the first time that they'd had to go in and clear out after a terrorist attack.

The schoolyard in front of the mission was empty. He had expected to see bodies there, much like those on the steps of the church, but there were none. He slowed Kimberlite, whose ears flicked from side to side, as if he too searched for a sound, for movement. He squeezed his legs, signalling for the horse to continue towards the door of the school rooms.

The doors were open, and he rode through, his Rhodesian Army-issued FN rifle ready at his shoulder in case he needed to use it, his bayonet attached for close combat if required.

There were no sounds, just an eerie silence. The building had escaped the shelling that the main church had sustained, and while some of the desks in one of the classes looked like they had once been in neat lines, they were now haphazardly positioned. There were still books on the desk and pencils strewn on the floor, as if the children who had been taking a lesson here had been disturbed. A few of the desks had been pushed up against the outside of the class, under the windows, as if they were used to shelter the children in case there was flying glass. He moved to the next room. Each one was the same.

He heard shots fired, and that there was contact somewhere on the mission grounds, the *pop-pop* sounds of the guns muffled by the thick walls of the building. He systematically cleared the last four school rooms, and although his heart beat wildly, he was relieved not to find any slain children. He wondered about their fate. They had obviously been there when the attack happened. It was school time, and the missions provided a valuable place in the small communities for an education. He had been fortunate to attend a village school on the farm next door to Delaware. His had been run by the government, not missionaries, and was nothing like Mike's fancy school in Bulawayo, which was only for white children.

He cleared the headmaster's office and what appeared to be a storeroom at the end, then exited the other side of the building, and went towards the gates where the rendezvous point was with the youngsters, being sure not to frighten them because of the contact he had heard.

He saw the mission's old Land Rover against a tree as he approached, and checked inside; the vehicle was abandoned, so he continued towards the youngsters.

He found their horses standing beside the bodies. Mealie-pup, Zack's horse, shivered, terrified. Zack had obviously been mounted when he was shot, and one of his feet was caught in the stirrup, its leather holding it as he slipped from his saddle. Henny had gone over the back of Dingo, who was splattered with his blood. Yet both horses were standing true; their training had won over fear, and they had not run off.

The strangest part was that Buffel's horse, Benga, was also there, but Buffel wasn't.

'Shit,' Enoch said, immediately turning around to check where Mike and Nick were. There was nothing he could do for his fellow Scouts. They were definitely dead, but perhaps he could help the rest of his *stick*.

He longed to get off his horse and attend to the horses who were standing in the open. Seeing a horse in stress was never easy to walk away from. 'Easy! Easy! I will be back in a moment. I must find Mike and the others, then I can attend to you —'

He was interrupted by a shot to his right. He ducked down low on Kimberlite and looked to where it had come from.

Mike stood in front of Buffel, his revolver pointed at him. Buffel seemed to step backwards, and then looked left towards the large tree they stood in front of. Buffel sank to his knees, and finally, Mike lowered his weapon. Enoch looked towards the tree.

Six bodies had been strung up by their feet as if it was a meat locker. Their weapons bound to their sides.

The sound of anguish that roared from Buffel was one Enoch knew he would never forget. He looked at Mike, who was still armed, and he could see the tension radiating from him as he rode up to them, putting Kimberlite directly between the two men. He didn't know what was happening, but he knew that he had to protect Mike from Buffel, no matter what.

He had made a promise to Mike all those years ago. Today was not going to be the day he broke such a sacred vow, even if there were FRELIMO guards keeping watch over them.

Enoch stayed awake.

Watching.

Waiting.

Ready to protect.

CHAPTER 18

Australia/New Zealand Top 6 Trophies

1. Dingo
2. Wapiti—bull elk
3. Camel
4. Captain Cook boar
5. Water buffalo
6. Man

CHAPTER 19

Chloe and Xo took turns keeping watch throughout the night, not convinced that the soldiers wouldn't turn on them. At first light, they heard a vehicle leave and were getting ready to exit the boma when Nick came into view. 'Chloe? Xo? You guys okay?'

'Tired from the broken sleep, but we're fine. At least the horses are well rested,' Chloe said.

Filipe was close behind him. 'I couldn't stop them coming to keep watch over the cargo. When they saw that you guys had the horses out and in the boma, they just split up and patrolled both parts of the camp. They were not here to cause trouble, just to keep us safe and make sure it got through their territory. The captain in charge here is ruthless, but he is not here—luckily our message got through to his men. They know that we are carrying goods worth a lot to someone, and even in times of war they know that there are a few cargos not worth getting involved with. A lot of drug shipments and big ivory caches get brought through here, and if there are any problems some really bad people will come to "fix" things. They were worried that if they didn't make sure we were safe, and anything happened to the cargo, they would be in trouble. The dead kind of trouble from the guy in charge, because it would reflect badly on him.'

'Those men patrolled all night!' Chloe said.

'Around the truck, too,' Nick said as he opened the boma and they led the horses out. Ethel walked out with Mike, getting him to walk a little and stretch before being cooped up in the vehicle again.

Nick took two lead reins and walked the horses back up the river to where the bank wasn't so steep. They climbed the small incline and walked down the road before standing together outside the truck while the horses were fed cubes and given water.

Chloe watched the fat belly of Pampero as she ate her food.

'When is she due?' Nick asked her.

'In about a month,' Chloe said.

'I hope this journey isn't too taxing on her and she doesn't deliver early. It's a lot to ask of a mare so heavy in foal,' Nick said.

Chloe frowned. 'It's not like we wanted to leave in a hurry. It's not like we knew that some idiot would come and attack us in our own home and get the SAP on our trail, and make our trip so much harder.'

Nick reached out and touched her arm softly. 'I know,' Nick said. 'I just meant that she's lucky she has you.'

Chloe looked at him and smiled in apology. She hadn't meant to be snappy, to go off like a banshee. But she wasn't sure what to say back to him, because now that his hand touched her, she seemed to have lost all words.

Pampero got up and shook all over, as if now that she'd rolled in the dirt, she wanted it all off her.

Enoch laughed, and Chloe looked towards him.

'Enoch's also lucky to have you. You all seem devoted to each other. He's always been such good friends with your dad; it's nice that you're all still together,' Nick said. 'Despite everything that's happened, it's good to see a friendship like theirs last through thick and thin.' He removed his hand.

Chloe ran her hand over the spot where his had been. She missed the warmth.

'I guess so, although we did spend a few months apart. After Dad was hurt, I drove him to South Africa. Enoch and Xo brought the horses through the bush so we could all be together again.'

'I'm almost afraid to ask, but what was his final diagnosis?' Nick asked.

'Brain damage and spinal injury. He'll never recover. There are certain things that set him off—like a change of routine, or a simple change of the weather—but there was little pattern to the other times. The first sign that he's having an episode is usually when he starts to rock back and forth uncontrollably. To be honest, I'm surprised that he's handling this trip so well.'

'You think it's because he doesn't know what's happening?'

Chloe shook her head. 'He's in there still, and he knows,' Chloe said. 'There's a calmness in him since we left that's been missing for a long time. The doctors at first predicted he could turn violent after his injuries, but instead Dad took the path of refusing to eat or drink, giving trouble when Enoch would try to bathe him. Instead of fighting an angry man, we fought to make the man inside want to live.'

'It must've been hard for you,' Nick said, putting his hand on her arm again, only this time he began patting it, almost subconsciously giving her comfort.

'If it wasn't for Enoch, Xo and Ethel, I wouldn't have finished school, let alone gone to varsity,' Chloe admitted. She liked the feel of his hand resting on her arm.

'Surely you tried a professional nurse? Didn't they help?' Nick asked.

'We had one with us when I left Zim. She didn't last long. We tried home care with various nursing sisters, but I think the isolation of where we lived tended to get to them much more than it got to us, even though they had been warned about it. Female nurses were always good for him; they saw things that Enoch, Xo and I didn't. Like he gets colder faster than we do. But in the end, they all left.

'Then one day Ethel came knocking on our door, asking for work. We were desperate, so although she was much older than any of the previous nurses and she never finished her training, we gave her a chance. And she was better than any registered nurse we'd hired. She understood the need to be in the same house as us so that she was on call all the time—not clock off and go to separate quarters at night. It was a big ask of her, but she fitted into our family just fine.'

His hand moved slightly, as if he was going to remove it. Then he hesitated, and instead of just resting his fingers, he now stroked her skin softly. It was a different sensation, and she realised that she didn't want him to move away; she wanted more of his touch.

'I've watched her with your dad. She's kind to him, never rough,' Nick said.

'Yes, but she isn't strong enough to bathe him, and he wouldn't like that anyway, so Enoch and Xo still attend to that every night when they come home after being out in the cattle truck, earning money. They usually take over after dinner and complete all the male stuff that needs doing.'

'You sound like you've had a really hard time looking after him. You've done a great job of it,' Nick said.

'It's not like we had a choice. You do what you have to when it's someone you love,' Chloe said.

'I really used to admire your dad,' Nick said, looking over to where Ethel was making Mike walk with his stick, encouraging him to keep going. 'I'm sorry that he got hurt so badly, and that you lost your dad and your mum so close to each other.'

'Thanks,' Chloe said. 'But I still have him—well, a part of him anyway.'

'Let's get breakfast, and then load these guys into the trailer so we can get moving,' Xo said as he came up behind them, interrupting their talk.

Nick moved his hand off Chloe's arm, and she immediately wished he would keep it there.

'If I remember right,' Khululani said, 'we only have to travel for another five hours before we arrive at Mapai for the crossing of the Limpopo.'

Filipe whistled from his watch post on top of the truck. A single soldier was walking back towards them.

'Get in the truck, Chloe,' Enoch said. 'Ethel, get inside with Mike. Nick, you too. They must not know we have white people out here with us.'

Filipe jumped off the top and walked towards the soldier.

Chloe watched the conversation through the cracks in the trailer, until finally, Filipe came back and took a carton of smokes from the truck, then returned and gave it to the soldier, who walked away. Filipe stood watching him go before turning back to the truck.

'He wanted to guide us the rest of the way to Mapai. According to him, they have set a lot of new landmines in the road, so we will be making our own track from now on, not using the old hunting roads that were here.'

'And he's not guiding us because ...?' Nick said.

'Because while I believe him about the landmines, I'm the guide, and it would look like I didn't know what FRELIMO were doing if we took another. They would suspect I'm RENAMO and kill me, and attack you guys,' Filipe said.

'Good enough reason,' Nick said.

'He drew a map in the sand, showing where the new mines are, and I showed him where I knew was mined. We both gave a little information. Hopefully, he was not lying, but it's a chance we have to take. It's going to be slower than it has been,' Filipe warned.

Khululani said, 'There is already a single-path elephant track that we will follow. But it is rough. I walked on part of it yesterday. But the truck needs two tracks, and there is lots of bush to pass through.'

'Damn,' Enoch said. 'We were doing so well.'

'At least we'll still get there,' Filipe said. 'And we know which of the roads have the new mines.'

'Knowing where they are is a big bonus,' Xo said.

'Let us get moving then and stop standing in the hot sun,' Enoch said. 'Time to load the horses.'

Xo and Enoch loaded the horses quickly, with Khululani keeping watch at the front, and Nick at the back. Xo grumbled that they were once again on trekking rations, and unable to have a hot breakfast.

Khululani, still in his Parks Board uniform, drove the truck—he sat next to Filipe and Enoch as they bounced their way through the bushveld, around downed trees and huge ant mounds following a winding elephant path.

When they heard a distant explosion, loud and deep sounding, Filipe said, 'Something just stepped on a mine. That FRELIMO guy warned that they do it all the time on this stretch of road. He said if it happens, to tell the villagers at Mapai to go check for fresh meat when we get there.'

'But you said it was mined,' Khululani said.

'It is, but apparently they have marked out a path to walk on. It is only a stranger to the area who will get blown up there or someone who tries to drive on the road,' Filipe said.

Chloe shuddered.

CHAPTER 20

Chloe jumped out of the truck, glad to be outside, and gazed around. Khululani had stopped the truck on a small rise. Looking down through the trees, she could see the village on the banks of the Limpopo River.

Enoch stood next to her. 'Too much water to cross without help, yet low enough that we can still get across.'

'It's going to be interesting getting the truck through. You sure you don't want to leave it on this side and we just swim the horses across?' Nick asked, standing close behind her.

Chloe shook her head. 'Not an option. It goes all the way home.'

'Okay,' Nick said. 'But that river looks like trouble to me.'

'We are just lucky it is not flooding,' Enoch said. 'Or we would not have got this far.' He turned around. 'Ethel, you can come out now; I will get Mike.'

Xo put the deck chair in the shade of the truck, and Enoch helped his friend into it. He then opened the back of the truck, and they all got busy unloading the horses.

'I'll head into the village,' Filipe said. 'You coming?'

Khululani nodded.

'Okay,' Chloe said. 'And check if they have a tin tub I can borrow. I would give anything for a hot bath!'

Xo laughed at her. 'With bubbles too, Your Highness?'

'You have no idea how much I want to say yes to that, but right now I would just settle for a bath.'

'And what about smelling like a male? Filipe still wants you to blend in as much as you can,' Nick reminded her.

'I'll stink quick enough in this heat,' she said, 'especially if I put these clothes back on. So, I don't see any reason to not at least be clean.'

Nick shook his head, but he was smiling.

Filipe and Khululani returned within half an hour. 'That was fast; did they have a bathtub?' Chloe asked.

'I did not get to ask them because we have a small problem. The chief of this village will not let the oxen into the water to pull the truck through because there is a big crocodile that has moved into the area. Unless we can kill the croc, we cannot get their help to cross,' Filipe said.

Enoch looked at Nick. 'We can try to shoot it.'

'That is what I told them we would do,' Filipe said with a grin.

Enoch, Nick and Khululani got their rifles and walked back towards the village with Filipe.

The children of the village were the first ones to want to know more about the horses. At first, they kept their distance, looking on, and peeking at them from behind the trees, but gradually they lost their inhibitions, and they came closer when they weren't chased away until a group of six stood watching them.

Chloe's heart broke. One girl was about three years old. She walked with two homemade crutches constructed from roughly cut wood. Her right leg was gone from the knee down. Bandages still wrapped around the wound, evidence that this was not an old injury. And that the landmines they had managed to avoid so far were a real threat to everyone in the area. Another boy who looked to be about eight was also on crutches, the stump shiny with scars as he too had part of his leg blown off.

Chloe silently thanked Filipe for guiding them safely through the area. She was grateful that they'd forged their own road in the last section of the journey, even though it had been slow going.

Xo beckoned the children to join them. '*Woza*, you can come and say hello, but you must approach from the front. Do not go behind the horses.'

The children cautiously approached Xo and the horses, wary of the zebras with no stripes.

A child who introduced herself as Malinda stood close to Chloe. She looked to be about fourteen, tall and at that stage where a girl became awkward while she tried to understand what was happening with her body. Chloe remembered that stage well. Only she hadn't carried a toddler of about two in a traditional, brightly coloured *capulana* hanging from her shoulder. 'Your child?'

Malinda shook her head and smiled widely. 'My sister, Perfect. I look after her.'

Chloe smiled. 'Copy me, put your hand out. The horse will smell your hand, and know you want to be friends.'

Malinda put her hand out, and little Perfect did the same.

Pampero reached forward with her nose and smelled the hand of Malinda. The girl pulled her hand back in fear, but Perfect left hers there, and when her palm touched Pampero's velvet nose, she wiggled her fingers and laughed.

The other children pressed inward. Chloe looked at Xo and smiled as he had the little girl with the blown-off leg on his hip and was introducing her to Sirocco.

'You're a natural with kids,' Chloe said.

'I should be. I had you around all the time, but I'm never having my own. There are already too many mouths to feed in this world,' Xo said.

Chloe smiled sadly and said, 'I always thought that maybe one day I would be called Aunty Chloe.'

'Sorry to kill your dreams, but it's not going to happen. If you want to get all maternal on us, get pregnant and have your own.'

Chloe laughed again.

The little one on Xo's hip leaned forward, and with both her hands on either side of Sirocco's nose, kissed him loudly.

Sirocco didn't pull away. He seemed to sense the precious moment and kept his head very still while the damaged girl laid her forehead on the top of his nose. He blew air out of his nose, and she pulled her head and hands back.

'*Nenga!*' she said.

'No, he isn't being disgusting, he's making friends, *zwana*,' Chloe said, and wished she had a camera to capture the tenderness and keep it close always.

Xo hugged the girl and bent down to place her on the ground again, before helping her with her crutches.

Malinda, seeing the younger child hadn't been hurt, put her hand out, and this time she left it there when Pampero breathed into it, and she giggled.

Chloe felt someone watching her. She looked up and caught the eyes of a man standing behind the children. They ran off, but he continued to watch her while she brushed the horses, rubbing them down with paraffin to keep the flies and bugs off.

Every time she looked up, he was staring at her.

'We have a man who is over-curious,' she eventually said to Xo.

'I think he's the village witchdoctor. He has realised that you are a female, and you are white, despite all the dirt on your skin.'

Xo turned to face the man who approached him. '*Salibonani*.'

The man greeted him back. '*Linjani. Unjani wena?*'

Xo said, '*Sikhona*. I am Xo.'

'*Tinyanga* Cassamo,' he introduced himself.

'*Tinyanga*, not *curandeiros*?' Xo asked, wanting to make sure that the man was a traditional medicine man and not a spirit-guided witchdoctor. He knew that he could not hurry along a traditional greeting, even if you wanted to get rid of the person, as it would be considered rude, even when you knew it was an old man just being nosy.

Cassamo smiled. 'I'm only *curandeiros* when there is a need; mostly I am the healer. The one who stops the bleeding in the children after the mines, and the one who makes the crutches and carts so that they can walk and get around.'

Xo nodded.

'What is wrong with your friend?'

'Mike?' Xo pointed. 'He can't talk anymore because he hurt his brain and his back, but Ethel helps him to keep moving around.'

'This is sad for a man to hurt his brain. Is there no medicine that can help him?'

'Nothing, he is too damaged,' Xo said.

Cassamo shook his head. 'Sometimes, even a *tinyanga* knows that a body is beyond his healing powers. Perhaps it is like that with the doctors where you came from?'

Xo nodded.

'But he is an *ibhiza-idlozi*, he can still talk with his *ibhiza*.'

Xo turned to see that Mike was still sitting in his chair; Diablo had wandered over and was nuzzling him, getting pats. The healer believed that Mike was a horse-spirit, someone who could communicate with horses.

'Yes, that's right,' Xo said.

The old man nodded. Then he pointed to Chloe. 'I think we both know that she is the first white woman these children have ever seen.'

Xo smiled. 'Chloe can't help that she's white.'

'True.'

'I have heard that the other men who travel with you have gone hunting for the crocodile.'

'That is right. Have you seen it?' Xo asked.

'Many times.'

'We were told that the crocodile attacks men in the water when they try to cross the river,' Xo said.

'Some days he swims around and does not take anyone; other times he will attack quickly.'

'You sure it's a he?' asked Xo.

'It is too mean to be female,' Cassamo said.

Chloe wanted to laugh, but was still unsure why the doctor had singled her out.

'You have nothing to fear in this village,' Cassamo said. 'When you leave, and I will be *curandeiros*, I will tell the people that you were never here, that they might have thought that they saw a white lady, but they did not. They will believe me, and they will tell the people chasing you that you were never here.'

'Why do you think we are being chased?' Xo asked.

'No one comes this far into Mozambique from South Africa, heading north through a war zone, unless they are running from something.'

'You see things that others do not,' Xo said.

'Perhaps. I came to ask if the ladies have any dresses, they do not want that they could give to the women in our village. Their clothing is old. I am thinking something nice because there is one woman who needs it; she is getting married, and a nice dress will help her, make her feel better about the wedding.'

'Doesn't she want to get married?' Xo asked.

'She wants a wedding, the *lobola* has been paid, it is just the man she wanted died,' Cassamo said. 'Her parents will not give back the *lobola*, so there has to be a wedding, so she will marry the brother.'

Chloe at last broke her silence. 'That's not fair to her; it's not her fault that the parents probably spent her *lobola* and can't pay it back. Now she's being punished not only by his death, but by marrying his brother.'

Ethel clicked her tongue in annoyance. 'How old is she?'

'Old enough to marry,' Cassamo said.

Chloe stilled. 'How old is the brother?'

'He is not as old as the chief,' Cassamo said.

'*Eish*,' Ethel said.

Chloe had to bite her tongue hard to stop herself from telling Cassamo that it was in his power to change what was about to happen to the poor girl —she shouldn't have to marry a leery old man—but the thought of her marrying Nick popped into her head, and she stumbled into Pampero, causing the horse to step backwards. 'I'll find her something, but know that I'm doing this for her, not for you, and not for the old man she's being forced to marry.'

Her mind was reeling at where it had suddenly gone as she went to rummage in her case.

Nick was an amazing man; he was strong, easy on the eye, perhaps a little over-protective. She certainly didn't think of him as a father figure, but then she wasn't sure what it was she thought of him as. He was Nick, and until her move to South Africa he had always been there. A little older than she and Xo were but hanging around with her dad and Enoch. Lately, she would turn her head and find him looking at her, and a feeling deep inside her stomach would flutter. Other times he would catch her watching him and give her this little smile that she'd never seen him gift any of the others. It made her heart sing, made her feel as if she was the only one he cared for.

She did a quick mental calculation—their age difference was probably under ten years, so it wasn't too bad. It wasn't like she was still in school, and he was cradle-snatching.

'Here, take this,' Chloe said as she handed over the only decent dress she possessed.

Cassamo shook it, unfolding the dress, while keeping it out of the dirt, to look at the full-length satin gown.

'Your matric dance dress?' Xo said. 'Are you sure?'

'Yes. A bride should look like a princess at her wedding,' Chloe said. 'Especially if she's having to enter into something she doesn't want.'

Ethel patted her on the arm. 'You have a good heart.'

Cassamo smiled. 'Ngiyabonga. Sala kuhle.'

'*Hamba kahle*,' Xo said, wishing him well as he left.

'*Hamba kahle*,' Chloe said, then in a quieter tone, 'He's thankful, *se voet*. I bet you he's the one marrying the young girl.'

'Maybe,' Xo said, 'but it's good to keep the local *curandeiros* on our side, just in case.'

CHAPTER 21

The beast lay in the water, half submerged, absorbing enough sunlight to warm his big body, but still keeping it cool. From the massive head, Enoch could see that the croc was probably between three and a half to four metres, a true monster. The prehistoric creature had always been at the top of the food chain out here in the bush. His size had kept him safe.

Even a farmer knew that an AK-47 was a really inaccurate weapon, which wouldn't necessarily penetrate a crocodile this size. Besides, many of the bullets that had made their way into the revolution in Mozambique were substandard, making the killing of a big croc difficult. But that wasn't what was stopping the villagers killing this beast. That was left to the superstitions around the crocodile.

There was also the small problem that sometimes a crocodile just didn't die from bullet wounds. Nick had heard of more than a few hunters that'd been taken by crocodiles that were thought to be dead—a crocodile could endure many shots from an AK-47, making it an extremely angry predator.

Even with the professional hunting weapons that Nick and Enoch carried, the croc might still be a challenge. If they were lucky, they'd get a brain shot and he would die, or they could go for a shot that would shatter the spinal column. But the crocodile's brain was tiny, just beneath the eye, slightly forward, and often missed, even by professional croc hunters. Alternatively, his heart was about halfway down his body, but you had to get in just where the tough scales turned to yellow and were a tiny bit weaker. And of course, you had to get him out of the water long enough to be able to make the shot. Crocodiles can see well, and will always slide back into the water, protecting their hearts first when they see something 'dangerous' coming towards them. To get this monster at its most vulnerable, he had to be at least three-quarters out of the water.

'I think we are close enough. From here we can shoot the nuisance,' Enoch said. Looking at the big croc as he lay on the bank, his mouth slightly open to regulate his temperature, he shuddered involuntarily.

Nick smiled. 'What is it with you guys and crocs? Remember that one that we had in that river with Mike, and how you wouldn't go in, even when he assured you that the croc was dead?'

'That was not because of the croc, it's because I cannot swim, you idiot. Do you not know us Matabele men? We never needed to swim!'

Nick chuckled quietly.

Khululani clapped his hands together silently and smiled too.

The crocodile became aware of their presence, or something else moving towards him, as he slightly closed his mouth and slipped backwards into the water. Too fast for them to react. He disappeared into the brown depths and they could no longer see him.

None of them approached the edge, knowing the danger of the croc's striking distance.

'Darn it. Now we'll need to bait him,' Nick said.

Khululani nodded. 'I have seen some pheasant in the bush; I can shoot one.'

'No, you will step on a mine. You do not know this area,' Filipe said.

One of the village men with them said, 'I will give you one *inkukhu* so you can kill this beast as you said you would. It is a good price to pay to have him dead, as he captured my son.'

'I am sorry that your son was lost. Thank you for your offer,' Enoch said.

'Wait here, I will bring it,' the man said as he disappeared into the bushes. When he returned, true to his word he brought a live chicken under his arm, and a long piece of nylon rope was tied to its feet.

The man said, 'When my son was captured, he was almost at the bank after falling in the water. There were two boys. The other boy, he saw the crocodile and he froze stiff; he did not move. My son, he wanted to reach the bank. Get to us and safety. He kicked as hard as he could with his legs and got closer to where I waited trying to reach him.' The man dashed tears from his eyes but continued. 'This crocodile, he didn't capture the still boy who was almost drowning. He took my son instead. You will need the live *inkukhu*.'

Khululani stepped forward, taking the *kaal*-necked chicken. '*Siyabonga*, and I am sorry he took your son. We will shoot this crocodile, and your son's spirit can finally rest.'

Khululani took his hunting knife, and spreading the wing out, he cut the flight feathers, and quickly stepped forward and threw the chicken into the water where the croc had been. 'Filipe, come behind me. Two pulling might be better than one; this croc is massive.'

The chicken flapped its wings trying to get out of the water. It splashed and squawked as it attempted to swim.

'Get ready,' Khululani said, tugging the rope in a little, almost as if he was fly fishing. The chicken could now reach the sand bottom with its feet, and clucking loudly, its wings still flapping, it made to run out of the water, but kept falling over as its feet were bound. It was pulled further up the bank, just out of the water.

'He is coming,' Khululani said.

The flatdog launched itself out of the water with speed, his jaws clamping down hard on the live bait. More than half his body now clearly out of the water as he tossed his head back, crushing the chicken between his powerful jaws.

Enoch and Nick simultaneously let off shots into the croc's head. He didn't have a chance against their high-powered guns and the accuracy of the seasoned hunters.

'Got him,' Enoch said, still holding the rope taut.

'Fine—you called it, you check him,' Nick said.

'Do I look like a fool?'

The man from the village ran towards the croc and, taking a handful of river sand, threw it all over his snout.

The croc didn't move.

The man lifted a rock and threw it. It landed with a dull *thunk* on the crocodile's head and stayed there.

'Guess he's really dead,' Nick said.

The man started dancing near the croc, while others ran down into the river to help put ropes around him to drag him out of the water and onto the bank.

'Will you feast with us tonight?' the chief of the village asked. 'It has been many years since we celebrated the waters being safe.'

'Are you sure there is only one?' Enoch asked.

'We have seen no babies, so we have no reason to think there is more than one.'

'Don't let your guard down. Just because this one's gone, doesn't mean another won't come and take its place. They're territorial, so he might just have been keeping the others away,' Nick warned.

'Perhaps the next one will be smaller, and we can kill it before it becomes a monster. Either way, if we pull your truck through the river this afternoon, tonight you can come back on the pontoon and feast with us. We have that fresh meat from a kudu landmine kill. We will not eat this crocodile as he has eaten lots of our villagers, and it is not our custom to eat humans, especially not our family. But the young men, they will drink the crocodile's bile in *utshwala* that Curandeiros Cassamo brews so that if another crocodile comes, they will have the strength to kill it. That the restless spirits of all people eaten would allow.'

'It'll be our honour, but first, we need to get the truck through the river,' Nick said. 'Once the men are done getting the croc up to the village for the women to skin, we do need to use your oxen to help the truck through the deeper water.'

The chief nodded. 'The horses, they will swim, but the truck, it will take a team of oxen to get it through the water. It is very heavy, that one.'

'That it is,' Enoch said. 'But I know that your oxen are strong, and they will get it through.' Then he turned and said quietly to Nick, 'Whatever you do, do not drink the homemade beer tonight; just trust me on this one. That stuff will make you sick, not give you strength, even when prepared properly.'

The six oxen were harnessed together, and the tow-leader walked at the front, encouraging the animals with a whip to pull. The water ran just above their bellies, and you could see the white of their eyes, terrified of the depth and what they knew once lurked there.

'*Donsa!*' called the tow-leader as his oxen strained with the weight of the truck. The men at the back pushed with all their might, and Enoch gently stepped on the accelerator. He had heard that in the first golden days of travel with cars in Africa, they often had removed the fan belt so that they didn't throw water on the plugs, but he didn't think it was necessary in modern vehicles. The truck got out of the deeper water with a lurch, and slowly made its way through the sluggish water that sucked at the metal, trying to claim it for itself.

'*Donsa!*' he heard the tow-leader call again as the oxen bellowed, the whip cracked once more, and the truck suddenly had enough traction to move under its own power. He slowly inched forward, taking the stress off the animals, as they began walking proudly in front of the truck, knowing that their job was done, their gait easier now that they no longer strained with the weight on their muscles. They reached the bank on the other side and went up the small incline, still with the oxen pulling just in case the truck got into trouble. But Enoch knew his truck would get through with no more problems.

Enoch stopped once he was up the bank and looked over the flat river. He switched off and watched as the head musterer uncoupled the oxen from the truck but kept them harnessed together as he drove them back into the water, back towards their side of the river, where Xo and Chloe still waited to bring the horses across.

He looked at his youngsters. They were not children anymore. He was so proud of the two of them. Despite all the darkness that he and Mike had inflicted on them, they were two determined young adults who fearlessly faced any challenge that was thrown their way. Always united, they worked together as if they were real siblings, not people separated by birth and colour.

They would need every ounce of that cooperation to cross the river. It was going to test their bond. And while he wanted to protect them and do it for them, he realised that he needed to let them do this one, be in charge of it and come out the other side stronger for it, no matter the consequences. Xo could swim, Enoch and Chloe had made sure he had lessons, and he'd often swum with Chloe in the river.

It made sense that Xo and Nick would be with Chloe when the horses crossed, and not him. He was just thankful that Khululani and Filipe had both chosen to cross with Mike and Ethel on the pontoon.

'The crossing won't be as easy as those oxen just made it look. River crossings never are,' Nick said as they approached the river.

'This looks the same as last time we crossed. The water is deceptive. It looks sluggish and slow, but the current beneath the surface is strong, carrying the unwary along with it,' Xo said.

'Come on, Xo, we've done enough preparation for events like this. All those steeple chases, and how many times did we take the horses swimming in the dam? We'll be fine. The horses are strong; those oxen didn't look like they struggled much—as long as we try to stick to where they crossed, we should be fine,' Chloe said.

'I've crossed many rivers with my brothers from the Scouts, but this is the mighty Limpopo. I don't think it's a river to be taken lightly,' Nick said.

'I'm not. That's why you're riding Marin. He doesn't like water much. Xo and I'll have Kimberlite and Diablo on lead reins. You'll need both hands to get Marin into the water.'

As if to prove her point the stallion bucked, trying again to unseat Nick.

'Cut that out,' Nick said firmly. 'Come on, it's only water, boy. You can do this,' Nick said, though he was glad they were all roped to the horses, just in case.

He watched as Xo entered the water first with Sirocco and Kimberlite followed with no problems.

Trying to keep close, Chloe took Pampero in and shortened her lead on Diablo, with no problems either. He saw her smile as she turned back to check on him.

Marin was prancing and stepping as if he was a horse on new shoes that were not comfortable. Unsure of the water, the highly strung Arab was not keen to enter. Then he bunched himself together and jumped into it, and ran into the chest-deep part, splashing water everywhere as he almost caught up to the other horses.

Chloe was laughing. Marin's antics had wet them before they'd even started. 'It's not a hot bath with bubbles, but it's water either way,' Chloe said.

Nick laughed with her. 'It's going to be interesting seeing him come out the other side if this is what he does on entry.'

'Bucking, farting and a possible spill from your saddle coming up,' Chloe said. She laughed. He could listen to her tinkle of a laugh all day. They could disguise her as much as they wanted, but when Chloe laughed it was totally woman, and any male would know it.

The water rose on the horses' bodies as they made their way across, and Chloe called to Xo, 'You're going off course; keep upstream. This isn't where the oxen crossed; it's deeper already.'

Xo adjusted.

Nick could see that Xo was trying hard to get the horses back on course, but the river was strong. A team of oxen yoked together was stronger than a single horse fighting the current—but they kept going, and the water got deeper.

Sirocco began swimming, and Xo turned around. Chloe was looking backwards, checking on how Marin was going.

Xo shouted, 'Chloe, careful that shelf drops off sudden—'

Pampero's back dipped suddenly, causing the unbalanced Chloe to slide off and go under. For the moment, she was still tied by a rope to Pampero's bridle. The horse was now swimming, totally out of her depth and unable to touch the bottom and dragging the full weight of Chloe.

'Shit,' Nick cursed as he watched from behind, hoping that the bridle didn't give or slip off the horse's head. He watched in slow motion as Chloe broke the surface of the muddy water, long enough to take a single breath before she was pulled under again, straining against the ropes that held her to Pampero.

Nick could feel when the rush of adrenaline kicked in. The hyper awareness of his situation. The steady beat of his own heart. The battle-trained calmness that overtook him. He urged Marin forward. They were already upstream from Pampero, as was Diablo, who now swam alone. Nick cut in between Pampero and Diablo and hoped that the old horse would keep on in the direction he was heading. He took the lead rein from Diablo as he passed.

Diablo tossed his head, not liking being fiddled with as he swam. Marin's strength was now helping as Nick urged him forward until he was almost neck to neck with Pampero, whose eyes were white with fright, and she began shaking her head, trying to shake the weight dragging her head into the water.

'Steady, girl. Steady,' Nick said as he attempted to calm Pampero. He grabbed her by the bridle, ensuring that even if it slipped now, he would have a hold of Chloe. He clipped the lead rein onto the bridle and let her go again. He wound the other end around his arm. 'You're going to be fine. Just find the bottom, put your feet down, girl, find the sand as soon as you can.'

Pampero continued to drag Chloe, who was still under the water. If he couldn't get her out in the next few seconds, she was in real danger of drowning.

Nick worked faster than he ever had. Pampero's neck was straining to hold the dead weight of Chloe, which made every movement of his desperate. He grabbed at Chloe's rope and began pulling it in. Using his whole body, he hauled the rope into his chest, then wrapped it around his arm, and repeated the motion, slowly winding Chloe in.

Chloe's head bobbed up again. She was trying to swim against the current but getting nowhere. Then a survival instinct so strong must have kicked in—she grabbed onto the rope with both hands, steadying her body as the water sucked at her, and began pulling herself back towards her horse.

'Come on, Chloe, pull!' Xo shouted.

'You can do this,' Nick shouted almost at the same time.

She pulled herself along, then pushed her legs downwards and found the riverbed. Finally, she was able to stand and continue walking—getting closer to Pampero, while Nick continued to wind her in on his arm.

Nick dragged her by the rope over Pampero's back. She swung her legs over her horse and gripped her mane so she could sit up, coughing and then vomiting out the muddy river water.

He saw that Xo had got Kimberlite to the shallows.

Chloe had stopped vomiting, while Nick untangled himself from Pampero. He led them out of the water, and Marin, as if sensing that there had been a major event in the river, behaved himself and didn't try to unseat Nick.

'Oh God, Chloe, I thought I lost you there. I thought we had lost you for sure,' Nick said as he hauled her off Pampero's back and into his arms.

'I'm okay, I'm okay. I thought I was lost there, too. I thought I was going to drown,' Chloe said as her arms snaked around Nick's waist and he held her tightly.

She was safe.

Enoch, who had been on the other side watching the whole scene unfold, ran down to the edge of the water and waded into the shallows. He grabbed Kimberlite's lead rein from Xo.

'Hurry, help Diablo; he is still trying to make it across,' Enoch said.

'On it,' Xo said, and turned Sirocco sharply, plunging back into the river.

As he watched Chloe come out of the water, he thought of how proud Mike would've been if he'd been able to comprehend what was going on. He knew that Sarah would've approved of the woman Chloe had become. He knew that he and Xo had spoiled her and tried to shield her from much, but he also knew that at her core she was stronger than they gave her credit for.

He watched as Nick came out, still guiding her with the lead rein, and immediately went to check on her. Then haul her into his arms. Nick didn't know it yet, but he was hooked, and while Enoch accepted that Nick was still fighting a demon within himself for what he and Mike had done, and Nick's choice that fateful day, he hoped that Nick would be man enough to overcome his reservation that Chloe was part of Mike, and see that she was now a woman in her own right.

Enoch still believed that what they had done that night had been the right thing to do as revenge for what had happened to Sarah. If one day Nick felt half as much for Chloe as Mike had for Sarah, he would understand the actions and perhaps find peace within himself.

Enoch walked towards them to check on Chloe. Kimberlite pushed his back with his nose, looking for some sort of acknowledgement for getting across the river and not causing anyone any dramas. Enoch moved to the side and waited for a single step till the horse's head was next to him, then scratched Kimberlite's ears as they walked. 'Thank you, boy. Hopefully, this should be the last time I ask you to cross this river.'

He thanked all the gods that everyone had made it across the Limpopo.

In about two days, at the rate they were going, they would be in Zimbabwe again. He couldn't relax yet—he could only hope that the rest of the journey went more smoothly than this part.

CHAPTER 22

On their second night in Mozambique, they camped on the other side of the river in RENAMO territory. Filipe and Khululani remained stationed at the camp with Mike, Ethel and the horses in case any soldiers came, while Chloe, Nick, Xo and Enoch kept their word and feasted with the villagers on the landmine kudu. But all had refused the homemade beer. It was late when they sat on the pontoon pulling on the steel cable to get across the river and saw the campfire in the distance.

'Do you see that fire on that *kopje*?' asked the chief's son, Julio.

'I see it. Do you know who it belongs to?' Enoch asked.

'That is the fire of the Caçador Escuro, the Dark Hunter. We avoid such fires when we see them.' Julio shook his head and made a cross on his chest as if to ward off evil.

Enoch frowned. 'Why?'

'These men are evil. They hunt people. Men, women, they don't care, but they're not soldiers. When we see the fires on the old elephant trail, we stay out of the bush. You shouldn't travel tomorrow. They will be out there looking for someone to hunt. You're better off here, near the village. You have kept us safe from the crocodile; now we must protect you from the Caçador Escuro. I will tell my father that I saw their fire tonight; tomorrow no one will leave the village, not until we see no fire again or we see the vultures in the sky as proof of his successful hunt.'

'Are they not scared of the RENAMO soldiers?' Xo asked.

'That hunter is not afraid of anything. He is *penga* in the head.'

'How do you know that he hunts people?' Enoch asked.

'When the vultures flew close to the village, we went to look to see what was there; if there was anything for us to scavenge. That was the first time we noticed him in our bush. We buried the bodies of two men that day. He always digs the bullets out of the heads—it is not a good sight to see, but we must face it. He does not give them a burial to help their spirits rest. He always leaves the body for the scavengers.'

'Has he killed anyone from your village?' Xo asked.

'Yes, the first time we knew he was out there. One was a woman of ours, the other a man who walked so far that he had got lost, and our woman had taken him back to the old elephant migration track to follow, to get home to Malawi. It took us a while to connect the fires and the killings. Now we keep a lookout for the big fires that tell us he is here.'

'This is interesting. We have someone who kills like this near Kruger Park, too. Our people call him Inthunzi Zingela—the Shadow Hunter. But I have not heard of him killing women, only men. Could you identify him?' Nick asked.

'No, we do not go close. He shoots anyone he can find in the bush. But he makes a fire like a signal on the hill, so that everyone can see it. As if he knows that there is nothing anyone can do about him being here. Hunting people here.'

Enoch nodded slowly. 'Only one man?'

Julio shook his head. 'The one man—he is always the same, with big feet, wears boots with a good tread. From the tracks in the sand, we can tell that the others change all the time. But mostly, if there is a killing of a man, there are always two sets of prints. When there is a woman killed, only one set of tracks, never two.'

'Do you know if he drives here, or do they walk in?' Nick asked.

'He drives on a track he has made slowly over time. RENAMO have not mined it; as he is not FRELIMO, they do not care.'

'Hasn't he shot any of them?' Filipe asked.

'Only those who do not stay with their group, deserters, people wanting to go back to their own villages.'

'Have the killings been going on for long?' Nick asked.

'It has been five years since he killed the woman from our village. He has killed twenty people since then that we have found the bodies of. I can show you each grave. Before that, the scavengers of the bush might have been cleaning up his kills. Even now, they might clean up before we can bury the dead.'

'Have you told your police?' Nick asked.

'There is a war here, and no one will care if one more man gets shot. We do not have any police in this area,' Julio said.

'Did you follow the track back to see where he came from?' Khululani asked.

'We stopped where it joins another road used by the South African hunters. RENAMO do not mine their roads. From there, he can drive to South Africa or Zimbabwe. We do not know,' Julio admitted. 'Because we cannot tell you what he looks like, only that he drives a white *bakkie*, and he never comes with a tracker. We cannot go to the police in either country to ask for help to stop him. This man knows enough about the bush that he can find people on the *Camino Dorado*, the Golden Road to Johannesburg and their gold mines, to shoot them.'

'Does he ever kill any animals?' Enoch asked.

'Not that we have seen, only people,' Julio said.

They finished the crossing in silence. When they were on the other side, Julio pulled two necklaces from his pocket. 'I made these for you to thank you for killing the beast. I have given you each one of his canine teeth for strength in your journey to come.'

Enoch shook his head. 'I cannot accept these. You need that for you, to make yourself stronger for next time.'

'No. Now I am strong. It is dead, and the villagers it had taken are avenged. If another one comes, we will be a strong enough village to kill it as soon as it arrives. We will have the courage next time because we drank its bile in the *utshwala* tonight.'

'I hope so. I'm all for living with nature,' Nick said, 'but if a croc is taking your people and your cattle, he's a menace and needs to go.'

'The Caçador Escuro is a menace and needs to go too,' Julio said.

'We do not kill people,' Enoch said, shaking his head. 'That would make us murderers, like them.'

'I understand,' Julio said. 'Travel well.'

They jumped off the pontoon onto dry land and pushed it back, then walked to where the truck was waiting for them, the horses restless and calling softly as they had heard them approaching. The boma they'd built around the whole camp area, with the horses free to move inside the truck for the night if they wanted to, would keep them safe from predators.

Enoch looked in the direction of the fire and frowned. Those he knew about, he could prepare for, but how did one defend against a two-legged predator who lurked in the night out there?

How did he keep his family safe from the Caçador Escuro?

It was late. Enoch and Filipe had gone out for another perimeter check, and Chloe was supposed to be sleeping till they woke her up for her watch. Instead, she threw another log on the fire, not caring that the supposed human hunter out there could see the light from afar. She pulled the soft sleeping bag around her and tried to stop her teeth from chattering.

Nick sat down next to her. 'You okay?'

She looked in the direction of the river. 'I don't know. I'm alive, so I should be happy with that, but the thought of almost drowning today makes me want to throw up,' she admitted.

'Come here,' he said as he put his arm around her shoulder, and she moved a little into his warmth. 'It's a natural reaction to something traumatic like that.'

'I know, but it keeps playing again in my head like a stuck record.'

His fingers moved on her shoulder. She rolled her head and winced at the pain.

'I'm not surprised that you are wound up tight like a cobra. Sit in front of me and I'll massage those shoulders.'

She adjusted her seating, and he began rubbing. At first it hurt, and she flinched. But then he softened his touch, and she began to relax.

'I wanted to say thank you for being there. I don't think I got a chance with everything that was happening.'

'If it'd been me in the drink, you'd have done the same.'

'I guess, but you did do it, and that's what matters.'

'It was my pleasure. I really didn't want to see you drown out there.'

'Gee thanks,' Chloe said, and moved her neck to the side for him to massage a little higher into her hairline.

'The horses were good. Shows their training was outstanding because they didn't panic either. You've done a good job with them.'

'Thanks,' Chloe said, 'but I can't claim all the credit. Xo and Enoch also train with them.'

'And with you. All Enoch's training helped you and Xo to stay calm in the water today. It's a credit to him. Most people would have panicked, let go of the rope and been lost in the river.'

She shuddered.

He leaned forward and wrapped his arms around her. 'I didn't mean to set you off again. It helps to talk about experiences like this.'

'I'll be okay.'

He started to rub her arms with his hands to warm her. She smiled as he returned to massaging her shoulders.

'What are you going to do with yourself when you get home to Delaware?'

'Take a long, very long, deep bubble bath,' she said. 'Filled so high with nice warm water that it slops on the floor, and I won't care.'

'Now that I can imagine,' he said, laughing quietly.

'And after that, I guess settle into rebuilding the farm. Enoch warned me that Aunty Grace isn't much of a farmer; she's only a caretaker. Enoch has had to keep giving her instructions over the phone, which she just passes on to everyone. He said he suspects that the farm isn't in as great shape as it could be.'

'Is that right? And you are going to do it differently? You didn't study farming—you did a Bachelor of Commerce.'

'Enoch will be there to look after the farm and teach me, while I look after the business side.'

'You think you're up for it, taking on a farm the size of Delaware at just twenty?'

'Twenty-one. I'll be twenty-two on the first of February,' she corrected him.

'Even if I have the year wrong, you know I don't forget your birthday.'

'I know.'

Nick smiled, and moved his hands further down her back to work on the next set of muscles that were bunched together.

'Have you thought about how the workers will react to the change?'

'I'm going to need to prove that I'm no longer little Chloe, the *baas*'s daughter. Then they'll work hard for me, like they did for Dad.'

'You have it all figured out.'

'Actually, no I haven't. I'm scared to get there and find that Aunty Grace has done such a great job that there's no need for me. No place for me. I'm scared that when I get there, that Xo will think there's nothing there for him either. He's probably given up the most of all of us. He was in the middle of high school, my dad was hurt, and his life was thrown into that of sticking with his own dad, looking out for mine. The life of a farm worker. And he never got the chance in South Africa to go and do anything. I went to varsity, and he stayed and worked with his dad. I'm worried and torn firstly, that when we get there, he'll want to move away from me. He might go to varsity in the city, but as much as I want that for him, to be independent, and successful, I don't think that I would cope living away from my brother. He's always been there. I know that is selfish, but I want him there with me, riding horses and just being there. He's only a year older than me, but he never got to do anything with his life.'

'I can't imagine how his life has been, not having a choice about being able to do what he wanted. Putting his life on hold for your family.'

'Said like that, it makes me feel even worse, thank you.'

'That wasn't my intention.'

'I know, it's just when it all happened, I never gave his future a thought. I was completely focused on my father and helping him. It didn't really sink in until I was in varsity that Xo had given his life up so I could keep studying. That he was the one doing all the farming things, the garden, the horses, and helping his dad with the cattle truck, making enough money to keep us from bankruptcy, at the sacrifice of furthering his education.'

'It was his choice. I'm sure if he'd wanted differently, you all would have made an alternative plan.'

'That's a nice thought, but I'm not so sure now.'

'Chloe, you're lots of things, but selfish isn't one of them. You all made your own choices.'

'I guess.'

They lapsed into silence for a few minutes and the fire crackled. Chloe watched the green flames as they danced along the dead wood, and then slowly turned blue and orange. Sparkes flew upwards as something in the wood ignited, and the light shone brighter, then darkened again. 'What about Enoch? I worry constantly how going home's going to affect him.'

'What do you mean?' Nick asked, his hands stopping.

'I still don't know what happened the night my dad was hurt. I have these vivid memories of you being there, but you were not with my dad and Enoch. It's all muddled in my head. There was a lot of shouting. It was such an emotional time. I just can't seem to remember it clearly.' Silently, her mind screamed at her to say something about Enoch burying something. About her dread that she had seen him burying a body, and that he had covered something up deep in the soil of Delaware.

'You really should ask Enoch about that night. You need to know what happened.'

She shook her head. 'I asked him once; he was adamant that I drop the subject and never bring it up again. I figured one day he might be ready to tell me, and then I figured what if I ask him and I don't like what I hear? I can never un-hear it.' She threw a stick she was dragging through the dirt into the fire.

'Sometimes the truth is hard, but it helps us understand the past. You need to talk to Enoch. He's the only one who can tell you everything that happened. Yes, I was there with you, but I didn't go out with them that day. It's his version of the story you need to hear, not mine. What you do with the information he tells you is up to you.'

'But it's never the right time, and it's as if he is avoiding the topic as much as I am.'

'No surprises there,' Nick said, his hands continuing their massage.

'I never know when I'll step on a landmine with him and the past. When I suggested that we come to you for help, Enoch was convinced that you wouldn't want to, that you would turn us away. Why would he think that?'

'There were many things that happened back then, Chloe. I was younger. I made my share of mistakes. So too did Enoch and Mike. At first, I also had a lot of anger, resentment, and admittedly hurt. It's taken all these years for me to realise that perhaps we were all just doing the best that we could during those trying times. For me, there's no who's right and who's wrong anymore. Life's too short to live like that. So, while I have begun to put the past behind me, and learned to live with the memories, perhaps he hasn't. Perhaps he still allows it to haunt him.'

His hands had stilled on her back while he was talking, and now she was feeling the coolness of the night instead. She shimmied back to recline against him for the warmth, and he wrapped his arms around her, resting his chin on the top of her head.

After a while, she took a deep breath and exhaled. After what he had done that day, if she was ever going to trust Nick, this was the time to tell him. To let him know about the ghost that haunted her memories. 'I think something else bad happened that night, and while my dad can't talk about it, Enoch chooses not to. I have flashes of memory: he's there when Xo and I stand next to each other and watch something being buried. You're there, and you have blood on you, like Enoch does. Something's in the back of the cattle truck; there is blood everywhere. But I can't remember enough to put it together. Then there is just Enoch, and he had a shovel and is stomping the ground, flattening it and putting the veld grasses back on top. Something is buried. Someone. I'm scared to know.'

'I'm sorry,' Nick said with a heavy sigh. 'I appreciate you confiding in me, but this is not my story to tell you, Chloe. You have to get Enoch to talk to you, and soon. If there is this Caçador Escuro out there, he could hunt any of our small party on this journey. None of us are safe. You need to know what happened before you get back to Delaware. But promise me that when Enoch does tell you, you listen with an open heart. I want you to know that even back then, before all the madness, you were special to me. And I would have helped you through this journey a million times, just because you asked me to. There is nothing that I wouldn't do for you.'

They sat in silence, lost in their own thoughts.

She pulled her hands from inside the sleeping bag and wrapped them around herself, over where his held her. 'I read every one of your Christmas and birthday cards over and over. Other than Aunty Grace's, yours were the only cards I received, and I loved them. I would get all excited when I saw your writing on the envelope.'

He moved his head slightly and gave the top of her head a whisper of a kiss. 'I'm glad. You know I thought about not sending them because I began to feel a little self-conscious when you were in varsity. You're so clever and studying a business degree. I thought that you might think the cards frivolous and stupid.'

'I never thought that.' She shook her head.

'I always bought them from the little store in Crocodile Bridge. There is an old couple there, Alice and Gil, who own it. One day, Alice asked me who it was that I bought the cards for, because I took so long deciding, reading each one in the shop.'

'Did you tell her?'

'I told her it was for someone I hadn't seen in many years, but whom I really wanted to see again.'

Chloe felt him alter the hug as if he needed her even closer to him, and the tightening of his arms matched the tightening of her stomach. 'What did she say to that?'

'Alice told me that I should get in my *bakkie* and drive to wherever you were, and hand-deliver the card.'

'But you didn't …'

He shook his head, and she could feel it as it moved over the top of her hair. 'I didn't. But I'm really glad that you called me.'

'Were you surprised?'

'I've been putting my numbers on your cards every year, just in case you needed them, but the fact that you did was a surprise. I had no idea you were in trouble, but I'm happy that you turned to me.'

'And finding that we were fleeing the law? Not exactly the behaviour of someone who's supposed to be clever enough to be at university, is it?'

'It was the best, wisest and most selfless decision you could ever make. Fleeing to save Enoch's life. It helped me realise what a fool I've been all these years.' He rested his head back on hers. 'I left Zimbabwe soon after that night, not knowing how badly hurt your dad was. I only heard later about his diagnosis. I was so mad at him and Enoch, and then at myself, that I could only see one solution, and that was to get as far away as I could. But you travel with your dad now, despite his condition, and doing what you are doing, it's helped heal something inside of me, too. I never hoped it would happen, but there's a calmness in me that has been missing for a long time.'

She could feel the heat from his arm under her hand, and the thick hair tickled her fingers as she explored the contours of his muscles. She'd been so busy watching over her father, making sure she did well in varsity, that she hadn't given herself permission to even get close to a man.

Nick had smashed through every barrier she'd ever erected to keep men out when he had helped save her from the river. They now shared something special. She knew she wanted to explore the friendship further. But she had to be careful; she could destroy their friendship if it went wrong, and she couldn't hurt Enoch in finding out if it was worth exploring.

'Are you and Enoch friends again?' she asked.

'I'd like to think so. I hope he considers me a friend, especially after all that we've been through on this journey home. Men don't talk about all of this stuff; we just drink a beer together and put the past away. When something is over and done, it's not worth speaking about. Men would rather talk cricket and who's ball tampering or not.'

She laughed then, and he hugged her closer. Just holding her.

She felt deep inside that just for that moment, there was no fear out in the dark; there was no room in her heart for anything except the feeling that Nick was the most precious person in her world.

They had planned to heed Julio's warning and spend the next day near the river, taking the opportunity to do washing and give the horses a rest. But just as dawn broke, they heard a single shot in the distance.

Everyone was up and discussing what calibre it was. They eventually settled on it probably being a .404 hollow point, but from an older hunting rifle. Obviously, the weapon of the Caçador Escuro, and not an AK-47—as would be expected if it was RENAMO out hunting for rations for their men.

Nick threw another log on the fire. 'I can't sit here and do nothing. We need a plan to go after this Caçador Escuro. He just murdered another person.'

'If we move any closer to his camp, we could get taken out too. My understanding was that he sits on his small rise over there and picks them off. The truly cowardly predator with a high-powered hunting rifle, probably complete with telescopic sights, preying on the unsuspecting migrants,' Khululani said, and spat into the sand.

'We can go around, sneak up behind him. Catch him,' Filipe said.

'We don't know if he checks all around. We don't even know what hill he's camped on. He's too far to see in the binoculars. Even with our skills, we'd be walking into a trap,' Nick warned.

'I hardly got any sleep thinking about him all night, lurking out there,' Enoch admitted.

Chloe said, 'He scares me. How do we hunt someone who has all the advantage in his environment, and is totally in his element?'

'You don't. You hide, and you stay here,' Nick said. 'We'd all be better out there hunting him if we know that you are here looking after yourself, Mike and Ethel, and your horses.'

'Sexist much,' Chloe said, and moved from sitting next to him to sit next to Xo instead.

Xo and Enoch laughed aloud.

'Oh, Nick, you really don't know the adult Chloe well enough yet,' Enoch said. 'You just flapped a challenge in her face, and she doesn't back down from a challenge. You thought that honey badger was bad ...'

'Not quite, but I'm not being left behind,' Chloe said, 'not just because I'm a woman. That's not a good enough excuse. I have just as much skill as you guys.'

'No one is deciding who does what yet,' Enoch said. 'Because we still do not know what IT is going to be.'

Nick nodded. 'This guy's killing near Kruger, too. The men who work at the Phalaborwa Gate no longer commute if they're not in a big group. He picks them off regularly if they're alone, even if they're in pairs. There have been others killed outside of the park perimeter, too, mostly near Phalaborwa township.'

'Really? And here I thought the park was a safe place, and it was just the animals we had to worry about,' Enoch said.

Nick shook his head. 'Not inside the park that we know of. Not yet. But we're all on edge about who he is and where he could be. When the teams go out into the bush, we all wonder if that will be the day that our number's up.'

Enoch frowned. 'What about the SAP? They have not found him yet?'

'No,' Nick said. 'He doesn't seem to hunt white people, or it would be in the paper, so maybe his killings are not a high priority. His name here supports this—the Dark Hunter.'

'If we have a chance to catch him, to stop him killing anyone else, should we not be doing something? Taking a chance and getting to him while he thinks he is safe?' Khululani asked.

'I am all for getting him,' Enoch said, 'but my priority is getting Mike, Chloe, Xo, Ethel, and those horses home to Delaware. Taking a side hunting trip was not part of the plan. We already spent precious time on their flatdog problem.'

'I too thought that at first,' Nick said. 'But how can we continue, knowing that he's out there? Here, in Mozambique. We could accidentally pass through another one of his hunting spots and all be dead before we realise what's happening. I foolishly thought he was only operating on the South African side of the park, that we didn't have anything to worry about in this area. I was wrong.' Nick pointed in the direction of the fire they could see smoking in the lightening sky.

'What's the plan?' Xo asked. 'Six of us, and I'm sure if we told the villagers we were going after him, they too would join in. Bet they have an arsenal of arms; they have to have one. They are residing in the middle of nowhere in a war zone. Julio seemed quite disappointed when we told him we wouldn't be hunting their hunter and helping them solve another of their problems.'

'He has a height advantage. We can't get close enough to study him without having him take a pot shot at us,' Nick said.

'We have to speak with Julio again,' Xo said. 'See if he has any pattern to his behaviour. Anything the hunter does when he's here that Julio hasn't already told us about.'

'We also need to find out how far around we need to go to get behind him, like Filipe said earlier,' Chloe said. 'You said that Julio mentioned that they tracked him before, which means they know where he parks his *bakkie*. He has the advantage up there, so we don't go after him on his *kopje*. We move around behind and ambush him when he returns after his hunting trip. When he thinks he's home free.'

'I wonder if Julio has any idea of the range of the hunter's gun?' Nick said.

'Perhaps I should go fetch him and any of the men from the village that want to join us?' Filipe said.

'Just Julio. In case there is someone in the village who is in his pocket and can warn him,' Enoch said.

Filipe nodded. 'Good thing that the crocodile is gone now from the river, because if I fall off those pontoon cables into the water, at least he can't eat me.'

Only Khululani laughed half-heartedly at Filipe's departing back.

But before Filipe could even begin his river antics, they saw the chief, Julio and the *tinyanga*, Cassamo, crossing the river on their pontoon with their oxcart and four oxen. Standing together on the bank, the group watched the progress across the water, until finally the pontoon bumped onto the sandy area on their side.

'The Caçador Escuro has left the area. There are vultures circling near where the fire was; he's killed someone and will have gone away again,' Julio said.

'That is sad news,' Enoch said as he cast his eyes downwards briefly in a sign of respect to those passed on. 'But are you sure that he is gone?'

'He never stays once he has killed his prey. He takes his bullets, and he leaves. Look,' Julio said, pointing, 'his fire is no longer smoking. He's getting ready to break up his camp.'

'This means we need to move fast. Julio, can you ride a horse?' Enoch asked.

'No, but I have ridden a donkey.'

'He can ride behind me,' Xo said. 'Sirocco can carry two; it's not that far.'

'What are you thinking?' Nick asked.

'We can move faster as a mounted unit. We want to hit him at his *bakkie*. Chloe is right. That might be the only place we will have a chance to get him. Julio, can you show us exactly where it is?' Enoch said.

'Yes,' Julio said, 'safe past the landmines, too. The way is marked.'

'If we ride hard, hopefully we can make it to his *bakkie* before he drives away, and we can capture him. If not, we can at least give chase and try to see a number plate. It is worth a try,' Enoch said.

'Saddle up,' Chloe said, turning to get the horses ready.

'We will continue as we always do,' Curandeiros Cassamo said. 'We will take our oxcart and bury the body today. No one deserves to have their spirit stuck between the worlds and not pass over to the other side because they did not have a proper burial and were eaten by scavengers. Perhaps if he sees the oxcart, he will not see the *ibhiza-idlozis* as they ride towards him and capture him.'

Nick nodded.

'You keep heading in that direction,' Enoch said. 'We will come back and find you once we have taken care of the Caçador Escuro, and we can help you bury the dead.'

Filipe shook his head. 'It is a bad idea to run towards evil with a rough plan. But even if there is a war, the cold murder of civilians should never be allowed to happen. I will ride with you.'

'No, Filipe, as much as I want you with us, I need you to watch over my dad and Ethel while we are gone,' Chloe said.

'We will stay here and watch the quiet *ibhiza-idlozi*, make sure no harm comes to him and his nurse,' the chief said. 'It is the least we can do while you help my people with my son. Go. Capture the Caçador Escuro. Or kill him. Either way, I will be happier if he is not around my people. When you return, then we can take the oxen and truck and bury the dead. Hopefully, there will be no more spirits to free today than who he has killed already.'

Chloe went to the chief and took both his hands in hers. '*Siyabonga kakulu!*' She bobbed in a quick bow to him, showing him the respect and gratitude of a younger person to an elder in the same tribe.

They quickly saddled the horses and took their weapons, and soon they were cantering through the bush.

They wound their way along the game trails at a healthy pace, the horses loving the freedom of running after being trapped in the trailer for so many days with only brief interludes of walking. Ducking for a branch of a mopani tree as they went past, Chloe could feel Pampero stretch beneath her and she patted her neck. 'That's it, girl, find your stride. We might be at this for a while. We'll get this bastard.'

Pampero's skin shuddered in response under Chloe's hand.

They rounded the *kopje* and Chloe could see Julio pointing to a piece of bush in front. Xo took a sharp left, almost unseating Julio. Enoch did the same turn, and Diablo and Pampero followed in Kimberlite's footsteps. Chloe could see why: a tree was downed and lying across the trail, but there was also a warthog burrow right in the path. That required evasive action to avoid breaking a horse's leg in the hole.

They continued for a while, and then she saw the white of the *bakkie* as it travelled along the bush road. It wasn't going at speed, just cruising along, as if the hunters knew that they were safe. Confident that once again they had got away from their hunting grounds with a souvenir dug from a person's head, and there was nothing that anyone could do about it.

Julio jumped off Sirocco, running next to him then rolled in the sand, leaving Xo alone. Xo increased Sirocco's speed as he took his hunting weapon from his holster, placed the barrel between Sirocco's ears, and stretched out over his horse's neck. Behind him, Enoch had his rifle out, almost at his shoulder. Chloe was not far behind, hers already between Pampero's ears, and as she heard the shot from Xo, she was already pressing Pampero faster, pulling to the right to ensure that she didn't shoot either Xo or Enoch in front of her when she noticed the *bakkie* speed up.

Enoch's shot was next, and she saw the back windscreen of the *bakkie* shatter with his bullet. The *bakkie* fishtailed but continued on the road.

Heart pounding, she took careful aim and squeezed the trigger of her .303. Pampero kept running, trained for just such a move. The *bakkie* swerved; she saw the man hold his shoulder and she knew that she'd hit him in his upper left arm.

The fourth shot from behind her was a surprise. Nick passed her on Marin, and Khululani was no longer riding double. Nick had his weapon on his shoulder, much like Enoch, and he took a shot, not at the driver, but at the vehicle's back wheel. The *bakkie* seemed to lift slightly as the tyre was blown, and then the driver got it under control again. He increased his speed, a dangerous move on gravel with one wheel shot out. Slower but still able to flee.

The four of them were close to each other now, thundering down the road. Xo shot again, and she saw the front windscreen spider. The driver was punching a hole in the glass with his right hand.

The passenger put the barrel of a rifle out the back and let off a shot. Chloe saw the barrel and was already veering off, out of the direct line of fire, as were the others.

Pampero was tiring. Though disappointed, Chloe pulled up and let the men go. There was no use losing her foal just to keep up with them. They were fine without her. She could be close behind, out of reach of the shotgun being used, but close enough that if she was needed, she could catch up.

Diablo thundered past her. Filipe had his AK-47 out and was still bouncing but had somehow managed to sit straight enough in the saddle and hold his weapon on his shoulder. A good thing too, as shooting from the hip would hit the horse's head and ears. But he was still behind the others, so he couldn't shoot yet. Diablo had automatically taken his place in the battle line-up.

Chloe heard a double shot from both Enoch and the deeper sound of Nick's weapon as they discharged into the *bakkie*. Xo on Sirocco broke off the gallop and slowed, as did Kimberlite. For a split second it seemed that Nick was the only one close to the *bakkie*, when the driver turned around and looked directly at him.

A second discharge came from the shotgun, and Nick pulled off to the left. The driver pressed the *bakkie* for still more speed, and his V6 engine gave it to him, increasing the distance between the horses and the vehicle.

There was no way for Nick to catch up at this speed. He pulled back after one last shot at the back of the car, and Chloe heard the tin sound of a hard nose going through metal. He dropped behind Filipe, and there was a round of AK-47 going off. She didn't know if any of the bullets being sprayed got the *bakkie*, but when the magazine was finished Filipe instructed Diablo to turn around and slow down.

Filipe was whooping like a hyena, having lost his hat somewhere along the route, and pure glee showed on his face as he trotted towards them. His gun was bouncing around as much as he was, and it was pointed directly at them.

'I think I have a new favourite hobby!' he shouted.

Chloe shook her head as she slowed Pampero, who had been gently cantering before coming to a complete stop. She had the butt of her .303 on her thigh and it pointed skywards.

'Raise your weapon so it won't accidentally shoot any of us, Filipe,' she said, and he looked at the rifle as if he'd forgotten that he had it attached to his arm and followed her example, putting the butt on his thigh.

Nick galloped to her side, and Marin stopped almost right next to her, as if he was a quarter horse, not an endurance stallion. His nose flared. Nick's gun was at the same angle as hers, safe from shooting anyone in their small group of riders.

'You okay, Chloe?' he asked as Marin brushed against Pampero with a small jolt.

'I'm good,' she said. 'And I'm sure that Pampero is fine. She enjoyed that run, but I think she'll do good to walk back to camp. She gave everything she could without taking anything from her foal.' She couldn't help smiling; she knew it was the adrenaline, but it felt so good.

He reached over for her and gave her a quick, unexpected hug. Holding her close, then letting her go.

'Seriously, I'm good,' she said again, reassuring him, her smile fading, her body on fire where it had touched his. She wanted to reach over and bring him back and press herself to him again to savour the feeling.

'Yes, but I needed to make sure for myself. That's the first time I have ridden into battle against a woman—that I know of. I thought she got you the first time she fired. I'm so glad that she missed.'

'She?'

'The passenger was a woman,' Nick said.

'You sure she didn't shoot you?' Chloe asked. Despite seeing that there was no blood, she still felt a need to check him.

'Not me.' He ran his hand over his own chest, then lay forward in his saddle and ran his hand quickly over the horse's chest. 'Marin seems fine, too.'

'You both okay?' Xo asked as he rode up to join them.

'Fine,' they said together.

Chloe asked, 'You?'

'Sirocco and I are both good. Dad?' Xo asked as Enoch rode up alongside them.

'You all okay? No one hurt?' Enoch said.

'Man, Chloe, that was some shot. You definitely got him in the shoulder. I think you got him too, Xo. You guys did so well,' Enoch said.

'He'll need medical treatment, but he still got away,' Xo said.

'Anyone get the numberplate?' Enoch asked.

'It's 443 409 H,' Chloe said, having committed it to memory before she started shooting.

'There was a big ZW sticker on his tailgate,' Xo added.

'The hunter is from Zimbabwe. We have one more lead that the SAP don't,' Nick said.

They turned their horses and started walking towards the road where Khululani and Julio were running towards them still.

Julio was clapping and doing a dance in the sand. 'You showed him, he'll never come back here. Even if you didn't kill him, you shot up his *bakkie* and he will think twice before coming hunting here again. Our people are safer thanks to you all.'

Chloe just shook her head.

Khululani walked up to Nick. 'Did you see his face close up? Was I right about it being the man we saw at the pan when we were fixing the pump?'

'Yes. He looked right at me. I think he recognised me, too,' Nick said.

Enoch looked from Khululani to Nick. 'You two know the hunter?'

'We've run into him in the Kruger. Up in the north part, close to where the park finishes, and the start of Coutada 16,' Nick said.

'It is at one of the last watering pans before you exit the park, right up in the mopani shrub veld,' Khululani added.

'It was barely six o'clock, and we wondered how he could've got to the pan as early as he had from any visitor's camp. The only reason we were in the area was because we'd slept in the bush not far from where we saw him. We reported him for suspicion of being in the park overnight and moving around outside of park hours. But there aren't as many staff policing the visitors in the north of the park as there are in the south. It's a lot less crowded. We learned later in the day that no one had him on their sign-in sheet either. We had him listed as a suspected poacher, a vehicle of interest at all the gates of the park.'

'He is an arrogant *tsotsi*,' Khululani said.

Nick smiled. 'When we arrived at the pan, he stood next to his vehicle, as if waiting for us to approach and reprimand him for being there. We had a lot to do that day, and if an idiot wanted to tempt fate and get eaten, then he was welcome to parade around in front of the lions in the park; it's his choice. When we simply ignored him and began to fit the new pump, he got in his *bakkie* with his passenger, another white male with a beard. He came around our side of the pan and drove close to us, staring at us the whole time, before tipping his hat and driving slowly north. He's with someone different this time, a woman; she's the one who fired back at us with a shotgun.'

'You think it's a coincidence that you see him here, in the middle of Mozambique?' Chloe asked.

'Absolutely. A bloody big one. But he clearly knows my face as well as I know his,' Nick said.

Enoch looked backwards. 'We should put some distance between them and us, in case they decide to regroup and retaliate.'

Xo reached down for Julio and pulled him up back onto Sirocco.

Khululani used Nick's foot and then stirrup to help him mount onto the back of Marin, as well as Nick pulling him up. He didn't manage to be half as elegant as Xo and Julio, though Sirocco was a fair bit shorter than Marin.

Chloe put her .303 away into its holster.

Enoch said, 'I think I will keep mine out. You never know ...'

They cantered back five abreast until they came to the tree and the warthog burrow, then they moved back into single-file formation to avoid a landmine area that they had apparently run through once already, according to a talkative Julio. Only when they were on the other side of the *kopje* did they slow to a walk.

They were with the chief and the medicine man when they found the corpse alongside a small campfire. He hadn't stood a chance. His empty cup was lying next to him; his morning tea had long soaked into the thirsty earth, and ants were making short work of his stick of biltong. As expected, he'd been shot in the head, his skull cracked open like a melon with a rock, to enable the Caçador Escuro to retrieve the bullet.

There were two sets of tracks.

'This hunter has big feet, size eleven,' Khululani said. 'The smaller boot prints look like a female tread to me. They are size six. Goes with what Nick said about the passenger being a woman.'

They dug a deep grave and buried what was left of the man, covering him with rocks so that the jackals and hyenas couldn't get to his body. The chief had fashioned a cross and placed it on top of the stones, and Curandeiros Cassamo performed a quick ceremony to allow the man's spirit to fly free from the binding that kept him in his body because of his violent death so that he could once again rejoin his family and assume his responsibilities.

Once it was done, Enoch, along with Nick, Khululani and Filipe, tracked them back to where the hunters' camp had been. They searched the area, looking for anything that could serve as evidence to help them identify who'd been there, but found nothing except a fire which had been extinguished a few hours before. The Caçador Escuro knew how to clean up after himself.

And that more than anything niggled at Enoch's mind.

They had the horses loaded and ready to go by lunchtime, and the villagers had all come out to wave them on their way. Deciding to press on hadn't been difficult for any of them. They wanted to put as much distance between the hunter and them as they could. The horses were more docile. After they had been for a cooling swim in the river and had a good rub-down, they seemed happier when being loaded.

The only thing remaining was to say their goodbyes to the chief, and then they could depart.

'At least we know that if we come across someone in a white—now beaten-up—*bakkie* in the bush, we must give them a wide berth,' Enoch said to the chief.

The chief nodded.

'We'll also be extra alert,' Nick said, 'ensuring that we check for him all the time in case he gives chase.'

'We cannot help you further with this Caçador Escuro, but we will keep what we have seen here in our thoughts. Perhaps one day we will have a way to find this man. We need to push through into Zimbabwe, but we will never forget your warning. We hope we scared him enough that he never comes back to your homeland. You keep your people safe and keep them close,' Enoch said as he shook the chief's hand. '*Sala kuhle,* my friend.'

'*Hamba kahle,*' the chief said, as he and Julio shook their visitors' hands.

When the chief shook Nick's hand, he said, 'Look after your missus and her horses. She's the best special cargo my village has hosted for many, many years.'

CHAPTER 23

They headed north-west for two hours, bumping along the old dirt road, before Filipe spotted the RENAMO soldiers blocking the way. As had become the practice, he got out and approached them alone.

Enoch and Xo watched from the front of the truck. There was lots of head shaking going on, and no back slapping.

Enoch said into the radio, 'It does not look like Filipe is winning this time.'

'Agreed,' Nick said, watching through the air holes in the top of the truck.

Khululani cocked his .303.

'No, wait; hopefully, it won't come to that,' Nick said.

Ethel put her hand on Mike's arm to reassure him, and Chloe smiled at her. Ethel had coped so wonderfully with the travelling, despite her years. Chloe thought maybe that Ethel had now found her calling, being a healing gypsy on safaris.

Filipe threw his hands in the air, then he walked back to the truck. He opened the passenger door and said into the radio, 'There has been a message from General Vareya. The soldiers here need to take the truck. They said we can keep the contents. They have to head south-east immediately. He apologised for borrowing your truck, but he said that he needs it, and he would not ask if it were not urgent. He said that as we are so close to Zimbabwe, the horses will be able to carry us from here. He guarantees that all the possessions you remove from the truck will be safe, and no one will take anything, and you can return with another vehicle from Zimbabwe and collect them once we get there. He also said that if he can ever return your truck, he will.'

'What? And you?' Enoch asked. 'What are his new plans for you?'

'I'm still your guide. I stay with you until the end, until you have come back and collected your belongings.'

Enoch climbed out of the truck and went to the back, opening the tailgate to let the others climb out. They all stood together, where the RENAMO soldiers couldn't see them.

'We are only a few more days' ride from the Zimbabwe border if we leave the excess from the truck here,' Enoch said. 'Once we are in Zimbabwe, we can call Grace. She will bring Delaware's cattle truck and collect us. We come back, fetch our belongings, and then go home.'

'And Vareya helps himself to a second truck?' Chloe said. 'Him breaking one promise and taking my truck is bad enough.'

'General Vareya would not do that,' Filipe said. 'He would not be taking this truck unless the need was very great. The debt he owed Khululani was very big.'

'But not big enough that he won't still take the truck?' Chloe said.

Filipe put his hand on his head. 'I tried to argue. I told them everything that I could, even that the Caçador Escuro was after us because we shot at him. But they are still taking the truck. We have to unpack. There is nothing more I can do,' Filipe said.

'Oh, you didn't fail. No, Filipe, like all of us, you answer to a higher man up the tree that just yanked the branch out from under you, that's all. It sucks. I'm angry at him, not at you,' Chloe explained.

'*Yebo*. It is sad that he is borrowing the truck,' Khululani said. 'But I know this man; he would only be in my debt again if his need was urgent. We are far along the track, and Zimbabwe is close. I agree with Enoch that we can make it from here inside a week.'

Chloe put her hand on Khululani's arm. 'I'm sorry. I really am. It was just all going so well. I thought we'd be home, and this would be over by now.'

Khululani put his hand on top of hers. 'We are all still alive, and that is more important than having a truck.'

He took his hand away and Chloe's eyes filled with tears.

Xo hugged Chloe. 'I know this is hard for you, but Khululani's right. Let's just get going.'

Chloe wiped her nose on the back of her hand. 'I don't even have a tissue!'

Nick passed her one that had been neatly folded, and she blew into it. 'Thank you.'

'Come on, it'll be alright, Chloe,' Nick said. 'The journey's almost over, and then the adventure really begins.'

Chloe put her hands on her hips and looked at Nick. 'Seriously, you're going to try feeding me shit like that. We're in spitting distance of home, and we lose our wheels. We're not safe from the SAP and SADF until we get home, and now we have to add an insane hunter who shoots people to the list. I'm a little angry about this! That truck's been our income for the last few years; it's brought in a steady flow of cash for us. Excuse me while I object to having it driven off into the bush to be used in a war and left burnt out on the side of a road somewhere, shot to shit. It's been a faithful truck.'

Nick looked down. 'It's crap that they are taking the truck, but we've been really lucky to have it for as long as we have. It's beyond our control. We have to face the facts and adjust our plans, Chloe.'

Tears welled in her eyes. 'But we're so close.'

'We'll make it all the way to Delaware,' Xo said as he drew her into a hug and held her close.

Nick walked up to Chloe and put his hand on her shoulder. 'Sorry you're losing your truck. I understand now how much it means to you.'

She took a few deep breaths, straightened her shoulders, sniffed and looked at Enoch. 'Okay, so there's nothing we can do about the truck. It's going. Where are we going to be crossing if we ride from here?'

'Just south of Gonarezhou is the Sengwe Communal Land, but it is a large hunting area, so we will need to be vigilant on the horses. There should be camps there that will have telephones or at least a vehicle to get us to a town where a phone can be found,' Enoch said.

'Perhaps we need to leave someone with the luggage that we can't take with us,' Xo said. 'I'll stay and guard it.'

'No,' Nick said. 'No one stays. We all go. We stay together. The threat of the Caçador Escuro is too great a risk.'

'I agree with Nick—it's just luggage,' Chloe said. 'We take the money and anything valuable that we can carry but keep things as light as we can.'

'Once we are home, I will come back with Filipe, and we will collect the rest of the luggage in a *bakkie*. The feed, which is taking up most of the room, can be dumped. The animals in this area will be happy for it, or the mice will have a cosy home,' Enoch said.

Chloe looked at the truck, and then at everyone around. 'I'm not happy donating our truck to General Vareya's cause. But I'm also thankful that we've got this far, so let's get moving and put some distance between those men taking our truck and us. And I'm seriously happy that he gave us Filipe because I know that we wouldn't have made it this far without your help.'

'There are eight of us and five horses,' Xo pointed out.

'And two of those horses are old,' Enoch said. 'Mike will need to ride most of the time. The rest of us, we will have to take turns walking. We were never going to be able to gallop home anyway. Slow and steady, we will get there,' Enoch said.

'Let's get the horses out, then we can decide what stays and what we carry,' Nick said. 'If we unload everything and then give them the truck, and make sure they leave, we can sort things without them knowing what's being left behind. Hopefully, reduce the chance of them being more interested in the luggage than in their general's orders.'

'No one says we have to ride this morning. It is almost teatime, and this is a good place to sort and store everything. We can start travelling again tomorrow morning. There is enough thornbush around here for a good boma,' Enoch said.

They unloaded the horses and secured them to a rope that they strung between two trees. There was green grass for them to nibble on, so they would be content to wait there while the truck was unloaded.

Filipe walked back up the road to the RENAMO soldiers to tell them what they were doing, and that they would get their truck soon enough. He came back to find that they had almost finished unloading. 'They want to know how much diesel you have left.'

Enoch said, 'We refilled the fuel tanks last night from the drums, so they have what is there, and about half a 44-gallon drum. We only had enough to get us into Zimbabwe, not trek all over Mozambique. There is water up on the roof, too, but we will be taking at least five of the jerry cans with us.'

Filipe nodded. 'They'll get to the next place they need to fill up on a full tank, and they'll be grateful for the water.'

'Good for them,' Chloe said sarcastically.

Filipe looked downwards, seeming embarrassed by what his general had done to them.

They watched the RENAMO soldiers drive away, and finally turned their backs on them. Except Filipe, who'd climbed a tree to watch the truck through binoculars to ensure it didn't come back towards them or stop and wait for them to leave before returning to take all their belongings.

Khululani said, 'I am going to take a walk around and see if there is a cave in those rocks, or if there is a big baobab tree, we can put everything in.'

'Good idea, I'll come with,' Nick said. 'Bring your .303. I don't think it's a good idea to be walking around here without them.'

Enoch nodded. 'While you two do that, Chloe and I will get things organised here. Chloe, get the backpacks. Each of us can carry one, and we can pack the guns, ammo, food, sleeping bags and personal items that cannot stay here. Let us keep one very light for Ethel. If we load most of the weight onto the horses, and we walk with them and travel light, I think we should be near civilisation within three days.'

'I can carry my share,' Ethel said.

Enoch touched her shoulder. 'I know you can, but I think we let the horse carry it for you, so you can watch over Mike. I know that we would all feel better knowing that you are there for him, and not tired.'

She nodded, and Chloe and Xo started to sort through the belongings piled next to where the truck had stood.

When Nick and Khululani returned, Nick was almost jumping with excitement. 'There's a cave not too far from here. It's covered in bushman paintings. I can't believe that they've survived as long as they have and not been damaged or vandalised. They've hunting pictures of spears and dead animals, and cattle, and herds of eland, and people. It's a true treasure. It doesn't look like the soldiers knew it was there—there doesn't seem to have been a fire inside it for a good few years. The entrance was hidden behind some thick bushes, but Khululani still managed to find it. It should work as a store for the stuff we can't take with us.'

'Finally, some good news,' Chloe said.

Enoch smiled. 'I will stay here with the horses; you two go have a look.' He motioned with his hands to Xo and Chloe. Then he yelled, 'Filipe. They gone yet?'

'Just a dusty dot on the horizon. But there are elephants coming our way,' Filipe shouted back. 'A big herd, moving slowly though. About an hour or so and they will get here.'

Enoch said, 'The cave will have to wait.'

'The cave is big enough to put the horses in. Let's let their introduction to the wildlife be a little less traumatic than having elephants walk through their camp on the first day out,' Nick said.

'Okay. Filipe, get down here and help move everything breakable into the cave. We can only hope your timing of them is right,' Enoch said.

They worked quickly, and soon, the belongings that mattered were in the cave. The first horse Chloe tried to coax into the cave was Pampero. However, she baulked at the confines of the entrance. 'Come on, girl, one last try.'

But the horse pulled back on her reins.

'Fine, be like that,' Chloe said. 'I bet you Diablo will come in, and he'll be safe from those big elephants, while you'll be outside.'

Chloe gave Pampero to Xo, who stood watching her, a silly grin on his face.

'Don't you dare laugh, Xo.' She took Diablo from him. 'Come on, old man, just show these others how it's done. Please.'

Diablo walked into the cave without hesitation. Xo followed with Pampero, and because he was so close behind Diablo, she walked in without any more fussing.

'We should have tried it this way the first time,' Chloe admitted. 'I should have known better.'

'Give yourself a break,' Xo said, 'it's been a full-on day.'

They went out and brought in Kimberlite, with Marin close behind him, and Sirocco really close behind Marin. The stallion baulked once.

Chloe brought out the horse cubes and bribed him. 'Come on, boy, you have to get in there.'

But it was Sirocco right behind as he pushed on Marin, trying to get to a few cubes, too, which manhandled and shamed the stallion into entering more than anything else. Chloe's nerves were frayed, and the horses could sense it.

'Stay with them. I'll bring in the food,' Xo said.

Chloe went to the back of the cave where Diablo stood as if he'd been housed in a cave all his life. Calm and still, he waited for her. She scratched his ears. 'Thank you,' she said, laying her head against his. The familiar earthy scent of Diablo washed over her, and her shoulders relaxed. The pain she felt inside abated for a moment.

'I know you have seen lots of death before, and smelled it, but today was a first for me,' she said quietly. 'I have to learn to live with knowing that I shot a man, and nothing in all my training prepared me for this feeling of guilt.'

Diablo whinnied and tossed his head.

'I know it's stupid; there shouldn't be any because he's a cold-blooded killer, but still. How can I be a decent human being if I don't feel bad for hurting someone else?' She stroked his face, drinking in the calmness.

Xo came back into the cave. 'I'll put their feed boxes out.'

'Thanks. I think we should give them an extra big helping of lucerne to keep them distracted.' She smiled, despite the feeling inside of her.

'Your wish is my command,' Xo said.

She laughed.

Taking the horse cubes from Xo so he could fetch the lucerne, she dished out the food, stroking each horse and talking to them as she went.

'You guys are so lucky you're at the back here; it's so nice and cool,' Chloe said. 'When you're done, you can look at all the splendour that surrounds you. I bet the men who painted those never expected a horse to shelter in this cave near their pictures. I doubt they ever got to even see a horse; they were here so long ago.'

Once the horses were settled, Chloe finally had the opportunity to study the cave. She'd seen a few caves on Delaware that'd had a bit of rock art, but nothing like this one. A hunter, painted in hues of brown, stood amidst a herd of impala, their brown bodies and white underbellies clearly visible. In another, a group of people ran together, their large bottoms and bellies showing as they chased a herd of elephants with huge tusks. Higher up on the cave wall, the bushmen had painted a scene of a large leopard. Its head shape and spots clearly indicating it was not a cheetah. Around that were clumps of animals—giraffe, zebra, wildebeest—and then layered on top again were even more impala, kudu with their large spiral horns, and more elephants with fat stomachs and long trunks. A rhino, with two long horns, completed the collection. Her gaze lingered on a group of people running towards a pride of lions.

There were so many paintings, and layers of paint, one on top of another, as if this cave had housed many artists over the years. In one, there was a change in colour to a blacker and more solid image, and a picture of a man on a horse with a hat on.

Chloe paused.

It looked out of place alongside the warthog, eagles and stylised figures of people with small bows and arrows, and lines of people dancing together, clapping.

The cave had been home to so many people, so much life, until the art had stopped in an era where modern men had taken over in Mozambique. With African exploration by the Europeans, then colonisation, their presence had led to the near disappearance of the San people. She reached out and traced a picture of a porcupine, its quills all pointing backwards. She remembered seeing many porcupines when she was growing up. Her dad had believed that you didn't mess with them, and just left them to their own business in their burrows on Delaware, but she'd spent hours around their den, collecting quills and putting them in a vase in her room. She wondered if the quills were still there, waiting at Delaware for her to come home, or if Aunty Grace had tossed them out and used her bedroom for something else.

'Chloe, we're going to climb up top to watch the elephants,' Nick said from the entrance. 'Are you coming?'

She turned, a refusal on the tip of her tongue, but Enoch had Mike on a makeshift bed, and Ethel was helping to settle him down for an afternoon rest.

'Go, I will watch the horses,' Enoch said. 'You will be close enough to slip inside if they smell the elephants and get restless.'

'Call me if they show any signs of distress,' Chloe insisted.

Enoch nodded.

Chloe, Xo, Nick and Khululani sat on top of the *kopje* that hid the cave and heard the elephants before they saw them, the rumblings of members of the herd communicating across the bushveld. Then the deserted bush suddenly exploded into life. Long grey trunks ripped trees apart as they went, eating the leaves and stripping the bark, almost like a large forest bulldozer. Chloe watched as one mischievous little elephant took a branch and attempted to break it from the tree, but the branch wouldn't come loose. It tried again, still to no avail. The little one eventually got the branch to break, and as testament to the fact he was stronger than it, he threw it on the ground and began stomping on it, as if to teach it a lesson.

Chloe chuckled, then put her hand over her mouth to stop the sound as the young calf looked in her direction before it ran back to its mother, leaving the now destroyed branch on the ground. The mother carried on eating, slowly plodding northwards.

'You know, your horses will get used to them pretty fast. To them, they are just another animal, and to the elephant, your horse is just missing its pyjamas,' Nick said.

Chloe grinned. 'It's not the horses I worry about; it's me. These guys are huge.'

'We're not going to purposely try to ride in their herd; we'll go around them—assuming we know they're there of course,' Nick said.

'I don't remember them being so large.'

'You just haven't been around them for such a long time,' Xo said.

'When you did the trip south through the bush, did you come across elephants?' Chloe asked.

Xo smiled. 'Lots of them, and the horses didn't mind. I think old Diablo and Kimberlite might even remember them.'

'I hope so. I'm counting on them to keep the others calm if we encounter them in the bush,' Chloe said.

They were still sitting up there watching the sky darken when they heard the gunfire, far off in the distance. It was so far away that they couldn't even identify the weapon, just that there were multiple shots, and an explosion. Then silence. The whole bush stopped and listened. Cicadas didn't scream, the crickets quietened, even the birds in their ritual calls of worship to life were silent.

After a moment, everything started up its chorus again, and other than a baboon barking in the distance, warning of some danger, the night sounds were natural.

A flash of orange fire leapt into the sky, then darkness and a grey smoky haze of a fuel-induced fire in the distance. But nothing else.

'You think that was our truck and they hit a landmine?' Chloe asked.

Nick shook his head. 'It's not the right way for where we saw the truck heading; it's more to the west. Quite far. They couldn't have got there already, even if they know where the road is mined and isn't.'

'It is back where we were this morning,' Khululani said. 'On the road that the Caçador Escuro sped away on.'

'You sure?' Xo asked.

Khululani nodded.

'Probably just the Mozambicans fighting each other. We've been really lucky to have seen nothing of the war in person,' Nick said.

'Enough about stupid wars and killings. I'm beat, and I need sleep. Let's go sort out some dinner then hit the sack,' Chloe said.

'Me too; I'm starving,' said Xo.

'You are always hungry,' Chloe said, and Xo gave her a playful punch in the arm.

'Surely not.'

She laughed and nodded. 'Always.'

Nick put his hand out and helped her as she slid off the granite dome and then began the climb down again. She smiled her thanks, and he seemed to hold onto her hand for a little longer than expected, before letting it go.

Their return had caused everyone outside to admit that it was supper time, and when they walked into the cave, Enoch and Ethel had a small fire going, and something smelled really nice in the cooking pot. A pot of *sadza* bubbled on the coals that Ethel had pulled away from the main heat of the fire, and Chloe sat down next to her dad in his deck chair.

She patted his leg and watched the fire as Ethel handed her a bowl, not bothering to give her a utensil. It was a stew, and she could eat it with her fingers. One less thing for them to have to wash up with their precious water.

Soon she was mopping up the last of the gravy with her *sadza*. 'What was in here? It tasted like goat.'

'Goat,' Ethel said, nodding. 'The *tinyanga*, Cassamo, he gave it to me when we were leaving. He said that he'd sacrificed it for us, to his gods and all his ancestors, because we had made his village a safer place. He has asked them to watch over us and keep us safe from the Caçador Escuro on our journey home.'

Chloe looked at Ethel with a frown.

Filipe shook his head. 'The meat was fresh, and I do not believe that Ethel would have accepted it if it was at all contaminated by anything he put on it.'

Ethel shook her head. 'I didn't trust him either, and I told him that. He gave me the knife and told me to *siga* the whole leg with the skin on and take it from the gutted goat. The sacrifice was his offering for the gods; he couldn't contaminate the meat.'

'What else did he give you?' Chloe asked.

'Nothing else, just the meat that was a gift to all of us to say thank you,' Ethel said.

'What did he ask for from you?' Chloe asked.

'Nothing,' Ethel said in a defensive tone.

'As long as that snake didn't try to give you a vulture's head or anything gross to wear to ward off evil. Despite everything, I still don't trust him.'

'I wouldn't accept anything like that,' Ethel said.

'Did he try to weasel another nice dress from you?'

Ethel smiled. 'I told him I did not have any smart dresses to give him, and he said that he did not want any of my maid's uniforms.'

Chloe shook her head. 'See, that's what I thought.'

'I was not giving him my favourite church dress. I want to wear it again when I get to my new home, to my new life,' Ethel said.

Chloe smiled. 'Good on you, Ethel. Thank you for an amazing dinner. I for one loved that stew, even if the meat came from that ratbag.'

Everyone else was also complimenting Ethel on the stew, and how nice it was to have eaten fresh meat for a change.

'You know, if we find anything edible along the way, we could always kill for the pot,' Nick suggested. 'We are out of the park area, and while we had the truck and were making decent progress, using the rations we carried made sense, but now, we'll have to change a few things, and eating fresh meat will need to be one of those changes.'

'Thank you for volunteering. That can be your job from now on, because we cannot carry all the food with us on the horses tomorrow,' Enoch said as they settled down for the night.

CHAPTER 24

Russian Top 6 Trophies

1. Wolf
2. Tur
3. Ibex
4. Snow leopard
5. Bear
6. Man

CHAPTER 25

Douglas looked at Nicole Schaffer.

'Nicole, can you hear me? You still with me?'

She was silent.

'Fuck!' He pulled to the side of the dirt road with difficulty as the *bakkie* was barely responding now with two tyres blown. He had driven as far as he could get from the danger. He jumped out and walked around to the passenger side and opened her door.

Nicole flopped out into his arms, unconscious. He had to find where she was bleeding and stop it.

He lay her on the side of the road, turned her over and shimmied her T-shirt upwards. He didn't have to search for where the entry wound was. Despite all the blood, he could see it at the base of her back. Her kidney. When she had told him she had been hit, she hadn't said where. The blood coming out of the wound was dark red.

He turned her over to check if there was an exit wound and saw the bullet had pulled part of her intestines along with it on the way out, and they were slowly beginning to protrude outwards.

He saw another exit hole in her shirt. He turned her again and, pulling her T-shirt over her arms, used that to wipe the whole of her back. About fifteen centimetres above the first wound, a second bullet had sliced into her liver, and probably her lungs, too. There was a third entry hole but no exit wound. One of the bullets was still inside.

He was losing her. There was no way they would make it to a hospital or a clinic.

He turned her back over and realised that he hadn't noticed the blood coming from her mouth as she drowned. Her body gave a last sigh, and then was still in his arms.

Not only had he lost his client, but he'd felt her last heartbeat. Been there to share her last breath. He had never experienced this feeling of loss before. Not even when Tommy had died had he felt that he had let his friend down. Nicole was his client, and he hadn't been able to protect her. He had failed at his job.

He had failed the 6th.

A *bakkie* went past, going towards Mozambique, then it stopped and reversed. A young black man got out and came to him. He was almost as tall as Douglas, but he hadn't had the years to fill out into his frame yet. '*Ag shame, man!* Some *skebengas* got your *bakkie*? Are you okay?'

Douglas looked up from where he still held Nicole. 'She's dead.'

'*Haw!* I'm so sorry, so sorry, man.' The driver took off his hat and put it on his chest as a sign of respect. 'Do you want me to go call anyone for help?'

Douglas began to shake his head. Right now, all he wanted was for the driver to leave him alone so he could turn his *bakkie* around and go back and kill the son-of-a-bitch Parks Board guys who'd done this to him. His life was over, but he was not leaving without their lives as payback for Nicole.

In the back of his mind, he remembered Kupua's promise to help the hunters if they asked, but he knew it was more a veiled threat than an offer of help.

The man was waiting. He needed more time to think. 'Do you have a pen and paper?'

The driver fetched a small schoolbook and a pencil that had been sharpened with a knife. Douglas lay Nicole down and made sure to drape her T-shirt over her chest, covering up her breasts.

He stood up and the driver passed the notebook to Douglas.

If he wrote this note and sent the fax to Bern, he was signing his own death warrant. He wouldn't get a chance to get even with the bastard game ranger before someone from the 6th came and ended his life.

He'd lost a client.

His life was already over.

But if he didn't send the fax, Kupua would eventually come after him anyway when he didn't check in, making sure everything was still in order. Since losing #5, they had tightened their control over the hunters. She would track him down, and he would be silenced because he had lost a client. It was the rule of the 6th.

Either way his life was over.

Except, maybe if they thought he was dead already …

'*Baas?*' the man asked. 'Do you need me to write for you?'

No, I need you to die for me.

Douglas looked up and down the road to ensure there was no traffic, then he grabbed the man, quickly overpowering him and breaking his neck. He put the body into the driver's seat and did up his seatbelt.

He picked up Nicole from the side of the road and put her back into the passenger's seat, righting her clothing. He pulled on her seatbelt and clicked it in place to hold her. There was nothing he could do for her now. She was dead anyway—but he could still avenge her killers.

He knew at least one was a game ranger from the Kruger. But he couldn't fathom how he'd followed him. Too much time had passed between when he had been with Heinz Koch, his German client in the Kruger when he happened upon those two rangers a second time. He had been back to Zimbabwe and into South Africa again before crossing in the Coutada 16 area for his 6th hunt with Nicole.

There was no way they could have followed him.

How had they found him?

The rangers were good, but there was no way they could have accomplished that feat. And the others? Why had they all attacked, and on horseback? None of it added up.

All he had to do was follow their trail and he'd find them. Clean up that loose end. Now that he had a chance to throw anyone off his trail, they would all think it was just him and Nicole in the burnt-out *bakkie*. Only when the cops looked closer would they discover that it was not his body. Or not, depending on how closely they looked at bodies that had obviously been in a war zone.

This would buy him the time to act.

Nobody hurt him or someone he was charged with protecting without consequences.

But the game rangers, and now those they rode with, must know he was the Inthunzi Zingela as they called him in the Kruger. There was no other explanation for their aggressiveness towards him.

They could recognise him. They could expose the 6th. His position within the 6th was already compromised. His life might end *if* they realised, he was alive, but if they didn't—if these attackers were gone, and didn't expose him—he might be able to slip deeper into Africa and live there, where no 6th master of the hunt would ever find him.

He had to find and kill every last one of them.

CHAPTER 26

Waking from a dark dream, Chloe could hear the deep murmur of men's voices talking, just outside the cave. She looked around. Other than the horses, her dad and Ethel, she was the only one still inside.

Blood thundered in her head, and the darkness in the cave threatened to close in on her. She shook her head, trying to dislodge the sensation. She wrapped her sleeping bag around herself and walked out into the early morning. She could see the golden light of the first rays as sunshine touched the treetops and bathed them all in a heavenly light. But it hurt her eyes. She closed them and tried to open them just a slit to walk carefully to where the voices were, letting them guide her.

'I guess we won't really understand what happened unless we double back, go take a look,' Nick said.

'That would be a waste of our time,' Enoch said. 'Better to press on, get into Zimbabwe, away from the war.'

'I would be happier knowing what that was. Khululani and I can get there and back easy. It'll take us a day and a night at most to check on it, and make sure it's nothing for us to worry about,' Nick said.

'It would be good to know exactly what it was, but are you sure about walking around an area when you don't know where the mines are is a good idea?' Filipe asked.

'Do not even think of joining them,' Enoch said. 'They are free to do what they want to do, but you need to ensure that the horses don't walk into any of those mined areas, so we will push forward.'

Nick was planning on leaving her?

Leaving them?

Her heart skipped a beat. She had got so used to him being there. What if something happened to him out there? What if he didn't get back to them and was lost forever in the bush somewhere? Her heart constricted, her breathing shallowed, and she became light-headed. She shook her head. Forced air into her lungs, trying to remain calm.

'No way, I'm not happy with this,' she said. 'How can you be so sure you can find us again, and we are not going to lose you? I know I was left out of this conversation for some stupid male chauvinistic reason, but I really don't like the idea of us separating out here.'

'Is it just me or is Chloe not speaking English?' Nick asked.

Enoch immediately came to her side.

'Don't try sucking up to me,' she told him.

'Xo, go find her migraine medication. I'll get her to lie down out here, hurry.'

'Migraine? Her speaking gibberish is a migraine?' Nick asked.

'I'm fine,' she said. 'I just want to know why you were conspiring behind my back and going to give me a fait accompli with us splitting up before we get to Delaware.' She tried to take a breath after telling them off, but there was no air around. Nothing was going in. She tried again.

Enoch took her sleeping bag and threw it on the ground, then physically pushed her downwards. 'Sit down before you fall down. And breathe, you are as white as white gets,' Enoch said.

'I'm trying to,' she said loudly, trying to explain.

'You're sure she can hear and understand what you are saying? She really doesn't look good,' Nick began, but saw Enoch's hand go up into a stop-talking position.

'Breathe,' Enoch said. 'You are going to pass out, Chloe.'

He was kneeling in front of her now. She could see him, but he was becoming fuzzy.

'Hurry, Xo,' Enoch called.

She closed her eyes and took a deep breath, and then she felt Nick sit next to her and take her hand. Her body knew it was Nick, and her heart began to race in response.

Nick looked at Enoch and asked, 'Does she suffer asthma when she gets a migraine?'

'Not for many years. I thought she had grown out of the asthma. Last time we had to buy a pump was about five years ago. The attacks stopped just after we settled in Howick. She has not had one since.'

'Can she understand what we're saying?'

'Yes,' Enoch said. 'But sometimes she will not remember everything.'

'Come on, Chloe, do as Enoch said, just breathe deeply. Breathe slowly. Regulate it again.'

She could feel the warmth of his fingers on the inside of her wrist, the fingers gentle despite his large hands being calloused from his style of outdoor work. She wanted his hands to stay there forever, making her feel secure. Safe. But he was going away; he was going to leave her —

The air was in her lungs, but she couldn't get it out.

'Don't think, Chloe, just let your body do what comes naturally,' Nick said. He was patting the back of her hand again, the rhythm gentle, reassuring. Soothing.

'Breathe. It is going to be okay,' Enoch said.

She opened her eyes and looked at Enoch. He was breathing deeply, trying to help her get into a normal rhythm again.

'Come on, Princess. Khululani is going to get a fire going, and we can have some sweet coffee and something to eat,' Enoch said.

She wanted to tell him that she didn't need coffee, or smoke, but there was no air in her lungs to speak, and when she opened her mouth, no words were coming out. Something was squeezing her head, making it explode. Something was stealing her oxygen and crushing her as it wrapped around her chest, too.

'I'm not so sure this is asthma. Can I try something? Do you remember that Mike used to help Sarah through the panic attacks she would get when everything was too overwhelming? It might just be one of those,' Nick said.

She heard Enoch give him permission, but they were fading away, and her vision was narrowing.

Nick gathered her in his arms, right up tight against his chest. 'Feel the rhythm of my breathing, Chloe, let your body feel mine. Don't try to do anything except breathe with me. Feel my warmth; it's all yours. You are safe. Feel my arms around you; they're not leaving you. You are safe. Feel my heartbeat.' His hands ran up and down her back as he spoke.

She could smell Nick's scent; she could feel his warmth. The rise and fall of his chest as his lungs breathed in air and let it out normally. His hands continued to rub, only now they were inside her T-shirt, and it was skin on skin.

Heat. Goosebumps. Nick was touching her, and it felt so good. She stopped fighting and relaxed into him.

The pounding in her head wasn't letting up, but feeling Nick against her was helping her chest. There was air coming into her lungs, and the giant coil that held her tightly began to relax.

'That's it,' Nick said. 'All you have to do is feel the rhythm. Relax, don't do anything —'

'Her colour's coming back,' Xo said, 'but we need to get these meds into her. As it is she might be out for a whole day. How's her temperature?'

'She's burning up,' Nick said. 'But her breathing's almost normal.'

'It'll get worse again,' Xo warned. 'Chloe, I'm going to put these in your mouth, and then give you some water to wash them down.'

She felt the pills on her tongue, and when Xo tipped the cup of water into her parched mouth, she tried to swallow. But they just seemed to swell and wouldn't go down her throat.

'Dammit, it took too long to find them,' Xo said. 'Hold her, I need to get them out.' She could feel Xo's fingers in her mouth pulling the pills from the back of her throat.

'Why did you not crush them?' Enoch asked.

'I thought she'd still be able to swallow.' He poured out half the water and threw the pills into the cup, swirling it around. He used his finger to stir it and make sure they had dissolved before carefully putting the cup against her lips and tipping it in.

'Swallow, Chloe,' Xo said, holding her nose closed.

She swallowed the bitter mixture.

He let go of her nose and she gasped for a breath.

Nick held her against him still and she snuggled into the warmth of his body, knowing somewhere in her head that in his arms, she was safe.

Nick held onto Chloe, even though he knew she had now fallen into a drugged sleep.

'She's going to sleep for a day or two at least,' Xo said. 'It's six o'clock now. Her next dose is due in four hours. If you lay her down, I'm happy to take the first watch. Once she is asleep, her temperature will continue to rise. She's been known to run above average temperatures for a week. We need to keep her as cool as we can over the next few days, despite the December heat.'

'It was a good place for one of her migraines to hit if it had to,' Enoch said. 'At least we have good shelter; the feed for the horses that we dumped will not all be gone, and we can use that instead of our stores while we wait it out.'

'We won't continue with her sick?' Nick asked.

Enoch shook his head. 'This is just the beginning. She is about to be really ill, and the cave will help us keep her temperature in check. I do not know why she was struggling to breathe though; that scares me more than her migraine.'

'The talking gibberish is normal?' Nick asked.

'One of her markers. For a few days, she will be totally out of it, drugged to help her. When she wakes up, she will vomit. Then another day to gain her strength after that, and then we can move again.'

'She has to get worse to get better?' Nick asked.

'*Yebo.* It would be good to have you here so that we can do patrols around, help Filipe keep watch while she rests, but I guess now if you and Khululani are still wanting to go see what that explosion was, given where you think it was, it would be a good time. We are not going anywhere, and there is no risk of you losing us in the bush. And if it's anything to do with that bastard, then it's better we know about it. But I fear I am supporting you going looking for trouble. There is a saying that I learned while in South Africa: *Jy krap met ń kort stokkie aan ń groot leeu se bal.*'

'What the heck does that mean?'

'Literally, you are scratching a big lion's bollocks with a short stick. But it really means you are going looking for trouble, you know, pushing your luck.'

'Shit, that's quite a saying. And I hope that you're wrong on this, I really do.'

Nick looked at the ground, then at Chloe in his arms. Her breathing was finally steady, and she was asleep, but he could feel the involuntary twitches in her body.

'What if she doesn't wake up?' Nick asked.

'She will. This one will follow the same path her migraines always have. All we need to do is keep her hydrated and cool, and let the drugs fight the migraine.'

'You sure you've got enough drugs?' Nick asked.

'Plenty,' Xo said. 'She always stocked at least enough for a week, and she hasn't used them in a while,' Xo said.

'I hate to admit that while I don't want to leave her, I don't want to ignore that explosion either. We are all uneasy knowing that the Caçador Escuro is out there, and he's deadly accurate with a rifle from a long way off. We know that he was shot at least in his shoulder, but it could just be a flesh wound. He could be out there already, tracking us, and he could pick us off one by one, and we would never find him.'

Enoch nodded. 'I have been thinking about that, too. But right now, I have to focus on Chloe. We cannot move her, not with what we have available to us. We need to also protect this site in case someone comes here, so three of us patrolling will be hard. It would be easier with five.'

'Two nights away at most, probably less,' Khululani said. 'It's not too far. We'll be back before she wakes up.'

'He's right,' Nick said. 'Khululani and I can move quickly through the bush; we've done it before.'

Enoch nodded. 'Then go. The quicker you leave the faster you are back, for Chloe's sake.'

'Right, Khululani, a quick breakfast then we carry minimal on our trek, and we get back here ASAP,' Nick said.

'Just ...' Enoch paused. 'Be safe and take care. Both of you.' He held out his hand and Nick shook it.

'Don't get shot,' Xo said. 'Chloe will kill me if she wakes up to find you dead. She'll say that I should have stopped you going. Not that anyone could, but she's really growing fond of having you around.'

Fond. Now there was an insipid and inadequate word for how Nick felt towards her.

Holding her again today had been hard. He hadn't wanted to ever let her go. She felt right fitting into him; her soft skin felt perfect against his.

But it was wrong. He couldn't start a relationship with her. Not now. It was his fault that her father was in the state that he was. If he'd gone with them that fateful day instead of staying behind, the outcome might have been different.

If he hadn't stood on his laurels, had been a better friend instead—like Enoch—the outcome with three riding into battle might have been different to having just two there. The odds would have been improved.

Even after all these years, he still didn't believe that the gold that Mike and Enoch had acquired was worth the price they had paid for it. And he didn't understand why Mike was so insistent about going after it in the first place.

Nick had closed his eyes to the death and destruction afterwards. Nothing could hide the fact that Mike was damaged forever. Who knew if his mind was trapped inside his body, or he was gone altogether and only his shell remained. Could he have prevented it? A niggle deep inside was still there. He didn't think that Mike and Enoch had told him everything. They had trusted him enough to ask him to join them, but not told him their whole plan. The motivation behind it, or what they were planning on doing with the gold when they had it.

That was the part that he still didn't understand. And that was what had made him turn his back on them. Leave and start again, away from them all.

It had taken a long time to put that day behind him. To start a new life away from the family. Only to be dragged back into it—and now he was falling for Mike's daughter.

He needed to get away from Chloe. His body had reacted like a man drowning in the scent of a woman when he'd held her. He had to get away. To put some distance between his body and hers so he could get his mind in order.

CHAPTER 27

Xo and Chloe sat under the stars near the dying fire outside the cave. Mike lay on the stretcher, Ethel next to him, giving his legs a rub, while Enoch and Filipe were doing another perimeter check.

'This was a bad one. You were out cold for two whole days, and you are still not looking so good with it. You sure you are okay?' Xo asked.

'Shakes are still here, but only slightly. Nothing compared to yesterday's lot. Otherwise doing good. Thank you as always for watching over me, and sorry for throwing up on you yet again.'

Xo smiled. 'Isn't that what brothers are for?' He raised his hand, and they knocked their fists together.

'I can't believe one hit me on this trek. We've wasted so much time having to stop. Four whole days; we could have been almost inside the Zimbabwe border by now,' she said.

'Not wasted. You've been through a lot lately. Dad took out the stitches in your leg while you were being a sleeping beauty. You didn't even flinch. We figured since it's been two whole weeks that it was time. And they looked ready.'

'I'm glad he did it when I couldn't see.' She rubbed her leg.

'If nothing else, this stop helped you heal. The bruising on your face is so much better, a few yellow patches left, but black eyes are mostly gone. If it wasn't for the short orange hair you would be almost back to normal.' Xo smiled and reached over to rub her arm. 'Besides, it gave Nick and Khululani time to go look for the Caçador Escuro.'

'You think that they're okay? Your dad said they were due back two nights ago. He seemed worried when I asked him. He changed to a different subject like he always does when he doesn't want to talk about something. He started asking me questions about Ethel and Dad and if they were okay.'

Xo smiled. 'He's so good at that, isn't he. Dad thinks they got sidetracked. He said Nick is not the best at simply following orders, and he likes to know the reason behind everything. But as long as Nick is with Khululani, he'll be okay. I'm still astounded at the agility of that old guy. You saw him when Nick needed him off Marin; he just jumped as if he was a youngster. *Eish*, seriously.'

'He's pretty amazing. But then your dad's nearly fifty and he's still so nimble. Must be something in the African genes,' Chloe said.

'Maybe, and even if I'm half as fit as he is when I grow old, then I'll be a happy man,' Xo said.

Chloe attempted to laugh. 'I can imagine you with grey hair, perhaps because Enoch's hair has gone really white in the last few years. And you two look so alike.'

'Thanks, Chloe,' Xo said. 'But I still can't decide who was braver, Khululani for bailing off the back of a horse like that or Marin for carrying them both into battle in the first place.'

'In my eyes, Marin wins hands down every time,' Chloe said. 'He's a good horse. We knew that when we found him. His endurance is outstanding.'

'He proved more than that when we went after the hunter. And I told him that when I groomed him.'

Chloe laughed. 'As if he could understand that, sure ...'

'*Eish*, we each talk to them in our own ways,' Xo said. 'You discuss feelings with them, and I tell them worldly truths.'

They heard a whistle from afar, followed by a guinea fowl, *ripp-peee-peeep-peep*, and Nick's voice came out of the darkness. 'Don't shoot me, I'm coming into range.'

Enoch shouted back, 'We hear you.'

About thirty minutes later, three men walked around the side of the cave.

Along with Enoch, there should have been four men. She frowned. 'Where's Khululani?'

'He's fine. He took a different route,' Nick said as he came and sat next to her. A little closer than where Xo sat on the other side. He reached out and put his hand on her shoulder and gave it a squeeze.

'Good to see you sitting up and talking sense,' he teased.

Chloe could feel the blush rising from her chest.

'You had us worried,' Nick said.

Ethel drew a small blanket over Mike, and then began stoking the fire.

'Thank you, Ethel, but I can fix my own dinner later,' Nick said. 'You're already busy.'

'Mike's asleep. I was just massaging his legs some more before Enoch moves him into the cave for the night. I'll do your dinner; you must be hungry,' she said.

'Thank you,' Nick said, and Ethel passed him a cup of cold tea that she had made earlier and left to steep.

Filipe crouched by the fire, and Enoch sat opposite them. Ethel passed them both some cold tea.

'Are you better now, Chloe?' Nick asked.

'Mostly. I threw up over Xo and have spent the last two days with the shakes, so that's not fantastic, but I hope we can start again tomorrow.'

'Sorry that Khululani and I had to go away.'

'I was sleeping. I didn't know you'd left,' Chloe admitted. 'What did you find? And I don't want to hear a watered-down girlie version. I want the truth.'

Nick nodded. 'We might be in more trouble than we originally thought with this guy.'

Enoch came and sat closer to Nick so he could hear better.

'The explosion was the Caçador Escuro destroying his own *bakkie*,' Nick said.

'*Eish*. That's nuts,' Xo said.

'He's one deranged individual. We cut through the bush to the area where we saw the explosion. He might've been able to burn his vehicle, but the metal still showed the bullet holes. He had burned the lady passenger and someone else, too, to make it look like he was dead as well. She was still in her seat at the time of his torching the vehicle, as we had to chase the hyenas away. They'd pulled her body halfway out of the back window. There were also another vehicle's tracks. It'd pulled over to the side of the road. The bad news is, he didn't go back to Zimbabwe or further into South Africa after he'd destroyed his *bakkie*. He backtracked towards Mapai and parked where he had for his last hunt. He's now on foot and Khululani and I think he's after us.'

'Fuck!' Xo said, putting his hands on his head.

'Watch your mouth,' Enoch said.

'Sorry, Dad,' Xo said immediately.

'He knows how to read spoor well. He followed ours, got a little confused at the grave site, and then trekked back to where our truck had parked. Once he knew we were travelling in a vehicle, he followed us to where the RENAMO guys' tracks crossed over ours and changed direction about an hour and a half north of Mapai, obviously thinking we had gone north, and then turned back. He made a mistake, thank God. He changed direction and followed the RENAMO soldiers in the truck. We followed him for another day, making sure he was heading away from us, then we decided to split up. I came back to continue to travel with you, help keep guard. Khululani is still following after the Caçador Escuro, to shadow him, see where he ends up. If it looks like he's turning our way, then he'll leg it here to give us warning.'

'No offence, but despite Khululani being amazing and fit, he's on foot. How's he supposed to race to us and find us once we move again?' Xo asked.

Nick smiled. 'That man is part of Africa; he can be a tree, he can be the water. He'll find us. The only reason he would ever give up and not keep his word is if he's dead. But the likelihood of that happening is slim. The Caçador Escuro won't even know that Khululani is shadowing him.'

'This is an interesting development,' Enoch said. 'When we left, we thought that if we could just get to Zimbabwe, we would be safe from the SAP. Now we have to get to Zimbabwe and make sure that this Caçador Escuro never finds us. It seems the further we go, the more trouble we get ourselves into. We really did poke the lion's balls!'

'What?' Chloe said.

Enoch quickly explained as they all started to laugh. It helped break the growing tension within the group.

Nick coughed. 'Trouble used to be my middle name, but I hope that with all of us watching, we can make sure that the Caçador Escuro doesn't get close enough.'

No longer laughing either, Enoch shook his head. 'This is worse than I thought could happen. We will be constantly wondering if we are in his crosshairs now.'

Chloe woke to the quiet murmur of Enoch and Nick speaking. She could feel that she was held tightly against Nick, his arm over her back, keeping her close to him. She could feel his breathing and the deep vibrations when he spoke as her head was on his chest. Not wanting to move but knowing that soon she would have to, she stayed still for a moment listening.

'You have to tell her, Enoch,' Nick was saying. 'She deserves to know what happened, and more importantly, why.'

'It's not your secret to tell. You made your decision then,' Enoch said.

'I did, and I have learned to live with the consequences of that. But if you get killed on this journey? What then?'

'Then you tell her,' Enoch said.

'I don't know everything. That's the point. And if we both die? It's not as if Mike can communicate and explain everything to her. What about Xo? You telling me you never discussed what happened with him either? He's a grown man.'

'Leave Xo out of it.'

'Why? If you die, doesn't some of the gold belong to him?'

'No. The gold is Mike's. It always has been,' Enoch said.

'Well, Mike can't exactly do anything with it now, can he? It's Chloe that'll have to answer any weird police charges if anyone remembers when you guys return.'

'*If* anyone remembers. Grace said there had only ever been one police officer come sniffing around.'

'That's one too many. Chloe has no idea what she's heading back into. You of all people must understand you might not have the luxury of time. The hunter is out there. There are dissidents rumoured to be Mugabe's 5th Brigade running around Matabeleland, murdering everyone. You were a Rhodesian

Grey's Scout. They'll think of you as a threat, too. I'm not so sure that Delaware is as safe as you all hope it will be.'

'I will tell her when I am ready,' Enoch said.

Chloe decided enough was enough. 'Tell me what?' she said.

'How much have you heard?' Enoch asked.

'Enough to know it's time you told Xo and me what happened,' she said. 'Because if you do die, there are so many things that will be left unsaid between us that you will not cross over to the other side. You will haunt the earth forever. A lost spirit.' She took a big breath. 'Enoch, we need to talk about what happened on the day Dad had his accident. The truth. I want to know the whole story.'

'Told you we should not have been talking with her close by,' Enoch said.

'I'm going to wake Xo, and you're going to have a family chat.'

Enoch's shoulders slumped. 'You are like a tsetse fly; you keep on and on. You are never going to allow me any peace if I do not, are you?'

'No,' Nick said, giving Chloe's shoulder a squeeze. 'Not anymore. I'm going into the cave and Xo is coming out. Talk. All your lives are in danger, and you can't have unfinished business and regrets if you die.'

'Nick, you need to come back and listen too; you are right. Perhaps by having this out in the open, it can help heal both you and me, because it certainly can't help Mike,' Enoch said.

'Thanks. There are questions I still have that are unanswered, too,' Nick admitted.

Enoch stared into the fire as they waited for Nick to return with Xo.

Within minutes, Xo walked out of the cave and went to sit next to his father. 'Dad, Nick just told me you want to talk to us about the day that Mike was hurt.'

Enoch shook his head. He stood up and paced a few steps before sitting down again. He chewed the side of his thumb nail.

'My son, and Chloe,' he began, 'the daughter who loves her father, and as a daughter who loves me, a simple black man. I need you both to know that deep down inside we were always good people. Before the madness.'

Chloe said, 'I know you are still a good person, Enoch.'

'Dad …' Xo's voice broke.

Enoch took in a deep breath and then let it out. 'I knew this day would come. I have dreaded each day waiting for you both to push for the answer. It eats inside me, like maggots on rotten flesh, but I dread telling you. I do not want to see the light that you both hold in your eyes for me dim and turn to hatred.'

Chloe reached across and took Enoch's hand. 'I can never hate you, but I need the truth, Enoch. I deserve to know what happened.'

'Whatever it is, Dad, you need to tell us. We're adults. You can stop trying to protect us. We can make up our own minds when you explain,' Xo said.

Enoch wiped the sweat from his forehead. 'This is mostly for Chloe. I tried so hard to keep you out of it. I never wanted you tainted, Xo.'

Xo nodded his head.

'I'm listening,' Chloe said.

Nick sat down on the other side of her and took her hand in his.

Enoch sighed. 'That day is burned into my memory …'

Mike passed Enoch a bottle of water from the Coleman. 'Chloe's going to love that last jump you and Xo constructed,' Mike said.

'I think they are nuts to jump up and out of a riverbed like that, but then I have become more cautious now that I am older, and do not bounce quite as well as the children,' Enoch said.

Mike laughed. 'It's been many years since either of us bounced. Now when I hit the dirt, it hurts like hell.'

'Who would have thought that we would be getting older,' Enoch said.

'Glad you said old*er*. I don't feel old. Not unless I fall off Diablo, then I feel as if every bone in my body is breaking.'

'That is because he is over sixteen hands tall. It is far for anyone to fall from up there.'

Mike laughed. 'I think Diablo must have been a throwback to some thoroughbred that was also loose on that farm. Seriously, Zonda couldn't be his sire.'

'That, or you overfed him as a foal. You bottle-fed him around the clock after his mum died! That's how he got so tall, too much milk.'

'That was a sad day when we lost that mare,' Mike said, shaking his head.

As they came towards the fence, the maid Milly was running towards them. '*Baas* Mike, *Baas* Mike. Telephone. The man said it is very urgent.'

Enoch watched Mike taking the steps two at a time, and running into the study area where the phone was. Enoch waited outside the door.

'We need to get to the hospital. Sarah's hurt,' Mike said as he headed back outside.

Enoch nodded, and together they ran for the *bakkie*. Enoch went to the driver's door and stopped Mike getting into the seat. 'I will drive; you are too upset.'

'Fine,' Mike said, 'you always drive faster anyway.'

They reached the hospital at breakneck speed and rushed into the ER waiting area.

'My name is Mike Mitchell. I was told my wife is here,' he said to the nurse at the counter.

She looked at a chart on the wall. 'They've taken her into surgery—they couldn't wait.'

Mike ran his hand through his hair. 'Can you tell me anything else?'

The nurse read the chart. 'She was unconscious when the ambulance brought her in. She was brought in with another patient, who's also in the emergency rooms, and there was a security guard—who's also in a bad state, who they took to Impendla Hospital.'

'Do you know anything about what happened?'

'Sorry, but I can let you through to wait in her cubicle. The doctor will come back there once she's finished in surgery.'

'Thanks,' Mike said as the nurse led them through to wait in the curtained-off portion of the ER, before going back to her desk.

Mike sat in the chair and Enoch stood.

'Wait a moment, she said "another patient". The only other white person at the mine this week was Andy Pryor because of the work stoppage. Andy is here too,' Mike said, beginning to walk through the emergency room, opening curtains one by one until he found him.

Andy had a bandage on his head, and the doctor was finishing putting plaster on his arms, which had been broken. A nasty cut above his left eye had already been stitched closed.

'What happened?' Mike asked.

'Mike,' Andy said.

'What happened?'

'I don't know. I don't remember.'

'Bullshit,' Mike said, taking a step towards him. 'What happened? Was there a riot? Yesterday it was just a peaceful work stoppage. What did you do to make it turn into a blood bath?'

'Sir, I'll have to ask you to leave—or I will get security to come and remove you,' the doctor was saying over and over.

Enoch tapped Mike on his elbow and tried to guide him back into the waiting area. 'Brother. Come with me.' His insistence eventually managed to break through the haze that Mike was in.

'This isn't finished. I want answers,' Mike said as he turned and walked away with Enoch.

'Come sit,' Enoch said when they were back in Sarah's cubicle. 'I think we will get more answers from the mine's security guard. You stay here, and I will go and talk to him in Impendla after we know what is happening with Sarah.'

Mike nodded and sat down. 'I know that Andy had something to do with it. That man is terrible to his staff. I want to know what he did that pushed those men over the edge and caused them to riot. To get Sarah hurt. This is his fault, and he's going to pin it on the workers; just wait. I bet you anything his bad work ethics won't be questioned here, and once again they'll all be swept under the mat.'

'We don't know that yet,' Enoch said. 'You'll need proof if you are going to say something like that against him.'

The doctor came into the emergency cubicle. 'Mr Mitchell, can you come with me, please?'

Enoch watched Mike walk into a private waiting room. He walked closer. With the mood Mike was in, anything could happen, and he would rather be on hand just in case.

Through the window, Enoch saw Mike kick a trolley full of medical equipment, which toppled over. Enoch burst into the room, taking the doctor by surprise as he held Mike in a grip around his arms, and while he didn't struggle, he was swearing and breathing hard.

Enoch looked at the doctor. 'What happened with Sarah?'

'She didn't make it,' the doctor said. 'I'm sorry—we did everything we could.'

'When can he see Sarah?' Enoch asked.

'That won't be possible,' the doctor said.

Enoch shook his head, still holding Mike. 'Make it happen, or I will let him loose.'

'I'll see what I can do,' the doctor said, backing down.

'Better,' Enoch said as the doctor left the room.

Mike had quietened and now sat on the edge of a chair, while Enoch stood close by.

Sometime later the doctor came back into the room. 'Follow me.'

They walked into a private ward, where a body with a sheet rested on the bed. The doctor left them in the room and excused himself.

Enoch's heart broke when he saw Mike lift the sheet to find Sarah's head wrapped in blood-stained bandages. Mike took the sheet down further. She was dressed in a hospital gown, and while all the tubes and needles had been removed, it was clear that she'd only been hastily cleaned to allow them to see her as quickly as possible.

At least Mike could hold her one last time as he sat on the bed next to her, put his nose to hers and broke down.

Enoch left him there and returned to the *bakkie*. He drove to Impendla Hospital, which was reserved for the black population—although that would hopefully change with the New Zimbabwe. He got directions to Sammy Mabiza's ward from the nurse on duty.

He found the security guard, Sammy, lying on a bed in a shared ward surrounded by beds filled with strangers. He had no family or friends around him for support. He had bandages around his head and chest, and his hands were both bandaged. His left shoulder was strapped to keep it upright. The man had taken a severe beating from what Enoch could see.

He approached the bed with respect.

'*Salibonani. Linjani?* Can I visit with you? I am a friend of Sarah Mitchell.'

The old man turned his head and nodded, and he smiled as best he could with his swollen lips and face. '*Siyaphila. Unjani wena?*'

'*Sikhona.*' Enoch smiled. Even though the old man was hurt, he was still sticking to their formal traditional greeting.

'How is Madam Sarah?' Sammy asked.

'She is on the other side now. But I can see that you are in great pain.'

Enoch watched as Sammy tried to hold in his emotions and failed, and tears welled in his yellowing eyes.

'*Uxolo*,' Sammy said. 'I tried to protect her, I tried.'

Enoch chose his words carefully. Although he and Mike treated each other as equals, he was still seen as 'Mike's boy' by many of the people in their country. A time would eventually come when that would hopefully change, but not today. Sammy was old, so Enoch needed to appeal to the man's traditional ways. Older people deserved respect, and they were not usually questioned.

'I see that,' Enoch said. 'That is what I came to ask you about. I wanted to know what happened at the mine. How my madam got hurt? I know my madam—she is a good woman. She is a friend to everyone. Why did the workers hurt her?'

'She tried to leave. *Baas* Pryor, he told me not to *vula* the gate if the men outside got cross. I told her to go back inside where it was made of bricks and it was safe. When they came through the fence, she couldn't get back inside.'

'How come?'

'It was locked from the inside. She was between all the workers and the door. I tried to protect her with my body, but they had shovels, *gwaza* and *knobkieries*. They were like *tokoloshe* and wouldn't listen because they had bad, bad news, and they were *ngxama*. Angry.'

'What news?'

'Jacob Ntuli, their representative, was killed during the night. Men came to his *ikhaya*, dragged him outside and beat him in front of his wife and children, then when he was dead, they drove away.'

'That's terrible,' Enoch said.

'The workers, they said it was a Sunshine Gold Mine *bakkie*. They are saying that *Baas* Andy organised for Jacob to be silenced.'

'Surely the police were called?' Enoch said. 'They will catch and punish whoever was responsible.'

'They do not believe that the police would do anything about one more black man who was dead. They are busy with more important matters.'

'But when they had gone into the building, how did the mine stop the riot if you were hurt?'

'The police came with the *inja*, but only after they had got inside the building. Madam Sarah and I were on the outside. Still, I was lying on top to protect her. I do not know what happened. When they got through the door, I dragged madam around the corner so that they could not hurt her anymore.'

'I am thankful for you trying to look after my madam, for attempting to keep her safe. I am indebted to you for taking it all on yourself to protect her with your life. You are not a young man; you will not get better fast from this beating. I will make sure that you have food and blankets in the hospital. Where is your wife and family? I can arrange for them to come here,' Enoch said.

'Your madam was lucky to have you in her life,' Sammy said, and told him where to find his wife.

Enoch nodded. 'I was lucky she was in the life of my white brother-but-one. But there is much I do not understand in what you have told me. I need to know who locked my madam out of the building. It is their fault that she is dead. They share equal blame with the miners who hurt both of you.'

The old man looked down. Understanding what Enoch was asking, but obviously torn between loyalty to his *baas,* the man who ensured he got paid, and telling the truth.

Enoch had his answer. 'Was there anyone else inside the building with *Baas* Andy Pryor?'

Sammy slowly shook his head.

CHAPTER 28

'Your mother, she was caught in the wrong place at the wrong time, and crushed by the workers when they were rioting,' Enoch said.

Chloe slumped back on the log.

'The manager of the mine, Andy Pryor, he caused the dispute, and then had the main instigators of the work stoppage beaten. Which in a country only just turned from white to black rule, was the worst thing to do. About a month after Sammy left hospital, his wife came to Delaware to tell us that men had come in the night, and he was also dead now.

'Your father, he visited Pryor at the mine and told him to pay compensation for Sarah's death and to Sammy's family, because he knew that Pryor had caused both deaths. But Pryor refused. Mike told Pryor that he needed to understand what it was like to have everything you love torn away from you because of the stupidity of another man. Pryor just laughed at him.

'Mike and I; we decided to teach Andy Pryor a lesson. We invited Nick to join us, as the plan really needed three people to make it work. Nick had lived through a lot in the Scouts. He was unbreakable, and he was dependable, but mostly, his mind was strong. He saw things during the war, and yet he would sleep through the night. His hands, I never saw them shake. He is like Mike, a good man. But we underestimated Nick's resolve. He would not have anything to do with the raid we had planned. He tried to talk us out of it. He told us that it would not work, and it was unfair on you two if we also died that day, or worse, if we were caught. That you both only had one parent each now, and that we needed to think of that, not Sarah. She was already dead, and nothing could hurt her anymore.

'On the day we went to raid the payroll of the mine, he stayed at Delaware to protect you two. We left Nick with documents signing over guardianship of Chloe, and a promise to look after Xo as he was already sixteen, along with instructions to leave the country if anything went wrong. To take you guys to safety.

'Mike knew that Grace would never leave the farm, so he could not leave Chloe to her, as much as the decision pained him. He did not want Chloe to hear anything bad in the papers or at school if we failed. Nick could keep you two away from the fallout if we were caught; he swore he would.'

'Nick was going to be my guardian?' Chloe asked.

'Only if we were caught, or dead, and that did not happen. Mike and I, we used our horses. We hurt Pryor where it counted. In his pocket. His only love was money, gold. That is what he held dearest. We took the gold as ransom for compensation for the death of Sarah and Sammy. But then things went wrong.

'Maria got shot by the guards and fell on top of Mike. He took her full weight when she rolled over him. Where most people would have died, his love for you, Chloe, was too strong. He would not leave you an orphan. Instead, he lived as a vegetable to pay for the crime. But Maria, she got up, like a true war horse. I pulled Mike onto Monsoon and Maria followed—she did not even scream then. When we got to the truck, I got them inside.

'In the end, we lost both Maria and Monsoon. They were injured badly by the guards but kept going. I could not save them and treat Mike, so I had to shoot our horses in the cattle truck, and then I brought Mike home, past the police who were rushing towards where we had just committed the crime. I did not think Mike would live, not with the weight that he had taken on his head, but I did not want to get us caught.

'I should have gone to the hospital first, but instead, I came home. Nick and I, we cleaned Mike up so that the police wouldn't suspect him. Then I drove him in the *bakkie* to the hospital, and said that he had fallen from his horse while riding on the farm. Nick stayed at Delaware to look after you and

Xo. Nick helped me to bury both horses that day, after I got back. Well, you know that part.' He looked at Nick.

'But you got the gold from Andy Pryor for the ransom?' Chloe asked.

Enoch nodded his head. 'Before I could contact Pryor and call him out for the ransom money, I found out that he was dead. I buried the gold. I paid some money to Sammy's wife every month until she died last year. I know that on that day, not only did I lose my best friend, but I lost my soul. Because what was supposed to be returned could not be, and therefore I had stolen. I had become a thief.'

Chloe and Xo both sat still, staring at Enoch. Nick squeezed Chloe's hand.

'That day—Chloe, you lost not only your mother and everything good that she stood for, but you lost your father, too. That gold, it is payment alright. It is payment from Pryor for three souls.'

'What happened to Andy Pryor?' Chloe asked.

'The workers of the mine took care of him. When he would not pay them, they came looking for him again, and he was not so lucky that time round. He had told the papers he believed it was an inside job and his workers did not deserve to be paid, that they had already taken enough gold. He never even accepted responsibility for Sarah's or Sammy's death. He died believing that he was a victim, but knowing that his precious gold was vulnerable. The next manager who came in paid off all the workers, and then shut down the mine. There were rumours that Andy Pryor had been embezzling from the mine, too, but Grace has followed the story and passed on the parts I needed to know about. Even after all this time, nothing has been proved, and the mine sits quiet and empty.'

Chloe pulled her hand out of Nick's. 'Nick, you knew that they were going after the gold, and you chose not to be a part of it? Not to help them?'

'Nick felt strongly that it was not the right way to go about sorting out the problem,' Enoch said. 'Please remember—we never meant to keep it. It was only meant as ransom until Andy Pryor admitted publicly that he was responsible for Sarah's death. Nick was never onboard with the idea of the robbery, nor the ransom and threatening of Andy Pryor. I cannot even remember if we told him that part. Mike was too consumed with grief and wanting revenge on Andy to consider the law, and I would have done anything I could to help Mike, even if it meant doing something crazy like we did.

'Nick was right. He said if we were patient, we could find another way to hurt Pryor, but we wouldn't listen. In the end, there was a lot of gold, much more than we thought there would be. Much more than for just the wage run of the mine. We never found out why there was so much there—I think that there was some truth in the rumours of Andy Pryor embezzling, and we happened to stumble into it. The only problem then, was if I went public with the find, Mike and I would be punished for our part, and whoever else had their fingers in the same pie as Pryor would never be held accountable either.'

'I would kill Pryor myself if he wasn't dead already,' Chloe said fiercely.

'No, Chloe. There has been enough killing,' Enoch said. 'This was never meant to affect you and Xo. It was a mistake, and this family has paid a big enough price.'

Chloe shook her head. 'That son of a bitch. He took my mother and father from me. I'm thinking that if I could get my hands on just one of the workers who hurt my mum, I would string him up,' she said as she slammed her fist into her open hand.

Enoch stood up, walked to her and wrapped his arms around her. He held her as she sobbed into his shoulder. 'It's not fair, Enoch. It's not fair.'

'No, it is not. But do not blame the workers. You need to know that your mother was never supposed to be hurt. She was not their target. Pryor failed to keep her safe that day, like he should have,' Enoch said as he comforted her. 'There is no use trying to take revenge. Learn from what happened to Mike and me. Learn from us that sometimes friends can be right about an outcome, even if you are blind to it and do not want to listen. Nick was adamant that there was a way we could prove that Pryor was guilty, but we did not want to take the time. We wanted instant gratification. To Mike and me, it was a simpler solution that appealed: he hurt Sarah, and we wanted him to hurt too.'

'You could've been killed,' Xo said quietly.

Enoch looked at his son. 'Mike was my brother. Skin colour never mattered to us. He would have looked after you, and we might even have landed up in the same town in South Africa looking for help to try to fix me if it had happened the other way round.' He reached out his hand, and Xo stood up and put his arms around both Chloe and Enoch.

'We still have the same problem. If we give the gold back, Dad's sacrifice is worth nothing,' Chloe said.

'If we give the gold back, then some other fat cat will profit from it,' Enoch said. 'The mine will never admit responsibility for your mother's death. And even now, returning it will not bring her back, will not undamage your father. Only if you decide to use it, it should ensure that we can always look after those who need help, like Sammy's wife.'

'Half of it is yours,' Chloe said. 'What are you going to do with it?'

'This was never about me owning any of the gold. I am just sorry that Pryor never acknowledged that he was the one responsible for Sarah's death. The mine should have been held accountable instead of all the workers. What happened after that night—Mike getting hurt, me burying the gold, destroying Nick's faith in us—none of that was ever supposed to happen.'

Chloe released her hold on Enoch and sat back down. 'We have bars of gold buried at Delaware—that's what I see in my nightmares. You are burying gold. All this time I thought maybe you had buried someone.'

'No. Never. We did not murder anyone,' Enoch said. 'Nick and I buried the horses, and he did not want to know where the gold was buried. I did not even show you and Xo because I did not want you tainted by it. Even if something happened to me, you were better off not knowing.'

'We have *bars*—as in multiple bars of gold?' Chloe asked.

'*Yebo*,' Enoch said.

'How do we cash it in without getting caught? Melted down, we could sell it, launder it into cash, and use it?' Chloe asked.

'You need to think on this very carefully,' Enoch warned. 'The glitter of gold and wealth from it is alluring, but some might believe that if you touch that gold, your soul is as dirty as mine, who stole it. Some might believe your father and I earned it. It's all a matter of perspective. You need to carefully consider the price you would be willing to pay, should the need arise,' Enoch said. 'I have not told you about the gold to make you see dollar signs in your eyes. I have told you because if I die on this journey home, I need to know that your nightmares have stopped, Chloe, and that I have made peace with both of you, that my spirit will not become trapped here on earth, and that one day, with much hard work, I will be forgiven by my ancestors for the foolish thing that Mike and I did.'

Chloe looked from Enoch to Nick and back again. 'So, if I go and dig up that gold, I'm damned in both your and Nick's eyes? Is that what this is all about?'

'You need to understand that when we get to Zim, the SAP might stop coming after me—but there is always a chance that the Zimbabwe Republic Police could for the theft of that gold, and while none of the men that we shot with the tranquilliser darts died, they were sick for a long time afterwards.'

'You shot them with tranquilliser darts?' Xo asked.

'Yes. The darts were Nick's idea so that we did not kill anyone by accident. We removed a lot of the opioid, too, so we wouldn't overdose anyone. It just took a while for one or two of them to go to sleep, so we could load the gold, and they got a radio message off that they were under attack. That was the part we underestimated in the whole plan. But looking back, I am glad that we never killed any of the guards.'

'That you know of. This doesn't mean I'm not still mad at you for doing such a stupid thing, Dad,' Xo said.

Enoch cupped the back of Xo's head and put his forehead against his son's. 'I'm still mad at me, too.'

Nick sat next to Chloe. He had both his hands resting underneath his chin, and he stared deep into the fire.

Chloe shook her head. 'All these years of nightmares, of being scared of something that wasn't real. And now finally knowing that you didn't kill anyone, Enoch, that I don't have to lie to protect you if anyone asks. I should feel relief, and I do, but it's tinged with a sadness that you took so long to trust Xo and me and tell us the whole story. I suppose it all doesn't matter now. Not when it's all nothing compared to the reality of knowing that now we're out in the open, on the run and definitely being hunted by a psychopathic killer.'

The luggage they were leaving behind was safely stored in the cave where they'd camped. Thornbushes had been piled up to hide the entrance once again, and all the tracks around brushed away so that anyone who came looking would hopefully not see that they had sheltered there for almost a week.

The feed that they'd left by the side of the road had already been scattered, and what hadn't been eaten by the elephants and horses would be found by the other animals of the bush soon enough.

They assembled their horses and pointed them in a north-west direction as they began their slow walk home.

With Khululani not needing a horse, that left them five horses, seven people and lots of luggage, including a fair share of ammunition that they wouldn't leave behind, to move through the bush.

Filipe scouted in front on foot. He carried his backpack and his AK-47 for protection as always.

Enoch led Kimberlite, who was packed with travel gear, while Chloe led Diablo with Mike sitting astride. Enoch had fashioned a strap to keep Mike's legs in the stirrup, so he was basically attached to his saddle. Mike looked around as if he knew where they were going. Next was Ethel sitting nervously on Pampero's back, and finally Xo followed with Marin and Sirocco. Nick, at the rear, was constantly checking for signs that the Caçador Escuro or anyone else might be following them.

The horses were loaded like pack mules of another era, and Enoch, Xo and Nick each wore backpacks. There was one strapped onto the outside of Marin's load, ready for Khululani when he caught up with them.

They walked for several hours at a steady pace along the track that the elephants had left, which kept them heading north, and while they went through thorn-tree forests, they saw their first big baobab tree, with its huge bottle bottom, sticks of branches reaching for the hot African sun. There were remnants of the blossoms that hung downwards. The once white petals were already browning, and some had slid down the pistils and fallen to the ground. A small duiker was eating in the shade of the great tree, but quickly darted away when it realised they were close.

'Good thing we are passing here during the day. These trees stink at night when they are in flower,' Enoch said.

'I've never seen one flower,' Chloe said as she gazed up into the tree, with its green leaves high above her.

'You see those big green nuts? They open at night and the flowers come out, ready for the insects and bats to pollinate them.'

'I remember eating these with Dad, and you, Xo, do you remember?' Chloe said.

'I do,' Xo said. 'They were bitter.'

'Look at the marks on the trunk,' Chloe said, 'what do you think did that?'

'Bullet holes,' Nick said as he walked closer to have a look. 'Someone used this tree for target practice. Doesn't seem to have gone too far in; the fibres are pretty tough,' Nick said as he ran his hand over a few of the marks.

'Guess we will start to see more as we enter into the lowveld area,' Enoch said, turning his back on the tree and carrying on.

They walked through thickets of bush, then on into an open area of sporadic grasslands, where Enoch called a break under some large trees at the edge.

'Filipe, did you see any water coming up? Any streams?' Enoch asked when Filipe walked back to rejoin them.

'No, nothing.'

Nick said, 'There must be water here somewhere. Those elephants who passed us by would not go for more than a day without water.'

Filipe nodded. 'I didn't see it, but it doesn't mean it's not there.'

They decanted water for the horses from one of the jerry cans they carried into the tub and watered them one by one.

'We only have enough water left to last for half a day at the most. The horses will need more water now that they are loaded. Perhaps you should scout ahead and find where it is,' Enoch said.

'On it,' Filipe said as he drained the last of his tea from his cup before carefully putting it back into his pack, along with a packet of sliced biltong that he had been nibbling on for lunch. 'I have seen no other signs of RENAMO in this area. It's as if they have just disappeared.'

Chloe shook her head. 'I'll leave them to you. Right now, I'm just trying to put one foot in front of the other.'

Xo grinned. 'Come on, it's not that bad. We've been through some stunning forests today. This is a beautiful land. The stone structures are incredible, and the wildlife—I can't believe there's still so much wildlife here, despite the war.'

Enoch said, 'We saw so little until now—either we are closer to Zimbabwe and the game reserve than we thought, or it could be that we are close to where there is water.'

'Aren't there fences around Gonarezhou?' Chloe asked.

'There are supposed to be, at least around some of it. But do not make the mistake of thinking that they are in any state of good repair. It has been closed for many years, through the Rhodesian Bush War. The last I heard, there was such bad poaching there that no one knew if there would be any animals left alive to be saved if they ever opened it again,' Enoch said.

Xo made sure that Ethel was once again seated comfortably on Pampero.

'That's really sad,' Chloe said as Xo put his hand out to pull her up from where she was still sitting on the ground. She dusted off her pants and picked up Xo's pack. 'You sure you don't want me to take this for a little while?'

'I'm sure. We can't chance your migraine coming back, but you can help put it on,' he said as she settled it onto his back. 'I'll let you know if I have any problems, promise.' He smiled as he took the lead reins from Nick.

Only once Enoch had checked everyone was safe, secure and ready, did he hoist his pack onto his back and take point again, walking out from under the coolness of the trees into the excessive heat of summer.

They were walking through a herd of impala. The animals milled around, snacking on the grass, their black-and-white tails flashing up and down as they stamped their feet to remove the annoying flies and other insects that buzzed around them. Chloe had always been a fan of the gentle impala with their shiny black noses when she was younger. She hadn't realised how much she'd missed seeing them when they had moved to Howick.

The impala didn't seem worried that the caravan of horses and people were travelling through their herd, and the horses didn't seem to mind the strange-looking miniature cattle.

Chloe tripped on some unseen hump under the trampled grass, and Diablo held his head steady as if waiting to help her if needed. She decided it'd be a good idea to keep her head down, her eyes on the ground, and concentrate on where to put her feet. So, when Enoch spoke, she visibly jumped.

'Keep your horse steady, breathe naturally, don't share your fear of seeing a lion with him,' Enoch warned as they walked.

'Where?' Chloe said, immediately looking up again and around.

'Lioness, at one o'clock, just walking along, minding her own business,' Enoch said as if seeing lions was an everyday affair.

Chloe took her rifle from her shoulder, chambered a round, then held it with the barrel facing upwards but ready, in case the big cat did something stupid, and she needed to fire a warning shot.

'Keep a steady pace,' Enoch said.

'Easy for you to say, Dad,' Xo said from behind her. 'Your horse knows lions. My two are not happy.'

'They will become accustomed to them,' Enoch said.

Chloe looked at the lioness again. She was ignoring them—for now. But where there was one lioness, there were usually more. She looked around, scanning the small grass land they were in. 'At three o'clock, there's another one sneaking through the grass.'

She put her finger in her mouth, covered it in spit then brought it out. The air felt cooler on the back of her finger. Good, they were downwind from the lions, so they wouldn't smell them, and probably couldn't hear them either.

'Seven o'clock, by the big, downed tree,' Xo said as he picked up another one. Chloe looked for the tell-tale sign of the lion. Sure enough, there was another lioness slinking down and moving into attack position near the herd.

This one could be trouble—it was downwind from them.

She caught the movement of the lioness at seven o'clock, in the corner of her vision, as her tail slammed down, and the cat began her chase. They could see that there was a young impala calf in trouble, skilfully separated from the herd by the lions who had now crossed in front of their caravan. It didn't take long before it was lying on the ground and the three lionesses were on top of it, finishing it off, its anguished bleating silenced.

The Impala herd slowed, and the ram barked to his harem. They seemed to mill around slowly and began to settle once again. The lionesses had something to eat, so the impala considered themselves off the menu—for now at least.

The lionesses were making short work of the small carcass when a male from their pride arrived. He was an impressive size, and a large black mane adorned his neck. He was battle-scarred across his nose, with patches of hair turned to scar tissue over the years. The lionesses snarled and sneered but gave up the carcass to him when he chased them away with a noisy roar of dominance. In typical male-lion style, he didn't want to share the meal. Snarling and swiping at the females, he moved on possessively to the small kill. But as the group watched, slowly, the lionesses came back one by one and continued to feast on the tender meat.

'That little snack is not going to keep them going for long,' Chloe said.

'No, and lions in the area are going to make camping tonight interesting,' Enoch said. 'We push on for another half an hour, then we set up camp. We have to have time to build a strong boma to keep the lions out. Hopefully, Filipe will have found us water by then.'

Chloe turned one last time to look at the kill as they walked out on the other side of the grassland and into some thick bushes. She always felt sad when she watched lions take down any animal, even though it was necessary for them to live. She put her hand on her own stomach and wondered what she would do for her child, if she ever had one, and if she would be like a mother impala and just leave it once the lions got hold of it, or if she would be more like the buffalo mothers, who would challenge the lions head-on, and fight them to try to save their baby. She hoped if it ever happened, that it was the latter.

An image of Nick with her child filled her mind, and she shook her head to get rid of it. She still wasn't sure what to make of the situation. After the stuff that Enoch had revealed, Nick had been distant from her. She had no idea how to broach it with him, but figured he would need to sort out whatever memories Enoch's confession had triggered in his own time. She would just have to hope that he knew she was there for him if he needed her.

CHAPTER 29

Kupua tapped her nail on her diary. Hunter #4 was late checking in from his hunt with member Nicole Schaffer. She heard the ring of the fax on the machine in her office and watched as it began printing.

'What have you got yourself into?' she murmured, walking out of her door and down the passage to the chairperson's office. She knocked quietly.

'Enter,' the chairperson said.

'*Guete morge*. Looks like we were right to keep a tighter control of the hunters. Hunter #4 is in trouble in Africa,' Kupua said, handing over the fax.

'This does not look good. Two bodies burnt in a truck. One identified as our member. The other has yet to be identified. Do you think it could be #4?'

'I have a feeling he is going to be craftier than that. There have been mounting reports of the South African Police looking into killings outside the Kruger Park area. Corpses with bullets dug out of them. There is no intelligence coming in from any of the surrounding countries. Other than Botswana, everyone else in that region is experiencing some form of civil war, so other priorities are taking preference at the moment. It's Africa.'

The chairperson massaged her temples. 'It displeases me that we were right. But I was expecting the next one in trouble to be the big Russian, not the Brit.'

'I think you underestimate the Russian. He will be the last one to need help. I must be honest—it surprises me that #4 is in this predicament in the first place. I am curious as to the story behind how he lost a member of the 6th. I'll fly out to South Africa and find out what has happened. I'll start at the morgue, then onto where the police reports came from, in a place called Phalaborwa. If he is not that other body in the truck, I will find him,' Kupua said.

'You have all the 6th contacts there in order to clean house if needed?'

'South Africa, Mozambique, Botswana and Zimbabwe should not be a problem. I'm confident that my contacts will have a way around any inconveniences.'

'Take the Society's jet. Wheels up within two hours if you can. The sooner you get there and sort out what is happening the better. I'm not happy he lost a client. What was he doing in Mozambique? What were they doing in a war zone?'

'Same thing the soldiers were doing, only not taking sides,' Kupua said as she made to leave the room.

'Kupua, be safe,' the chairperson said. 'The last thing we need is for our master of the hunt to be in jeopardy.'

'I will be fine, Madame,' Kupua said. 'When have I ever let my Hawaiian ancestors down? I am Kupua. I may not be a demigod, but I'm the best at what I do. We will get the outcome we require for the good of the Society. It won't be long before I'll be back home to Bern, my hunters in line again.'

CHAPTER 30

Asian Top 6 Trophies

1. Tur
2. Red stag
3. Roe deer
4. Marco Polo argali
5. Brown bear
6. Man

Indian Top 6 Trophies

1. Black, brown and sloth bear
2. Gaur
3. Indian rhino
4. Asian elephant
5. Indian tiger
6. Man

CHAPTER 31

They had been walking through the bush for four days since leaving the cave. Luckily, the evening thunderstorm on the first night out had provided them with catchment water to fill the jerry cans, but once again, they were running low. Today, they finally walked through the tall reeds that grew along the bank and let the horses drink from the water running slowly in the narrow river that wound through the vast tracts of sand. The river would be formidable when in flood, but for now, it was a welcome relief.

'This is the Nuanetsi River,' Enoch said as he looked at the map they carried with them.

'I'd say we're about here,' Nick said. 'A stone's throw from the Zimbabwe border.'

Filipe nodded his head.

'We follow this and we're home?' Chloe asked.

'Not quite. We will go into Sengwe Communal Land. At least someone there will have a telephone, or they will have a bus that can take us to one. I thought we were further north than we are, and this might actually make it easier,' Enoch said.

'Not easier. There are more mines here than further north,' Filipe said. 'Now that we are travelling on the animal tracks, it's going faster, but I worry about booby traps as we get closer to the border.'

'We need to be vigilant, watch for spoor in the tracks, look for any small mounds. The rain might have washed the looser disturbed sand away, anything that does not look right. I would rather be more cautious than run into trouble,' Enoch said.

'As long as the trails are used by game, the chances of us stepping on a mine are slim, so if we stick to the used ones, we'll be okay,' Filipe said.

'So, we take turns being in the front?' Xo asked.

'It is not always the first person to step on the mine,' Enoch said.

'Oh great,' Xo said.

'I'm safe up here from them,' Ethel said, 'and so is Mike. The worst we can do is fall off if the horse steps on one, which wouldn't be good either.'

The small group got themselves reorganised, and soon were walking in single file down the animal track, alongside the river. They saw no one for the next two days. They pushed hard to get as far as they could during the day, knowing that the Caçador Escuro could have changed directions at any time and be coming after them.

They passed through some beautiful country, but now they were more focused on looking for moving shadows. With Filipe scouting ahead, they could often cut across bows in the river and make their journey even shorter. But this time, it would also take them through a valley, between two small *kopjes*.

'This is the ideal place for an ambush; be ready, everyone,' Enoch said, just as he had a million times before, but still they walked through it because they didn't have a choice.

The single shot came out of nowhere. It pierced through the air and in the next instant, Ethel fell to the ground next to Pampero.

The horse whinnied and tossed her head, bunching up into Diablo, who gave a small jump to get away from her, and jolted Mike. Chloe lost grip of his lead rein, and Diablo jumped again as Pampero slammed into the back of him. Marin's high-pitched neigh behind Pampero made her step to the side of Diablo, and she bolted.

Chloe saw her gallop full tilt into the bush ahead, bucking as she went. Marin was close behind, his lead rein trailing, the cargo on his back being ripped at by the thorns as he ran into the scrub.

A second shot followed with a deadening sound, but Chloe was focused on Diablo, who now was bolting after the other two horses.

'Whoa, whoa,' Xo called, hanging onto Sirocco with both hands.

Chloe was running after Diablo, watching her father bob in his saddle, knowing that any moment Diablo could go under a tree and her father would be seriously injured. 'Diablo. Stop. Stop right now,' she commanded.

Diablo halted just before the thick bush.

'Back up and turn around,' she said, her voice low, her fear disguised in her bravado.

He did what she asked, and she reached out her hand and grabbed his rein. He shuddered. She looked at his eyes, and white was showing. The danger was still present.

'Get your dad down, quickly!' Enoch was shouting at her.

She fumbled with the strap on his leg, and Diablo danced a little, trying to keep still, but remained seriously spooked. 'Wait, calm down,' she tried to reassure him. 'I just need to get Dad.' Diablo continued to dance around her, prancing, huffing out his breath as he looked all around for the danger he knew was out there, somewhere in the bush.

Nick appeared right next to her and held Diablo on both sides of his bit. 'Stay still. Contact.'

Diablo's whole stance changed. Something inside of him recognised the tone of the old command. He stood perfectly still while Chloe tore at the strap holding her father in on the right-hand side, then rushed around back to the left and pulled her father down. He landed hard on top of her, with Nick still standing in front of Diablo, keeping him motionless.

'Flat down,' Nick commanded.

Diablo folded his legs and lay flat on his side. He put his head on the ground, making himself as small a target as he could.

'Good boy,' Nick said as he crawled behind him to help Chloe with her dad.

Mike was heavy, and although she'd managed to catch him, it had been a dead weight falling onto her. Her back muscles screamed as she moved him now to ensure that he lay down behind Diablo, away from the direction of the first shot.

Nick tucked in Mike's arm that was over the top of the horse, and then lay on the other side of him. 'You okay?'

'As good as I can be, you?'

'I'm alive.'

She nodded, but she was still checking her dad. He seemed to be aware that there was trouble, but his pupils were dilated. She was worried that the jarring had probably started the bleeding in his head again, causing the pressure to build. But he wasn't thrashing around. He seemed to be weirdly calm, lying still beside her.

She turned on her back with her head against Diablo, making sure his shoulder area was higher than her head. 'Xo, you okay?'

'Good. Dad, you still with us?'

'Scanning for the bastard now,' Enoch said. 'Not seeing him in my sights. But Kimberlite and I are lying down.'

'Ethel?' Chloe called. 'You okay after your fall?'

Silence answered her.

'She was the target. She didn't make it,' Xo said. 'I can see her. She's gone. There is no use me even going over to check. It's a head shot. I'm in the same position as you, Sirocco lay down when asked. It's just Marin and Pampero who're in the wind.'

They heard a third shot from a different direction. It echoed around them, and then there was a second follow-up one in quick succession.

'Khululani's weapon,' Nick said. 'He's shooting at the hunter. I hope he gets him.'

There was silence again, and then the sound of return fire from the original direction, this time towards Khululani, as the sound was different, not as close to them.

Enoch let off a quick double tap from his rifle, and all was quiet.

The *pop-pop* of an AK-47 dominated for a few minutes, and then once again silence.

Chloe could hear the blood as it rushed through her ears. Her heart thumped so loudly she was sure that the whole of Africa could hear it.

'Stay here, Chloe, don't move until we tell you it's safe,' Nick instructed as he belly-slid to where Enoch was behind Kimberlite.

There was murmuring coming from them, and Enoch called out, 'Xo, can you get to your rifle?'

'I have it already; just can't see them up on that *kopje*, even with my scope.'

'Keep it trained up there; don't let anything get down here alive,' Enoch said.

'Khululani?' Nick called.

Silence.

'Filipe?'

Silence.

'They probably don't want to give away their positions,' Xo said.

Enoch and Nick got to a crouch and ran together to the closest tree, then they zig-zagged away and didn't call anymore.

'Chloe, are you armed?' Xo asked.

'Just with my knife. My rifle was on Marin,' she said, pulling her hunting knife out from its sheath on her belt. The blade was sharp, and although only about six inches long, she was confident in her ability to bring someone down with it if she had to. The thought of her shooting the hunter flashed into her mind, and she pushed it aside.

'Where's your 9mm?' Xo asked.

'In the pack lying under Diablo,' she said.

'You okay there with your dad, or must I come over?'

'No, keep watching up that *kopje*.'

'I'm scanning and the only thing I have seen has been a fat pheasant run away from where I think Filipe has dug down and is waiting.'

'Can you see Khululani?'

'No, Nick was right, that man's a ghost,' Xo said.

They settled into silence as they waited for something to happen.

Nothing.

Doves began to coo their love song once again.

'Don't move, or I'll shoot you in the head!' Filipe shouted.

'Filipe has him. I can see Filipe and the hunter. He's putting his rifle down,' Xo said. 'There's Dad and Nick; they are right next to Filipe. I wouldn't want to be that hunter,' Xo said.

'Can you see Khululani?'

'No.'

'They're bringing him down the side of the *kopje*—none too gently. He's definitely injured. Looks like you did a good job with his shoulder—the blood on his shirt is already old and brown, but there's new blood there, too. And on his arm as well—*eina,* that doesn't look pretty,' Xo was giving her a running commentary.

'So, he's still very much alive?'

'For sure,' Xo said.

'Shit. That means we have to drag him with us until we find some police to hand him over to. We'll have to feed him and keep him alive. I'm not sure I can do that, Xo, knowing that he killed Ethel. Can I get Diablo up yet?' Chloe asked.

'Not until Dad or Nick says it's safe,' Xo said.

She watched him continue to follow the progress of them all down the *kopje*. Before they got much closer, Enoch stopped them. 'Xo, bring rope so I can tie this bastard up.'

'Rope's on Marin,' Xo said.

'Here,' Chloe said, throwing him the lead rein from Diablo.

Xo walked to where the men stood together and handed the rope to Enoch, before he turned away and jogged back to Sirocco.

'You can get up now, Chloe,' Enoch called.

'Up,' commanded Chloe and Diablo stood. Shaking himself, he waited for her next command. 'Steady, just stay here, I need something,' Chloe said as she put her knife between her legs and clamped them tightly together to hold it in place. She fished her 9mm out of the pouch on her dad's saddle with her right hand.

'Don't move, okay, boy,' she whispered, and using both hands did up the holster buckle once the belt was around her waist, and the weapon rested comfortably on her hip. Only then did she slide her knife away from its resting place and clip it back into its little pouch. 'Right, let's find your chair, Dad, or at least let me get you a pillow. Hang in there; I'll be right back,' she said as she walked towards Xo. 'Do you have his chair or anything I can make him a little bit more comfortable with?'

Sirocco was also on his feet, looking around for grass to eat. 'Sure, here you go,' Xo said as he unstrapped a bundle of dish towels. 'These will do for now.'

She took them and walked back to her dad.

Only once she was sure that her father was comfortable, did she then go to where Ethel lay.

Chloe turned Ethel from her side and onto her back. The shot had gone through her temple. There was no exit wound. Chloe used her fingers to close Ethel's eyelids, then she took two small plasters from her first-aid kit on Diablo and taped them closed. She straightened the crumpled body and crossed her arms over her chest. A tear rolled down her nose and dripped onto Ethel. She wiped at the next one with the back of her hand to try to stop it, but it too fell in silence, splashing onto Ethel's face.

'I'm so sorry, Ethel,' she said, forcing her emotions back deep inside. Ethel's wasn't the first dead body she'd seen. She remembered standing in the funeral parlour between her dad and Xo, with Enoch on the other side. She remembered how her mother's body was cold when she reached into the white satin coffin and touched her hand. Her mother had been refrigerated in the artificial surroundings where she got to view her and say her last goodbyes.

Ethel was still warm.

Her mother had been made up with makeup to look beautiful, forever in a peaceful sleep. An artificial tranquillity created around her, that until now, she'd never appreciated.

Ethel had blood splattered on her face, and dirt from where she'd fallen on the ground, and a fly had already smelled the blood and come calling.

Chloe reached forward with her hand and attempted to shoo the fly away as another joined it. 'Xo, throw me another towel,' she said.

Catching it, she draped it over Ethel's face to try to at least protect it from the harsh African environment.

'I need to go fetch Pampero and Marin so we can get your church dress to bury you in,' she told Ethel quietly. Then taking a deep breath, she exhaled slowly and called, 'Enoch, can I go look for the other horses?'

'Take Xo with you,' Enoch said.

'But he's looking after Dad.'

'I'll watch your father,' Khululani said from nearby. 'Go get your horses back.'

She jumped and let out a small involuntary scream. 'You scared the shit out of me!' she said, her hand over her heart, staring at him. He was full of leaves and bushes and twigs and looked like a moving tree. Although he was pulling pieces off already.

'Chloe?' Nick called.

'She's fine just got a fright from me,' Khululani said.

'Here, take Sirocco and make a temporary hitch for them. You'll need to do Kimberlite as well,' Xo said, leaving Khululani holding the lead rein. 'Welcome back.'

'Just keep Diablo and Sirocco away from where Dad is lying,' she said, 'and thank you, for being here, for catching that murdering bastard.'

'I am so sorry that he got Ethel,' Khululani said. 'And that I was not quick enough to stop his bullet.'

Chloe nodded and Xo took her hand and led her in the direction the horses had gone. 'Come on, let's hope those two haven't ventured too far.' He slung his rifle over his shoulder and walked ahead.

Chloe had to run a little to keep up. Her back hurt, her head throbbed, and she had a constant feeling that she couldn't breathe properly, but she let him lead her away while pushing her fear and sorrow deep down.

She looked ahead, scanning the bushes for signs of where the horses had run, following their footprints in the grass and the sand. Just because they hadn't seen any more lions or leopards since that morning, didn't mean they were not there. She had already lost one precious person today; she really didn't think that her heart could take losing her horse to a lion, too.

CHAPTER 32

'Fucking hell, leave me the fuck alone, you fucking weasel,' Douglas swore as the small soldier in camo who had crept up on him shoved the barrel into his back again.

How had he not seen that they had another person ghosting them? Protecting their flank and back? A rooky mistake. He knew better. He was trained better, or so he had thought, and yet he had made the mistake anyway.

That black game ranger who was a good tracker—he couldn't see him in the valley; it had to be him.

His hand throbbed where the splinters from the butt of the gun had penetrated his skin, and probably broken a bone or two. About a millisecond after he had got his shot off and killed the black bitch who pampered the old man as if he was her lover, someone else's bullet had hit the butt of his rifle, and it had exploded from the impact, sending shrapnel everywhere. In the last few days watching them, watching the way she attended to him had made him want to vomit. Always massaging him, hand feeding him. It was as if the man had no control over himself. She did everything for him.

The white game ranger and a big black man had their arms around Douglas's biceps and were frogmarching him down the *kopje*. The smaller man poked him again with his AK-47. Douglas was sure there was an imprint left of the round barrel in his back.

Douglas cursed. 'Fucking unbelievable.'

'Shut up,' the big black man said.

'You going to make me? Hey, you stupid *kaffir*? Fucking tell me how? You don't even have the guts to shoot me with no one around as a witness, you yellow-bellied cowards. You're going to pay for this. You're *all* going to pay for this. I'm going to kill every single one of you, and fuck that orange-haired bitch —'

The white game ranger took a step in front of him and stopped them all. 'Listen to me, you son of a bitch,' he accented each point with a hard finger poke to Douglas's hurt shoulder, ensuring that he felt each one, 'you're lucky we didn't just shoot you and leave you in the bush for the scavengers, like you do to the innocent people you kill. You're lucky we're more civilised than you and are taking you to the police. We won't be goaded into killing you, so you might as well stop your crap now. Stop talking. Stop fighting us; just walk. Be a good prisoner and just cooperate. That way you might get to die of old age in jail.'

Douglas spat in his face.

The game ranger punched him hard in his and broke his nose.

For a second, the burn between his eyes was worse than that in his shoulder, then he opened his eyes again, and while his vision cleared, he knew they were still dragging him down the side of the small hill, and into their camp.

One thing about distance surveillance was that although you couldn't hear everything, you could learn how people interacted with each other. Now he was about to get the chance.

He looked forward to ending the lives of all these people. Every one of them deserved to die, and when he got away from them, he was going to give them exactly that.

For Nicole, the client he had failed.

For the 6th, whom he needed to protect.

For himself and his own life. He would relish digging the bullet out of that game ranger's head when he collected his trophy from him. He might even wear that one around his neck on a chain.

He spat the blood out of his mouth. 'You are going to fucking pay for that,' he muttered. 'Just wait.'

'Come on, Dad, you can sit in the chair and watch us get everything here sorted before we move camp. You'll be more comfortable and then you can see where we are going to let Ethel rest.' Chloe waited, lost in her own thoughts. 'I still can't believe she's gone, and that he shot her, but then one thing I'm learning fast is that no one lives forever—and none of us get to choose how we go. At least it was fast. She didn't suffer,' she said and then sniffed.

She got her dad lifted up into his chair, but he didn't seem to be helping much. Then his legs collapsed under him.

She frowned. 'Okay, let's give those legs of yours a massage. Think maybe I left you lying down for too long.'

She took off his shoes and started on his feet. One limb at a time. Then her hands moved up higher on his left leg and stopped. She checked his right leg: there were bumps where it should have been smooth. She tried to push his pants up to have a look, but they were too tight.

'Enoch, come here,' Chloe called as she sat with her dad.

'What's wrong?' Enoch said, having jogged over to her.

'Feel here.' She took his hand to where she had found the huge bump.

'*Eish.* I need to get his pants off. Give us a minute, then come back.'

Chloe walked a little away, watching the men digging Ethel's grave instead. The ground was rocky, hard. They were having to use their single pick to make any sort of dent in it. The hole was taking a long time to progress.

She glanced to where the Caçador Escuro was tied to a mopani tree. And quickly looked away again. Not trusting herself to confront the man, and what he stood for. Not wanting to look at the person who had killed Ethel and the traveller they had buried at Mapai.

As if realising that he had an audience, the Caçador Escuro started up again like a set of bagpipes. He'd been screaming abuse and swearing constantly, generally carrying on like a lunatic since they had brought him off the *kopje*.

She looked at the rope that held him. From his neck to his knees was criss-crossed rope binding him, holding him in place.

'You fucking think you're so clever, riding a horse, shooting at me. At us. You killed her. What do you think I'm going to tell the police when you take me to them? I'll tell them you shot her. You. And you shot me, you fucking bitch, look at my shoulder. It's still bleeding and you don't even care that I could bleed to death here.'

His venomous spurting carried loud and clear to her.

'If you even get me that far. I'm going to get out of these ropes and I'm going to slit your throats, all of you, but you, I might have some fun before I kill you. You, I might kill slowly, with a knife —'

'You can come back, Chloe,' Enoch called.

'Chloe, that's your name. Ch-llllll-oooo-eee. I'm going to kill you, Ch-llllll-oooo-eee, and that boyfriend of yours for breaking my nose. He can watch me fuck you before he dies too.'

Chloe shook her head. She'd had enough of his filth and his obnoxious behaviour. 'Anyone care if we gag him? Shut him up?'

'It will be my pleasure,' Khululani said, walking up beside her. He had one of the dish towels that had been propping up her dad's head, and he was winding it up.

'Fitting to clean a dirty pot,' she said, and turned her back as Khululani sorted out the foul-mouthed prisoner.

She went to where Enoch sat next to her dad, now with a towel over his lap, covering up the adult nappy that they had chosen to use for the journey.

'Keep far away from him, Chloe. That man is demented. And strong. I worry he might get out of his ropes, and you are no match for him, even wounded. Do not antagonise him. Do not go near him,' Enoch warned.

'I hadn't planned to—he gives me nightmares while I'm awake. There is no soul in him when you look at his eyes, just nothing.'

'Filipe, Khululani and Nick will take care of him. He is going to make the last few days even more challenging, that is for sure. Keeping us all on our toes all the time.'

'What's up with Dad's legs?'

'The bruising is really bad, look here,' Enoch said as he showed Chloe where the straps they had fashioned to keep him in the saddle had worked, but had also caused a problem when Diablo had bolted. On both his calves and on his thighs, there were clear strap marks. And in one place, the skin had begun to rub away, causing what looked like a gravel-rash graze.

'I don't like the look of this,' she said, pointing to one part that was already black and swelling.

'Me either. Not only will that be hurting Mike, but we will not be able to have him travel on Diablo anymore.'

'We can shift the packs around, and he can double with me. Marin will be able to carry us both; he's strong,' Chloe suggested.

'Marin is carrying a heavy load. It's too much to shift it all onto old Diablo. We would need to give a little to Pampero, also. You going to be okay with that?'

'I have to be; what else are we going to do?'

'We can make a travois to drag behind, but doubling up might be easier. We will have to take turns, because it will tax your arm muscles holding onto him all the time in front of you. We cannot tie him on as that would be too dangerous.'

'Let's see how I go. I don't like the idea of a travois. It could hit a mine buried deep that we don't notice.'

'I see your point. Do not worry, Chloe, we will get him home,' Enoch said, reaching out and touching her cheek.

Chloe smiled and put her hand over his. 'I know. But I also think this is probably hurting him something chronic and once again he can't tell us. I'll rub some arnica oil on then bandage it to try to keep the swelling down.'

'It might help, but I suspect that this is going to look a lot worse in a few hours than it does now,' Enoch said. 'The bruising is only just starting to show.'

'Enoch, he's going to be okay, isn't he? This isn't something worse than just bruises?'

'Let us hope not. We can only treat it as we see it.'

Burying a stranger was hard. Burying a friend was agonising.

Chloe had got Ethel's body ready. She'd found Ethel's best church clothes, and dressed her for her journey into the afterlife, and then wrapped her in her own sleeping bag as well, since they had no coffin to put her in. But when the time came, watching Ethel be put into the ground, and seeing the men throw sand on her, covering her up deep inside the earth, had Chloe sobbing uncontrollably. Her moment to mourn had arrived, and she cried for her adopted family member. For a black woman who had become such an integral part of her life and filled a void in her heart that she didn't even know she had.

Nick stepped closer to her and drew her into his arms. He rubbed her back and made comforting noises.

Chloe could feel the warmth from him, but her shakes wouldn't stop. 'This could have been any of us. I'm not sure why it was Ethel. She was looking forward to her new life so much, loving the adventure. Do you know that other than going to Durban to train as a nurse, Ethel had never travelled? She's never even been out of Natal and the Transkei. I once bought her some sea water and shells in a bottle from the ocean. Something so small, and yet when I gave it over, she reacted as if I had given her the moon. She was so humble. Never once did I hear her complain about what we asked her to do. Not even a single time. And this is what happens when she was so looking forward —'

'It's not your fault,' Nick tried to comfort her.

'She chose to come with us, and because of that, she's dead,' Chloe said, just as a hiccup hit. Followed by another.

'At least she died free,' Enoch said. 'She was not being dictated to about what she could do, or where she could live, or who she could sleep next to. Even though she has passed on, she was happy when she died. You were with her this morning when she was eager to climb back onto Pampero and face another day, because she knew that soon she would have a better life. You gave her that, Chloe, and that is what you need to focus on.'

A loud unladylike squeak escaped out of Chloe.

Nick smiled. 'You sound like a cross between a bat and an annoyed tree squirrel.'

'Thank-*squeak*-you very much,' she said, and stepped away from him. She felt his hand linger on her shoulder as a coldness of air and reality rushed between them again. She stepped back into Nick's warmth and put her head on his chest, listening to the beat of his heart in the hope that it would help block out the scenes replaying inside her head.

'None of what's happened has been your fault,' Nick said. 'This monster needs to take responsibility for the harm he's caused. Ethel's death is squarely at his feet, no one else's.'

Chloe leaned against Nick.

Enoch placed a rough cross into the ground as they began to pile stones onto Ethel's grave. Chloe bent down and helped cover the grave as fresh tears flowed from her eyes.

'I think Ethel would have appreciated you getting those at her graveside,' Xo said. 'Remember the time she was trying to get your dad to sleep, and you got hiccups, and she eventually chased you out of his room because you couldn't keep them quiet?'

'I remember,' Chloe said.

'That's what she would want, you guys to remember her, remember fun things that she did, not her death,' Nick said.

'You-*squeak*-might be right there,' Chloe said as she threw another stone onto Ethel's grave so that it was protected from wild dogs, leopards, hyenas and any other feral animal that wanted to dig her up. 'As long as she doesn't fade from memory, then she lives forever free, even if it's just inside my heart.'

They pushed on for a couple more hours before they found a place that was okay to stop for the night. While Filipe scouted around and made sure they were totally alone, Khululani walked behind them all with the prisoner, his arms bound tightly, his mouth gagged. There was no need for any of them to deal with his abuse and taunting.

Enoch, Nick and Khululani had bandaged the Caçador Escuro's wounds as best they could, but there was nothing they could do for his broken arm; it needed medical attention. They could keep the flies off it so that it didn't fester and get maggots, but they were not exactly feeling hospitable and in a talkative mood towards their prisoner.

Khululani said that every step he took, the pain would remind him that he shouldn't have been taking people's lives and snuffing out precious souls. Chloe doubted that the Caçador Escuro would care about the pain that he'd caused others.

That night, Nick cooked the evening meal. A simple *sadza* and stew made with biltong and a few spices. There was very little conversation. Khululani took a plate and disappeared to where he had the hunter tied up against a tree —gagged once again, so that they didn't have to listen to him shouting any obscenities and idle threats at them. Chloe chose to look in the opposite direction.

Douglas closed his eyes. Although he was tied with his hands and feet together, he decided he might as well get some much-needed rest and regain his strength. Heal as fast as he could. Escaping could happen another time. He still had much to learn about his captors.

So far, only the men looked after him. Brought him food and water, took his gag off for him to eat, and then put it back on. They would allow him one hand loose to go to the toilet, so he didn't piss in his pants, and gave him toilet paper to crap in the bush. As captives went, he couldn't complain about his treatment, but all the time he was silenced. He watched them. Studied them instead.

He got to know who was who in their hierarchy.

It was Chloe who ruled the roost and had every man in the group doing everything for her, although it didn't appear that way at first. He had already learned that each man still appeared to have his allocated place.

Filipe was the outsider. The one who was guiding them. He was also a fanatic and totally loyal to his general somewhere and wouldn't be the weakest in the pyramid.

Enoch appeared to be a second father figure to Chloe, but it was Nick-the-game-ranger who held her heart.

Xo was quiet compared to the rest, and the unknown in the group. He kept close to Chloe all the time, but allowed Nick into his space. Much like a young lion who hadn't yet fought for his mating rights in a pride, or one that was about to fight and be tossed out into the wilderness on its own. Other than Chloe, with her obvious lack of strength being a female, he looked to be the next youngest, and the weakest of them all. He was the one to watch, the one who would make a mistake, if any of them did. And when he did, Douglas would be ready.

Khululani was a seasoned bushman and Douglas still admired the way he walked, the way he knew what was happening around him by the sounds of the birds, the whisper of the wind, but he seemed to be dedicated to Nick. He was also the arsehole that had shot his rifle to shit and broken his arm.

The invalid, spastic old man, as he now knew him to be, was Chloe's father, Mike, and everyone except Filipe would help him.

Nick and Khululani were going to be the first to die. Without them, the others were nothing. And next would be that Mozambique freedom fighter Filipe.

He adjusted his body to fit more comfortably, and knew that while he slept, one of those other suckers had to now stay awake to watch him.

Life was a bitch if you took a prisoner instead of killing them.

The caravan continued to push through the bush, with Chloe, Enoch and Xo taking turns riding with Mike. Sometimes the Caçador Escuro was in front with one of the men; sometimes they had him trailing behind. Never the same routine.

The next day, they smelled the cooking fires. Filipe ran ahead to investigate, while the rest of the group remained hidden under the tall trees that surrounded the banks of the river. Ready to cross into it, if they needed to.

When Filipe returned, he was smiling. 'We're in Zimbabwe,' he said. 'The people, they are from a village called Malipati, but they belong to a hunting safari company who have a camp along the river. They are looking for some men who went hunting for kudu from their small village outside of that area but did not return when they should have. The men are three days late.'

'Do they have a vehicle?' Enoch asked.

'They do, it's old, but they'll take you to the nearest telephone,' Filipe said. 'They asked that we keep an eye out for their missing hunters in a blue Mazda *bakkie*.'

'Of course we will,' Nick said. 'Please tell me you didn't mention that we have the Caçador Escuro in our custody.'

'I didn't, but they don't know how lucky they are that they don't have to worry about him shooting their guys,' Filipe said. 'Hopefully, they are just having vehicle trouble.'

'I will go and call Grace, once I find out exactly where we are. I think for now we should stay in this area, so I can find you when I come back. Chloe, you stay out of sight no matter what. Promise me,' Enoch said.

'I promise,' she said as she hugged Enoch. 'Take some of the money; you'll need to pay them for their help. Please buy us a Coke when you come back; I'd kill for one right now.'

Enoch smiled. 'I will do that for you. Nick, make sure that our prisoner does not get away.'

Nick nodded.

Xo shook his dad's hand, and then both Enoch and Filipe made their way back into the bushes towards the village.

'If we're staying here, we'll need another strong boma to protect the horses. Those there are lion tracks if I'm not mistaken,' Chloe said.

Nick looked at where she was pointing and nodded. 'Right you are. Boma first—then sort out our new camp. Xo, you with me or looking after that piece of shit so Khululani can haul thorn trees?'

'I'm with you and Chloe. Sorry, Khululani, he's all yours. I'd rather cut boma bushes than have to spend a minute alone with that snake.'

The fire was banked high, and they had collected enough wood to see them through the next few days just in case Enoch and Filipe took a while to get back. They weren't too worried about rhino coming in to try to stamp out the fire; they were all too painfully aware that the attempt to reintroduce black rhino into Gonarezhou in the 1960s had failed horribly with all the rhino being poached for their horns, so there were none left to come blundering out of the bush.

Khululani had set up the Caçador Escuro a little away from the campfire, as had become the norm since the first night when he had become abusive when the gag was taken off to sleep. Now it stayed on.

Nick threw a small stick he'd been whittling away during the final watch for the night into the fire and watched it burn. The noises of the bush surrounded him in predawn quietness. The shrieks of both grey and brown-headed parrots flying down to the river for some early-morning water; the frogs calling, trying desperately to mate and get their breeding in the shallow ponds completed before the water dried up and the riverbed became an empty desert once more. A spotted hyena grunted close by, and then the chilling roar of a lion, too close for comfort, followed by an answering call from another in the pride.

He stilled, putting his head to the side, and listened carefully. The horses whinnied, safe in their boma.

'Darn,' Nick muttered. 'Perhaps it would have been wiser to all be inside the boma again tonight with the horses, instead of out here where we can have a three-hundred-and-sixty-degree view around the camp with these lions so close. But I didn't want the horses near the Caçador Escuro.'

'Can you see them?' Khululani asked, already climbing out of his sleeping bag not far from the fire. No matter how many times Nick told him to use a pup tent to protect himself against animals, Khululani still avoided them whenever he could.

'No, but they're around,' Nick said, getting his torch and beginning to sweep it along the bush line they had near their camp. No eyes reflected back at him, but that didn't mean they were not there.

'How close?' Chloe asked as she unzipped her tent. 'That sounded almost on top of us.'

'It gave me chills, even in my sleep,' Xo said as he emerged from his tent, and lifted his rifle from where it had lain next to him, before re-zipping his tent closed behind him.

The horses whinnied again.

'I need to check on them,' Chloe said.

'Where's your rifle?' Xo asked her.

Chloe reached back into her tent for it. 'Got it now. Are you coming with me, Xo?'

'Xo will need to watch both Mike's and the Caçador Escuro's tents. Khululani and I are going to walk a perimeter check, so don't shoot us.'

'I'll try not to … today. But I can't promise about the Caçador Escuro. I have had enough of him and his foul mouth every time Khululani takes his gag off,' Chloe said.

'Just don't. He isn't worth having his blood on your conscience forever. Believe me, it's not worth killing him,' Nick said.

'We'll walk you to the boma—but don't come out till we come fetch you again, Chloe,' Nick said.

'I don't plan to,' Chloe said. 'You guys saw the size of those footprints. The lions here look massive.'

The horses neighed again, louder this time. 'Come on, guys, walk faster,' Chloe said, 'those horses are not happy.'

Nick shone his torch back and forth over the area as they approached the boma, and Khululani moved some of the branches aside to gain access. They scanned inside first, with Chloe still behind them. But there was nothing there.

'Right, Chloe, you're armed, and you have my torch. Be safe,' Nick said, and touched her arm as he came out.

She nodded and walked inside. Scanning quickly away from the horses with the torch, ensuring that there was nothing in the boma with them, double-checking the men.

'Can't see anything either,' she said loudly as she walked to where the horses were bunched together. 'Hey, guys,' Chloe spoke softly. 'What's going on? The lions are outside the boma; they can't get to you.'

She heard the scraping of the thornbushes on the ground as Khululani closed the boma back up behind her.

Chloe shone the light on the floor, not into the horses' eyes. They were skittish. She walked up to Diablo and stroked him. 'Come on, boy, help me settle the others. You know that we'll always protect you.'

The lions roared again. Chloe stopped to listen. They sounded strained, hoarse, then louder, an almost hollow sound carrying clearly in the quiet night.

She could hear one was to the left of the boma, while the answering call came from the opposite side. A third one joined in. It was as if they were all checking in on each other, wanting to know where they were in the darkness. Coordinating an attack …

Kimberlite stood next to Diablo. His skin was twitching, and he neighed softly, as if trying to alert her to danger. He certainly knew what the lions were, and while she could see the white of his eyes, he was not prancing around like Marin.

'Come on, Marin, you need to settle,' Chloe said. Reaching out her hand towards him, she took hold of his halter. He reared up, and she let it go, stepping backwards out of the way. 'No, Marin, that wasn't necessary. Come on, come here.'

He backed away from her, his nostrils flared.

'You know, it's just a lion. You're safe inside this boma. Come on, come here to my side, Marin,' she said in her calmest voice.

Marin pawed the ground.

'Don't be stubborn, come here,' she said a little firmer. 'There's no danger in here. Nick and Khululani are out there, and they'll protect us. Xo is watching that *totsie* from near the fire to make sure they don't eat him, because despite him deserving it, we do want him to rot in jail and think about what he did to Ethel for the rest of his miserable life. And any day now, Enoch and Filipe will come back with Aunty Grace, and she'll bring the cattle truck and we'll go home.'

Marin approached her, tossing his head, stepping closer.

The shot took her by surprise. She jumped at the loudness of the .303 in the night.

Marin thundered past her, running in circles around the inside of the boma. The other horses had their heads up, ears forward, attentive to the noise, but didn't run. She could see they were unnerved. Except Diablo and Kimberlite, they looked like they understood that the sooner the fighting started, the sooner the danger would be over.

She heard Nick shout to Khululani and knew that they were both okay. She looked at the sky, hoping that dawn would lighten the darkness and make it easier to see what was going on.

'What happened?' she called out at the top of her voice.

'Khululani gave them a warning shot. They were too close. They ran away,' Nick said. 'These lions are used to hunters; they know gunfire enough to be afraid of it.'

She breathed a sigh of relief and began trying to get Marin under control again. 'Come on, boy, steady. Steady now.'

He seemed to realise that the danger had passed, and he stopped running and came right up to her, tucking his head next to her body and breathing softly into her cupped palm. 'You are too highly strung for your own good,' she chastised him. 'It was just Khululani scaring away the lions.'

She patted the stallion, and could feel him settling. He still tossed his head, but his skin no longer shuddered, and he didn't paw the ground. She moved away to check that the other horses were all okay, rubbing her hands over Pampero's neck and tummy.

'Hey, girl, you're doing well protecting your baby from all this madness. Soon we'll be home, and there's a nice stable for you to have this little one in. I can see you already loving it there.' She moved on to Sirocco. 'Hey, boy, you know Xo wanted to come and be with you, but he's watching that *skelm* so that I don't have to face him at all,' she said, and gave him a hug.

Kimberlite and Diablo came to her, and she reassured them that she was still in the boma with them—she hadn't abandoned them.

'You okay in there?' Nick asked from outside the boma entrance.

'Some warning would have been nice,' Chloe said. 'I nearly jumped out of my jeans!'

She could hear the amusement in his voice when he said, 'Khululani's going to go make tea, you want?'

'Please,' Chloe said. 'With lots of sugar!'

This time Nick actually laughed as he walked away.

The noises of the morning continued to grow as the birds once again chattered amongst themselves, and the cicadas screamed. The bush returned to normal around her, and as she breathed in the scent of Marin, she thanked the universe that they had gotten through one more night as the dawn at last began lightening the horizon.

Douglas waited for the men to leave, and realised that there was only Xo keeping watch. This could be his chance. He slipped out of his sleeping bag, and belly-crawled to the tent zip fastener. He used his teeth to begin unzipping the tent, only to find it was shut tight. Obviously closed with wire or something on the outside. He couldn't get it to budge.

'Go ahead. Give me an excuse to shoot you, you son of a bitch,' Xo said, putting his rifle against Douglas's head through the nylon.

Douglas snaked himself back into his bed. But now he knew that the next night, if they were still there, and when everything was calm, he would have to create some diversion to get out of the tent, then he could overpower the kid—if they left him there alone again.

He had begun testing their defences.

During the morning, they reinforced the boma with more thornbushes and kept watch throughout the day. At the darkest part of the night, when the moon was almost gone and the sun had not shown its face to the African continent yet, the lions began roaring.

Chloe looked up from where she sat near the fire and into the dark bushes.

'They are still far away,' Khululani said.

But after a while, as the roaring got louder, they knew the lions were closer. Khululani picked up his hunting rifle and loaded it.

Nick scanned the area with his torch until he finally caught some reflective eyes in the bush, on the opposite side to where the horses were in the boma. They looked defiantly at him. 'There you are.' Slowly, he moved the light around. 'I can't see any more lions waiting in the grass around them.'

Chloe stared at the lioness, which just stared back.

Xo added more wood to the fire. The horses neighed. 'I don't know about you, but I'm not keen on going out there with those lions about.'

'She seems to be alone,' Nick said as he continued to search with his torch for more lions, then came back to her again, shining the torch in her eyes. 'The males we can hear might not be part of her pride.'

The lioness stood up and walked away, as if realising she was not getting a meal from the humans there tonight.

'Holy shit, she's huge,' Chloe said.

'That she is and look at those muscles. Well fed, too. She can't be alone to be in such good condition. She must be part of a pride that works well together.'

The lioness turned sideways and was highlighted in Nick's spotlight. 'Look, suckle marks on her undercarriage. She'll be hunting alone while her cubs are hidden from the pride. Good girl, you go find some easier prey than us.'

'That's sweet that she has cubs and is looking after them, but good girl?' Chloe challenged. 'She would almost take me at hip height, and you say good girl like she's some domestic kitten.'

'Healthy lions are essential to keep the natural balance of the game right. They weed out the weak and the old. So yes, good girl, she's a mum looking after her cubs, just doing what comes naturally. They've been successful predators for a long time, but even their existence is threatened by humans. One day soon, people will realise that they can't keep taking the predators out of the food chain without having a disastrous effect,' Nick said. 'She's cunning and a good hunter, obviously. Maybe you should go check on the horses and make sure she didn't stand up on her hind legs and work out a way to use those big paws to open the boma to feed them to her cubs.'

Khululani laughed when he saw the reaction on Chloe's face. 'You need to learn when Nick is bullshitting you.'

'Nick! You're a *domkop*!' Chloe said. 'How can you start a story with one line of truth and then spout all that rubbish? I should know better; you have been doing that all my life!'

Nick laughed. 'Come on, Xo, you and I'll go do a perimeter check around the boma. The likelihood of us having to scare more lions away with a shot again is real high, even if that mama has moved on.'

'This time he is not joking,' Khululani said.

Xo nodded and stood up. 'I think Chloe got it. I'll go with Nick to check on the horses; you guys keep the fire nice and high. And make sure those lions don't get to the Caçador Escuro, as much as that would be justice.'

Douglas settled in; he had to be patient and wait. They had switched it up and not left the kid alone again. Not even with Chloe in camp to keep him company. The kid and the woman, he had a chance against. Khululani alone

—the likelihood of a successful escape was slim. Not with a shot shoulder, a broken arm and his face still throbbing from his busted nose.

His window to freedom was shrinking.

Using his feet as they gripped the nylon in the tent's corners, and further where each peg held it securely to the ground, he quietly lifted the peg so that when the time came, he was ready to roll the whole thing, even into the fire if necessary, to get away.

'Stop moving in there, go to sleep!' Khululani said; then he was outside the tent and stomping on the pegs, pushing them back in the ground, and moving large boulders onto the corners.

Enoch and Filipe would be back soon, and they would move on. He would be given over to the Zimbabwe police. And while he knew some of them were corrupt, many were dedicated men and women, and proud, too. He wasn't sure that even the promise of a well-paid bribe would get him out. He had to get away. He had to escape.

He dozed, waiting for the next changeover of the guards, when he could shift the rocks and try again, but it never came.

They heard a whistle, and an excited Xo answered in return. 'Enoch's back!' Chloe said aloud.

He walked into their camp and both Xo and Chloe threw themselves into his arms.

'You guys are all up, and here I thought I was walking in early,' Enoch said.

'We've had lions visit us,' Chloe said.

'If you pack up and ride out of here, the truck is about two hours away, and you can leave the lions to live their own lives, away from you.'

'That's fantastic news,' Chloe said.

'And,' Enoch said, 'this is for you.' He dug in his small pack and handed her a bottle of Coke.

'Awesome,' she said, hugging him again. 'Thank you, thank you!'

'And ours?' Xo asked.

'What? You think I would bring her one and not you?' Enoch said, handing them out to the rest of the group.

'No, but that is going to taste like nectar right now,' Xo said, getting his knife out and opening the bottles.

'To a journey almost over,' Chloe said, standing next to Mike.

'I'll drink to that,' Nick said.

The Cokes didn't last long, and they put the empties back into Enoch's pack before they got busy dismantling the camp.

As they were riding away, Enoch and Filipe had the Caçador Escuro on his short rope out in front and the horses a way behind. Xo first, then Chloe riding Marin with her father balanced in front and held tightly, and up the back came Nick. Ever dependable Nick who had stayed by her side, and done everything he could when she asked, and whom she knew she was falling in love with. They needed so much more time together to get to know each other as adults, time away from the stress of trekking, and away from the watching eyes of the Caçador Escuro.

Chloe turned around to look past Nick, at the site that would be their last outdoor camp. Delaware was close now.

At last, she would be able to relax, and they would all be safe.

An old male lion walked into the area they had so recently vacated, sniffing around for scraps of food left behind. His face was tattooed with scars from fights—perhaps for glory of his right to mate, or for his territory, but the latest sores were unhealed and more recent. His mane was just as magnificent as when he'd perhaps been king of that area and had his pride around him. Supported. Strong.

Instead of how he was now—isolated and alone.

His ribs showed like ripples on water against his tawny skin as he walked, carefully picking up one huge paw and placing it down, as if each step was a mission of its own to accomplish.

He sniffed around the fire, and finding nothing, moved to the tree the Caçador Escuro had been tied to during the day. He sniffed the ground, and the air, and then lay down under the canopy of leaves in the shade.

Tears formed in Chloe's eyes as she looked forward, and she squeezed her dad's waist as she held him in front of her.

Aunty Grace was sitting in a deck chair next to a cattle truck, her sunglasses and large hat shading her from the sun. There were also two men flanking her, standing as if the mid-afternoon sun was nothing and they were guarding someone of great importance. They wore camo colours, and their guns were pointed towards the riders. They may have sneaked up on her aunt, but not her guards.

'Oh, come on, I'm sure she told you we were coming,' Chloe said, and they immediately lowered their weapons at the female voice.

'Chloe!' Aunty Grace said as she stood up. 'I was just having a nap.'

Chloe looked at the lady standing in front of her. She couldn't help feeling that she was looking into a mirror thirty years in the future. Grace was as tall as Chloe, with silver hair and a face that belonged to someone who'd experienced a lot of trauma very early in their life. The family resemblance was very clear to anyone who saw them together. She held herself with an understated elegance, despite the T-shirt and cut-off denim shorts that she wore.

'Aunty Grace!'

'It really is you, Chloe!'

Enoch was there to take the weight of Mike from her as she slid him off Marin and then she jumped off and ran to her aunt. They hugged until Grace said, 'Okay, enough. Get your horses loaded so we can get you home. Was that Mike up there riding with you?'

'Yeah, but he isn't doing so well,' Chloe said, walking with her aunt to where Mike was lying on the ground.

Grace threw her arms around him and hugged him.

Mike half lifted his arm, and while Chloe could see him try, he wasn't able to put it around Grace fully, but it was close. She hadn't seen him do that to anyone else, aside from her.

'He recognises you,' Chloe said excitedly. But the excitement had already sapped all Mike's energy, and she watched as his face once again showed pain, and his arm flopped to his side.

Enoch was there in a heartbeat, picking him up and carrying him to sit in the front of the truck.

Grace frowned. 'It's been a while since we were all together. Come on, let's go home.'

'It's so close we can almost smell it!' Chloe said. Their trip had not gone as smoothly as she had hoped, but they were in Zimbabwe now. The SAP couldn't touch them here, and within a few hours, they would be home—safe at Delaware.

'First, we need to get Dad to a doctor, and then we need a police station; we have a prisoner travelling with us.'

CHAPTER 33

Chloe nodded to her aunt's two militia as they circled the perimeter of the school grounds again. Christmas was only five days away, and the roof had been decorated with bits of tinsel and greenery from the bush, and the yard was immaculately swept, showing the pride that the school had been chosen to host the medical clinic. Chloe looked at everyone patiently waiting.

News of the medical team had spread fast, with many of the people travelling for hours, and in some cases days, to see a doctor. They were thankful for the extra care they were receiving, but also worried about what other drama might follow the visitors.

The people were frightened. The dissident war was raging around them; family and friends, even work colleagues, were going missing in the night, and entire villages were being slaughtered and buried. But still they came—to wait in the hot sun, hoping that they would be seen by the doctor or the clinic sister.

For all the trouble that her beloved country was going through, the people themselves were always the same: friendly and patient, believing that tomorrow might be a better day. Chloe looked towards the toilet block building and smiled.

Dr Lily Winters walked up to stand next to her on the veranda, two cups of tea in her hands. She passed one to Chloe and indicated that they sit on the step.

'Thank you,' Chloe said, lowering herself down. Obviously, the doctor wanted to talk.

'I have always loved hot tea on a warm day. Not sure why, but I think it reminds me of my roots. I grew up in South Africa, and even though I moved away, something always calls me back,' Lily said. 'But you also need the hydration, the way you have been walking up and down outside the classroom all this time.'

'Sorry. Enoch says I pace around the house when I'm stressed.'

'Surprised there isn't a furrow in the concrete.' Lily smiled, softening the words. 'Two things. First, your prisoner.'

'He's not just mine,' Chloe protested.

'He says his name is Douglas Jones, and he's a Zimbabwean professional hunter and you have taken him hostage for no reason and treated him unfairly. He wants me to save him from you lot. Your men standing in the rooms all the time with us, Filipe, Nick and Khulani, they told me not to listen to his lies and I'm more inclined to believe them. However, it is not for me to judge. There is no phone here, so I can't call the police. You need to know that my colleagues have told me that the closest police station to here if you head north-ish is at Matibis. It's called Chikombedzi Police Station. Or if you are heading west, the bigger one is at Beitbridge, the Dulibadzimu Base.'

'We'll head to the Beitbridge one. It's on the way home,' Chloe said. 'Travelling on the roads, they will lead us south-west to the border town and then head north again.'

'That's what your men said too,' Lily said. 'That your farm Delaware is in Mazunga.'

'That it is,' Chloe said.

'But to me, prisoner or not, his health comes first. The shoulder that took a bullet will be fine. It's just a flesh wound. Between you all that seems to have been kept pretty clean, and it is already healing. I gave him a few stitches to help close it up faster. It's too late to reset his nose without surgery. But his arm's a different story. He needs to go to a hospital. It's been shattered by a bullet, as well as having splinters embedded quite deep in his hand. To be honest, I'm not sure how he kept walking the distance you say he's covered without passing out, even with his arm immobilised in the rope sling. He clearly has an extremely high threshold for pain.'

'We'll let the police know when we drop him off,' Chloe said. 'And the sooner we offload him, the better.'

Lily nodded. 'It is what it is. I have put a temporary cast on to help stabilise it. Now, about your dad. I'm sure you know that your father could've done without this additional trauma to his legs.'

'Obviously I know that, and I would've done anything to have it different, but circumstances are what they are, and he sustained these massive bruises.'

'I do understand. There isn't much more I can do for him. The nurses are bandaging his legs, and we have given him some pain relief. I'm worried that this is more than just bruising, though, that he has DVT.'

'Deep Vein Thrombosis? You sure?'

'Trauma like he's endured can cause major clotting. Without an MRI or a CT scan, or even a contrast venography, where I can inject dye into his feet and then use an X-ray to see the veins in his legs, I can't give you a proper diagnosis out here. Normally, I'd prescribe anticoagulant medicines to thin the blood, but ...'

'The doctors in South Africa said he can't take those.'

'I suspected as much. He'd be susceptible to bleeding on his brain, based on what you've told me. He needs tests run—I'd suggest that you take him to the hospital in Bulawayo. They might have the equipment working for the scans, but I would still caution against any anticoagulants if they recommend them.'

'What will happen if it's DVT?'

'There's a lot of clotting in the veins in his legs. There's already a lot of inflammation, what we call phlebitis, and he's already showing the signs of starting a leg ulcer. These are easy enough to treat—the danger is if the clot leaves the leg vein. If it travels through the circulatory system, he could suffer from what's called a pulmonary embolism, which is when the clot blocks off the main artery to the lungs or one of its major branches.'

'And if that happens?' Chloe asked.

'About one-third of the patients this happens to don't make it,' Lily said.

Chloe was shaking her head. 'So how do I stop it breaking off, if he can't have the drugs to make it flow better?'

'You can't. You can only hope it doesn't break off,' Lily said.

'So, there's nothing I can do? It's just a waiting game?'

'That's right. I'm sorry I've been so blunt, but I figured that you must be tired of people giving you false hope with your father's health these last few years. I won't be one to add to your list. Your father is basically hanging on by sheer determination now. My advice would be to get him home to where he might recognise things and keep him calm. Keep on with the physiotherapy, elevate his legs as much as possible and just wait for the swelling to go down. Hopefully, the clots will all be reabsorbed into his body. I also suspect that the jarring he sustained has started the bleeding on his brain again.'

Chloe bit the inside of her cheek and stared out at the landscape. 'Thank you for being honest. At least now the last part of the trip is in a vehicle where we can watch him better. And once we are home, he'll be in his own bedroom again by tonight.'

'You know, you should be real proud of what you've accomplished with your father, and how you have kept him with you all this time. Many people would have just institutionalised him and walked away,' Lily said.

'I could never do that, and neither could Enoch.'

'He's a lucky man to have you both,' Lily said, and she downed the last of her tea. 'Right, tea is finished, and I need to get back to other patients. No rest for the wicked.'

Chloe grinned and stood up with her. She put out her hand. 'Thank you for being here. Otherwise, our journey to find help would have been a nightmare.'

'We are the lucky ones to be included in this medical outreach. Quintin and I were not sure we would make this clinic, but I'm glad we did.'

'How many people have come through?' Chloe asked, looking around her at the crowds sitting outside.

'About fifteen hundred in four days, and one more day to go, despite it being a Sunday tomorrow. Between the local guy and the three Australian doctors, they can still only see about three hundred a day, so the hard part for the triage nurses is making the call as to whether the patient sees the nursing sisters or goes through to the doctors. I feel for them; some have camped here for days to see a doctor.'

'And we just drive in and yet they don't make a fuss.'

'They know medical emergencies come first,' Lily said. 'We've had more than a few of those this time. It's quite sad. We knew coming in that we would be collecting important data on the spread of HIV in Africa. When we did this same outreach clinic just two years ago, we were mostly treating everyday ailments, but now it's mostly HIV and TB related. I suppose I shouldn't be surprised; we know that HIV is spreading, but the rate of spread is frightening.'

'That's scary,' Chloe said.

'It's going to destroy Africa's population at this rate,' Lily said. 'This disease is devastating, and I wish things were different for these poor people. I think we'll see many millions of people die, and perhaps eventually see the birth rate drop, too. Many of the children here today will not ever get to my age, perhaps not even your age. It is a sad reality.'

Quintin Cornelius, Lily's husband and world-famous musician, who'd been the first one to come to the cattle truck and see Chloe and the others when they arrived, came up behind Lily and hugged her, landing a loud kiss on her cheek.

Lily blushed. 'I'm just glad we were here to help you.'

Chloe remembered her parents having the same easy relationship, touching whenever they sat near, holding hands and hugging a lot. She hadn't thought about it for a while, but it all came flooding back, and she understood why her father had wanted to make the slimeball from the mine pay dearly for her mother's death.

'Thank you again, Lily, and nice to meet you, Quintin. Have a merry Christmas,' Chloe said.

'You too,' Quintin said.

'Take your father home,' Lily said. 'And good luck.'

Enoch waved to her from across the yard where he was walking the horses with Xo. She beckoned him over, watching him give the lead reins to Xo, then jog to where she stood.

In that second, a *bakkie* drove through the gate and skidded to a stop in front of the school, spraying dust all over them and only missing Enoch by a smidge as he jumped out of the way.

'Hey, Doc, the veterinarians have run into a small problem,' the driver said, climbing out of the car and leaving the door open.

'What'd they do this time, Walter?' Lily asked.

'The blond one, Michael, he fell into the dip tank when he was helping the cattle through and broke his leg. After hosing him down, I brought him to you. He's lying in the back, and all I can hope is that he did not swallow any of the dip. Hope you can set it without him needing to fly to Bulawayo for an X-ray.'

'Oh my God, he still stinks of dip and cow shit,' Quintin said. 'I thought you said you hosed him down.'

'I did!' Walter protested.

'Come on, they have enough on their plate,' Chloe told Enoch. 'Lily said we could take Dad home. I'll fill you in on the way.'

'They are angels in my eyes, coming to our country and helping our people without expecting payment. Everyone always wants a handout somewhere along the line, and yet, they come to help, expecting nothing in return,' Enoch said.

'There's a little bit more to their research visit, but yes, I agree with you wholeheartedly,' Chloe said.

'Right, let us get Mike and that Caçador Escuro out of here, and then next stop, Beitbridge Police Station to drop off our prized cargo,' Enoch said. 'If all goes well, we will be home before three o'clock.'

CHAPTER 34

Kupua shook her head. Douglas Jones had made a bloody mess of things across southern Africa.

She tapped into her sources in the South African Police and reviewed their file. Douglas had been heading for exposure, even before he had cooked his client. She looked at the pictures of his *bakkie* and of the body of the woman, Nicole Schaffer. Kupua remembered her clearly. What was left of her body was still at the morgue.

Kupua read the autopsy report. The police suspected that she'd been burned after being killed as there were bullet wounds in both kidneys and the lungs. One AK-47 round had been recovered from her lungs. Poor woman hadn't stood a chance. At least she was dead before Douglas had torched her.

A second round had been found on her, which looked like it'd been in a pocket or inside her bra. It didn't match the AK-47 slug that killed her. It was a soft nose, most likely from a hunting rifle. It was an anomaly in the report and underlined by the examining doctor in their notes.

Douglas hadn't made sure that her trophy had been destroyed. That was just sloppy.

The other body had been identified as belonging to a black person.

Kupua wrote in purple pen *Not dead* in the margin and underlined it. Then she wrote: *Why pretend?*

She continued reading the report. Someone had found the bodies after the predators had begun dining on them, wrapped them individually in sections of a small camping tent they had cut apart, and piled thornbushes over them, trying to protect them. *WHY* and *WHO* were put in capital letters on the report.

Kupua underlined those.

She was relatively certain that Douglas wasn't the one who had tried to preserve Nicole's or the black man's bodies. This was a cruel side of him she didn't know about, and that was a problem for the 6th.

If he was still alive, Kupua needed to find him. She needed to know what had actually happened that day, and why he had chosen to not only try to deceive the police, but also the 6th.

Why had he walked away from his burnt-out, shot-to-shit vehicle?

Did he really think he could outsmart her, pretending to be dead?

She needed to understand him better. He lived just outside Bulawayo, Zimbabwe. Closing the file, Kupua locked it in her white briefcase with purple trim.

Time to change countries.

She suspected that the hourglass on Douglas's life was running out of sand, if it hadn't already.

Douglas was sweating.

The painkillers the doctor had given him had long since worn off, even before he had escaped. Thanks to his temporary cast, the police had been unable to put his hand behind his back. The hard bandages on his hand had made a perfect tool to knock out and then strangle the first cop who had walked him out to the waiting transport. He had been able to arm himself and threaten the second one to show him the placement of the anti-hijack switch on the *bakkie*, before he'd broken his neck, and thrown both men in the back.

Time was ticking too fast.

Kupua would find him and end his life, but he needed to get to those responsible first.

He needed to finish what he had started.

They all deserved to die.

He was grateful that finally after all his goading, and performing and threatening, it had been so simple to manipulate a doctor into helping him find out exactly where they were heading when he was at the clinic.

The Mazunga area.

He had hunted the lowveld often, and his tracker Virgil was already in that area, ready for his next hunt in the new year. He had a cache of weapons and other interesting articles he'd managed to accumulate buried on the hunting concession Lindani Conservancy. And he even knew their farm, Delaware. It was not right next door to the conservancy, but close enough that he was aware of its existence. The middle-aged woman who lived there was quite a looker; he'd seen her around. Grace, they had called her.

The police van he'd stolen was the perfect disguise. He'd stripped one of the two dead police officers in the back; his uniform would be the master key to his plan. His ticket through their security.

He listened carefully to the police radio, hearing nothing about his escape or his failure to appear in Bulawayo as a prisoner transfer. He had lived in the country long enough to know that Zimbabwe's political powers that be would never publicly acknowledge that someone had stolen a police vehicle, so the people on the farm would not know any differently.

'So, your plan is to go into their home territory, shoot them all, and then clear out again?' he said aloud into the cool night air.

'Correct,' he answered himself. Then he drummed a little beat on the steering wheel with his good hand in celebration before he turned off the main road, on to the Lindani Conservancy.

He had work to do tonight. Preparations to make.

By first light, they would all be dead.

CHAPTER 35

The first thing Nick noticed at Delaware, once they had finished unloading the horses and having a much-needed shower, was the familiar sound of a working farm. It called to him as he walked around. The mooing of the cows, a stockman cracking a whip, men singing in harmony as they brought in a few dairy cows to be milked for the evening. The constant buzz of flies and other insects were all sounds he loved and had grown up with, and lately hadn't heard enough of as he'd been more involved as a game ranger in Kruger. Sounds that were definitely not of the bush.

Delaware had changed since he'd last seen it. The paint looked faded and peeling, and there were fences that were not as tight as they should be. While the cattle they had passed as they drove in were numerous, they didn't seem as fat as they should be at this time of year. Granted, they had arrived during a drought, but they were still surviving off the veld, and there were no signs that they were being supplement-fed.

He looked across at the slightly raised position of the house, close to the huge horse barn, and peeking out beyond that was the equipment shed. A little further to the left was the workers' compound. Everything was surrounded by Delaware's signature eight-foot security fence that had become the norm during the war years, which was even more essential now with the dissident war raging.

The only place that Nick had ever seen that had the workers' compound inside its own fence was on Mike's farm. He remembered asking Mike about it years before and being told that his workers were vital to the running of the place, so they needed the same security as they had at the house. At the time, Nick hadn't thought too much about it, but now he realised that Enoch's house had been in that compound, and it had been Mike's way of keeping his best friend safe.

His eyes came back to the horses they'd brought home, which were out in the paddocks alongside the barn. His eyes followed Chloe's mare, Pampero, her coat shimmering in the evening light after a good grooming. She stood a little away from the other horses, her pregnant stomach clearly visible. She held herself as if she was proud to be in her new home. He wondered if perhaps she was dressage trained because she moved with such grace and poise. Then he looked at Mike's horse, Diablo.

He remembered a time when that horse had been such an essential part of their stick in the Grey's Scouts, a member of their unit. He had cursed the night he'd had to help Enoch bury Maria and Monsoon. In a way, it was kinder to Mike not to know what'd happened to his beloved Maria, given that he'd broken her in after capturing her as a wild horse in the Matopos.

He looked further away, into the outer paddock, and the horse there caught his eye. A big bay stallion sniffed the air and pawed the ground, knowing that Chloe's stallion, Marin, was now in his territory. He ran up and down the wooden fence, whinnying and challenging his rival from a paddock away.

'You watching Pampero?' Chloe had walked up to stand beside him.

'I'm watching that bay stallion. He's something,' Nick said.

Chloe frowned.

'You scared of him?'

'Not scared,' Chloe said. 'Just cautious. That's Buran. His father was Zonda, the stallion that we captured wild in the Matopos when I was eight. Buran was one of the last sired from him before he died. Despite the closeness to Diablo, Buran was left with Grace because he was only a tiny foal when Enoch and Xo brought the horses through to South Africa and he might not have survived the long journey. It nearly broke Enoch's heart to make the decision. I know that Enoch always hoped to get back here one day. The boys told me that Buran is wild, and they don't ride him like they do the other stock horses. They say he breaks a lot of bones. He throws every rider, and from the sounds of it, he's not even green broke yet.'

'Caution sounds good and wise in your case. He's stunning.'

'That he is. You're welcome to take a closer look. He's gentle to talk to, just not to ride apparently.' They began walking towards the horses in the corral, but then halfway there, Chloe stopped. Nick bumped into her and put his hand out and touched her arm.

That was a big mistake.

An electrical current went through his hand, and he pulled it away. He could still feel an echo of her soft skin tingling in his fingertips while she remained suddenly distracted. He needed to keep fighting his attraction to her—he couldn't let her know how he felt now. Not when he had to go back to Kruger Park. When he had to leave her.

Chloe stood quietly, then she appeared to straighten up as if she was facing an enemy and needed to show her full height. She looked at him, reminding him that she was as flexible as a lioness. And she was just as feisty—he needed to take care around her. He could see her annoyance wasn't directed at him but couldn't see the source.

'It's so frustrating that we had to leave here. Seeing the differences now that we've returned hurts. Delaware is falling apart. There's so much in disrepair—I look at it and see all the potential.'

'Stop beating yourself up at what was. You need to focus on what's ahead, not look back. Looking back is a dangerous game; it can keep you trapped in the past.'

'Is that where you still are?' she asked.

He stood unmoving and opened his mouth to answer and say no, but it wouldn't come out. Was he trapped in the past? Was he guilty of letting the past rule his present life?

No. He was shit scared of the future. Of the depth of his feelings for Chloe, and everything that he knew he was willing to give up just to be near her.

Chloe put her head on the top plank of the horse fence and called to Buran. She looked every bit the typical cowgirl, with her jungle hat on her head, her button-up shirt, jeans and boots, but it was her attitude that defined her as the heir apparent to Delaware. A confidence about her now that she was home. He looked towards the horses again to distract himself from dwelling on their parting, which he knew was imminent.

The bay looked at her, then looked at where his challenge to Marin was going unnoticed, then decided Chloe was the better option and trotted up to the fence, tossing his head.

She stretched out her hand, and the bay smelled it, and then his breathing changed as if he recognised her.

Chloe got through the fence and stood next to him, her arms around his neck. She patted him and spoke to him in a constant stream of soothing words. The stallion continued to toss his head but started to rest it occasionally against her for a moment—before going back to the tossing. Eventually, he calmed right down, making little noises and leaning his head against her body.

Nick stood and watched the pair's reunion after the years apart until Chloe's voice sliced into his thoughts.

'I watched Buran being born right in those stables one night. I was home from boarding school, and it was freezing. We stayed with his mother, Flicker, all through the night as she moved constantly, trying to ease her contractions. In the morning that little rubber-legged colt was born. He came out in his sack and Dad let me help pull it off him to make sure that he could breathe okay.'

'Buran, another wind, I get that, but Flicker, you kidding me, right?'

'She came with that name—someone obviously loved books. Buran was such a beautiful foal—he was so tame. I used to spend hours with him,' she said. 'They shouldn't have tried to turn him into a stock horse. He's so much better than that.'

Nick smiled as he remembered seeing her with a palomino when he'd visited, and how it had gone everywhere with her, even following her into the house, until Sarah had shut that one down.

'I remember Enoch telling Grace on the phone one day that under no circumstances were they to castrate him. Enoch might have left him behind, but I think he also missed seeing this little one grow up.'

She patted the horse one last time on his neck, climbed back through the fence, and turned to walk towards the stables.

Nick looked around inside the huge building.

Chloe ran her hand along the wall of the barn. 'These stables were rebuilt when I was five. Not sure if you remember that. The old wooden one was damaged by a fire that burned out more than half our farm. When my dad and Enoch rebuilt it, they made sure that it would stand up to almost anything, and the horses would be safe. I used to have my own fort built in the loft. I might show it to you one day.'

He laughed.

Chloe grinned. 'Seriously, Xo eventually made it with me. He got tired of me running away, so he built me a place to go away from the house, which was still close by. That way, he didn't have to track me into the bush all the time. I was really quite a brat, and he was the one tasked with entertaining me when I was younger. Poor guy, he was only a year older, and I was like this little girl hanging around him all the time.'

'You are such good friends, though; I can't imagine you running away from him,' Nick said.

'It wasn't from him. Some of my best childhood memories are when he and I would go out on the horses, or just walk. We'd track and watch the game, shoot something or trap a pheasant for lunch if we wanted to. We'd cook it on a fire we'd made. I loved those times. I can't even remember what I was always running away from.'

One of the grooms came over and shook Chloe's hand in both of his. 'It is good to see you home, Miss Chloe.'

Chloe smiled. 'Nick, remember Seth, he's been with our family for many years.'

'It is good that you are home again. We are all very excited for your return,' Seth said.

'Thank you,' Chloe said.

They walked past one of the young stable hands who was spreading hay into a stable. He couldn't have been more than thirteen years old and was at that stage of a gangly teenager where limbs grew faster than the rest of the body. Nick remembered that stage only too well.

'Miss Chloe.'

'Good grief. Isaac, is that you? Look how tall you are!'

He grinned and stood at his full height.

Chloe said, 'Thanks for getting the stable ready for the horses. I know that they'll all sleep really well tonight knowing they are safe and home again at last, and the new ones will love it here.'

'*Ngiyabonga*, thank you,' Isaac said.

Chloe smiled. 'Please say hi to your mum for me. She was always so nice. I remember eating *sadza* at her fire many times.'

Isaac smiled, and Nick realised that he seemed to preen because she'd noticed him and knew his name without having anyone remind her, even after being away for five years. A few things had changed on the farm, but one thing that hadn't was that Chloe was the boss's daughter, and she would be shown the respect due to her.

It didn't hurt that Chloe was a people person and could talk to everyone as if she hadn't been away. In his heart Nick knew that this was where Chloe belonged. Not in some snot-nosed accounting firm in a high rise in South Africa. She was home.

Nick kept a step behind her as she continued their walk, just watching the sway of her body. He longed to have the right to hug her right there, but he knew he didn't, and he probably never would. Their time together over the last three weeks had been just an adventure. Nothing more.

Eventually, they were out on the other side of the building, and as they stepped side by side, they kept their own silences while they walked up to the homestead.

The sun had set, dinner was over, and the moon was already busy dusting the acacia trees with silver moonlight when Nick walked into the lounge and sat down next to Chloe. 'You okay?'

He could hardly recognise her. Gone was the dirty traveller and in her place sat a beautiful young woman in T-shirt and shorts, with a faint smell of apples still lingering on her freshly shampooed hair. He'd got used to the street urchin. She looked her age now, and she looked amazing.

He was reminded again of the gap in their ages—he was an old man at twenty-eight and she was still so young at twenty-one. Well, almost twenty-two as she would have reminded him.

'I'm perfect. I'm home,' Chloe said, smiling.

'Where's Mike?'

'Enoch got him bathed and into his bed with his legs elevated. I'm sleeping in the room right next door. I can only hope that he sleeps well now that he's home again.'

'But things aren't quite as you thought they'd be, are they?' Nick asked.

Chloe shook her head. 'No, but I don't mind. Aunty Grace and I had a long talk. She's had a really hard time looking after Delaware. I often asked her to come visit us in Howick, and she always said that the reason she couldn't make it was because she couldn't leave the farm for more than a day. Turns out there was always more to this. My aunty couldn't bear the thought of my mother lying here all alone, and because she wasn't with her when she died in hospital, she feels too guilty to leave her grave. That's why she never visited and wouldn't come with me when I left with Dad.'

'That's sad and yet beautiful at the same time,' Nick said. 'Devotion like that is rare nowadays.'

Chloe nodded. 'She has her own house. It's not like we've moved back into her space, but I just feel so sad for her that while I was living my life for the last five years, she's been in such a sad frame of mind. I don't believe that's what my mum would have wanted.'

'It's sad, but if that is what she chooses, then you need to respect that,' Nick said.

'I do, but she's stuck in the past,' Chloe said. 'She wanted Enoch and Xo to live in the servants' compound. I said no, they live in the same house as Dad and me now, and that's not up for discussion. I had to explain to her how Enoch takes Dad to the toilet at night. And that I'll need to get a maid to help with everything once he's ready in the mornings, but Enoch and Xo are the ones to bathe him and help him dress. She didn't understand how bad my dad was.'

'I think he looks better now than when we started out,' Nick said.

'I think he enjoyed being out in the bush again,' Chloe said. 'Having the sun on his face.'

'Was she upset?'

'A little. She says my mum wouldn't have liked it. I tried to explain that for us it's normal, and while I do a lot for my dad, without them over the last few years, I wouldn't have managed.'

'Where are Enoch and Xo now?'

'She has allowed other workers to live in their house anyway, so it was an argument she wasn't going to win. They're in the old guest bedrooms. I have to have them close to Dad. We didn't travel all these miles to start that segregation bullshit again. She'll have to get used to it.'

Nick smiled. 'I'm sure she will, but you need to remember that Delaware's her home, too.'

'I know.'

'Where do her security guards sleep?' Nick asked.

'She's built them an *ikhaya* inside the security fence, next to her house. Apparently, none of the militia get to sleep in the main houses; they all have that arrangement.'

'Now that you're home, they'll want to issue you guards, too. I can't see you "sharing" militia. What're you going to do about that?' Nick asked.

'I don't know—that's a problem for another day. Tonight, I just want to sit in my old chair and enjoy the smell of home, listen to the sounds outside and know that Enoch is safe, and the troubles that followed Sebastian's death can't reach us here. And that the darn murderer is behind bars and not out there, lining us up in his crosshairs again.'

'I can understand that. It's probably not a great time to bring this up, but you need to know that Khululani and I can't stay here for long. We need to go back to the Kruger. We got you guys home, safe and sound, but now we need to face the music back at work—about where we've been for the last three weeks. Our leave is officially over in another week, but they must still be wondering what's going on. Knowing that I travelled north in a truck, they must be quite confused as to why they still have one sitting in the garage at Crocodile Bridge.'

Chloe smiled. 'Thank you for helping us. I really do appreciate it. I'm not sure we would've made it without you. I just wish you didn't have to leave … so soon.'

Nick smiled and took her hand in his. 'I've loved spending the time with you and seeing what an amazing person you've become. I remembered you from all those years ago as a wild child. Determined and headstrong—but a hellraiser, nevertheless. I feel privileged to know you now as an adult, and glad I could help see you home safely.'

Tears welled in Chloe's eyes. 'But you're leaving, and it's only five sleeps to Christmas. Can't you just stay till then? I know you have to go, but I've got so used to having you around. I sort of hoped you'd stay.'

Nick shook his head. He was so tempted to stay. He reached over and wiped a tear from her eyes. 'I have responsibilities in the Kruger, a job. Khululani has responsibilities. We can't just both walk away.'

He had finally got it into his head that the seven-year age gap between them didn't make him a cradle-snatcher. He could even get it out of his head that he would have been her legal guardian if Mike had died five years ago. He could even rest easy with his decision not to be involved in the physical aspect of that fateful day now. After Enoch had opened up to Chloe about the day her father was injured and burying the gold, he had felt a lot happier with his decisions.

He finally understood how Mike's mind had worked, that he had loved Sarah so deeply, he had put his own life on the line for her memory, to get her the justice she deserved. And finally, he knew without a doubt that what he felt was just like that: he was in love with Chloe.

Given the chance, they could take their relationship to the next level, and he would be the happiest man on earth. But there was the issue of the gold. She was willing to spend it, and he still didn't want any part of it.

He leaned over and gently put his lips to hers. When she looked into his eyes, her own widened and immediately softened.

It didn't bother him that they hadn't fluttered closed, that she was looking at their first proper kiss like everything else, with her eyes wide open. He brought his hand up to the back of her head and pulled her closer. He felt the intake of her breath. Her eyes at last relaxed and closed as he slid his tongue slowly along her lips, and they opened for him. Sometime during that exploration, he realised that her arms were wrapped around his neck, and she was holding him just as tightly as he was holding her.

He pulled back and rested his forehead against hers. 'And that is why I can't stay—I need to go back to South Africa, tie up loose ends,' Nick said, but he still held her tightly. 'I'm so proud of you. Not many women would have undertaken a journey like we just did or have been prepared to undertake a trek like that in the first place. You've just found your wings. I want so much to see you fly with them and enjoy your life, forge your own path, but I have to return to the Kruger.'

'I hope we can still call each other. You'll be there on the other end of the phone, won't you?' she whispered.

'Always,' Nick said, reaching forward to move a stray piece of hair from her face and tuck it behind her ear.

'I know it's only been a few intense weeks, but I'm going to miss you. You've always been so good to me.'

'An illusion, a fond memory,' he said with a wry smile.

'It's always been real to me,' Chloe said quietly.

Nick smiled, then hugged her. 'You've got a farm to get working, horses to breed. Dreams to achieve. You'll forget about me in no time.'

She snuggled into him, and he kissed the top of her head.

'I really don't want you to go, but when you come back, promise me that you'll bring Khululani with you. You're both always welcome here.'

'He and I are inseparable, believe me,' Nick said. 'Just like you and Xo.'

'Xo and I are not inseparable—he's my brother.'

'You have a great brother there. Hold onto him. He's fiercely protective of you, and living here, you're going to need a friend like him.'

Chloe smiled. 'I will.'

'Tomorrow when Enoch, Xo and Filipe go back into Mozambique to collect the rest of the possessions, they'll drop us near a bus stop so we can start our journey home. The longer I stay here, the harder it'll be to leave.'

His head screamed at him that if he delayed, he'd never leave, and never return to Kruger. And if he stayed, he would have to confront her about the use of the gold.

CHAPTER 36

England's Top 6 Trophies

1. Fox
2. Woodcock, forest hens and geese
3. Pheasant
4. Roe deer
5. Red deer
6. Man

Ireland's Top 6 Trophies

1. Fox
2. Red grouse, partridge and wild ducks
3. Pheasant
4. Fallow and sika deer
5. Native red deer
6. Man

CHAPTER 37

The sound of dogs going mad outside woke Chloe from an already troubled sleep. She went to the window to look out. It was still dark. A vehicle had pulled up at the gate, and the militia was opening it.

'What the hell?' she muttered, throwing on a tracksuit top and some canvas slip-on *takkies*. She pulled open her door—and found Enoch about to knock on it.

'Good, you are awake. The police just arrived.'

She squinted at her watch. 'It's two o'clock in the morning.'

'That is true,' he said as they walked onto the veranda. The floodlights were on all around the security fence, and they could clearly see where two policemen stood by their vehicle. One was speaking with a militia as another guard jogged towards them, having closed the gates.

The way one of the men held himself looked familiar to Chloe. But she couldn't quite place it. He stood taller than the black man who was talking, and when they had switched on a light, he had turned his back to them.

She didn't hear anything, but suddenly both militia fell to the ground. Then the police officer looked up directly at her.

'Oh my God,' Chloe gasped. 'It's the Caçador Escuro. He's here.'

'Contact! Contact!' shouted Enoch, pushing Chloe below the small wall of the veranda, just as a spray of bullets zinged over them and sank into the plaster on the outside wall, showering them in debris.

'Get into the lounge,' Enoch instructed.

But before she could take off on her hands and knees, there was another spray of bullets above them.

'Where are you guys?' Nick called from inside the house.

'Pinned down on the front veranda. Lit up like this he can see us clear as day. You need to kill the lights,' Enoch said.

'On it,' Khululani answered, and suddenly the floodlights were exploding as he took out each one in turn. Last to go were the veranda lights, but those went off together, so obviously someone had found the switch inside for them.

'Go now,' Enoch said.

Filipe materialised next to Chloe. He put his AK-47 above the small wall and pulled the trigger, returning fire in the general direction they had last seen the men, giving Chloe and Enoch enough cover to get back inside the house. Filipe moved backwards through the door, still crouching and firing.

Only when he was through, did Enoch slam the heavy wooden door shut. He reached up and locked it. 'This is not going to keep them out for long.'

'How many?' Filipe asked.

'Just two that we could see,' Enoch said. 'The Caçador Escuro and a black guy, both dressed as policemen.'

'Shit,' Xo said from behind them.

'Keep all the lights off. We know the house layout. It's our tactical advantage if we can get him to come inside,' Enoch said.

'I will go out the back, through a window, try to get behind them,' Khululani said.

'Okay,' Enoch said. 'Xo, get Mike and help him into the old cellar. Chloe will go there now. You all heard him when he was ranting; what he will do to her if he catches her. We can't take that risk. Chloe, despite your training, this is your time to hide. Keep your dad safe down there. Until you get the all clear from us.'

Chloe nodded. This was real. There was no time to argue.

She watched as Xo crouched low and ran for her father's room, and she went to move the furniture in the lounge to access the old cellar.

She heard Enoch behind her. 'Fucking hell, this shitbag is never going to give up. We need to drop this bastard dead, once and for all. Shoot to kill.'

Seconds turned to long minutes as Chloe attempted to push the heavy billiards table off the trap door to the cellar. She remembered practising this move again and again as a child; in case their farm came under attack by terrorists. She had no idea then that she would be doing that routine now as an adult.

Back then, the table hadn't been sitting on the trap door. Now a small carpet covered the area, partly concealing it, and the table leg was directly on the trap door. She tried again, but even with all her strength she couldn't move it.

Chloe could hear soft footsteps just outside the lounge. The door creaked as it opened, and in the light from the passageway she could make out a double barrel of a shotgun as it peeked around the wood.

She already knew it wasn't one of them; they knew she was in the room. Xo would have come in bent over, dragging her dad, not standing.

It was confirmed by his pungent odour. She could smell the man before he even stepped into the lounge. Not only did he have bad body odour, but he'd obviously been baiting traps or something before coming to their farm, because the smell of decaying meat hung around him and made her want to gag.

She crouched down behind the large table leg and pulled her tracksuit top over her nose. He took a step inside and hesitated, as if waiting for his eyes to adjust and to perhaps find a light switch. He was fumbling along the inside wall with his hand.

If she didn't react now, he would see her. She knew this room and everything in it. She did the only thing she could do. She leapt up, grabbed one of the silver castings of a pheasant that sat on top of the table, and she rushed him.

Using the heavy ornament as a weapon, she hit him on the side of his head with both hands, wielding it like a club as she came at him from the side.

He let off one shot with his shotgun, still facing forwards, and began screaming.

She hit him hard on the side of his neck with her hands clasped tightly around the pheasant, and as he fell, she brought her knee up and connected with his nose, smashing it.

He dropped his weapon as he brought his hands to his nose.

She dropped the pheasant and used her elbow to smack the back of his neck. As she heard a crunching sound, he dropped to the floor. Immediately, she grabbed at his free arm and bent it as far behind his back as she could while kicking the shotgun away.

He screamed again.

Nick burst into the room at full speed, his rifle on his shoulder, ready to kill.

'I'm okay, I'm okay, don't shoot me,' she said, recognising his silhouette.

'Oh thank God,' he said, taking a step inside.

'He's down but not dead. Turn the light on. I don't think this one is the Caçador Escuro. He's too small.'

Nick flashed on the light—and then quickly flicked it off again.

'It's not him,' she said.

'Okay, but now we have given away our location in the house, we can expect him,' Nick said, smacking the man on the back of the head with the butt of his hunting rifle. 'He's out now. Quick, pass me the telephone. We can use the cord to tie him up.'

Chloe grabbed the phone, pulled the cord out of the wall and took it to Nick.

Just as he finished tying the man up tight, the door opened with the same creak as before.

Xo's back appeared and he was dragging Mike, half on his shoulders, half on the floor. 'Chloe, you ready with that door open?' he called softly.

'Shit, Xo, couldn't you hear the commotion going on in here?' Chloe said.

'No, I was across the hall with the door closed. I thought it was in the other rooms, obviously. What's that smell? Are you okay?'

'I'm fine. So is Nick. One of them got in here!' she whispered. 'I couldn't move the table. One of its legs is on the trap door …'

'Come on, Xo, put Mike down. You and I should be able to shift it,' Nick said, and they went to the table.

The door opened just as Nick and Xo began to push.

Nick grabbed his rifle off the top of the table but was a split second too late.

'Drop it. Don't move or you're dead,' the voice of the Caçador Escuro said. He turned on the light.

Chloe could see that his hunting rifle was pointed directly at Nick.

'Hands on your head. I told you I would kill you, didn't I,' the Caçador Escuro snarled.

Nick still had his rifle in his hand.

'I said, drop it,' the Caçador Escuro repeated.

Nick said, 'I'm dead either way, what's the difference?'

'The difference is me having the pleasure of seeing your face when I fuck your girlfriend, Chhhhh-lllllll-ooooo-eeee, and there is nothing you can do about it.'

A strange noise came from somewhere near the door. It sounded raw. Guttural. Unnatural. Only once before had Chloe ever heard her father make it, and that day had ended with Sebastian dying.

'No, Dad,' she called at the exact moment Caçador Escuro cursed, 'What the fuck!'

Chloe could see her father's outline as he gripped the fallen silver pheasant and used its tail to stab into the Caçador Escuro's leg, just above his boots. He was jerking the projectile downwards now that it was in. Still hanging onto it.

At Caçador Escuro's curse, Xo spun on the balls of his feet and rushed him so fast that Xo was almost on top of him before a shot went off.

Chloe screamed. 'No!'

At that moment, the Caçador Escuro slid to his knees. But he didn't go any further. Filipe stood behind him, his bayonet protruding out the front of the man, holding him in place.

'It is over. He is dead. I can go home now. I have kept my promise to my general and protected your life, Miss Chloe.'

CHAPTER 38

TEN DAYS LATER

Chloe woke to the familiar sounds of the farm. The crowing of a cockerel somewhere in the compound, and the answering cock-a-doodle-do from a rooster closer to the house. She heard the men whistling as they moved cattle that bellowed in protest at being roused from their sleep, and the bells of the billy goats that clanged so that the herd boy could find them when they wandered away while grazing. From somewhere closer came the rhythmic sound of someone sweeping back and forth with a broom.

Sounds of home.

But one sound was missing. That of her father being moved around in the next room. Of Enoch's deep voice as he attended to Mike's needs early in the morning.

She dragged herself out of bed.

She still couldn't believe that they'd travelled so far, only to lose her dad on the night they got home, his head receiving its final fatal blow. She would never forget the sacrifice he'd made to save her, Nick and Xo.

After checking the time, she showered and got herself ready for the burial of his ashes.

She wondered what had happened to the body of the Caçador Escuro, if he had family somewhere to mourn him. She hoped not. She wanted his spirit forever lost, forever tortured for the hurt and misery he had caused her family, and so many other families. Killers like him should not be allowed to have rest and redemption in the afterlife.

She took a deep breath as they all gathered. Nick stood close to her and held out his hand. She grasped it tightly and looked at the others. Xo wore a pained expression. Next to him, Aunty Grace's quiet tears tore at Chloe's heart. She knew that her aunt had cared deeply for her dad, and she had done everything she could to help him. Including living alone on his land, so far from any town.

Now he was gone.

Khululani stood beside Nick, and Filipe was notable by his absence, having disappeared before they could even call the police after the attack. She hated that he hadn't said goodbye. That she hadn't got to thank him. She hadn't even got to give him a Christmas present. But she could understand why he had left.

Enoch was in the middle of the area marked off by the small iron chain where her mother was buried. Her grave was covered in white quartz stones and outlined with whitewashed rocks. Rosebushes had been planted close by, and on the grave itself grew African daisies. Now they were to the side, and Enoch had dug a hole about half a metre deep. He stood with the spade next to him.

There was no piper to make her cry by playing 'Taps' on his bagpipes as there had been at the formal military service that had been held for her dad. The forlorn 'Day Is Done' song got her every time. There were no Grey's Scouts' flags to decorate the area, or people she hadn't seen before offering their condolences for her dad. Just the people who cared enough to be there to place him in the deep ground and reunite him with his beloved Sarah.

Chloe said, 'I love you, Dad. I'm glad we managed to get you back here so you and Mum can be together again. I'm going to miss you.' She stepped forward to place the urn in the hole, then looked up. 'Anyone want to say anything else?'

Xo kissed his fingers and pointed to the urn.

Grace said, 'May he at last rest in peace.'

Enoch took the urn from her, and kneeling in the dirt, reached deep into the hole and gently placed it inside. 'Rest now, my brother.'

As he began to fill the hole, silent tears fell from Chloe's eyes and ran freely down her cheeks. She looked around. At the top of the gravesite, Grace had organised a small white plaque that said:

Sarah Elizabeth Mitchell

6th April 1939 – 5th May 1980

'Gone to fly with the angels too soon.

Loved and missed by all of us.'

She would have to get the wording changed now so that it had both her mum and dad together.

'Thanks,' Chloe said as she watched Enoch close up the hole and put the quartz and flowers back in place. When he was done, he placed the spade on the ground, pulled his feet together as he snapped to attention, and saluted the grave. Something she had never seen him do.

'Farewell, Corporal Mike Mitchell.' He dug in his pocket and removed a horseshoe which he placed next to the white plaque.

Nick saluted the grave as well.

She saw tears in Enoch's eyes as he turned from the grave and walked away. She ran to catch up with him and hugged him tightly. He stood still for a moment then enveloped her in a bear hug, and Xo and Nick joined in.

She didn't know if everything was going to be okay. There was still so much uncertainty, but while their epic run back to Zimbabwe was going to make their lives different, the closeness that they'd shared as a family had survived the ordeal, and together they could all face a new future.

CHAPTER 39

Chloe sat on the stable floor watching as Pampero delivered her foal. It was the best New Year's Eve gift any horse could give to her owner.

Knowing that the time was coming, they'd brought her into the birthing stable to keep an eye on her. It couldn't have been a day more filled with contrast if Chloe had planned it.

Her father's burial had been filled with a heart-wrenching sadness that would always be there, but it had also brought her so much peace. Knowing that he'd been there to protect her as a daughter, right to his last breath, was a gift she would never forget, but it also brought into focus everything he'd done. She understood her father had done it all for love. She knew that he had been trying to make things right when he was hurt, and this incident had helped her to comprehend fully the depth of the love he must have felt for her mother. Knowing that at last he was no longer in pain, stuck inside a body that didn't respond to him, that his mind was very much still there, in the present with them at the end, had made the last five years of hardships worth it.

She was now totally alone in the world, but the knowledge that he rested beside her mother, and they would forever be together filled her with an unexpected joy. Her parents were reunited.

She sniffed. It was all so emotional, and a sad close to their year.

At least with the birth of Pampero's baby, not everything was doom and gloom.

As much as Chloe hated interfering with nature, having Pampero foal out in the paddocks was risky. There were too many predators on the farm—leopards, jackals and even hyenas. She had to give her horses—both mums and foals—the best chance possible, and this was the only way to ensure that they weren't attacked while giving birth.

Chloe knew from experience that sometimes the birthing would take an hour and be over, and sometimes it would stretch on for ages. It just depended on the horse's stamina and the confidence of the mare.

Pampero had been restless until finally lying down for a while. The stable cat, Sparta, meowed and rubbed up against Pampero as if to comfort her. The cat was friends with all the horses, and while Chloe patted her horse, she gave the cat an affectionate stroke, too.

The cat was diligent with its duties in the stables: catching the mice and other vermin, which included the odd snake delivered to the grooms, and now, being there for Pampero to give birth, apparently. Encouraging the mare along with helpful meowing and a brush of affection, including the occasional headbutt as they progressed along. Sparta was part of their team, and Chloe hadn't seen a single horse object to having her in the stables.

Pampero stood up again. Pawing the ground. Her breathing changed, and the little bag-bubble started to appear. While Chloe had managed with assisted births before, she couldn't stop herself as she crossed her fingers, hoping she wouldn't have to with this one. She so wanted it to be all natural. Sparta jumped up onto the wooden side of the stable to be out of her way and began to sharpen her claws, meowing all the while.

With a heave, Pampero buckled her front legs and went down gently, then lay on her side on the fresh hay that had been put down for her. She lay flat, and Chloe could hear her clearly heaving as her waters poured out, and she grunted as her contractions gained in strength.

With much effort, the front legs of the foal came out, and after a few more pushes a little nose began to crown. 'Come on, girl,' Chloe said.

Sparta, as if realising that the horse needed encouragement again, jumped down and rubbed along Pampero's neck.

Pampero grunted as the next contraction rippled through her. The full head was out, followed quickly by a little black body. Chloe removed the sack from the foal's nose then face to clear it away as the newborn started to move its head.

'Your baby is breathing; it's going to be okay,' Chloe said. 'Come on, girl, you can do this.'

As if understanding that her foal was being watched over by Chloe, and she and the foal were safe, Pampero rested—she could afford to have a little break. Sparta gave her some more encouragement, rubbing her again, only this time on her velvet nose. After about a five-minute rest, the young mother lifted herself up and looked backwards.

Her foal lay still attached to her in the sack. But it wanted its freedom, so it put its little front legs out, using its hooves for the first time, and attempted to move to get its nose closer to its mother's.

Pampero struggled, trying hard to expel the foal's legs from her birth chamber. Her baby planted its feet forward and attempted to stand, but with its back legs still inside Pampero, it wasn't going anywhere.

Chloe wanted to rush forward and remove what was left of the sack, to help the little tyke, but she'd once been told that the foal needed to fight the sack itself, and to use that time to know that it could move and get itself acquainted with its own muscles. It made sense, as much as moths needed to break out of their cocoons themselves, giving them the strength needed to fly with their wings. She didn't interfere—just continued encouraging Pampero with words as she sat a little way from her and her foal.

Pampero watched her baby as it struggled to achieve the coordination to complete the job, taking the time to regain her breath and rest, knowing that for the next few months, she was going to be an active mum with the little one at her tail end.

The foal eventually moved its legs and wiggled its body enough that it was facing away from her. It managed to pull its legs out of the canal, and then break the sack with its sharp hooves.

Pampero grunted as the foal kicked at the sack, which was almost totally off now. She gave her baby an encouraging soft kick with her hoof, but she didn't stand up just yet. Her foal collapsed back to lie flat on the hay, grunting and moaning, tired from the birthing experience. The little one gave itself one final heave with its little rubbery legs, and its nose touched Pampero's.

Chloe watched as mother and child met each other for the first time, tears of joy running down her cheeks.

Sparta plonked herself into Chloe's lap in a ball and purred, content. 'Come on, Sparta, they've done well; let's get out of here and give them some time alone—our job here is done.'

But she continued to sit, leaning her back against the wooden panel as the little foal and Pampero touched and bonded. Eventually, it got itself up on its little rubber legs, and Pampero stood and began to nurse her new baby for the first time.

'This never gets old,' Enoch said from behind her.

'Hey—how long have you been standing there?' she asked.

'A while. You and that cat were content, so I did not want to disturb you.'

'But you are always welcome to join me,' she said. Sparta continued purring, happy to have a warm human lap to sit in.

Enoch entered the stable, closing the door behind him, and sat down next to Chloe. 'What are you going to call this one?'

Chloe said, 'I was thinking of calling him Alexandrite.'

'Like Kimberlite,' Enoch said, before falling silent for a while. Then he said, 'Kimberlite and Diablo, they saw a lot of Africa with your dad and me. We travelled many, many kilometres together. From when we first captured them in the Matopos.'

'Yes, and now you are all home again, and the new generation is here. Little Alexandrite here has got big hooves to fill, hopefully under the watchful eyes of both those special horses,' Chloe said. 'It's hard to believe so much time has gone so fast since that day of the capture. But I still remember it.'

'Me too.'

She put her head on Enoch's shoulder, and they sat in silence, watching Pampero and Alexandrite as they got to know each other.

'Why are you sitting here alone? Where is Nick?'

'In the house, I guess. Probably getting ready to pack up and leave tomorrow now that Dad's at rest.'

'Did he tell you that was still his plan?'

'He didn't tell me otherwise,' Chloe said.

'I am an old black man, and not good with showing gestures of love. I fail horribly at those. I am lucky Xo is a boy and I did not have to deal with two emotional people these last few years. But I do know that despite your smile, not having Nick here tonight is hurting you. And I know that he will be sorry that he missed this birth,' Enoch said, reaching over and giving Sparta a scratch behind the ears.

'Guess at least we were here for it. That's what matters.'

'You should have told him this was happening. He would have been here with you, and the two of you could have talked. Lord knows you need time alone together,' Enoch said.

'I'm not so sure,' Chloe said. 'I don't think he realises that I love him. I don't want anyone else. I never have, and I don't think I ever will.'

'When you love someone the way you and Nick do, I do not know if you will ever need anyone else,' Enoch said softly.

'Nick doesn't love me.'

'What? Did he say that?'

'No, not outright. But when we got here, he was so keen to leave, get away from me again, go back to the Kruger. The only thing that kept him here this long was the fact that Dad died, and we had to have a funeral and a burial.'

'You are wrong. He does love you. I saw his face that very first day he saw you as a little girl. You were tiny when Sarah and Mike brought you home wrapped up in a pink blanket. He got to hold you then, and he watched you with the eyes of someone who was dumbstruck.'

'Dumbstruck because he couldn't believe I was a girl.'

'No, as in he was lost to you already. He was just seven, you were only ten days old. You were an angel to him. He wanted to protect you then. He was already sunk. I saw his face the night he left you here, after your father's accident. The determination that it took him to drag himself away from you then. I saw his face at Nigel's house, when he saw you again all black and blue after Sebastian's attack. If he could have killed that man there and then, I believe he would have.'

'Good thing he was already dead, then,' Chloe said.

'I suppose so.'

'If he really loves me, do you think he would stay?' Chloe said.

Enoch smiled. 'So, like your mother. Proud. Strong. So independent. So stubborn. I remember when your father fell in love with her, and how they almost did not become a couple because pride got in their way, too. Be careful, Chloe. Unless you spell it out really carefully to Nick that you are in love with him, he is just a man; he will not know.'

'I know,' said a voice from behind them. 'That's why I followed you here and have been eavesdropping just outside the stable, but I can't do that anymore. I need to tell you, Chloe, I'm not planning on going anywhere. I couldn't leave you.'

Nick was already coming through the stable door and met her halfway as she jumped up, dislodging Sparta from her lap in her attempt to get to him.

He hugged her tightly.

'I love you,' Chloe said.

'I know. You've shown me that a million times with the way you are towards me, but I could never form the words for you, and I was a chicken-shit and scared,' Nick admitted.

'That doesn't matter, I can wait. What matters is that you're not leaving,' she said, hugging him again.

'Right, I am out of here. You two have a lot to talk about,' Enoch said as he walked away and closed the stable door behind him.

They hugged for a time, with no words between them. Chloe reached up and touched Nick's face.

Nick smiled. 'Come on, sit, there is much to say.'

They sat close together in the straw, with their backs against the wall, holding hands. 'You're not the reason I was resisting staying,' Nick admitted. 'Mostly, it was the problem of the gold.'

'You wanted to leave me because of the gold? That's unfair. That's not something I had control over.'

He nodded. 'I realised that just because I don't believe that you should touch the gold—and because I made it my mission to turn my back on it and everything that it represented—you are entitled to just as much of an opinion as to what you do with it, given that it's your mother's and father's blood on that gold.'

Chloe frowned.

'You are not your father—you were not the one who plotted and committed the offence of taking the gold. Now that I know and understand his love for your mother, and I know what the gold stood for, I'm beginning to look at it a little differently, too …' He hesitated. 'I thought that I needed time to process everything alone, away from us. I was wrong. I was the one who believed all these years that if I had taken up arms again that day and helped with the robbery, that the outcome might have been different. Being told the reasoning behind why Mike and Enoch were going after it, and that they never meant to keep it, but blackmail the mine into admitting their liability, changed things. They never told me that part years ago. It lifted some of the burden, but not all of it. I was still involved, even if not physically, in taking that gold. I always believed that I was as guilty as both of them because I was the plan B for you and Xo if things went south. Then to top it all, I fell in love with you. I had this stupid idea in my head that I had to go away from you to ensure that it was you I loved. Not the idea that at least I could help you, I could play a part in your life, not be simply a plan B that your father once intended for me. But when you were threatened by the Caçador Escuro, and it was life and death, I would have chosen death rather than live without you, and that scared me more than ever.'

'Oh my God, and Enoch thinks I'm the stubborn one,' Chloe said. She moved and sat on Nick's outstretched legs, facing him and took both his hands in hers, holding them close to her chest.

They sat eye to eye.

Nick said, 'I don't know if I could've managed seeing you dig that gold up, even if you plan on using it to help others, because of what it represented before. Now, I'm not so sure what I feel, but I know that I don't want this hanging between us, keeping us apart. And then there is another issue.'

Chloe dropped her head. 'What else?'

'Your dad, he was heroic. Even in the end, he sacrificed himself for you, and I like to believe for us. I would like to believe that in those last moments when he did what he did, it was not only to save you, but to save the family that was there in the lounge together.

'My dad was a class A shit. He beat my mum, he was a drunk and he beat me, too. When he left, it was the best thing that ever happened to my mum and me. You are young, you will want kids. What if I'm like that deep inside me? What if I am just as bad as he was, and it all comes out only after we are together, or worse, when there is a kid screaming in the night and I'm trying to sleep, and I hurt it? What then? What if, like Mike and Enoch, I don't trust enough and I keep secrets that hurt the people I love, who I didn't intend to hurt?'

'Listen to me, you are not your father. You are not my father, and you are not Enoch. You are your own person. Just because these things happened to you, doesn't mean you will be like your father. Just because Mike and Enoch kept secrets from you and me, doesn't mean we will be like them. We are our own people. We make our own decisions, and we learn from the consequences of those decisions. We'll be fine, together, you and me. We will learn to talk to each other about things. We won't have these mammoth secrets.'

'I wish I was as sure as you, just make a decision and go with it,' he admitted.

'Not always. And as for the gold, if it staying buried means so much to you, then we leave it there. I don't need to dig it up.'

'That's a lot of money to leave buried.'

Chloe smiled. 'You need to believe in me when I say that gold stash is not going to change me. I have our family bank accounts, and there is plenty in those for us to restore Delaware to its former glory.'

'What are you saying?' Nick asked.

'I have enough money to pretty much do whatever I want to do, without digging up that gold. It can stay in the ground if that's what will help your conscience.'

'Are you serious? You are going to just leave it there because I ask you to? Because I'm not comfortable with it?'

'Yes, that's what I'm trying to tell you. Why would I access something that will cause you anguish? We have both had enough of that.'

'What? How? What type of wealth do you have to be able to afford to do that?' Nick spluttered.

'It's old family money. I wasn't sure how to process all this info that I was given and I'm still working through a lot of it. I didn't want to tell you because I still didn't know if you loved me for who I am. But apparently, my great-great-grandfather was in shipping and loved Africa. I only learned about it all last week when I was with the lawyers for my father's will.'

'You're a constant source of surprise; I'm so glad that I told you I loved you before you told me that.'

'You can't take it back; you said it,' Chloe said.

'I'm not taking anything back. I'm in love with you. Not your money.' He put his palm under her chin, then cupped her cheek tenderly.

Chloe reached out and touched Nick's face. While it looked tired, now it was at ease, as if a heavy burden had been lifted, and he was now free.

'I love you. I always have. I don't want to waste another day of our lives.' Nick leaned forward and kissed her on the lips. Softly at first, but then the burn of desire that had been simmering between them ignited. She could feel the exact same response from Nick's body as he increased the pressure and urgency of the kiss.

She knew that while they were both really stubborn, they were in for an interesting life.

Together.

CHAPTER 40

BULAWAYO, ZIMBABWE

Zimbabwe was a country of contradictions. While the not-so-new president tried to hoodwink the world that he wasn't creating a one-party Marxist/Leninist-like state, and that his country wasn't already starting its slide into an economic crisis caused by these socialistic reforms, the older colonial world still had influence on the surface to create a bubble of illusion, with its infrastructure of roads, railways, telephones and electricity already in place. An almost self-sufficient economy boosted by industries and mines, and international business investments. But Zimbabwe also had the ability to feed itself and export surpluses because of its mainly white commercial farmers. The country appeared to still be transitioning into its supposed multi-racial society that the same president was promoting, but at the same time, thunderclouds rumbled in the distance with their president's anti-American sentiments becoming bolder and more frequent.

Kupua watched a great example of this infrastructure now through her binoculars while she sat on the roof of Meikle's store, right next door to which was the beautiful Bulawayo Police Station, with its stunning architecture of sizeable sandstone blocks and large windows. She looked down into the inner courtyard.

Despite knowing that Douglas hadn't spilt any information about the 6th in his interview at Beitbridge, everything he had done still didn't make sense to her.

The report from the police made no sense either. Looking at the layout of the building from the outside, anyone could see that they had lied and were covering something up.

There was no way that Douglas had escaped them in Bulawayo Police Station, unless he had walked out the front door. He had to have got out of their custody between Beitbridge and Bulawayo to have got to the family in Mazunga, and the fact that he had a police van with him at the time of the attack proved that. Only there was nothing in their report about the stolen vehicle—that was information she had gained independently.

There had been nothing in their reports about the two dead police officers either.

Africa was proving to be a provocative continent, the people full of secrets and deceptions, lies and conspiracies committed by many, and ignored by others, as a thin veil of decency was hung over everything, making it all appear more civil than it actually was.

BERN, SWITZERLAND

Kupua stood in front of the chairperson. 'I do not believe that there is any problem left in Africa.'

'You certain?' the chairperson said, looking up from the report on her desk.

'There was nothing to clean up. He imploded.'

'And the family that he attacked?' the chairperson asked.

'As far as they are concerned, he's dead and gone, and they can continue their lives,' Kupua said. 'This family were just in the wrong place at the wrong time, and Hunter #4 lost control. It cost him his life and that of one of our members.'

The elders were seated on the velvet-cushioned chairs, and the meeting had been going on for a while. The purple-robed woman, Kupua, had seated everyone around the table, then ghosted out as always, her footsteps hardly audible on the plush carpet before the meeting started.

The hunters all looked at the empty chair where #4 usually sat.

'Lastly,' the chairperson at the head of the table said, 'we've had cause to believe that Hunter #4 at no time jeopardised our organisation. His client was killed in a terrorist attack, and later, Hunter #4 was killed in a different assault. Our rules are ancient, and they protect everyone within the Society.'

There was silence around the table.

'We would like to introduce to you, our new Hunter #4 ...'

GLOSSARY

ag shame - ag is a filler word like 'um'; *shame* is to express pity or sympathy; general slang term in Southern Africa.
baas - boss; Afrikaans, but used as a general term in Southern Africa.
bakkie - truck/ ute; Afrikaans, but used as a general term in Southern Africa.
beheer - control; Afrikaans.
bliksem - hit; Afrikaans.
Boerestaat - a farmer's state; Afrikaans.
boet - brother; Afrikaans.
Caçador Escuro - Dark Hunter; Portuguese.
Camino Doroda - the Golden Road to Johannesburg; Portuguese.
capulana - a fabric 'sarong' used as clothing by both men and women in Mozambique; Portuguese.
curandeiros - spirit healer in Mozambique using both mixture of rituals of sortilege and religion; Portuguese.
deurlopers - illegal migrants who come through the bush into South Africa; Afrikaans.
domkop - idiot; Afrikaans.
donsa - draw/ drag/ pull/ haul; Ndebele.
doos - a really derogatory Afrikaans term for 'idiot'; also used instead of the 'c' word for a female genital.
eina - ouch; Afrikaans, but now generally accepted Southern African slang.
eish (pronounced Eye-Sh or Eh-eesh) -surprise/ awe/ shock/ exasperation/ excitement/ resignation; generally accepted Southern African slang (derived from Xhosa originally).
ek is jammer - I am sorry; Afrikaans.
flatdog - a crocodile; Southern African slang.
gatvol (pronounced gaaat-fall) - full to the brim (literally gut full); Afrikaans, but now generally accepted South African slang.
guete morge - good morning; Swiss-German.
gwaza - spear, stab; Ndebele.
hamba kahle - go well/ goodbye (said by the person staying behind); Ndebele.

haw - an expression of disbelief; general South African slang.
ibhiza-idolzi:-spirit/ soul horse (person who can communicate with a horse's spirit); Ndebele.
ifela - died a natural death; Ndebele.
in the drink - in the water.
inja - dog; Zulu, used generally in Southern Africa.
inkukhu - chicken/ poultry; Ndebele.
Inthunzi Zingela - Shadow Hunter; Zulu/Ndebele.
izzit - really, is that so; generally accepted South African slang.
ja - yes; Afrikaans.
jammer - sorry; Afrikaans.
jislaaik - exclamation, usually for something unbelievable; Afrikaans, but generally accepted South African.
jol - party; generally accepted South African slang.
Jy krap met ń kort stokkie aan ń groot leeu se bal -
you are scratching a big lion's bollocks with a short stick; Afrikaans saying.
kaal-necked chicken - a chicken with no feathers on its neck. *Kaal*—meaning bare, naked or nude in Afrikaans.
kaffir - the term kaffir has now evolved into an offensive term for black people. But it was previously a neutral term for black people in Southern Africa. Also was used in the term of a nonbeliever—referring to the black people not being of Christian upbringing. In this instance when I use it in my book, it is offensive.
kakulu - very much, a lot; Ndebele.
knobkierie - an African club. These are typically made from wood with a large knob (wood knot) at one end and a long stick protruding from that. They can be used for fighting (smashing someone's head) or throwing at animals during hunting. Ideal size to also be used as a walking stick; Afrikaans.
kopje - a small hill rising up from the African veld; Afrikaans—accepted as general by all.
kraal - an area where animals are kept, usually found inside an African village/settlement and usually circular with barricades and the stock inside. Can also refer to an African cluster of huts; Afrikaans, but generally accepted Southern African terminology.
Kupua - a trickster in Hawaiian folk stories, often demigods who possess shape-shifting abilities.

lekker - good, nice; Afrikaans—accepted as general by all.
lindani - watch over/ keep watch; Ndebele.
linjani - how are you? Ndebele.
lobola - an African tradition of an arranged payment between a groom and the bride's family, in exchange for their daughter. Can be paid in cattle or cash, and the higher the *lobola,* the greater value the bride is held in the groom's eyes. This payment is the groom's way of thanking the parents for raising a good daughter. It is still applicable to many South African traditional weddings; Zulu.
maak 'n plan - Whole saying is: ''N boer maak 'n plan'—which literally translated means 'the farmer makes a plan'. Farmers are known to be resilient and just find another way to do things, no matter what. Adapted from Afrikaans saying.
Maria (pronounced Mariah) - a mythical wind from the musical *Paint Your Wagon.*
Matopos Hills or Matobo Hills - Bald Heads—granite hills in the area outside or Matobo hills: of Bulawayo; Ndebele.
maywe - oh no/ oh my goodness/ oh dear; slang, accepted in general Southern African population.
mbulala - killer; Ndebele.
melktert - milk tart containing boiled milk, egg and flour, usually dusted with cinnamon; Afrikaans.
nenga - offend/ nauseate/ disgust; Ndebele.
ngiyabonga - I am thankful/ thank you; Ndebele.
nguni - cattle; Zulu/ Ndebele.
ngxama - be very angry; Ndebele.
nkhunsi - African milky eagle-owl (scientific name: *Bubo Lacteus*); Zulu; viewed by the Shangaan as being a messenger of death, sent by an evil person. It is believed that the only way to stop/ reverse the death spell is to catch the owl and cut off its head. This would then cause either the person who sent it, or their family member's death instead; Shangaan folklore.
oke (pronounced oak) - male or a person, usually someone you don't know; generally accepted South African slang.
ons is jammer - we are sorry; Afrikaans.
pan - a body of water (sometimes pumped in), as in a waterhole, used in game reserves where animals gather.

pangas - a really large knife.
pas op - beware; Afrikaans, but generally accepted into South African slang and used by all.
penga - mad, not right in the head; origins within the Bantu languages, but a general term in Southern Africa.
plaas - farm; Afrikaans.
quartering - a method for getting a clean and clear shot to an animal's vital organs when they are facing you. The front leg is used to line up where to shoot.
sadza - staple maize meal food in Zimbabwe, made into a thick porridge; Shona.
sala kuhle - stay well/ goodbye (said by the person leaving); Ndebele.
salibonani - hello; Ndebele.
se voet - like bloody hell; Afrikaans.
sheeesh - expression when there are no words, it's too sore, and you haven't learned to swear yet.
siga - cut; Zulu.
sikhona - I am fine (literally means 'I am here'); Ndebele.
situasie - situation; Afrikaans.
siyabonga - we thank you; Ndebele.
siyaphila - I am fine (usually said first in a traditional greeting); Ndebele.
skebengas - gangster; a Zulu word, but generally used in South Africa for anyone who is on the wrong side of the law/ trouble making/ a bad guy.
skelm - rascal or sneaky person; Afrikaans.
sondebok - scapegoat; Afrikaans.
stick - a unit of men on horseback deployed in the Grey's Scouts, comprised of six to eight men.
takkie - trainers; Afrikaans—but generally accepted South African slang now.
terugkeer - return; Afrikaans.
thula - be quiet/ shut up; Xhosa/ Zulu/ Ndebele—generally accepted South African slang.
tinyanga - (plural for *inyanga*) a traditional healer (witchdoctor) in Mozambique. Different to a *curandeiros* (Portuguese) (spirit healer).
tokoloshe - a really bad spirit; it can resemble a zombie, or a poltergeist, or a gremlin, any demon-like thing; Zulu.
tsotsi - naughty person/gangster/layabout; a general term in Southern Africa.

umntwana - child/ children; Zulu.
unjani wena - how are you (response); Ndebele.
utshwala - traditionally brewed beer; Zulu.
uxolo - sorry; Ndebele.
vetkoek - deep-fried dough bread bun; Afrikaans.
vriende - friends; Afrikaans.
vrous - women; Afrikaans.
vula - open; Ndebele.
wag-'n-bietjie - the Buffalo-Thorn Tree (*Ziziphus mucronata*); any of several plants having sharp, often hooked thorns; literal Afrikaans translation is wait-a-minute.
when-we - a derogatory term used for Rhodesians, because after they left Rhodesia, they would always talk about being back there, saying 'when we were ...'; generally accepted South African slang.
woza - come; Ndebele.
yebo - yes; Zulu, now generally accepted South African term.
zero(ed) - a hunting term for setting your scopes and making sure your rifle is accurate, usually done after travelling.
zingela - hunter/ to hunt animals or people; Ndebele.
zwana - friendly, to listen to each other; Ndebele.

FACT VS FICTION

Fact

There are smaller gold mine operators all over Zimbabwe. There was a real problem in 1980 when the mines were charging rent for mining housing that was substandard.

Fiction

Sunshine Gold Mine doesn't exist.

Fact

Mission outreaches to Zimbabwe do occur, as do aid volunteer holidays.

Fiction

Lily and Quintin's medical outreach clinic is not real.

Fact

Professional hunting of wildlife in Zimbabwe is legal, and there are concessions to control the animal quotas taken. There is a professional body that has tried hard to regulate a difficult industry.

Fiction

Professional hunters in Zimbabwe hunting people.

Fact

The Afrikaner Weerstandsbeweging (AWB), Afrikaner Resistance Movement, is a South African neo-Nazi separatist political and paramilitary organisation, often described as a white supremacist group.

Fiction

Afrikaner Partisans are not real, neither are their ideals and they are not part of the AWB.

Fact

After the Rhodesia Bush War ended, there were Grey's Scouts' horses who travelled through the bush from Zimbabwe to South Africa to join their ex-Grey's Scouts owner, who lived in Kokstad. A Ndebele groom brought these horses down. I was fortunate enough to be allowed to ride these beautiful animals as a teenager. This is not their story.

Fiction

The horses and journey back to Zimbabwe through the bush.

Fact

Missions were attacked during the Rhodesian Bush War; one of the worst was Emmanuel Secondary School, run by Elim Mission, of a Pentecostal Church, based in Cheltenham, England. Twelve European missionaries were killed, including a three-week-old baby.

Fiction

Shilo Mission's attack in my book.

Fiction

The 6th Society.

ACKNOWLEDGEMENTS

There are many minds that go into making a book—it is not a journey I take alone by any means.

Louis Olivier, retired game ranger, Kruger National Park (forty-five years' service), not only for your dedication to the park and the animals inside that fence, but for all the help in my research. And for conspiring with me to plan an escape through the park and then through Mozambique, for maps, 'inside' info and even helping write the bones of the route for me. Thank you, I so appreciate your generosity with your time and sharing your knowledge. One day I hope to meet you and shake your hand in person.

Robyn Grady, Amy Andrews and Gayle Ash, long-time writing friends who continue to shake pom-poms my way all the time. You girls rock and I so appreciate the support.

My beta readers: Siobhan Graham, Petro Grobbelaar (who also checked my Afrikaans) and Sam Eeles. Many thanks for your help in various edit stages.

Alli Sinclair, who is on the other end of the 'interwebs' all the time. Thanks for being there, for the bad and the good, the tears of both happiness and dramas, but mostly the friendship where text conversation can continue over days and still not need a formal hello.

My cousin Jeremy Wilde and his patient wife, Caren, for putting up with all my questions on professional hunting, and for talking out different scenarios with me, even though we are still so many miles away from each other. Diesel vs Petrol engine mistake fixed in this edition… Much, much appreciated!

Skinny Wood, as always, for checking my Ndebele.

Original Publishing Team:

The team at Harlequin Mira: Rachael Donovan, for helping me write a better book, and being my 'door monitor' for what gets put out into the world. Also, for the first time, naming my book.

Thank you. My original editors, Laurie Ormond and Alex Nahlous, for taking an okay story and helping turn it into a book worthy of giving to readers to enjoy. Thank you for your help and your expertise.

Michelle Zaiter, cover fairy, for the lion cover.

My 2024 Publishing team:

My independent editing company, Creating Ink, for the new update.

My independent cover designer, Mecha. Love this cover too!

My sons, Kyle and Barry, for putting up with me writing and being off in my own world, even while on an overseas holiday this time.

Kyle, whose turn it was to do my mud maps. (Have to admit, it's so handy having kids who can use graphics programs!)

2018:

Lastly, to my husband, Shaun. For still loving me after all these years. Thank you for the freedom to stretch my wings and fly beside you.

2024: For learning new programs to help me spread my writer wings and figure out Independent Publishing. I can't say that our life is ever monotonous or boring! x

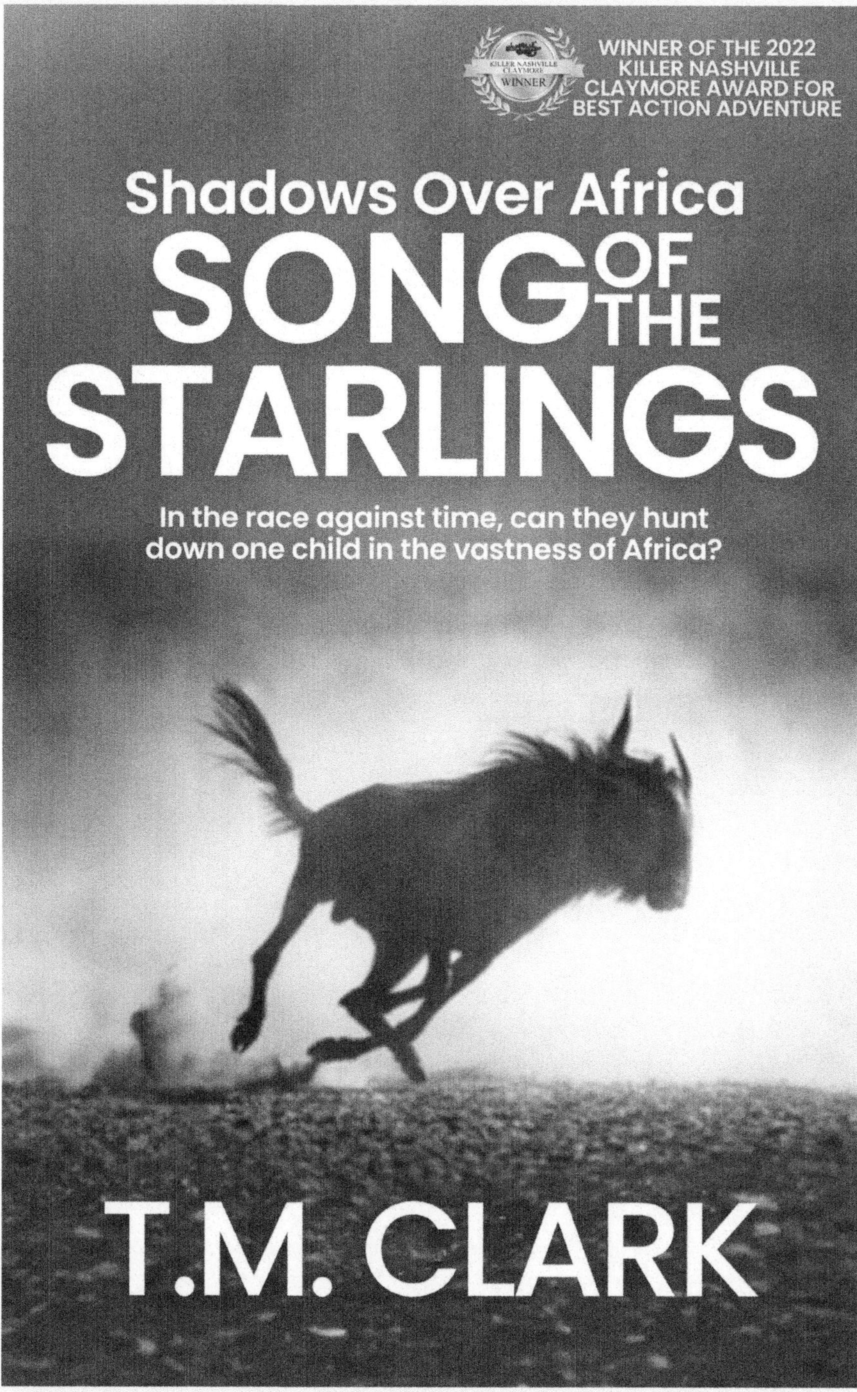
KILLER NASHVILLE CLAYMORE WINNER
WINNER OF THE 2022 KILLER NASHVILLE CLAYMORE AWARD FOR BEST ACTION ADVENTURE
Shadows Over Africa
SONG OF THE STARLINGS
In the race against time, can they hunt down one child in the vastness of Africa?
T.M. CLARK

CHAPTER 1

Saliebos Farm, Thabazimbi, Northern Transvaal, South Africa

1987

Lightning split the African night sky and cracked through the bushveld. It shimmered; then the rumbling could be heard, tumbling over the *koppies,* growing in volume. Rain lashed the windows in sheets, rattling the panes of glass held in wooden frames by old putty.

Ben sensed his grandchild's presence in his bedroom before he heard the floorboard creak, despite her three-year-old featherweight and the storm raging outside. Having her in the house was enough to keep him awake.

He found he was always listening to ensure she was alright in her new room, and not trying to run away. Three years of her life had been stolen from him, but now that he knew about Chrystal, there was no way he would let any harm come to her.

They could start afresh and make good memories.

Ben wouldn't make the same mistakes with her that he had with her mother.

This time around, he would get it right.

He'd been given a second chance at parenting, and he was going to embrace it.

"You can come in." Ben lifted himself and turned slowly toward the door, pushing the photo album he'd been flicking through only moments before onto the quilt.

Chrystal stood there in her little white nightdress, a tatty knitted horse, which had once belonged to her mother, held firmly under her arm, and his heart became even more broken than it already was. Her blue eyes were too large and sunken deeply with black circles, her face showing more bone than was healthy for a girl her age. Her pallor was almost translucent. A vein throbbed in her forehead.

He could see the resemblance to his daughter Avril, and his darling wife, Ella. The same silver-blonde hair that they had both had. He knew it would change into a more golden color as Chrystal grew older.

Her hair was neglected, wild, and matted. Another sin to lay at his drug addict daughter's feet. Chrystal was as skittish as a newly born foal. There was no way she'd let a social worker near enough to touch her hair, and she certainly wouldn't let him.

God knew she didn't trust anyone. Of that, he had no doubt.

The social worker had said that it would be more traumatic for her hair to be brushed than left unruly, so they had left it.

So much had changed in her little life so fast.

Her mother dying.

Him collecting her from Cape Town this morning and bringing her home to live on *Saliebos* in the Northern Transvaal. He wished he'd been able to bring Avril home alive too. He had tried often enough and never gave up hope.

How could it all have gone so wrong?

A week ago, when Avril called and begged for his help, it was already too late. For Avril, but not for his granddaughter. He could still help her. Bring her into his life and give her the childhood she should have had. Not the life she'd had to endure with her mother in the decay of the city.

It was almost four years since Avril had disappeared from the last rehab center he'd paid for in Johannesburg.

Four years of no contact. A constant void.

Four years of total anguish.

During that time, she'd given birth to Chrystal.

Of all her betrayals, that was the one that hurt the most.

He had a grandchild he'd been denied knowing.

Avril had been found dead in the tiny flat in Woodstock outside of Cape Town. He'd never expected the call from the child services welfare officer contacting him about his granddaughter. The social worker was adamant that Avril had been clean for her pregnancy at least, and that while Chrystal was neglected, she didn't appear to have had any drugs forced into her little veins.

Chrystal shifted from one foot to another as if waiting for something. She bit her lip.

Waiting.

He cursed his daughter for keeping this little girl away.

"I can see that Mr. Nag there is a bit scared of the storm. Do you think we should tuck him in this nice big bed alongside us? We can protect him. I can put my hand over his ears to block out the noise, and you can stroke his mane to calm him," he said as a deep roll of thunder shook the homestead.

Of all the days for nature to unleash its fury on the African landscape, did it have to be the night I brought her home?

Chrystal nodded slowly and walked to the side of the bed, but she didn't climb up. Instead, she put the knitted toy in the air, as if expecting him to take it from her.

Ben frowned.

The welfare workers had told him that she hadn't spoken since the day the police had found her sitting next to her mother's body. They weren't even sure if she could talk.

When he'd first seen her in the flesh, all he'd wanted to do was hold her close. Hug her. His little gem that his screwed-up daughter had left behind. His last precious glimpse of his darling Ella. His grandchild.

Lost and alone.

But he was here now, and he would help heal those uncertainties and those nightmarish memories. Replace them with happier ones. Push them far back in her little mind until they were forgotten. He took Mr. Nag and put him on the bed.

"You want my help to climb up here next to Mr. Nag? I bet he would like that."

A loud clap of thunder had her scrambling up the side of the bed. Ben tucked her stuffed toy between them and made sure that the sheets and blankets were pulled up high under her little chin, her head on the large white pillow.

"When your mom was young like you, and the storms would roll in, she would hop in this bed with Grandma Ella and me. We would look at the photo albums of where we had been on holiday together and plan our next great adventure. That's what I was doing when you came in. Do you want to see the photographs of your mom when she was a little bit older than you are now? She was five when we traveled to England."

She nodded her head.

A louder and closer bolt sizzled as it struck near the house; the room lit up blue momentarily as the electricity transferred from the heavens to the earth.

Her eyes grew larger and she bit her lip while clutching Mr. Nag tight. Her attempt to control the fear that threatened to overwhelm her body and her soul was both disturbing and heroic to watch. He remembered Avril at that age; her emotional outburst would have been visible to all.

His grandchild was already strong.

His heart wept when he thought about how much she must have already witnessed to be able to control fear like this.

"Your Grandma Ella and I took your mum with us and we traveled to England on a big airplane, like the one we flew in today."

She silently looked at the ceiling as if studying the knots on the wood poles that supported the thatched roof.

"If you look here, you can see a picture of your mum," he said, opening the page for her to look.

Chrystal peered at the photo album.

He smiled. He had her attention. He continued, pointing to the pictures as they went through. "See this one here, she is standing with one of the lion statues in Trafalgar Square, and you can see the pigeons all over her. Can you see how big those pigeons were compared to her hand?"

She sat back up in the bed and leaned forward, looking at the pictures.

He brought the album closer to them and pointed to the next picture. "See here, this is a highland cow. We were in Scotland. That's your mum feeding it with a bottle. It's a calf, mind you. There's its mother standing close by watching, making sure everything is okay. Your mum loved those cows. When we got home, she asked me to buy her a Nguni cow with big horns, which I did.

It took a lot to say no to your mother. She was my little girl. I wanted to give her everything, even the moon if I could have. I still have Nguni cows out there on the farm. Would you like to go look at them tomorrow?"

He watched as Chrystal reached hesitantly toward the album. "You can touch the pictures."

She traced the large horns of the strange shaggy cow as he carried on. "From that day on, your mother collected anything to do with cows. Remind me to look in the old barn, and we can find her figurine collection in there, one of these days. I packed them up and put them away when she got older. I didn't want her to sell…" Ben trailed off, not wanting to upset Chrystal more than she already was.

They continued their journey through the yellowed album, Chrystal silently turning the pages when each story had been told.

On the last page was one of his favorite pictures that Ella had taken. Avril had been ill and running a fever with a twenty-four-hour tummy bug while they were still in Cardiff. He'd been sitting in a chair next to her bed and had fallen asleep from exhaustion, having spent the night awake watching over his daughter. While he'd been dozing, Avril had climbed into his lap and eventually fallen asleep there.

"Your mum would always sit on my lap when she was scared or lonely," he said. "She always said it was because I had a bit of padding on my bones, unlike your grandma. She was thin as a willow tree but strong like ironwood. Your grandma said it was because your mum could hear the sound of my heart beating, and it drowned out all her worries, so she didn't have to think about being sick or lonely."

The storm had been building in intensity and was still unleashing its fury on the ranch. The lightning glowed blue once more, and a loud crack shook the house at the same time.

"The storm is right on top of us. Once this lot passes, it should start to calm down," he said. The thunder rolled loudly. Chrystal jumped, her whole body moving in a jerky motion.

"You know, I bet that if you snuggle up here, you can hear my heartbeat louder than that thunder like your mum used to do. You want a listen?' He tapped his chest, indicating where his heart was.

She looked at him, hesitant.

He held his breath as Chrystal got on her knees on the top of the bed and leaned toward him. She put her ear against the white T-shirt that he wore to bed.

He could hear the blood pulse through his own body as he held still, not wanting to frighten her. Not wanting to move in case she bolted.

He felt the moment that she trusted him, and climbed into his lap, like her mother had done in the picture, and snuggled closer. She put her arms around him and held tightly, her ear against his chest. Only then did he slowly wrap his arms around her and hold his granddaughter for the very first time.

"It's okay, Chrystal. You're safe here. I'll watch over you. I swear it with my own life. Nothing bad will happen to you ever again."

"Can I stay here forever?" she asked.

His granddaughter had spoken. "This is your home. You can stay here, forever and ever," he whispered as a tear rolled down his cheek. His heart felt like it might burst, from love for the grandchild he finally held in his arms and a deep grief over the daughter he'd lost.

ALSO BY T.M. CLARK

ADULT BOOKS

Shadows Over Africa series

- Child of Africa
- Cry of the Firebird
- My Brother-But-One
- Nature of the Lion
- Shooting Butterflies
- Song of the Starlings
- Tears of the Cheetah
- The Avoidable Orphan

COMING SOON

- Daughter of Africa

PICTURE BOOKS

- Slowly! Slowly!
- Quickly! Quickly!

Printed in Dunstable, United Kingdom

81431121R00184